PRAISE FOR
The Conductors

"*The Conductors* is a seamless blending of magic, mystery, and history, creating power and wonder with its rarefied glimpse of Black life in the late 1800s. The Vigilance Society and the magic-wielding couple at the core of this story are a welcome addition to the growing chorus of voices in Black speculative fiction. Glover's worldbuilding, characters, and attention to historical detail create a delightfully genre-bending debut!"

—Tananarive Due, American Book Award winner
and author of *Ghost Summer: Stories*

"Community dynamics mixed with a magical alternate Reconstruction-era mystery. *The Conductors* has all the elements I was looking for in a good story."

—Mary Robinette Kowal, Hugo Award–winning
author of *The Calculating Stars*

"Nicole Glover blends historical detail and magical elements into an unforgettable debut. *The Conductors* is a wholly original and thoroughly riveting story. This is no doubt the first of many brilliant books to come."

—Deanna Raybourn, *New York Times* best-selling
author of *A Murderous Relation*

"With *The Conductors*, Nicole Glover creates a fascinating world where even magic is segregated. She effortlessly weaves both the constellation-based magical system and the real-life struggles of being Black in post–Civil War America. The characters, led by former Underground Railroad conductors Hetty and Benjy Rhodes, are as intriguing as the mystery. It's hard to believe this is Glover's first book. I found it as enchanting as one of Hetty's spells."

—Kellye Garrett, winner of the Anthony, Agatha, and Lefty awards and
author of *Hollywood Homicide* and *Hollywood Ending*

"*The Conductors* is a conjured novel. Reimagining a past [to help] us navigate our present, it weaves a rich tapestry of history and magic to create a story of resilience and resistance through the power of Black girl magic. It's the perfect book for our times."

—Maurice Broaddus, author of *Pimp My Airship*

"*The Conductors* is a wildly inventive alternate history that combines compelling characters, a propulsive plot, and lots of intrigue. It is also radical as hell. Thought-provoking and powerful, Glover's novel is a must-read."

—Cadwell Turnbull, author of *The Lesson*

"Inventively mixing mystery, magic, and alternate history, Glover's nail-biting debut takes readers to Reconstruction-era Philadelphia . . . Glover is a writer to watch."

—*Publishers Weekly*, starred review

The Undertakers

The UNDERTAKERS

NICOLE GLOVER

A JOHN JOSEPH ADAMS BOOK
MARINER BOOKS
An Imprint of HarperCollins*Publishers*
Boston   New York

marinerbooks.com

Library of Congress Cataloging-in-Publication Data has been applied for.
ISBN 9780358197102 (paperback)
ISBN 9780358181804 (ebook)
ISBN 9780358581949 (audiobook)

Book design by Emily Snyder

Printed in the United States of America
1 2021
4500837987

*For every kid who has their
library card number memorized*

I find at times the imprecise and rather loose application of Celestial magic is its best quality. Yes, it may be true that there is no uniformity or standard spells. But that is its greatest strength. Whatever the magic needs to accomplish can be done as long as a person is willing to try. Such potential in my view is what moves white men to write laws to have it banned. But you cannot ban magic. You cannot limit magic. Just as you cannot force laws upon nature. It is part of every living creature in this world. It is even crueler to ban our magic, the magic of the newly freed, who are now just spreading their wings to explore all the wonders of the world.

— FROM THE PRIVATE JOURNALS OF RAIMOND CECIL DUVAL

FEBRUARY 19, 1871

The latest fire in town occurred last night on Powell near Fifteenth Street, centered around a boardinghouse. Severe property damage has displaced many, left dozens injured, and caused one death — Olmstead Secondary's beloved alchemistry teacher, Raimond Duval. Subscribers of this paper are no stranger to the many stories about Duval's work, and all of us at the *Observer* mourn with the community for this great loss.

An inquest will be held. Any news about what started the fire or anything of unusual nature should be sent to the interested parties known as Sparrow and Finch.

— *EVENTIDE OBSERVER*

JUNE 16, 1871

The Undertakers

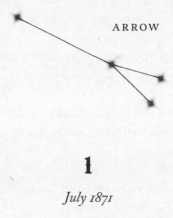

ARROW

1

July 1871

PHILADELPHIA, PENNSYLVANIA

Hᴇx, ᴄᴜʀsᴇ, ᴏʀ ᴄʜᴀʀᴍ?" Hetty asked as they strode down Barclay Street. "Don't say that hex and curse are the same. There are nuances, you know."

"Of course there are," her husband replied. Benjy took a moment to consider the question before replying. "I think it's a jinx."

"That wasn't a choice!"

"Should be. There's got to be a reason that place is still standing." Benjy pointed to the only house on this end of the street. Despite its neighbors being reduced to piles of rubble, this home was untouched by the fire. A state that was quite unnerving given that even the still-standing homes of the street had shown some signs of the fire.

Since the end of May, news of a fire had reached their ears twice a week, and sometimes more. While small fires around a single home or a building were not uncommon, these fires were different. They engulfed both sides of a street, and once they started they raged until they burned themselves out. Such fires led people to craft charms and potions to keep their homes safe.

And the ones that didn't make their own bought them from charlatans who touted fire-proofing potions that could barely quell a candle's flame.

While reports of this fire would have brought them to this street anyway, Hetty and Benjy got word of it in a somewhat different matter.

Just after midday, Hetty had found a card left in their postbox. A card with a sun and a crescent moon drawn on one side, and on the other a brief message:

> *Last night a fire took eight homes on Barclay Street and scorched more than a few, but one home stands untouched by the flames.*

Such a message wasn't just odd. It was downright *peculiar*.

And peculiar was their business.

Although the day was still young, the fire itself was a distant memory, with only traces of smoke left in the air. What it left in its wake was still evident.

Buildings here were mostly made of wood, and were home to several families both large and small. While this wasn't the slums, neither were the people rich. Some homes were divided so that as many as six families occupied a building, and most people rented out a spare room to any interested boarder.

While only eight houses had burned down, every building on the street, save the one miraculously spared, was damaged. This meant of course the street was filled with people. There were those who lived on this street, making light repairs to their home and casting spells of protection. There were people tending to the dead and wounded, people checking on neighbors to see what survived the fire, and others jealously guarding piles of recovered possessions.

As Hetty and Benjy walked the length of the street, several people called out to Benjy for help. This was not unusual. The blacksmith shop Benjy used to work at was not far from here, and he was generous with his time and repairs. It wasn't surprising that so many recognized him on sight as the person likely to lend a helping hand. Not that he was hard to forget, in Hetty's humble opinion. He cut a handsome figure, even in plain attire of shirt-sleeves and suspenders. Although, more appealing was the easy air of competence and unsatiable curiosity in the world. While Benjy often pretended that other people's problems held no interest to him, they had gotten involved in mystery solving because deep down he couldn't help but care.

"You take this end of the street, and I'll take the other," Benjy said to Hetty. "We'll meet at the still-standing house."

"Why not go there first?" Hetty asked.

"Because there are plenty more interesting questions to ask before we do."

With that, Benjy crossed the street to assist a man dragging a trunk out from the rubble, already asking about what had happened last night.

Hetty should do the same, but she was a bit reluctant.

It was never easy asking questions about the fires.

People lied to her face, or were too wearied to give a proper answer. A handful were rude, and quite a few were wondering why she even cared.

A fire was a fire.

A tragedy that ruined what strangled hopes they had for a better tomorrow. A fire that pushed them to move in with friends, with families, with strangers, or finally convince them it was time to leave the city. What caused the fire and why mattered little to people who had more than their fair share of things to grieve.

However, not all fires were accidents.

Something more than a mere fire occurred here. She could feel it in her bones.

At the end of the street, two dozen bodies were stretched out in neat lines. Most were badly burned and bearing mortal injuries that no healing magic could cure. The rest were people who died from breathing in too much smoke and fell unconscious. The group was mostly adults, and the youngest person was on the edge of adulthood. No children. Good fortune, one would think, until you remembered what happened to orphaned children. Babies and the very young would find new homes easily, but the older ones would have a much harder time of things.

Hetty saw a handful now, huddled on the corner, and she wondered if any of them had lost family in the fire.

As Hetty looked on, she found a trio of elderly women sitting on the steps of a nearby building, watching her closely.

So closely that even when they realized Hetty had noticed them, they kept on staring. They reminded Hetty of a gossiping trio that was the bane of her existence at church. But gossips weren't all bad. Gossips always had the most interesting news and were more than willing to share. It was no surprise at all that when Hetty approached the small group, they started talking before she asked a single question.

Their home had not been impacted by the fire. Not by luck, they quickly assured Hetty. The building was owned by someone who knew his magic. Spells were put in place to repel flames, and were replaced regularly. The other buildings didn't have that in their favor.

"What happened here was an accident," one of the women, Paula, assured Hetty. "Started from a candle that got knocked over. No mystery here."

"Not even that we had to deal with the flames ourselves," grumbled Emmeline.

"No fire company showed up?" Hetty asked.

"Nobody showed up, legitimate or otherwise!"

Until last December, volunteer fire companies had the run of the city. They put out fires, but usually for a fee, and they often took their time arriving. And more than a few were aligned with gangs to such a degree that the only difference between the groups was access to hoses and water. Which was why when the city finally set up their own fire company there was great rejoicing. But the volunteer companies were not going away quietly, especially not when elected officials didn't mind them running amuck in Black-majority neighborhoods. While some, such as Moyamensing Hose, were notorious for sparking riots and violence, the worst group in Hetty's opinion was Beatty Hose, which targeted magical practitioners. Rumor had it that Beatty Hose was behind most of the fires that had sprung up without a clear cause, and used Sorcery to ensure that flames did not die easily.

"How do you know a candle started the fire?" Hetty asked.

The gossipy air of the trio changed then, as they looked over at Hetty rather keenly.

"What it's to you?" Iola asked. Her lips, already thin with suspicion, flattened even more with undisguised scorn. "You don't live on this street."

"And you don't look like you will anytime soon," Paula added, eyeing the delicate embroidery on Hetty's pale green dress.

With ease Hetty replied, "I make it my business to know about odd things. Have you heard about the sparrow that lives on Juniper Street?"

While Paula and Iola blinked on in confusion, Emmeline's eyes widened.

Hetty hid a smile.

There was always one.

Emmeline sputtered as she addressed Hetty with new admiration in her eyes.

"I've heard the stories. You take care of things. Clean up messes. Make sure the dead aren't forgotten," Emmeline said. "You're the Sparrow!"

"And my husband is the Finch," Hetty said. "We've been looking into these fires and hope to do something about them."

These words got Hetty more stories from the trio. They were similar to what they'd already told Hetty, but the missing details that Hetty suspected earlier had now quietly been slipped back in.

Overall, nothing tugged at Hetty's curiosity, except for one thing:

"You saw a stranger last night?"

"Yes," Iola said. "My hip was bothering me again. I was up trying to find something to settle these old bones. Then I heard it." She rapped her knuckles against the steps she sat on. "A knock on the door. At that hour I wasn't opening the door for anybody, not even kin, but I peeped out the window. There was a man out there I hadn't seen before."

"As I told you," Emmeline interjected, "that was the new neighbor!"

"Ain't nobody new on this street!"

As the women began to argue between themselves about the veracity of this fact, Hetty gently cut in.

"What can you tell me about the house that didn't burn down?"

The arguing stopped midsentence, and Emmeline answered:

"A fellow owns it. Haven't seen him much lately. Although I don't think it's the man going inside right now."

Hetty spun around to look.

She didn't see whoever stepped inside, but she saw a door slide shut. While that was fine on its own, less so was the ripple of magic that followed.

"You look like somebody stole the flowers off your grave. Something the matter, child?" Iola asked. "What do you know about the house?"

"Not much, but I plan to find out more."

Leaving the trio behind, Hetty crossed the street, taking care to go slowly to avoid drawing any more attention than she already had.

Standing on its own, the house appeared much like a lost, lonely duckling missing its siblings. Although from a distance it seemed untouched, as Hetty climbed the front steps she saw she was wrong in that regard. Soot dusted the exterior of the house, turning the house gray, and left the windows looking dusty and forlorn. Even the flower box, devoid of any growing things, had a fine layer of ash. The door had scratches along the doorknob and scuffs on the lower portion as if someone had kicked in the door when they couldn't unlock it.

"Aren't you going to come inside?"

Benjy's voice called out to her.

Hetty pushed the door open and found Benjy standing in the hallway frowning at the florid wallpaper before him.

Hiding her relief that the stranger the old women had seen was only her husband, Hetty jabbed a finger at the door.

"Did you do this?"

He looked over at her, barely glancing at the doorway. "Why would I do that?"

"Because no one lives here."

Hetty gestured around the hall, not bothering to point to any specific spot. The evidence was all around. From the debris that stirred as she walked in the hall, the musty air of a room that had been shut up too tightly, and the old water stains in the corner. Not to mention the chandelier above their heads that held sunlight in the cobwebs stretched between its candle posts.

"Someone does," Benjy corrected her. "They just haven't been around in a while."

Hetty stopped at the foot of a staircase. She stood there with one hand on the railing, frowning up at the shadows that swallowed up most of the upper level. "Let's hope they'll be gone for a while. It'll be hard even for me to spin a tale explaining things."

He didn't answer her, and when Hetty looked back, she found he had vanished.

But he hadn't gone far.

In the next room, Benjy had his ear pressed against the wall. The tiny blue bundles of flowers framed by golden double rings was perhaps the ugliest wallpaper Hetty had ever seen. Distracted by the overwhelming urge to rip the wallpaper from the walls, she had to force herself to notice anything else about the room. There were a few stiff-back chairs scattered in the room. While they were made from the same dark wood, they were all vastly different, sitting higher or lower, with different arched backs that made it clear they had come from different dining sets. There was a rug on a floor, its colors faded from the dust, and sunlight attempted to stream through the closed curtains. But the most interesting bit was a table holding slightly melted candles sitting in a dish. They appeared to be more ornamental instead of used for magic protections, but their placement was still rather unusual.

"There's something here," Benjy said as he tapped the wall.

"Does the wallpaper cover a door?" Hetty asked, not bothering to rap the wall as well. "I wouldn't be surprised. That would be just about the only reason I would put up something so ugly. Who could notice anything else?"

"There's no door. The wallpaper covers the sigils carved into the walls." Benjy pressed his hand down against the wallpaper so the form of a circle could be seen through it. It was nearly as big as his fist.

"Sweet stars above," Hetty whispered. "Maybe it was a bad idea to come in here after all."

"I think we'll be fine. I spoke to a neighbor who witnessed the owner carving the walls one night and then papering over them with this horrid wallpaper. It must be to ward against fire, but it's hard to say for certain. But ever since then the neighbor has heard noises at the oddest of hours."

Because Hetty could never pass up a chance to tease him, she quipped gleefully, "Sounds like a ghost to me!"

Benjy rolled his eyes skyward.

They'd been hearing stories about all manner of ghosts around the city, even more since they got into the undertaking business. Strange rattles, cups knocked over on a table, unexplained patches of cold air. People who said they saw the faces of the dead, both loved and hated, staring out at them from windows. Tales of ghosts entering a store and walking through the shelves. And the whispers of the dead leading the living through crossroads and into the great beyond.

Hetty didn't fully believe a spirit would want to linger on this bitter earth, but she had seen enough of this world to know that anything was possible.

Benjy, on the other hand, had far greater reservations.

"Ghosts don't exist. It's more likely there's a curse on the house that's causing trouble," he said as he resumed his tapping.

"Well, we won't find it dithering away in here." Hetty gave the room one last look. "I'm going to go explore the rest of the house."

"Don't go upstairs without me," Benjy called after her.

Hetty was tempted to do so anyway just to be petty, but when she stepped back into the hallway a partially open door caught her attention.

The door creaked slightly as she stepped inside. Like the other room, the curtains were also drawn tightly closed. While there were many beautiful things in the room, Hetty's attention went straight toward the desk. It was a hulking thing, more like a piano than a desk. The hutch loomed overhead, its countless tiny shelves filled with nothing more than dust. The shiny drawer knobs seemed to wink as she walked passed, calling to her like a siren hidden in the seas.

Hetty tapped the cloth band at her neck. The choker had two purposes. It satisfied her vanity by covering the old jagged scars that ran around her neck. And it kept her magic in reserve.

With a single finger, Hetty traced the delicate embroidery and stirred to life the Dove star sigil she had hidden in her stitches.

The spell took on the form of a dove, but not a true one. From beak to tail feathers, it was midnight blue and speckled with starlight. When the bird flapped its wings, wisps of magic swirled around it. But that magic stayed a neutral blue and did not change even when it fluttered down to rest atop the desk.

How very interesting.

Hetty snapped her fingers, dissipating her spell. No star sigils were etched in the wood of the desk, nor did she detect any trace of magic. Did it mean it was harmless? Intrigued, Hetty placed her hand on the desk.

Not a moment later, she yanked it back.

It was like she had plunged her hand into ice water.

No, not ice water. Something colder, something stronger. Like going ice-skating and suddenly there's no ice. Only plunging into the frigid depths with no hope of seeing the surface.

How did touching a desk feel like that?

Hetty put her hand back on the desk.

The chilling cold swept along her palm, inching up her arm.

But she held firm.

Hetty kept her hand pressed flat against the wood, and suddenly light exploded around her.

Protection spells rose up from every stitch in her clothing, encasing her in delicately spun glass. It hardened, buckled, and then shattered.

Hetty jumped back from the desk, and to her horror, an angry mass of bubbling red magic hurtled toward her.

She held up her hands to brace against the attack, but no attack ever came.

The mass of magic hovered inches from her face, held back by a protective barrier.

"I think you have your answer." Benjy appeared behind her in the doorway, his mild tone undercutting the potentially dire circumstances. "It's a hex."

His left hand was clenched into a fist, small sparks of green light jumping between his fingers. Although he should have been watching the orb of dangerous magic, his eyes rested on her.

"What did you do?" Benjy asked.

"I touched the desk," Hetty freely admitted, and before he could share his opinion, she added: "I know it was foolish."

"Glad you know that."

Hetty fumed even though she deserved the rebuke.

She took a step closer to the hex and it moved *away* from her.

"Look at what it's doing." Hetty lifted her hand and the hex followed. "Let it go."

"That's a terrible idea," Benjy grunted.

"Don't worry," Hetty reassured him, "I'll make sure you won't get hurt."

He rolled his eyes, but relaxed his left hand in the end.

With the restraints gone, the hex started to charge. Hetty drew sigils in the air, but Benjy was quicker. The Taurus star sigil rammed itself into the hex. Catching it by the horns, the star-speckled bull shook its head mightily and sent the hex flying.

Guided by Benjy, the bull chased after the hex. The spells bounced from wall to wall, the splash of colors mixing and clashing.

At first Hetty watched this heady chase with concern. There was no way to know what sort of hex it was, but it didn't seem like any intruder spells she'd encountered before. It didn't act like any she knew, either. Was it trying to attack them or escape to warn whoever set the spell originally?

"Why was this left behind?" Hetty asked.

"You're asking the wrong question. You should be asking who left it." Benjy slammed his hands together.

A second sigil that Hetty hadn't even noticed fluttered into view. Aries. Together, the two star sigils squashed the hex like a bit of heated metal caught between a hammer and anvil.

The light from the collision was dazzling—a piercing white light with the power of a small sun—and once it vanished it left the world even duller.

Except for the patch of bright green under their feet.

A path.

A trail of green moved along the floor, slithering much like a snake down the hall and illuminating the path the caster had taken. Magical residue, revealed by the second spell Benjy had cast.

"I don't think whoever left this hex is the owner," Hetty remarked. "It might be the work of the intruder."

"Why don't we see where this leads first before we make that assumption?"

This path didn't lead outside. The trail of magic veered down the hall and into a kitchen until it stopped at the pantry.

Mostly empty shelves greeted them when they opened the door. There were a few dusty cans and jars on the shelves, with scattered mouse droppings nearby.

On the floor, the green line continued until it reached the wall.

"Do we go outside, then?" Hetty asked.

But as she moved away, Benjy brushed past her to step inside the pantry. He placed a hand against the wall and pushed.

A soft click whispered in the air, and the wall and its shelves sank into the floor, revealing a passageway with a set of stairs curling in a downward spiral into the unknown.

Benjy whistled as he peered down into the opening. "I wonder where it leads."

"Only one way to find out." Hetty drew Eridanus into the air next to her. The River star sigil twinkled as it spilled through the stairway, lighting the way and warning of any trouble that lay ahead. "You first into the abyss!"

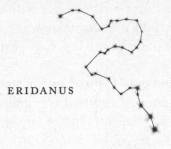

ERIDANUS

2

HETTY FOLLOWED HER HUSBAND, nudging the river of stars forward, but it helped little. It was a spiral staircase, which meant, light or no light, it was hard to see anything beyond what was in front of her. The staircase wasn't as tight as Hetty first feared. They couldn't walk down side by side, but there was room enough that they could walk without feeling like they were being squeezed into a vise. A vast improvement over some of the tunnels Hetty had been in before.

The first tunnels under the city started with the express purpose of smuggling goods out of sight of British eyes during the Revolutionary War. They started at the rivers and linked up with the taverns. As it happens with any good idea, new tunnels were made, and over time they smuggled more than liquor in and out of the city.

The tunnels that Hetty had walked through previously didn't run from one end of the city to the other. They were merely links between churches and the basements of select houses, allowing people fleeing to safety, and those assisting them, to avoid detection. Some of those tunnels might still be in use, but most of the ones that Hetty knew of ran in unfriendly territories, had collapsed, or had been personally sealed off by Benjy.

This tunnel was something entirely different.

It shouldn't exist at all.

Hetty had never heard of a tunnel being under Barclay Street before, or anyone using a tunnel in this area. Which wasn't a bad thing on its own, but that all depended on what they found.

As they reached the bottom of the stairs, the tunnel expanded. Not only did they have a choice of turning left or right, but the tunnel swept upward into an arched ceiling well above their heads.

"This was carved out with care." Benjy swept his arm toward the ceiling as they took the leftward path first. "Great skill, too. Something important was moved down here. What it was depends on who used this tunnel."

"You have doubts?" Hetty asked with some surprise.

"I have a few ideas but they rely on people using the staircase back into the house."

Hetty had an idea of one possibility as she glanced at the ground. The light from the star sigil above them revealed deep wheel ruts cut into the dirt.

A wagon with heavy cargo? Or had countless wagons come through here?

"If only there was a bit of mess. It would have made things easier." Hetty tapped her boot against the ground. The tunnel was fairly clean. No cobwebs, no musty air, and no signs of debris lying around.

"I disagree."

Benjy had stopped not far in front of her. At first she thought he was waiting for her to catch up. But as she drew near, she found she was wrong.

They could go no further.

Densely packed rock and rubble blocked the way ahead. The light from the river of stars flowed along it, illuminating the stones that had settled in a fashion that would be impossible to move.

"Interesting," Benjy said. He leaned forward to study it, but thankfully made no move to touch a single stone. "This is recent."

"Did any of the neighbors mention something like an earth-quake?" Hetty asked.

"No. But we're deep enough that it might not be a concern."

"What if those star sigils dampen things?"

"Possibly. The hex bothers me more," Benjy replied absently. "It nearly caught you—and you're an expert at magical detection. I don't know if this is connected to the fire, but the possibility is high."

They retraced their steps, passing the stairwell as they turned their attention to the other side of the tunnel.

It was much the same, although they did manage to walk for a longer period of time before they were stopped by a solid sheet of rock.

This time, Benjy pressed a hand against the wall. He barely touched it before the wall swung outward.

Hetty peered out into a small side street. At first it looked no different than the dozens she'd seen before. Then she heard the bells—church bells that she recognized at once.

"This opens next to St. Gregorious." Craning her head, Hetty recognized the gates of the tiny Greek church that showed up in several of her friend Darlene's paintings. "This is only a few blocks away. We didn't travel that far at all."

"Still close enough for trouble. This is the end of the tunnel. The rest is blocked."

Hetty turned around, pressing her back against the stone archway to better look up at her husband. "Should we try to get through the blockage?"

"I wouldn't try it with magic." Benjy tapped his fingers against the wall. "There's a risk of tunnel collapse if I do it by hand."

"You just don't want to do it," Hetty said as she poked him in the chest. "Or you can't."

"Oh, I certainly can," he said swiftly, his full attention swinging back to her. "I just see no reason why I should." Benjy leaned toward her, leaving a playful gap between them. "Unless you can convince me?"

He said the words softly, and for a long moment the idea was tempting, because she was curious about where the tunnel went. And given a few moments, she could be quite persuasive. Yet . . .

"It doesn't matter where the tunnel leads if we can't connect it to the fire or hex," Hetty said.

Benjy nodded, pleased at these words. "The trail of magical residue didn't flow into here. It stopped midway on the stairs. So I'm more curious if there are other hexes left in the house."

If there were, they didn't get a chance to find them.

When they ascended the stairs back into the kitchen, it became very clear that Benjy had been right.

The house was occupied. They had been back in the kitchen for mere moments before the owner appeared in the doorway, the surprise in his face turning to confusion when he saw them in the pantry.

While it was hard to say if Benjy was surprised, Hetty was quite alarmed. They had left spells behind to warn them if someone had entered the house, and those spells had somehow failed when they never had before.

The man stared at them for what felt like a long time before speaking. "What are you doing here?"

He was a bit older, with streaks of gray in his hair that gave him a dignified air. He was handsome, with a squarish face and a neatly trimmed beard. A fact he was well aware of, for there were traces of his vanity about him, such as the tailored cut of his jacket. Although his skin was a warm dark brown, his features hinted at a complicated ancestry. He had an easy grin that only grew as he took notice of Hetty's study of him.

"We're looking into reasons for the fire. This house caught our attention since it's the only one still standing," Hetty said. "I'm sorry that we just barged in here."

"What were you doing in my pantry?" he asked. "Although, I won't complain about finding such a lovely woman in my home." He turned on the charm with these words, seemingly heedless of Benjy's presence at her side.

"You live here," Benjy said rather sternly. "How are you so lucky that the house still stands? Your neighbors' homes are nothing but dust and ashes."

Benjy met the man's gaze with a rather foreboding expression.

He was very good at this. A simple look that was a mixture of disdain, scorn, and impatience was just enough to silence all conversation and to have people reconsidering their choices in life.

While Hetty doubted Benjy took offense to the man's flirting, he did a good job at playing a jealous husband. It was a ruse they used often to great effect, because playing into expectations was always easier than bucking them.

"A well-placed spell." The man's pleasant smile could not hide how vague that answer was. "And a good deal of luck."

"I heard a candle was the cause of the fire," Hetty said.

The man snorted. "I don't believe an ordinary candle did this! I saw splotches of magic around when I checked on my neighbors. If any candle did this, it was etched with star sigils."

Candles were often carved with star sigils, and like the designs she sewed in her clothes or the etchings Benjy added to various metalworks, they could be used to amplify or ground spells.

It wasn't unusual magic, but it was unusual for Hetty to talk about it in conversation with a stranger. As long as magic did its job, few people cared to discuss the whys and hows.

"Are you familiar with such things?" Hetty asked.

"Not as much as I could have been," the man admitted. "My father was a scholar of magic."

"Of Celestial magic?" Hetty's surprise got away from her. There were many branches of magic in the world, but Celestial magic wasn't one that was closely studied. Formed during captivity and enslavement, Celestial magic was a curiosity to some, an abomination to others, and a mystery even to those that claimed it as a birthright. Constellations were the basis for sigils, and the rules on how to use them varied a great deal, as most instructions were passed along in stories and songs. Having become adept in such spells over the years, Hetty was confident in saying she had few equals in spellcasting. But in serious academic study, she wouldn't know where to begin.

"Yes. My father devoted as much as he could in this study. He's well known in certain circles about it."

Hetty wrinkled her nose. "Certain circles" always meant those elite and insular groups that seldom invited the likes of her into their ranks.

"Then I haven't heard of him."

"Are you sure about that?" he asked. "My father was Raimond Duval."

The man held himself ready to face an onslaught of questions. But there was no need to worry. Hetty had none, because that name told her everything she needed to know.

Raimond Duval died in the fire on Powell Street last month. While the fire, the destruction, and his death were recounted in the newspapers, a few details weren't mentioned.

Such as Raimond was badly burned on the chest and arms, but his clothes were intact enough that what they were able to retrieve showed precise tears in the flesh of his torso that looked like a knife wound. Or that the building rubble had layers of magical residue mixed in the ashes. Or that Duval's body moved through the coroner's office at such an alarming pace that the only thing Hetty and Benjy could study was the report file, which was riddled with half truths. Or that the only eyewitness had been a drunk—a woman sober enough to recognize the unofficial badge of a Beatty Hose volunteer making the rounds and who ended up floating in the Schuylkill not long after sharing this statement.

Everything pointed to Beatty Hose's involvement. And everything made sense. So they'd closed the case and moved on.

But nothing felt *right* about it.

And here she was, standing in front of another Duval.

This couldn't be by chance.

"Raimond Duval," Hetty said softly. "I know who he is. I didn't know he was a scholar of magic."

"One of the few. The name's Valentine. Who do I have the pleasure of speaking to?"

"Henrietta Rhodes."

Valentine grinned at her. "And Miss Rhodes, are you also a scholar in Celestial magic?"

This time, Benjy wasn't pretending any annoyance as he corrected the older man. "My wife is an extraordinary talent with magic."

Valentine exclaimed, "No wonder the name Rhodes sounded familiar to my ear! If she's Henrietta, you must be Ben Rhodes —you're well known in the Seventh, for the murder that often surrounds you."

"I would hope so," Benjy replied. "It's what happens when my wife feeds crows as often as she does. She enjoys seeing a large murder at our door."

Valentine didn't even blink. "Ha! This is the sort of wordplay I expect from Winston Smalls. Are you a member of the Edmonstone Club?"

"A sometimes member," Benjy admitted.

"Sometimes?"

"Yes, I sometimes show up for meetings when there's a topic of interest."

Valentine's laugh was both genuine and endearing. "I wish I could say you were wrong, but you got the right idea of it. These days, though, I've been giving my time to another group. Maybe you can join me at a meeting with like-minded individuals, regarding magic rights?"

Hetty coughed into her hand.

"Both of you," Valentine amended. "Women are not excluded. Some of the brightest people I work with have the moon's favor."

His well-meaning words were met with silence, and his smile wavered.

"Brother, who are you talking to?"

A woman poked her head in the doorway, frowning at Valentine and mostly ignoring Hetty and Benjy.

Her dress was dark gray, but made of material light enough for summer. The fine embroidery on her bodice pointed to the work of the Garden Tailors, who were infamous for certain swirls in their stitches. She had the wan look of someone who forgot a meal or two while distracted with other work. Brother and sister weren't identical, but there were faint echoes of each other in their features. Her long hair was kept back in a single plait that swung between her shoulders, and looking at the two of them, Hetty thought that the siblings likely had Native American relatives.

"Adelaide, this is Benjamin Rhodes, and his wife, Henrietta."

"Rhodes?" Valentine's sister echoed with some surprise. "I have heard the most extraordinary stories about you and your husband. My father—" She stopped for a beat, grasping the glasses that dangled from the delicate chain at her neck. She lifted them to her eyes and peered at Hetty and Benjy with clear fascination. "My father said you're one of the best practitioners of Celestial magic in the city. Some would say *the* best, given all the tales about you. I'm Adelaide Duval, and it's a pleasure to meet you."

"*Pleasure's* not the word I would use." In strolled a man who was some years younger than the siblings, although still much older than Hetty and Benjy. Accented French rolled along his speech, and if that didn't betray him as a Louisiana Creole, then his light complexion, light eyes, and a casual disdain of everything and everyone around him did that for him.

"Our cousin," Valentine said without looking back, "Horace, who shouldn't have come if he was only here to complain."

"I was curious"—Horace's eyes roved around the kitchen— "and I paid dearly for it. Are these your intruders?"

"We just came in to see if there was trouble," Hetty interjected. "The door was kicked in."

"Perhaps by the neighbors." Valentine nodded. "I have been traveling until recently, and since I got back I've spent my nights in my father's home. But I had spells set here, and knew something had gone wrong."

"Don't tell them your business, brother dear." Adelaide wasn't as rude as their cousin, but there was wary caution about her. Earned, perhaps, as there really wasn't a good excuse for Hetty and Benjy to be there. But there was something else. Something in the way the woman stuck her hands in the pockets of her skirts to hide the balling of fists.

The presence of strangers was not only a surprise. It was quite unwanted, almost enough to raise a fuss.

"I'm sure the whole street knows my business. I have not been here for a while, and if I had been—"

"The house would have burned down too," snorted Horace. "What a loss that would be! The house, I mean, not you."

"Horace," Adelaide snapped. "Why don't you go back to Father's house. We will talk then."

Her cousin shook his head. "You know what I came for."

Adelaide turned to her brother, one eyebrow raised in question.

"Upstairs," Valentine said. "In the wardrobe in the bedroom."

She nodded, and then glowered at their cousin. "Follow me."

When they left the room, all signs of ease in Valentine went away, leaving him tired and worn.

"I apologize for my cousin's rudeness, but it's been a trying time since my father's death. And this little fire is of concern. I know this was no accident. None of these fires have been accidents."

"That's why we're looking into them," Benjy said.

"Why would you be interested in such things?"

"You know who we are," Benjy said. "Since you are a sometimes member of the Vigilance Society."

Valentine smiled and something else in his face changed. Instead of the genial older man with a taste for inappropriate flirting, there stood a man who had seen his fair share of adventures. "The stories are true, then? You *are* that good."

"Just a good memory for details," Benjy said airily.

"I don't recall hearing anything about your work," Hetty said.

"I didn't do anything worth boasting about."

"Don't be so humble. Surely you have wonderful stories to tell," Hetty encouraged. "You must tell me how you got your start!"

"Brought into the family business. My father's people are from New Orleans. They've been free for generations, but unlike his siblings he didn't turn a blind eye to the slave trading going on. He went down to the auctions, placed bids, and made arrangements to get them their papers. My father freed my sister and myself this way. We were the last ones he had done this ploy with, and we stayed with him as he fled north with the aid of the Vigilance Society, which he joined later. When I grew older I took up the work alongside him. This house ended up in my possession because of the tunnel you can enter through the pantry." This last pointed remark was said with a small smile, confirming they had never truly fooled him in the first place.

"No regrets about the work?" Benjy asked.

"A few, but whatever you lost can hardly compare to all the lives you helped. Or so Bernice Tanner tells me."

"She would say so," Hetty grunted, "after all the assignments we took without question!"

"Such as Sarah Jacobs? Forgive me," Valentine said when they both looked on with surprise. "I remember that one because I had gotten an urgent message to give assistance, but I missed you by several days."

"Speed was important in that case," Hetty said as she turned to old, almost forgotten memories. "Someone was after Sarah Jacobs. We even had to rescue her children first, as she wouldn't leave without them. Luckily she had marked them." Hetty lifted her hand and drew a circle along the inside of her wrist. "So we knew who they were. With the children in hand, we returned to Philadelphia, met up with Sarah, and brought them all to safety."

"Is that the whole story?"

Hetty had heard many rude things in her life, but this ranked high among the worst offenders.

"The whole of what? That was not a proper story! Only a recounting of memories nearly forgotten. If you wanted the true story, I can tell you of a flight taken in haste. Of magic that silenced the wolves at our heels. A story with a villain who had a hundred faces that he slipped on like a mask. They didn't all fit, but some he wore rather well as he fooled all sorts of people."

"Tell me the proper story, then. There is more I haven't heard, it seems." Valentine smiled at Hetty as he said these words.

But there wasn't anything genuine about that smile. He wanted something.

That was fine.

Everyone wanted something. Although what he was after was hard to say. Nothing in his manner gave his true aim away.

"Let me start from the beginning." Hetty dropped her voice into a harsh whisper. "In the weeks before the war broke out, the North Wind blew an assignment into my lap. There was a woman in need of safe passage, but her children were taken from her, and she would not go to safety without them . . ."

CANIS MINOR

INTERLUDE

March 1861

PHILADELPHIA, PENNSYLVANIA

"WHERE ARE THE BOWS?"

"Bows?" Hetty echoed, her bland smile fading at the girl's words.

Making dresses for spoiled young misses, especially ones visiting from the South, was not something she wanted to do anymore.

But Hetty needed money. She needed any money she could slip into her pocket if she was going to make another trip to find her sister. This dress that the little miss wanted was worth three times Hetty's regular work. For that much money, Hetty would remake the dress in a night—but not with bows.

"There are no bows. They should be there. Not big ones, but here and here." Clarice pointed to places that would ruin the elegant lines of the dress.

The young miss looked at Hetty expectantly.

Hetty cleared her throat, searching for the words that wouldn't get her tossed out of the hotel room.

"They wouldn't look good there," she said finally.

"You have no imagination for that, clearly." Clarice took her wand and waved it in the air. Garish orange bows appeared like mushrooms on the bodice and underskirt. "Ah, much better."

"I suppose this could—" Hetty began.

"I don't like this color." Clarice held up the underskirt. "It's too dark. It should be lighter. How about pink?"

"The underskirt is to complement . . ."

"There is pink in the trimming."

"To tease out the colors!"

Clarice swung her wand around. The tip was near enough to Hetty's face that she could see the grooves in the wood.

Hetty's words caught in her throat, for this was what her old mistress did before she activated the collar around Hetty's neck.

It took all of Hetty's strength to keep from pressing a hand to her neck to prove the metal ring was long gone and only her scars remained.

"This is not what I wanted." Clarice's voice pulled Hetty out of her memories. The girl tapped her wand on the bodice. "Did you put any of your Primal magic in this?"

"No," Hetty lied, urged on by a stab of anger at hearing the offensive name for Celestial magic. There was magic in the stitches, but only a basic preservation charm, to keep the color from fading and strengthen against minor tears. Now she wished she hadn't even bothered.

"She wouldn't do such a thing." Clarice's Yankee cousin, Elspeth, finally looked up from her book. Her reassuring smile did not have an audience. If there was anyone to blame for Hetty being in this room at all, it would be Elspeth. The older girl fancied herself an abolitionist simply because her family hadn't owned slaves since her grandfather freed them in his will. When Hetty arrived at the Grand Laurel Hotel, Elspeth led her inside through the front doors and paraded Hetty about to the scandal of the other hotel guests. The girl's antics even drew the attention of the hotel staff, as well as the servants attending to their employers.

"Primal magic is harmless," Elspeth said. "It can't be complicated, since the practitioners hardly have the wits to make it do anything. They learned magic from us, after all. None of the Africans I've seen at the zoo know anything like this."

"What do you know? I've seen them in my daddy's fields, jumping and spinning around—they're doing something." Clarice turned to Hetty. "I hear there is magic that lets you communicate with the dead! Can you do that?"

The girl beamed at Hetty, and Hetty promptly forgot all about bows and dresses.

She was free, Hetty reminded herself. She had run away and made it to freedom. She returned to the South by her own choice and made it back up north with others, safe and sound. She'd lost everything and forged a new life. The words of this spoiled young miss were nothing compared to all of that.

"There is a way." Hetty dropped her voice to a loud whisper. "But it's a taboo."

Clarice's eyes grew as round as the moon. "You can talk to the dead?"

Hetty clutched her hands to her chest and made a show of rubbing them over and over, as if she were afraid to do even that. "Miss Reeves, I shouldn't say such things. It ain't proper. Or safe."

Clarice's chin went up. "You will try. If you want to be paid."

"Then all I can say . . ." Hetty kept her speech stumbling, to make it seem like she was terrified of her own words. "All I can rightly say is, don't go whistling by a grave. Any kind of noise stirs bones, but whistling calls to them. It brings them here. And they want to hear what you have to say. Try not to do it while wearing another's shoes."

Clarice swallowed and her eyes trailed down to the dainty things on her feet. The same shoes Hetty had overheard belonged to the girl's dead sister.

"Shoes?" Clarice said in a very tiny voice.

"Anything, really. But shoes most of all. Because they tell where you have been and what you have done."

Hetty might have said more to spook the girls to next Tuesday, but a door snapped open and a maid came back into the room.

It was Sarah, an enslaved woman not much older than Hetty. Wearing a homespun dress dyed ink black, and white gloves. Her hair was hidden under a cap. But the first thing anyone saw about her was the silver collar around her neck.

"Miss, Mr. Adam Thompson is here—"

Clarice let out a squeal, far away from the fright she had been in moments before. The girl bounded toward her cousin.

"I knew he would show up!" Clarice gleefully clapped her hands together. "I told you he would!"

"Maybe he is here to see me!" Elspeth teased.

"Well, if he is, he'll soon cast favor to me." Clarice batted her eyes. Moving toward the door, both girls had already forgotten about Hetty, the dress, and the payment for Hetty's work.

Hetty thought of calling after them, but knew better.

She would be expected to wait if she wanted her money. The silly girl probably even expected the bows to be put in place in her absence.

Bows! Those ugly things!

Hetty snapped her fingers.

The eyesores vanished in a flash of light.

A barely suppressed squeak behind Hetty reminded her that she was not completely alone.

Sarah had stopped tidying the room. Her eyes were locked on Hetty as her hand clenched around a dusting rag.

Hetty had waited all week for this gaze.

It was the reason she stretched the work on the dress and suffered the chatter of the young misses.

"I'd never seen magic like that," Sarah whispered. "So quick, so bright. I guess that's what you learn up here."

"No, I taught myself." Hetty pulled at her shirt collar, revealing the ring of scarred flesh. Scars that came not from just wearing a collar but from the punishments she suffered from using magic.

Sarah's eyes widened. "Yes," Hetty said, answering the unspoken question. "I was just like you. Do you want to be like me?"

Hope flared in Sarah's eyes, but it died like rain dripping on a candle. "I can't."

"You can. You can choose. I have friends in place ready to help."

Again hope flared before Sarah shook her head. "It's not just me."

"Family," Hetty said with sudden understanding.

"My babies."

"Back on the Reeves Plantation?"

"At a nearby farm, close enough I can walk on Sundays to see them. Two girls. If I leave with you, I'll never have them in my arms again."

"Not if we bring them to you." The promise rolled off Hetty's tongue without a moment's thought. "The little heiress is here for how long?"

"Quite some time. There was a scandal back home," Sarah said faintly.

"Then you stay, we bring back your children, and then we all leave together."

Sarah gazed at Hetty with a dizzying amount of disbelief. "Is that possible?"

"As possible as the sun rising the next morning!"

On that note, Hetty slipped out the room.

She found the laundry cart that Darlene Needham had left for her. Taking ahold of it, Hetty pushed the cart toward the lift and squeezed it and herself inside.

When the lift arrived in the laundry room, Hetty steered the empty cart around the corner. Darlene stood just out of sight, folding and sorting linen. She didn't stop even as Hetty fell into place next to her.

Darlene lifted the topmost layer of clothes. After staring down at the empty cart, she glared up at Hetty as if Hetty had ripped a lace shawl in half in front of her.

"Where is she?" Darlene asked.

"She has children," Hetty whispered. "She won't leave without them. I promised to bring them north."

Darlene cut her eyes at Hetty. "Bernice won't like this. It's not the plan."

"Who cares what she's planning. I don't work for her."

"I do. Why do you think I'm working in this hotel? I was put in place to help any servants who want to flee bondage. And it's not an easy task. It takes careful planning. There are things in place right now, and your foolish promise has ruined everything."

"Not yet."

Darlene was not impressed. "If we wait even ten days there might be trouble."

"I'll bring her children back in less time."

"Will you?" Darlene looked over the rim of her glasses, giving Hetty the same dismissive glance she made when Mrs. Evans first brought Hetty to properly meet the rest of the Vigilance Society members. The one that dismissed Hetty's adventures as luck and saw her as a nuisance instead of help. "You're only here to gain information about your sister. Are you saying if you learn about her location today, you'll still help Sarah?"

"That is an unkind question!"

"Maybe, but it's a fair one. Don't worry." Darlene wrenched

control of the cart from Hetty. "Someone else will take care of this."

Someone probably could, but when Hetty had made that promise it wasn't on a whim. She was going to bring Sarah's children back and get the family to freedom. Hetty just needed assistance, and from someone more helpful than Darlene Needham.

A jingling bell hanging above the blacksmith's door announced Hetty's entrance.

"Back here. If it's urgent I can—" Benjy looked up from the bench and his face folded into a scowl. "What do you want?"

"How do you know I'm not just here to talk?" Hetty came to a stop at the table, eyes on the items waiting their turn to be fixed.

Benjy waggled the hammer in his hand at her, irritation coming off of him in waves. "You don't turn up here without asking for some sort of favor."

"I do not!" Hetty pouted.

Benjy shut his eyes, grumbling like an old man. "I don't have time for your nonsense today!"

Although he was merely the blacksmith's apprentice, Benjy had the run of the shop overseeing all the fixes and creations that came out of the forge. The only problem was that no matter how good his work was, he didn't look like the blacksmith people expected. Too young, too easily distracted, and too willing to give opinions on things no one cared about.

Mrs. Evans had said something about him having potential, whatever that meant. Hetty didn't dare ask. The older woman had this funny notion in her head to play matchmaker. Which should have been annoying, but Mrs. Evans was all gentle about it, considering anyone else would have forced them to get married when they returned to Philadelphia after months of traveling together. Instead, Mrs. Evans only teased that Benjy might be sweet on her. But Hetty had her doubts about that, since nearly every time they talked he shooed her away like an annoying fly.

Hetty tapped the lantern sitting on the table as she tried to figure out the right words. She had only one chance to ask this right before he ripped her words apart. "It's not a favor but a question—"

"Don't touch that!"

Hetty made a show of moving her hands away and then turned them over. The Libra star sigil flashed and the lantern floated into the air next to her.

She looked at him pointedly, and he said nothing but gave her a look that could curdle milk.

"I need your help," Hetty said as she placed the lantern back on the table. "There is a woman who needs passage north. It's been arranged for her, but she won't leave without her children. They are down in Tennessee. I need to get there and back here in ten days."

"You want my help?" he scoffed, turning to a dented teakettle. He swung his hammer down on it hard enough that the clash rang in the air. "Take a train." He went on to strike the poor teakettle a few more times, the resounding clangs taking the space of whatever angry words he had. Hetty sighed, uncertain if this was better than being fussed at.

Then he stopped mid-swing. "No, that won't work. You need to move quickly and quietly. The children are blackmail." He blinked. "Who is this woman that you would press on the heels of time for such a task?"

"Someone who needs help," Hetty said. Seeing his skeptical expression, she added, "If I do this, I'll get information about my sister."

"That's your objective with everything," Benjy said. But he was no longer thinking about her as he spoke, having moved on to the problem at hand. "I think I might know a way to get there in less time. You won't like it, though."

"I doubt that."

Instead of explaining further, he pointed upward.

Hetty tilted her head back. Above them was a basket the size of a wagon hanging from the ceiling. There was something metal next to it that looked like a lantern. But it was only when Hetty saw the fabric tied up next to it that she realized what it was.

"An air balloon!" Hetty exclaimed. "Did you steal this? No, I don't care if you did! How fast does it travel?"

"Shouldn't you be asking if it's safe?" Benjy asked. "Or if it works?"

"If you put it together it has to work, and as for being safe, well, I trust you."

He blinked, and for a moment Hetty thought she'd said the wrong thing.

It was occurring to her that in her eagerness to keep her promise to Sarah Jacobs and prove Darlene wrong, she forgot one small thing.

She hadn't asked if he wanted to take part.

It was one thing to ask him for ideas. Quite another to ask for more help than that.

But she couldn't operate this air balloon on her own. And if she was being honest, she couldn't head back south on her own either. Nor did she want to.

It was easier to have someone with her to watch the road and guard her back, but she couldn't ask. Not when he hadn't been brought into the fold with the Vigilance Society. Not when they weren't truly friends.

Then, to her surprise, something that never happened before occurred: he smiled.

"*Safe* isn't quite the word I'd use, but it will fly," Benjy said. "There is a small hole in the balloon envelope. If you sew it up, we can leave by nightfall."

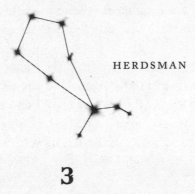

HERDSMAN

3

BENJY WAS QUIET WHEN they finally put the strange fires, secret tunnels, the Duvals, and everything else behind them.

Retreating to a broody silence, Benjy remained unresponsive
to Hetty's few attempts at pleasant conversation. In the end, she
fell into her own silence, thinking not just of Sarah Jacobs, but
the circumstances around the case. The incident was the first official work they'd had with the Vigilance Society. The one in which
Hetty had been properly introduced to Darlene, though they
would not become good friends until years later. Not to mention the work that cemented the partnership she had developed
with Benjy. Which was an odd thing to say, since they had already
traveled together along a dangerous and difficult road. But ferry-
ing Sarah Jacobs and all that followed turned what had been a
question into the beginning of their adventures together.

Benjy went to where they'd left their bicycles leaning against
a pole. With a flick of his fingers, the spell making the bicycles
an uninteresting sight went away. He wheeled them both as he
walked back toward her, gently pushing hers ahead.

"Why didn't he ask about his father?" Benjy asked abruptly.
"Why bother asking for stories when there was a better use of
his time?"

Used to these outbursts that were often interjected into un-related conversation, Hetty merely shrugged. "Why would he ask us?"

"He knew who we were from the moment he saw us."

"I doubt that," Hetty began. "He said—"

"He said a lot of things. The most important bits were near the end, when he was looking for answers from us."

Hetty placed her hands on her bicycle's handlebars but did not mount. "You're saying three different things at once. Tell me so I can follow."

"Valentine Duval knows who we are and that we looked into his father's death."

"I don't remember him coming to our door asking for help. Or even meeting him at his father's funeral. How did you know about him?"

"I pay attention to such things," Benjy said without malice, and he went back to his brooding.

Hetty let him be. There would be plenty of time to find out what exactly was on his mind, and answer his lingering questions.

Hetty swung up on her bicycle and led the way home.

The house on Juniper Street was a narrow building inlaid with beautiful dark red brick. The shutters around the windows were a dark blue, and the rooftop was flat enough that Hetty could set up her telescope on it. Their home shared its front steps with the house next door, and the postboxes acted as a dividing line. There were a few bushes out in front, with a sign for their funeral home poking out. As theirs was the end unit, access to the backyard was through the gate that opened both to the street and to the narrow alley that ran behind the line of row houses.

They'd owned this house for a couple months now, and spent quite a bit of time renovating it to their tastes, from the small-est nail in the floorboards to the cream-colored paint that now graced the main rooms. Still, whenever Hetty approached it and saw faces in the windows and heard conversation trickling to the streets, she felt like a guest coming for a visit.

"Why are there people in our house?" Hetty asked as she skidded to a stop in the middle of the street.

"Are we doing a play tonight?" Benjy asked.

About once a week they gathered with their friends to put on a play. What that play was varied in both scope and scale. Sometimes it was a full production with costumes and props, and other times they simply read favorite fragments of different plays. Either way, the plays were always performed with great enthusiasm. The gatherings were really about spending time together. Although Hetty wasn't a fan at the start, she enjoyed the evenings they put on plays very much, even when she'd rather come home to peace and quiet.

"We never picked one last time," Hetty reminded him. "Oliver wanted us to do the play he wrote, and George was against it on principle, and—"

"Everyone argued all night. I remember that part. Not sure that explains why they're here so early. They usually come around after sunset."

"Because they have keys," Hetty grumbled.

"That was your excellent idea," Benjy said with some glee. "You argued strongly for it when I disagreed. But if you want me to, I can get rid of them."

"It won't be easy."

"Doesn't hurt to try. I'll put the bicycles up—"

"No." Hetty grabbed his handlebars, nearly toppling off her own bicycle as she did so. "I'll do it!" she said. Before he could reply, she added, "I'd rather do this than deal with them. And you've always been better at shooing people out without magic."

"It's a gift." Benjy shrugged, easily taken in by the compliment.

As Benjy headed for the front door, Hetty slipped through the gate, leading the bicycles into the back. After sliding the bicycles into their spot behind the house, she went to the far corner of the yard and poked at the shed hidden under a thick veil of her magic to see if the spells had been disturbed or not. Assured they hadn't, she turned to the house and spotted the curtains in the kitchen shifting aside. Within moments, the back door opened and Penelope skipped out.

Penelope's hair was twisted and held in place with a butterfly hairpin. She wore a plain white blouse and a dark skirt, both of which had a dusting of dirt and smelled of wildflowers. She also wore a belt that had a few dangling pouches tied to it, which meant she had come right from the herbal shop she worked at. Penelope liked fancy clothes, and liked even more dressing to show off her fuller figure, which she couldn't do when wearing an apron.

"About time you showed up," Hetty's best friend declared with a grin. "We were all getting dreadfully bored waiting for you. We even talked about bullying Thomas into fixing us dinner as the afternoon came to an end."

"I wish him the greatest luck with that, since there isn't much. But if it was that boring waiting for us, maybe you should rethink showing up when we aren't here?"

Penelope placed a hand against her chest in feigned offense. "I was in the garden most of the afternoon! Everyone else just showed up on a mere whim."

While both bits were unsurprising, Penelope often came after work to tend to the garden. The backyard was in theory Hetty's to design to her liking, but she'd just handed the whole thing over to Penelope to manage. Half the yard had been tamed under Penelope's gentle hand into a tidy garden — although her friend refused to say if any poisons would bloom there. Questions on the subject received a wry smile but no firm denials. The other half was enough space for them to actually use the yard for entertaining and other amusements. There was even a metal bench where Hetty often sat feeding the birds. What lay in the far corner protected by her wards was a secret for now.

"Is Sy here?"

Penelope shook her head at the mention of her cousin. Penelope had several cousins living in Philadelphia. While Hetty had little love for a few of them, there were some she rather liked, and Sy was among that number. The young man had apprenticed under Benjy at the blacksmith's shop. However, when Benjy lost that job earlier this year, Sy had quit in solidarity. Though, truly, it was for the best. Sy had many talents, but being a blacksmith was not one of them.

Though Sy wasn't working for Benjy anymore, he often acted as their assistant even when they couldn't pay him anything more than a good meal and a story.

"Sy's coming around tomorrow. He'll be bringing"—Penelope lowered her voice—"the boxes."

"The boxes" was the term they agreed on using in case Benjy was around to eavesdrop.

When he was fired from his blacksmith job, Benjy had been running the place on his own, as the owner left all the work and responsibilities on Benjy's capable shoulders. His work and talent were what brought customers in, and with Benjy no longer there, his old employer found very quickly just how loyal customers were. With outstanding debts to pay, the shop had quietly closed at the start of the month, with the owner selling off equipment. Hetty had waltzed right in, unbeknownst to Benjy, and bought everything that she could.

She couldn't bring everything home, however. If she had, Benjy surely would have discovered it and spoiled the surprise before it was ready. That was where Sy came in. What Hetty couldn't handle herself, he hid for her.

"He can't come soon enough," Hetty lamented. "Do you know how hard it is to keep a secret from my husband?"

"You kept secrets before."

Hetty scoffed. "But he knew about the existence of the secrets and played along to amuse me. I want to take him by surprise, just once!"

"Well, you're not going to if we stay out here any longer," Penelope laughed.

Entering her kitchen, Hetty stopped short at the sight of three cauldrons merrily brewing away on her stove. The one on the left held familiar medicinal smells from Penelope's signature healing salve. The other two set off plumes of purple and blue respectively. Those were also familiar, but were less welcome.

"Did I say you could brew up potions in here?" Hetty asked.

Penelope thought for a moment before she grinned. "You never said I couldn't!"

Hetty tried to glare, but it was a futile effort. Hetty had had a sister once. Esther: an expert in herbs, a devoted healer, and the dearest person in Hetty's life. They had lost each other when they escaped to find freedom. While Hetty would never reunite with her sister, Hetty had a fair idea of what Esther could have become in Penelope, as her friend had slipped right into the role with surprising ease.

Penelope was kind when Hetty was not, prone to excitement when Hetty was unimpressed, and more forgiving than Hetty would ever be. Hetty had other friends that were better listeners, but Penelope was the only person Hetty could speak to candidly and be completely unafraid of what would follow.

"I suppose it'll be fine. We do use up a great deal of healing salve." Hetty glanced at the table. Unsurprisingly, the basket held the elemental pistols Penelope had recently crafted. "Will you be leaving those here?"

"Of course." Penelope picked up one of the pistols. Though it looked like a regular gun, instead of firing bullets, it fired magic. There was a glass orb on the back that held the potion that fueled it. The only one that worked was the ice pistol. The rest Penelope had varying success with, to which Hetty's kitchen could bear witness.

Penelope shook the pistol gently so the purple liquid in the orb canister swirled around. "I made some modifications. The kickback when the wind element is activated isn't as bad as it was before."

"I'd like to try it. But not inside." Hetty pointed to a small dent in the kitchen door.

Penelope pouted. "That was an accident."

In the past few months a number of "accidents" resulted in something being set on fire in the cellar, the backyard, the kitchen, and once in the hallway—although that last incident was Benjy's fault. Though Benjy was not an alchemist like Penelope, his interest in tinkering with magic, metal, and machines led him to be a willing partner in Penelope's experiments. And as long as they didn't burn down the house, Hetty wasn't about to stop her two favorite people from spending time together.

Leaving the kitchen behind, Hetty nearly bumped into Darlene in the hallway.

A mixture of contradictions, Darlene was both practical and imaginative, stubborn and easily persuaded, mousy but with the courage of a lioness. On the outside she was a model example of the new ideal that was growing in their community—married, with a baby, and a husband who provided for the household. However, a closer look revealed that Darlene had adopted her daughter, that George took on an equal amount of time in childcare duties, and that Darlene was currently working outside the home as an artist's assistant.

She never begged for dresses like Penelope, but slyly showed Hetty a dress design and presented a challenge to Hetty of turning it into reality. Such a dress was one Darlene wore at the moment, a pink so dark that it was the color of wine, with delicate lace along the collar and sleeves that had buttons so Darlene could easily slide them upward.

"Ah, I wondered where you were!" Darlene pushed up her round spectacles as she looked at Hetty. "Where have you and Benjy been?"

"He didn't say?" Hetty asked.

Darlene shrugged. "He stepped in and got swallowed up into a conversation about tonight's entertainments. Oliver is trying to get Benjy to box in tonight's match."

"Won't say there's betting involved," Penelope added, "but there probably is."

"Probably." Hetty nodded. "Why are you here? It's Tuesday, and we don't usually have plays on Tuesdays."

"I came looking for Penelope," Darlene started, but then just as quick she stopped without saying a word more.

As this was never a good sign, Hetty prompted, "Looking for Penelope to . . ."

"Go see a medium," Penelope cheerfully supplied.

"Just where will you find a medium?" Hetty asked.

"In New Jersey."

"There's a traveling show that arrived with an assortment of attractions. We're going this evening," Darlene explained. "It looked interesting."

"More than interesting!" Penelope declared. "I don't know anyone dead I'd like to talk to, but according to the poster I saw, Eudora Mason can summon all sorts of ghosts during her séances. Famous people, pirates, queens, even presidents!"

"I know all about this sort of nonsense." Hetty's words came bristling out, dimming their smiles. This was the first time she had heard about such a trip, which sounded like it had been planned for some time without her. "These spirits only seem to visit the drawing rooms of the white and wealthy!"

"Don't be like that, Hetty," Penelope said. "And it's not a white medium. She's Colored like us."

"As if that makes it better. Only fools call upon ghosts!"

"I'm not trying to! The only ghosts are the ones that the living let linger."

"If you think that, why are you going?"

Penelope shrugged. "To observe how she is fooling all these people."

"And if she's not a fraud?" Hetty asked.

Penelope waggled her eyebrows. "Won't it make an interesting story?"

"We'll make sure to tell you all about it," Darlene said.

"Why would you do that?" Hetty asked. "Can't I come along?"

Her answer was only silence and guilty looks.

Hetty struggled to keep back her bristling complaints. Being told things last was happening more often these days, and it seemed that since Hetty moved she only heard about the tedious little things in her friends' lives instead of the things of greater interest.

"We didn't think you'd want to come," Penelope admitted.

"I do want to come! I will come. When are you leaving?"

"Soon," Penelope said.

"Good," Hetty grunted. "Come find me before you go."

Leaving them, Hetty went to the study to take a calming breath before she sought out the rest of her friends.

Although her home was a palace compared to the room she had lived in the past few years, it was smaller in a different way. Their bedroom was in the attic, and the second floor held four other bedrooms, though only one was a guest room. The rest acted as storage for various odds and ends.

On this level, they used the kitchen and the study for their personal use, leaving the rest of the ground floor and the cellar for the funeral home. In the parlor she would greet people who came for funerals and conduct all other manner of business. The dining room was set up to show off caskets.

Their study was tucked into the back of the house, and most of their waking hours were spent in the room. Benjy had widened the doorway to get his piano in, and it was a good thing he did, for it was often moved in and out of the room. The study was the only room besides their bedroom that had a rug reaching from wall to wall. A small couch was their main seating, and a couple chairs were nearby to be pulled in as needed. The desk where Hetty worked on the accounts had a newfangled typewriter on top of it. Several lamps were tucked here and there around the room. A couple of Penelope's plants rested on the windowsill; the purple flowers brightened the room and were definitely not poisonous. Benjy had built bookshelves into the far wall from floor to ceiling, with plans to add more shelves around the room when the need arose. Hetty had laughed at such ambition, but since the end of spring, they had books on every shelf, and the topmost level was packed tightly. While Benjy might think his growing library the center focus of the room, for Hetty it would always be the map.

With colored thread dangling from her old sewing pins, the map marked various places across Philadelphia related to odd incidents and small mysteries they were working on. Their usage of the map was simple. Unrelated incidents got different colors, while pins used for a single case were unified by color. They also had a rule about removing pins when a case was settled.

Although it took the death of Raimond Duval for them to finally define what a settled case was.

Where there once had been a pin for the house fire that took

Raimond Duval's life, there was now a large, slightly jagged hole in the map.

Hetty ran her fingers around the torn edges.

Benjy had ripped it out when they finally put the case aside. He hadn't yelled, he hadn't raised his voice, but his opinion was clear. This case was over because there were no leads, no matter how they felt about its conclusion.

But was the case truly over?

They had met Valentine Duval. In their short conversation he'd made sure to communicate several things. He hinted that the fires that had torched his neighbors' homes were as deliberate as the other fires around town. He talked about his father in depth, in a way that went beyond conversation with mere strangers. He also brought up Sarah Jacobs. That was an odd topic to speak on, even if he had once worked for the Vigilance Society. Even odder for him to ask for the story about something that happened so long ago.

While this was a troubling thing, what drew Hetty's attention was the tunnel. A tunnel that should not be there, with hexes left behind in the house.

She should have asked for more information about it when they spoke. Valentine knew about it; he made sure to communicate that to them. But what he knew about the blockage in the tunnel, the connection to the hex, or anything else remained a mystery.

Next time she saw him, Hetty decided as she stuck a pin with bright green string on Valentine's home, she would most definitely ask.

SEA MONSTER

4

HETTY WASN'T SURE WHAT she expected when she poked her head into the dining room, but it wasn't her friends gathered around the long and ornate table that took center stage in the room. Or that the large chandelier above their heads was fully lit up despite plenty of sunlight trickling through the window.

On the table was an open case for a fiddle. Benjy loomed over the instrument, giving it the full weight of his scrutiny. Nearby, Thomas was in the middle of a rapid-fire explanation about the fiddle's origins. Oliver sat in one of the straight-back chairs, rubbing at his short beard, his expression much like whenever Hetty and Benjy brought a murder victim for him to study. Disapproving, concerned, and unable to stop himself from getting involved. Although the magnitude of his concern appeared greater than usual. A circumstance that only occurred when Thomas was involved. Watching Oliver for a moment longer, Hetty could only ponder what that expression meant. Oliver always worried about Thomas, and these days he did so with a particular keenness because he and Thomas had spent over half a year apart due to a combination of stubbornness and unwillingness to listen on both sides.

Sitting apart from this set piece, George flipped through the pages of a book, absently moving it away from the baby in his lap, who kept reaching for it. George's frown only seemed to deepen, and it didn't seem related to what he was reading. Across from her husband and daughter, Darlene idly sketched what must be the scene before her in her sketchbook. On the other end of the table sat Cora and Jay. Neither appeared too concerned about the fiddle as they spoke softly to the other, their heads bent in a whispered conference. But they were the only ones who noticed Hetty as she slipped inside and quietly shut the door behind her.

Both Cora and her husband, Pastor Jay Evans, had worked with the Vigilance Society as station masters in the years leading up to the war. They housed many runaways like Hetty who were struggling to figure out what it meant to be free. While many had come and gone, only Hetty remained long enough to call their house a home. She had gotten on well with the older couple, becoming a part of their lives outside of the Vigilance Society, living with them until her marriage. Having no children of their own, they often claimed Hetty as their adopted daughter. Hetty once had a mother and father, and held on to the memories through the stories she told. Cora and Jay would never replace them, but they filled the void in her heart.

Hetty was halfway across the room when Benjy asked, without looking up from the fiddle, "Do you think the wood itself could be enchanted, Hetty?"

Heads spun in Hetty's direction, surprise on the others' faces. Hetty ignored them all as she stepped to the table, reminded of the times they'd found a dead body in the middle of the night. Up close, the fiddle wasn't as nice-looking as she'd first thought. A few scratches and worn spots proved it was well used, but not valuable.

"It depends on the method," Hetty said. "The wood could be soaked in a potion. Or grown from a tree that's been enchanted."

Hetty reached out a hand. She didn't touch the fiddle, but merely held her hand over it.

She could almost feel the magic, but that might be her mind pulling a trick on her.

There was too much ambient spellwork around her in this room to allow her to pinpoint what made this fiddle special. And she wouldn't risk finding out in a more direct fashion, crowded as she was with her dear friends.

"Where did this come from?" Hetty asked.

"It's mine," Thomas said. The right side of his face was a web of old scars, and made his already worried expression hold even greater concern. "Or . . . not mine exactly, but it came into my possession."

"I told him not to take it," Oliver grunted. The snarl of his words didn't hide the glimmer of fear behind his eyes. Of all of their friends, Oliver assisted them the most directly because he was an embalmer. And in the course of looking at dead bodies, he'd witnessed his fair share of magical mishaps. Thomas, despite all he'd seen, didn't share his partner's caution. It was a trait that appeared in the number of failed ventures Thomas had started over the years, and explained how he rushed into things with too little information. Including the mail-order business he was running out of his living room.

"I didn't pick it up off the streets," Thomas said wearily. "Someone wanted me to mail it for them."

"Is this about the Pony Post again?" Hetty asked.

"In a roundabout way," Thomas insisted.

"Did an instrument maker want you to send this?"

Thomas swallowed and carefully avoided Oliver's eyes. "No, just someone who had it in his possession."

Together, Hetty and Benjy cried: "It's stolen!"

Oliver put his head in his hands, groaning about foolishness and foolhardy men. Meanwhile, Thomas looked around for allies.

George was still pretending to read his book. Darlene sniffed and looked away. Jay shook his head with gentle reproof. Which left Cora.

Cora peered at the fiddle for a long moment, but then sat back even more disinterested than she was at the start. "What made you bring this here? It's not causing trouble." She waved a hand around the room. "The wards Henrietta and Benjamin placed on their home wouldn't have let you in if it was dangerous. This fiddle's been here for hours now, and it's done nothing to be concerned about."

"But it could," Thomas said.

There was an almost stubborn quality to his words. While Hetty was ready to dismiss the fiddle as harmless, Thomas clearly wasn't ready to do the same.

Benjy shut the instrument's case. "I could keep it for a while. Take a closer look."

"You don't think it's dangerous?" Darlene asked.

"No, but a closer look will help." Benjy carried it out of the room. Hetty waited for a moment before she followed him.

"Why the big production?" she asked the moment they were alone in the hallway. "We both know it's harmless."

Benjy tapped his fingers against the instrument case. "I know, but Thomas is worried about something. A tricky enchantment is the least annoying thing I can deal with."

"We," Hetty corrected. "I'm curious too."

"And it is worth looking into just to be safe. Think Penelope has a potion that can find something our spells can't?"

"Penelope always has a potion we can try."

But when they went back to the kitchen, not only had the table been cleared and the kitchen tidied, but Penelope was nowhere to be seen.

They even went into the study, just in case Penelope had gone in there to restock the jars of healing salve, but she was not there, either.

"She might be upstairs freshening up," Hetty said, although she made no move to check, choosing instead to perch on one end of the couch. "I'm going to New Jersey in a bit. Penelope and Darlene want to see a medium. The great Eudora Mason. She speaks to ghosts and sends messages to loved ones."

Her husband's expression was everything she had imagined and somehow more. The perfect amount of disgust and mild disbelief filled his face.

"Ghosts aren't real," Benjy declared. "And if they were, why would they speak to the living?"

"To bestow knowledge, give wisdom, maybe even tell people who killed them?"

"If they did that, it'd take all the fun out of mystery solving." He paused for effect. "If they were real!"

Hetty laughed off his concerns. "I believe the medium is a fraud, but it's Darlene who wants to go."

"Who died recently for her to be that interested?"

"Her father's been dead for the past three years, but he died rather peacefully."

"Maybe she wanted to introduce him to her baby."

Hetty rolled her eyes as Benjy chuckled at his own joke. "If you're that curious, you're welcome to join us."

"I have plans for the evening, although I'm just learning about them."

"I heard Oliver is keen on getting you in the boxing ring tonight."

Benjy leaned the instrument against the wall. "He's trying to convince me."

"Convince you?" Hetty laughed. "Did he bet his house and a great deal of money on you?"

"No, but he was telling me about Wildcat James. The man's been talking nonsense about being the defending champ, even though the last time we fought it was hardly a match."

"I know." Hetty hid a smile as he fumed, clearly bothered by the blatant lies. "I was there."

In Hetty's biased opinion, Benjy had no equal in the boxing ring, but even so, no one could deny his superior skills when he sent the Wildcat flying out the ring by the end of the second round.

"Are you doing the match, then?" Hetty asked. "To correct this very wrong opinion?"

"It's just that I didn't plan on it," Benjy began. "I haven't made up my mind."

That was a lie.

Benjy may have started taking part in these matches because of the outrageous bets made by an old friend, but he enjoyed it. The money their friends placed on him, the harsh words spat by other opponents, the lure of riches to be made—these were of little matter. He did it because he liked it, and that was that.

"You should box," Hetty said. "I don't like hearing such tales spread about you. And we could do with the extra money."

"There are easier ways."

"No, *this* is the easiest. You don't have to put on a grand show. I won't even engage in the usual antics."

Benjy chuckled at that. "People are starting to catch on."

"But that's what makes it so fun! I just stand there twisting a handkerchief around. It's not my fault people change their bets based on the quiver of my lip."

"They aren't the only ones watching for that," Benjy said.

"I know, because you're the primary audience," Hetty teased. "So yes or no?"

Benjy stood above her, leaning over so the gap between them wasn't so great. For all his protesting, his brown eyes were alight with amusement. The promise of something else lurked there as well, which was equally exciting to Hetty. "I shall think about it. After all, I should keep busy while you're away."

"One would think you would be busy regardless!"

Jay's voice had cut into the conversation, chilling the warm summer evening. Benjy stepped away from her at once, as Hetty quickly jumped off her own couch as if they were children caught being naughty.

The door swung quietly behind him, and the pastor stood brimming with as much disapproval as he had done a month ago and in the weeks since.

Jay was not here about boxing matches or mediums. Hetty knew what subject brought him to seek them out.

"There was another fire today—did you hear about that?" Jay demanded.

"We did," Hetty began, only to have her words quelled with a stern look.

"Another strange fire," Jay continued. "Just like the one that Raimond was murdered in."

"Officially, it was an accident," Hetty said, as easily and calmly as she could. Benjy had stiffened at this twist of the conversation, forcing his face into a neutral mask. "There is no murderer to bring to justice."

"That might be true," Jay grunted. "But to leave it at that when I know you two can and have—"

"We did all we could." Benjy's voice was quiet as he interrupted the pastor, but he was firm and unyielding. "We poked and we prodded. There is nothing more to find."

"There is always something more."

"Not this time. There are no more answers. All roads lead to Beatty Hose." Benjy spat out the name as if he hoped it would shut down all conversation.

Jay just shook his head, far from deterred. "It's Beatty Hose. They are always behind things. All these fires going on . . ."

"What do you wish for us to do about it?" Benjy asked, even as Hetty tried to hush him. "Perform last rites for the dead?"

Jay didn't take the bait. "I want you to admit that this is a pattern! These so-called firefighters are standing by and letting homes burn on purpose!"

"I know how terrible they are," Hetty said.

"No, you do not!" Jay cried, and the pictures on the wall rattled around them as ambient magic swirled in the air. "You were not even alive when the fire companies banded together to stop us from forming a Negro fire company—and they didn't simply refuse to look at our charter. They set buildings on fire and placed hexes to keep us from dousing them. Then they turned around and said we couldn't handle fighting even the smallest of fires. There's no magic to divine the future. But I'm seeing the signs of this city once more careening back into a past I thought the war had snuffed out. When I wasn't much younger than you, I could vote in this city. But they changed the rules when folks upstate started shaking in their boots when word of revolts on plantations reached their ears. I've seen it all. The rise of taboos, and cursed sigils, and race laws placed on the books. And it's happening again. I'm not sure if I'm a fool for thinking it all settled."

"No one's a fool for wishing for the best."

Cora walked into the study, her voice serene and bringing a cool misting rain to the heated tempers in the room. She reached over to place a hand on Jay's arm. As she did, her touch softened the lines along his jaw.

Jay slumped, the anger directed at the world around them vanishing.

"Another friend of mine died last week in a collision with a wagon," Jay said, softer this time. "It reminded me of Raimond.

Seems like it was an accident, but I can't be sure. But maybe I'm wrong. I'm sorry to have bothered you with an old man's worries. You young folk, you deserve an evening of distractions. The chances are so rare these days."

Jay turned and left the room. Cora looked back at them for a moment and nodded at Hetty in sympathy before she followed after the pastor.

Like a tree, Benjy remained rooted where he stood, his arms folded across his chest and his gaze fixed on the framed photograph across from him.

Last month, a photographer had been at one of the church's excursions. A nephew of one of the deacons, the young man had set a very cheap price for portraits — so cheap that nearly everyone that was interested sat before the camera. Hetty and all of her friends had portraits done in a variety of numbers and configurations. After some serious portraits, they had a bit of fun, attempting to see what spells they cast could be captured in a photograph. The best attempt, a star-speckled crow fluttering down to Hetty's hand, hung in their bedroom. But the portrait in the study featured the four of them arranged in front of a large oak tree. Hetty and Cora sat on the little bench while Benjy and Jay stood behind them. They all managed a bit of a smile, but Hetty was beaming. A family portrait, the young photographer had said, and no one corrected him.

"He can ask for answers," Benjy said finally, his voice strained and tired. "But he won't like what he gets."

SAGITTARIUS

5

With the wind coming off the river and clouds turning the sky gray, the summer heat receded. Hetty leaned against the railing, watching the landscape shift around her. The ferry to Camden wasn't her favorite mode of transportation. It was a bit too slow for her taste. But it was the cheapest way to cross, and in the summertime traveling this way could be quite pleasant compared to the train.

While Hetty still had her doubts about seeing a medium, she was willing to do anything to get out of the house for a moment to put all mentions of the Duvals, fires, and the conflict brewing between Benjy and Jay aside. To say Jay had not been happy about the conclusion of Raimond Duval's case missed a world of nuance in his displeasure. It was a quiet displeasure, less angry heated words and more cool and cutting comments, that caused a strain in their relationship. It was stronger on Benjy's end, because of his pride when it came to mystery solving. But also because the case was a bit too perfectly closed for their taste. Blaming Beatty Hose was easy, but it didn't feel right for that case. Yet that was the only answer they landed at.

"I heard all about the secret plot with Benjy's shack," Darlene said, leaning along the rail next to Hetty, interrupting her brooding. "I can't believe you pulled it off!"

"I haven't quite yet—not all of the tools have arrived," Hetty said.

"But it's just in that corner, right?"

There was a level of care in Darlene's voice that lifted Hetty's gaze off from the horizon and toward her friend.

Hetty's mild curiosity only increased as she noted how Penelope, standing on Darlene's other side, pointedly looked away.

"Why is that of interest?" Hetty asked.

"I'm thinking if I set up a number of lights floating around, it would be a wonderful spot for the next E. W. Harper meeting."

"No, it wouldn't," Hetty said. "My neighbor will make it unpleasant."

Darlene was undeterred. "Then inside. You're finished with renovations and you can't say you don't have the space."

There was plenty of space. Hetty just refused to get involved as it meant inviting an untold number of strangers into her house.

Her friends were part of the E. W. Harper Literary Club, which met frequently to discuss books and poems, as well as a variety of topics including politics, art, scientific advancements, magic, and even community projects. The group had been started by Eunice Loring, who often played host to such gatherings. Because Hetty did not get on well with Eunice, she made excuses to avoid going to the meetings. However, there was no longer a need to put them off. Eunice, uneasy at the thought of staying around the very people her husband had hurt back in May, left Philadelphia for a fresh start at Fisk University.

"Why do you want to have it at my home?" Hetty asked. "You have plenty of space, especially with the schoolroom below your apartment."

Darlene swallowed then, suddenly quite stricken. But it was

Penelope who answered with a rather flippant air: "They sold the classroom."

"What!" Hetty cried, loud enough to draw attention from the other passengers on the ferry. She made an effort to lower her voice. "When did this happen?"

"Rather recently," Darlene said weakly. "We'll have new neighbors before the end of the summer, and if we're lucky, we will have moved into a new place as well."

"You're moving," Hetty added, recalling Penelope rented a room nearly for free from Darlene. "You both are."

"It won't be for a while," Darlene said. "Our living above the school was meant to be temporary. George always said he wanted to turn it into a school building when we had enough funds and buy a little house somewhere else. It took a while to realize that wasn't going to happen. If adopting Lorene wasn't enough, recent events told us we shouldn't put off things to a future that might not arrive. And I have to admit, I am a bit jealous of you. All that natural light was enviable enough, but you transformed the rooms on the main floor. I can hardly believe it used to be Oliver and Thomas's home. All of us can actually sit and rest comfortably."

"They weren't inclined to entertain people often," Hetty said, unmoved by such kind words, stuck on the fact that yet again she was the last to know about important things. "I'm starting to see they had a very good reason. You may flatter me all you like, but I'm not hosting your little club!"

"You can read us the astronomy paper you sent to that magazine," Penelope coyly suggested.

"Again?" Hetty brightened at this. "Are you sure? I read the earlier version to you, and there weren't that many changes with what I sent off."

"Astronomy is a very popular topic with E. W. Harper." Penelope jabbed Darlene in the arm.

Darlene forced a smile onto her face, so she didn't quite sound sincere when she said: "I would love to hear it again."

The idea was tempting, and Hetty found herself reconsidering her stance. Most of her friends' interest in astronomy went as far as the constellations used for their magic, but beyond that only Benjy would peer through a telescope pointed to the sky—and that was mostly for the pleasure of her company. There were very few people she could discuss astronomy with. Maybe this meeting could change that?

"I don't want too many people in the house, but if you keep it small—"

"I'll only invite people you know!" Darlene cried.

"Then it'll be fine. When's the next meeting?" Hetty asked.

"Thursday after next."

"That should work. And while they're there I can let them know about my funeral home services."

Darlene started to nod but stopped. "That's not a good idea."

"Why not? They'll be there already," Hetty asked, rather puzzled.

Darlene hesitated a bit before she said, "You tend to be a bit forceful about—"

"I always forget about that island!" Penelope exclaimed. "I heard they're putting in a naval yard."

Hetty glanced at the dot of land passing by. "As long as they leave Stars Haven alone it will be fine."

"I haven't been there before. What's its story?"

Well aware that Penelope was trying to distract her, Hetty took the bait anyway, as she could never pass up telling a story when asked.

"Stars Haven's story begins when the island was purchased by a Quaker, who turned it into a small settlement. On his deathbed, Friend Matthew returned the land to the few descendants with ties to the Lenape still left in the area. And they, as well as a few runaways, turned it into a haven, a fort, and the site of the grandest escape you'll ever hear about. But that's not the most interesting story about it."

"It's not?" Penelope wondered.

"It saw the arrival of its most esteemed guests." Hetty pointed to herself. "Benjy and I stopped there on the way back into Philadelphia a few times during the war. We would take a rowboat and work it through the river to avoid detection of soldiers."

"But Union soldiers occupied the fort," Penelope said.

"Didn't matter." Hetty shrugged. "Union soldiers thought we were spies for the other side. The Confederates thought the same."

"But didn't you act as spies at one point?" Penelope's eyes were big. "When you spent all that time in Virginia. You and Benjy—"

"Stop interrupting the story," Hetty chided playfully. "I'm telling you about daring naval escapades. We can save the spy stories for another time."

"Don't let her fool you." Darlene cleaned the lenses of her glasses, her smile full of indulgence as she spoke. "They had help. Mostly from me, because I was always tapped to give aid."

"You could have refused," Hetty pointed out.

"I suppose I should have," Darlene admitted. She attempted to sound stern, but she failed at it. "But in my youth I had bravado and thoughts of adventure."

"You never lose bravado when adventure isn't far away," Hetty said.

"For you, perhaps," Darlene said.

"It's true for you, too," Hetty said. "You count yourself among my friends, don't you?"

Hetty didn't finish telling Penelope about Stars Haven, for soon the ferry docked, marking their arrival.

The traveling show wasn't in Camden proper, but on the outskirts a bit. It was much smaller than Hetty expected, and the paltry showing didn't quite do justice to the sum she had paid for her entrance. But the air was much like a carnival. A carnival where each attraction was a sideshow and every sideshow was a less interesting delight. Others appeared to take an interest despite the lackluster appeal, but Hetty and her friends weren't here to take in the sights.

They came for one reason, even if a number of things got in the way first.

Like the man standing on a highly decorated wagon, holding a jar of touted miracles to the passing crowd.

They had missed the short skit that preceded it, and only heard the man talk about a "miracle potion." The list of cures ran long and perplexing, half being obviously false even without Penelope's grumbling reminding her otherwise.

"What a disgrace." Penelope shook her head. "I can't even sell herbs openly some days, and this flimflam gets sold on the streets without a problem."

Darlene shook her head in equal disgust. "This is why magic bans are being floated around. Because of people like this. And like that woman who used to be in the streets with her little brews."

Penelope snapped her fingers. "Geraldine Browne, that's her name. Only a handful of her potions actually worked."

"I never liked her much," Darlene said with some heat. "She used to do things like this. Selling your heart's desire, leaving you with only pain. I haven't seen her in a while."

"Because she's in jail."

Hetty's voice cut in the conversation, hardly amused at their words. "Her husband was killed and she had no choice but to sell more of her potions. Funny thing, though. The batch that landed her in jail actually worked. Geraldine mixed up something that put people on the edge of death on purpose. Her reasons were sound. She needed the money to take care of her daughter. But she was wrong to trust a white man would give her any sort of protection. Half of the proposed bans on potions are because of her."

"She was behind the Clover Street Sleep?" Penelope said. "Why didn't you say anything? Why didn't you stop her?"

Hetty blinked. "That's not what I do. And I only learned she was involved afterward, during another case."

"Remember," Darlene said quietly, "this happened at the end of May."

Penelope's scowl faded and she turned contrite. "That's right. I'm sorry. I forgot."

May had ended in a rush of excitement. They moved, Benjy had been recovering from a broken arm, Hetty learned of her sister's death, and news reached them that a man who tried to kill them died in jail by apparent suicide. A busy time all around.

And a time that clearly weighed on her friends.

As a wary look passed between her, Penelope, and Darlene, Hetty suddenly found herself wishing she hadn't insisted on coming along on this jaunt.

"Well, is there something I should know about—" Hetty's words faltered as she stared at the large green tent in front of her.

A tent that had not been there when they passed moments before, and appeared without the usual fanfare.

"Tell me that you see this too?" Darlene whispered.

"The work of a don't-notice-me spell," Hetty attempted to reassure her. None of the usual marks of Celestial magic were clear to her eye. "Nothing to fear."

"Who said 'fear'?" Penelope swallowed hard, her lips trembling. "Sweet stars above, what's wrong with this? Should I be worried?"

"It's nothing to be worried about," Hetty protested, but her words held little heat.

Several others drifted toward the tent, their swift movements showing that they, too, were lying in wait.

They fell behind others in a line, where a barrel-chested man stood at the opening. He nodded, pulling aside the curtain flaps.

"You will be the last. In you go."

Inside the tent was a large round table covered with a delicate lace tablecloth of faded ivory. The lace trim had swirls that were a bit more yellow than the rest of the cloth.

Star sigils sewed into the stitches.

Relief washed over her.

This was magic she was familiar with.

The tent was dimly lit, with tiny lights floating over them casting them in a soft amber glow. Yet despite these lights, a large fat candle sat in the middle of the table, but its flame didn't bend or move around as it should. Around the table were eight other people. They whispered softly to each other, except for one, a woman who sat stiffly apart from everyone, her arms wrapped around a box. Her hair was pure white, and her neck gleamed with pearls a bit too fine for this outing.

As Hetty took her seat, a woman stepped through a set of curtains that partitioned the tent. Her clothes were more like a costume: loose and flowing, with billowing sleeves common two decades previously, like the castoffs from an old mistress altered and given use. Her hair was covered in a kerchief, and she clutched a lace scarf along her shoulders. She was not young, but not old, either, as the faint wrinkles around her eyes attested. But she moved with care as she sat down in the last chair, beaded necklaces around her neck softly clicking together as she did.

This was clearly Eudora Mason, as the moment she sat down, conversation stopped in the room even before she lifted her hands into the air.

"All who gather in my tent, know this. You expect me to summon a ghost, but ghosts don't come when they are called—they come when they wish. All you need to do is create a space for them to appear. Breathe deeply and allow the spirits to come in. They will reach out when called."

Her arms lowered, and she extended a hand out to each of them, swept around the tent. When she faced Hetty, her arm dropped to her side completely as if she'd lost track of what she was doing. Although Eudora's expression didn't change, something in her eyes shifted. Not fear, not recognition, but something else that was gone too quickly for Hetty to name.

"You!" Eudora rasped and she turned to the woman holding a box. "What do you bring to me?"

"Something my friend left me." The woman placed her box onto the table. "A ghost is inside."

Eudora drifted over to the woman. "How do you know this?"

"Just look at it. It rattles and shakes and when I speak to it—it answers, with raps!"

"Spirits do not communicate like that," Eudora said. "They do not—" She staggered, a hand darting to her chest. And when she spoke again her voice was higher pitched, with a squeaky quality. "Madeline, you need to tell the truth about what you have done."

The box shook again, but this time it was from the woman's shaking hands and not any supposed spirits trapped inside.

This dialogue went on for a bit, and Hetty found herself watching the woman instead of Eudora.

After working with Benjy to make a spectacle at his boxing matches, it was easy to spot the lie in the performance before her. The overperformance, the playing to the crowd, the deliberate sleight of hand that mixed magic with practical effects.

The more Hetty watched this pantomime, the more she moved from annoyance to anger.

It was one thing to trick people, but there was something malicious about using people this way. The woman with the box wasn't part of a scheme. Hetty could see it in her eyes, that genuine hope there. Hope that the fake medium was cruelly exploiting.

As the farce came to an end, Hetty stole the moment of silence that had fallen. "Madam Eudora. I come seeking someone I lost. Can you help me?" She let her voice tremble, as she pretended to grab a pendant hidden underneath layers of fabric.

Next to her, both Darlene and Penelope shifted forward with great alarm.

"Who is it that you seek?" Eudora demanded. "Who is it that you wish to speak to?"

"Someone very dear to my heart. Someone I didn't just lose —he lost me."

Penelope settled back into her chair, relaxing a bit, but Darlene kept twisting a handkerchief between her hands.

"Now you wish to speak to him once more. I think I can feel a presence around you, heavily lined with regret. I see a man standing near you, guilt in his face. Someone dear to you as you say, lost behind when he ran from a plantation. Who left you to your fate?"

"He didn't mean to," Hetty exclaimed.

"There was a choice." Eudora's voice grew confident. "There is always a choice, back then as there is now. Not as great, but a choice to pick whether to die before you even lived, or live while you die. This man, your brother, he made this choice, and his regrets lie with you. To tell you, he went on so you could live. And he—" Eudora staggered as if a hammer had been dropped on her foot. She grasped the table as she fell forward. When she spoke her voice was a deep growl. "I'm sorry, sister. Forgive me for not taking you with me. No one would notice me missing, but for you they would have sent the dogs after. They would kill you if there was chance enough, and make you an example to the others."

Eudora hadn't even finished speaking before Hetty forgot about the ruse entirely.

In fact she forgot everything except for something Benjy had once told her during a case that involved a baseball player they confronted over the murder of his father. Every word out of the man's mouth had been a lie. Yet despite the lies they were able to figure it out.

"There is truth in lies," Benjy had said as his magic suspended the frightened man in the air. "Because to make a believable lie, you need to weave enough truth in it. And that truth is the thread you pull to find your answer."

Then, Hetty thought it a clever way to find out useful information from seasoned crooks, but now she saw how it could be used against her.

As if Hetty had been stripped of her protective spells, Eudora's words peeled away all the lies to the soft underbelly of truth that lay there. Hetty did not have a missing brother, but she did have a sister she would never see again. Once again all the regrets she pushed back bubbled up to reveal only one thought. Esther would be alive if they hadn't run. If they'd stayed, if Hetty hadn't broken her collar, if she hadn't learned magic—

"It's all right." Penelope's voice was distant, yet soft and assuring. "It's all in the past."

She held out a handkerchief and Hetty realized her face was wet.

Embarrassment rose to cover her grief. Hetty had one of two choices.

She could pretend to faint, or flee.

She chose the latter.

With a small squeak, she covered her face with the handkerchief and ran out of the tent.

Hetty got surprisingly far before her friends came after her. But her face was dry by then, and she stood facing an empty tent with a swinging sign inviting guests to come back later.

"I'm sorry," Darlene sputtered.

"What is there for you to be sorry about? I started all of this when I opened my mouth and started to spin a tale."

"Did you want to speak to your sister?" Penelope asked.

Hetty stared, thinking it a poor joke. But Penelope never joked about Esther, not in moments like this.

"I'd rather not talk to her through a medium," Hetty said. This should have settled the matter, but the concerns that filled her friends' faces had not diminished by even the slightest bit.

Hetty's face warmed. Her friends meant well, she knew that. But she didn't like the feeling that they were waiting for her to fall apart.

She was the one that looked after them.

Struggling to find a way to change the conversation, Hetty spotted a young man some distance away, clutching a vial in his hand.

It was uncorked, and judging by the defeat on his face, he knew lies lay inside.

Eager for any distraction, Hetty called, "Do you need help?"

He blinked, nearly dropping the vial, but answered all the same. "I'm looking for a healer."

"You'll find no cures here. There's nothing but charlatans around."

"I know." He gripped the vial. "This is just some watered-down ale. This is not going to help my niece. I can't seem to find anyone willing to go out to Stars Haven. I have my rowboat, and it's not that far."

"I am a healer," Penelope said. "I might be able to help, depending on what ails her."

The young man's eyes started to well with tears. "You could? Oh, thank the stars! I don't know what else to do."

The rest of his words had gotten choked up in his throat, and while Hetty was inclined to be wary of strangers with tales of woe, his distress appeared genuine enough.

"We can't pay much in way of money," he put in before Penelope cut him off: "What you can spare will be fine enough."

Darlene pulled Penelope aside, not as willing as Hetty to trust the young man. "Are you sure about this? You don't know how long it will take; it'll be night before you know it."

"When people need help it doesn't matter how long something will take," Penelope retorted.

"Then I suppose there's only one option left," Hetty said. "We're coming with you."

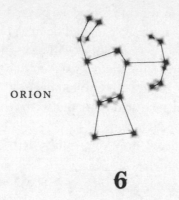

ORION

6

As the young man, Timothy, rowed them to the island, he told them more about the strange illness that had struck his niece. Hetty didn't pay much attention to his words, but it sounded like something rather ordinary. The little girl was a victim due to location more than anything else.

Stars Haven was a tiny spit of an island that you didn't visit unless you knew someone there. It wasn't much of a town, just several families who lived fairly close to each other and a store that was more like a trading post. The people who lived there made a living elsewhere, and more people left each year. But the island was still home to many. It had been a few years since Hetty had visited, and little had changed. Children had grown, the old were grayer, and buildings were marked only by the spray of the river.

Timothy's sister lived in the central cluster of homes. She greeted them, more out of politeness than any true interest.

Penelope disappeared into the sickroom and Timothy went out to collect the plants Penelope had told him to gather.

This left Hetty and Darlene alone in the kitchen with nothing more to do than tidy up, make tea, and see if their help was needed.

Wanting to keep things light, Hetty asked as she stirred her tea, "How is your painting job going at the art school—"

"I am sorry about what happened with the medium," Darlene interrupted. "You wouldn't have had an old wound poked at if we hadn't gone."

Hetty grimaced into her tea. "Or if I'd kept my mouth shut. But enough about me. Who died recently that you wanted to be put in contact with?"

"I can't tell you."

"Those are words that make me even more concerned and more likely to pry. Do you want me to mention something to Benjy? Because he'll figure it out without asking you three questions."

"That many?"

"He likes to be certain. Tell me what it is."

"I suppose there is no harm in telling you." Darlene's hand tightened around her cup as she took a moment before she started to speak. "I went to see the medium in hopes of speaking to the ghost of Raimond Duval."

Not expecting that name, Hetty nearly dropped her cup. "Well, this requires stronger drink than tea!"

"It's not how it sounds!" Darlene's words came out in a rush. "George's new job is the post that Raimond Duval held at Olmstead. When we closed our little school, I prayed that George would find a job that would pay enough so I could pursue an art career and paint what I wanted instead of the things that sold well. When I heard Raimond died so terribly in that fire, I felt my ill thoughts killed him as surely as a bullet."

"How would talking to a medium help with that?" Hetty asked. "Did you want to apologize?"

Darlene actually started to seriously answer before she stopped herself. "You shouldn't make fun like that!"

"I'm sorry," Hetty said, so insincerely that Darlene grunted.

"It's just that Penelope didn't think the medium was real, and I doubted the woman's ability, but you . . . you believed."

"It would be silly not to! We know only a fraction of how the world works. The bit that we claim to know might not be certain at all."

The kitchen door opened. Timothy entered from outside, clutching a few plants in his hands, the tangled roots holding clumps of dirt like grasping fingers. "How are things?"

"Haven't heard anything yet," Hetty said.

Timothy slumped into his chair and put his head into his hands. "I need one good piece of news. Anything to put me at ease. I have no one to turn to and I have no place to go for solace, after the church fire."

Hetty perked up at that word. "Fire? How much damage was there?"

"Mostly smoke. Someone saw it before it could spread. It's funny, though. The fire was in the cellar, but none of the protections on the church's door had been destroyed. No one knows where it started."

"It started in the cellar, because there's a tunnel that leads out to the coast," Hetty said.

"How do you know that!" Timothy exclaimed.

"I walked through it myself," Hetty added. "You see, I was one of the conductors that came through here in years past. The last time I was here was largely spent in that tunnel."

"You were. I see. A tunnel," the young man said faintly. "How many others know about this?"

That was a good question, and one Hetty was already turning over. This was the second time that day that tunnels had become a point of conversation. And she was willing to bet this one saw some sort of trouble as well.

· · ·

"Have you been on the island before?" Hetty asked Darlene as they strode along the neat path, walking past homes that had been there since the Revolutionary days. The sun was starting to sink in the sky, and golden light danced along the roofs.

"Somewhat, when I was with Marion Watts the night we ran after a slave catcher. Although, she did most of the work. I just kept the boat from sinking."

"What a very modest story, considering I heard a different version."

"Not everyone has a flair for your dramatics," Darlene added rather sharply. "Why are you interested in this?"

"It's odd," Hetty admitted. "Odd like the tunnel I found earlier today. It might be something, it might not be, but I learned it's better to poke around now when I have the time and inclination for it."

"Don't want to make another trip out here?"

"Rather not need to," Hetty said. "Here we are."

Hetty studied the rocky ground beneath their feet. It looked different with sunlight around her, but the entrance of the tunnel was right where Hetty had remembered it. The ground was still uneven and its location marked by an oddly shaped rock with moss on its north side.

Hetty tapped her boot against the side, and the rock shimmered to reveal a weathered door with a snake on it.

Brushing her thumb along her choker, Hetty stirred the magic bound to the star sigil for the Herdsman. A star-speckled woman dropped to the ground next to them. Urging the star sigil forward, Hetty sought first to find traces of the magic that lay there, as well as any traps that might be lurking.

Nothing glimmered, nothing shimmered, but something stirred.

Then it leapt out at Hetty.

Hetty could only see the shape of the star sigil before the Herdsman swung out her staff.

The staff struck and magic clashed.

When Hetty could look again, the star-speckled woman held in her hands a struggling sea monster. The star sigil flailed about, glowing so brightly that the actual constellation inside it became visible. Not good. Hetty's spell should have contained it, but light sparked along the Sea Serpent and it appeared about to explode.

Using the Herdsman as the anchor for her spell, Hetty drew out into the air the star sigils of Canis Minor and Aries to help keep it in place, and then pressed down.

"What are you doing?" Darlene called.

"Overwhelming it!" Hetty shifted forward, both hands curled into fists as she held on to the spells. "If it's not a trap, it's a signal, and we can't let it go far!"

With a nod Darlene drew her own spells, her fingers flashing to form the Swan star sigil. The majestic bird of stars swooped in and swiped at the Sea Serpent. This burst of the magic weighed the scales in their favor, because the moment the bird joined in, the sea monster vanished in a puff of smoke.

"Stay here," Hetty said to her friend. "I'll be right back."

"You're going in there?"

"Yes" was all Hetty said as she stepped through the tunnel.

There was no need for such concerns. There was nothing down here except for musty, ill-used air, and a surprising amount of dust. She smelled only smoke as she neared the tunnel's end. Only then did she see signs of disturbances. Not just from the fire, but for the reason the tunnel still existed.

"Wheel ruts," she murmured, running her boot along them. "Moving something very heavy. They're deep."

Hetty followed the tracks through the tunnel, her eyes skirting along the rock as she remembered the last time she was here.

It was not long after the end of the war, in the early summer of '65. They had spent nearly two years away from Philadelphia as shifting battles in the war, leads for Hetty's sister, and a variety of adventures made returning home tricky, and they were finally coming home.

Somewhere around Wilmington they stole a rowboat and paddled up the river. Benjy did most of the paddling, Hetty remembered. A secretary to a Confederate general had escaped from Fort Delaware that night—something that Hetty would learn later. Though they were unaware of it that night, it had added another layer of danger as they crept past torches and sorcery. Hetty kept her magic primed for any disturbance. Luckily they met nothing along the way, and when they arrived at Stars Haven they dragged the boat with them into this tunnel.

Hetty could still see the scratches in the wall from dragging the boat through the tunnel until they dropped it at the foot of the stairs.

There was no boat here now, of course. And the stairs swayed and creaked underneath her feet as she climbed them. This was age and wear, but the fire couldn't have helped much.

The smell of smoke was thickest here.

Wrinkling her nose, Hetty did her best to ignore it, only to stop when she felt a chill sweep past her.

The chill of skating along thin ice.

This was familiar.

More familiar than she liked.

Hetty drew forward, more than a bit curious. With the trap at Valentine Duval's home still fresh on her mind, she ran a finger along the band at her neck, stirring up the magic that remained there.

This time she would be better prepared. And if there was no trap, well, she wasn't going to complain.

Carefully, Hetty placed her hand on the door.

The door was locked, but there was no magic on it. No wards, either, but Hetty expected that.

She pressed hard, uncertain what her next move would be.

Then she heard a scream.

Darlene.

Hetty spun, abandoning her questions as she ran back to the tunnel's entrance.

Outside, Darlene clung desperately to a rock. Strands of thick red light pulled her by the ankles out to the river. It was a strong spell. Darlene was lifted parallel to the ground. It was not yet successful, but it would be. The rock was slowly moving in the ground and Darlene's grip was slipping despite her desperate attempts to hang on.

"Hetty!" Darlene cried. "Help!"

And that was all her friend needed to say.

Hetty drew the Arrow star sigil. Several star-speckled arrows appeared in the air next to her. She flung them at the hex. The first bounced off the red strands, but the second and third had some effect. But not enough to fully destroy them.

She needed to go bigger. Find the source, overwhelm the hex.

Hetty glanced over to where land met the river. The magic ran all the way into the water.

What was doing this?

Hetty flicked her fingers in the air to form Orion. The star-speckled hunter took form next to her and she directed him across the river.

"Go stop it," she commanded. "One more thing. Your sword."

Orion stopped in the water, turned, and tossed a glittering sword at Hetty.

She caught it. Not by grasping the hilt, but by manipulating the magical energies so that it hovered over her hands. She flipped her hands to line up the sword with the rope made of magic.

"Don't move," Hetty urged Darlene.

Hetty brought Orion's sword down exactly where the magic and Darlene's ankles parted ways.

The hex vanished in a puff of smoke, and Darlene fell to the ground with a soft thud.

"Stars," Darlene moaned, as she lay there gripping the rock. "Stars above!"

Taking this as a sign that Darlene wasn't hurt in a meaningful way, Hetty gazed back out toward the river.

It was steadily growing dark, but in the distance she thought she saw something on the water. It could be the last ferry making its way back to Philadelphia for the evening. It could be fishermen. Or it could be someone else who happened to be on the water, improbably waiting and watching for someone to disturb this tunnel.

"I hope you found what you're looking for." Darlene's glasses were askew as she clambered to her feet. Her voice trembled, but she didn't look like she was going to throw up.

"Not exactly," Hetty admitted. "I hoped to find something interesting, and I found something a bit more. A case. This tunnel is a curious thing," Hetty settled on saying. "And I want to look into it."

"Of course you do." Darlene sighed. "Why do I even ask?"

"Because you like to know." Hetty grinned.

"Most of the time." Darlene brushed her hands against her dress. "When do you plan to start poking around in other tunnels?"

Hetty affected innocence. "Why would I do that? I don't even know where all the tunnels are!"

"But I do." Darlene tapped her nose. "I know all the tunnels like this that were used by the Vigilance Society. I could draw you a map."

"You'd do that?"

"Of course. Isn't it easier to know where you're going instead of stumbling around?"

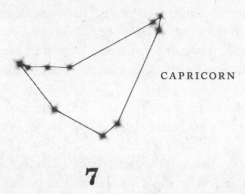

7

Wʜᴇɴ ʜᴇᴛᴛʏ ᴡᴀʟᴋᴇᴅ ɪɴᴛᴏ the house on Juniper Street, the sun had been down for an hour, so it was only slightly surprising to find no lights on.

Benjy only turned on lights in the room he was currently in. When he needed to go into another room, he just conjured an orb of light and had it bob over his shoulder.

Drawing a star sigil to summon her own light, Hetty was pulling off her shoes when she saw the scrap of paper left on the side table by the door.

Boxing tonight. Might end up losing the match if you aren't there.

With a grin, Hetty blew out the light and headed back out into the night.

After a few high-profile boxing matches that brought a little too much attention, the organizers had shifted to a new venue, a saloon off of Seventh Street. To Hetty's eye, very little had changed. Same stage, same patrons tossing down bad liquor, and same management who asked too many questions and made things more than difficult than they needed to be.

"You can't come in." The doorman extended his arm to block

the way. He didn't touch or push her back. But there was a gentle threat in the words as he spoke. "You have to wait—"

"To be personally escorted in." Quentin Mills stepped out of the side door, beaming, as if he had been waiting to see Hetty all night.

"This is Mrs. Ross," he said using the fake name that Hetty went under at these matches. "Bender Ross's wife," he added, which got the boy's notice.

The doorman swallowed, staring at Hetty.

She smiled as she slipped into the persona she crafted for Lottie Ross. A much gentler woman whose teasing never went deeper than the surface and only had eyes for her husband. A softer version of herself anchored around a single truth.

"Nice to meet you." Hetty directed a syrupy smile at the doorman. "I hope we'll see more of each other!"

Quentin escorted her in, and didn't do it quickly. He led her through the crowd, ensuring that she was seen.

"I didn't think you were coming tonight," he said in a low tone. Quentin was perhaps the only one who worked here that knew their real names, and he made sure that didn't change, since he knew how important their privacy was to them. He owned the venue, paying for it with the money he made by well-placed bets on Benjy's matches. Quentin also was the one that taught Benjy how to box properly. Although Hetty didn't quite trust him, she didn't fully dislike him, either.

"I had plans of my own. Didn't think anyone would miss me."

"Miss you?" Quentin exclaimed. "The mere turn of your head just changed seven bets! Watch around us for ripples. People know who you are and what it means."

"My husband wins all his matches."

"But the matches are a bit more exciting whenever you are in the room."

"Why, Mr. Mills!" Hetty clutched a hand to her chest with an exaggerated gasp. "Are you accusing me of cheating?"

"All I can say is that some matches hit all the marks of a good show, and the others are a spectacle. Tonight will be the latter."

Quentin left her in the middle of the room, but he hadn't left her alone. Across from her was a table occupied with familiar faces, and at least one set of eyes that had seen her the moment she had stepped into the room.

"I thought you were boxing," Hetty said to her husband as a chair was found for her.

"I'm the last match. There's a floor show beforehand—when it starts I'll leave to get ready."

"Until then," Oliver said, "we make it known that he's here and help raise the bets. Isn't that right, Thomas?"

Thomas didn't say anything right away. He had his hat pulled over the right side of his face to hide his scars. But even that didn't fully hide how his attention had drifted across the room.

Oliver reached over and placed a hand on Thomas's arm. The simple touch brought Thomas back to their little group.

Thomas looked around until his eyes stopped on Hetty. "Why, the missus is here!" he declared with a playful grin. "What's the name you use here again? Cassandra? Elizabeth?"

"Either of those names would be better than Lottie." Benjy shuddered.

Hetty bumped him lightly with her elbow. "It's too late to change it now."

"I don't see why you bothered at all with fake names." Oliver drew a star sigil in the air to summon a flame to light his pipe. "Wouldn't it help your popularity around town if they know who you really are?"

"Would you come to a funeral home of a well-known boxer?" Benjy asked.

"I would. Makes a great deal of sense."

"Not to me."

Oliver waved the smoking pipe around the room. "You could make a career out of this."

Benjy shook his head. "Things are only fun when I know I can walk away."

The lights dimmed a bit and noise shifted as attention went to the boxing setup in the room.

"That is my cue," Benjy said. To Hetty he asked, "No antics tonight?"

It wasn't as much of a question as it was a confirmation.

Hetty patted his arm. "No, just beat the Wildcat."

He leaned over to kiss her then.

While they kissed for show at his matches, it was like the plays they put on with their friends. Exaggerated and made to play up to the crowd's expectations.

This kiss was nothing like that.

This was just for her. This kiss was for her to know that despite teasing and pretense, he wanted her here.

When Benjy pulled away, he paused for just a moment longer. As she peered into a face she knew even better than her own, she knew that this was the reason she came to the matches.

"Was that necessary?" Oliver remarked when Benjy finally left. His face was wrinkled as if he were drinking a glass of lemonade that was more sour than sweet. "That won't change the bets that much."

"Not everything is about money," Hetty said rather absently, watching the crowd until Benjy was out of sight. "Neither does everything have to be about what you want."

Oliver huffed, but he knew better than to step on the trap she'd laid for him.

"Want to get closer to watch?" Thomas asked. "Now would be a good time to find a place."

Hetty looked to Oliver, but he had already jumped to his feet.

"I'm going to add some money into the fray. You being here might even convince the reluctant ones."

"You're not going to watch?" Thomas asked.

"Why?" Oliver absently flicked Thomas's hat as he passed, smirking. "The real game is the bets."

Thomas pushed the hat back into place, but Oliver had hurried off before he could retaliate.

"You shouldn't put up with such things," Hetty teased.

Thomas shrugged. "I don't mind seeing him in a good mood."

Hetty looked back at Oliver, crouched over as he spoke to a group some tables away.

"That's a good mood?"

"He's enjoying himself," Thomas said, rising from his seat. "We should move closer."

That suggestion by itself did not cause Hetty much concern.

They always moved closer at the start of Benjy's matches. But there was an insistence in how Thomas repeated himself that made it more than a bit noteworthy.

Then it was how he moved through the crowd.

Thomas usually walked with her, trailing at her side like her guard. This night, however, he guided her. Guided her through the crowd in a rather deliberate manner.

They ended up not as close to the ring as they could have been. They were still near some tables, where a trio of white men sat with drinks, keeping to themselves and ignoring the match setup. That too was quite normal. The men were common laborers fresh from work, by the look of their stained and rough clothes. There weren't many white men who came here for the matches. But the few that did were hardly trouble. They ate, they drank, and they placed bets. Any rudeness or fighting was settled outside or in the ring, with proxy fights.

But there was something odd tonight about this rare sighting.

Thomas kept tugging down his hat. Enough for Hetty to finally ask:

"You didn't come here for the match, did you?"

Thomas stopped tugging, but his attention didn't fully return to her. "I'm here because I didn't tell you everything about the fiddle I got."

"I figured. Give me the short story—we can fill out the details later."

"It's not much. Just that items I had been shipping had gone missing. And they're magical items. Potions and herbs, and items charmed with spells."

The noise around her grew louder, overshadowing the rest of Thomas's words. In the ring, the last fighters made an exit, but instead of a musician or some other performer, a man hawking pocket watches climbed into the ring.

"The fiddle," Thomas continued, "was enchanted by me. I was trying to get your attention without making a fuss."

"You succeeded so well, Oliver was quite on his way to getting upset. Why not just tell us the truth?"

"It's complicated."

Hetty sighed, unsurprised by this answer. "What do you need help with?"

"With this."

Thomas nodded to the three white men. A young boy had made his way to that table. He said something to them. Then all three stood up and followed the boy out of the room.

"I know him," Thomas whispered. "I've seen that boy around when I sent out packages. Not all the time. But often."

"Then let's go see why he's here."

Hetty and Thomas weaved their way through the crowd and headed toward the door, her curiosity and his desperation making the distance vanish quickly.

When they reached the door, the announcement for the final

match of the evening was made and cheers were already pouring out, even before the boxers' names were called.

Quentin Mills had not exaggerated the impact Benjy would make by his appearance tonight. She could hear the crowd, the roar of approval.

His popularity had shifted the tides of bets on more than one occasion. While Benjy won often, even the few matches he did lose were always rousing until the end. His good looks didn't hurt, either. With grace and quiet strength, every move Benjy made caught and held attention, transforming what should have been a brutal and coarse sport into something a bit more elevated.

She almost didn't leave after Benjy climbed into the ring.

Like his opponent he was stripped to the waist, but that was their only similarity. Benjy was half a head taller than the Wildcat, broader in the shoulder, with a more impressive form. He stood still with his arms crossed over his chest, while the Wildcat postured for the crowd. While the distance made it hard to tell, Hetty knew he was smirking at the Wildcat. Wildcat James won matches, but out of luck, not skill — and by exploiting weaknesses of his opponent. Tricks he clearly forgot didn't work on Benjy.

The announcer called out their names to the awaiting crowd, and a gong sang in the air.

Benjy slammed his left fist into his right palm and violet light swirled around his hand. His color for this match, and any match he fought. Despite Hetty's wishes otherwise, boxing was not quite a duel of magic. But the colors that swirled around the boxers' fists did more than help make it easy to follow the flow of events. The spells protected the fighters both from their opponent and their own exertions.

Before the first blow could strike, however, Thomas hissed Hetty's name into her ear.

Hetty tore her eyes from the match and followed Thomas into the corridor.

The door shut away the noise of the boxing match and warmth of the room, leaving only silence before them.

The white men had gotten far ahead. But they were still near enough that Hetty could hear the voices ahead of them.

Thomas moved forward, but Hetty caught his arm. "Careful," she whispered, brushing her free hand at the band at her neck. Her magic fell around them as she unraveled a spell to hide them from sight. "This goes out where there is no place to hide, except on a nearby roof. Stay here. I'll go ahead."

"No. This is my business. Besides"—Thomas gave her a lopsided grin—"he'll kill me if something happens to you."

With magic covering them, they approached the end of the hallway to the door that led out into a narrow alleyway.

The space, small to begin with, shrank even more with the presence of a cart at the end and the several men waiting around it.

The young boy they saw earlier sat in the cart. Not only were the three white men there, but they were outnumbered by five others working in and around the cart, picking up and moving crates. Even more interesting: the white men didn't appear to be the ones in charge.

Hetty tapped Thomas's arm and pointed to a nearby roof.

He nodded, understanding, and moved with her to the wall. Thomas bent down, cupping his hands, clearly meaning to help Hetty onto the roof. Hetty just shook her head and turned a hand over, allowing her magic to gently fly her onto the rooftop.

Thomas scrambled up with far less grace, hitting the edge hard enough to startle the men below.

Everyone froze, except for Hetty. She slapped a hand across Thomas's mouth, and refocused her spell of invisibility.

"What was that?" a voice called.

"Nothing, probably a rat."

"That sounded like no rat I've ever heard!"

Hetty watched as the man hurried to check, a lantern held up high to see anything or anyone lurking in the corners.

Hetty lowered her hand, letting go of Thomas.

Sheepishly, Thomas knelt next to her at the roof's edge as the action resumed below them.

One of the crates was open and displaying its wares for the small group. One of the objects that emerged from its depths was a small jewelry box. The young boy presented it to the white man with a beard.

"Is it empty?" the bearded man asked.

"No, there are vials and amulets inside," the boy replied.

"Show them, don't just tell them about it." This new voice entered the air from a man still on the cart. The tone of authority stilled hands and got all eyes turned toward him.

He jumped off the wagon and snatched the jewelry box from the boy. "These are the amulets and potions we got. No need to work any magic. Any of you can use them without trouble."

The man said something else.

He could have been sharing the secrets of Celestial magic to these white men and it wouldn't have mattered.

Nothing mattered once Hetty recognized the man who vowed to give her a long and painful death.

He wasn't the first person to threaten to kill her or worse. But she had dragged a knife across his face and that was the least of his reasons for wanting her dead.

He still had the same lethal slender frame, but the puckered scar was worse than she remembered. A thin ripple of pale skin cutting diagonally through brown skin from chin to forehead. The face of one man, and one alone.

Nathan Payne.

A man who had once traveled across state lines during a war just on the rumor that Hetty and Benjy were in the area. A man who delivered runaways to the bounty hunters he worked for. A man that Hetty should have killed years ago when she had the chance.

Her hands were not completely clean of blood. But the spots that were there came from situations where there was no better choice.

Shooting Nathan Payne the last time she saw him would not have been the best choice. A gunshot blast in that moment would have drawn attention and put others in great peril.

But killing Payne then would have meant not seeing him now.

A hand pressed down hard on her shoulder, pushing her flush against the rooftop.

Panic slowed her reactions, so much that the only thing Hetty could do was place a hand on one of her hairpins. At the touch of the bird balanced on a tree branch, her sensation of the world flooded back to her. This was the hairpin Benjy had made especially for her, and while it didn't have any particular magical qualities, the love it was made with was the strongest charm in her possession.

As she began to breathe easily again, she saw Thomas's frightened face.

Dragging her free hand against the stone, she cast a spell using Canis Minor, the simplest star sigil she could think of. She replaced the invisibility charm over them, hoping that the telltale glow wouldn't be noticeable this low on the roof.

They waited there, not moving, scarcely breathing, until they were sure the conversation below them didn't pause.

It kept going, as Nathan Payne showed off all the vials and amulets he had stolen, proclaiming the abilities of each, and offering prices. Goods changed hands, and what wasn't sold was put back on the cart. Nathan Payne and his young associate jumped onto it to leave. The men, both white and Black, left, and in moments the narrow alley was empty once more.

Thomas sat up. "Is that who I think it was?"

"That was no one."

"Your face says otherwise."

Thomas's words caught Hetty without a ready excuse.

"Your spells unraveled at the sight of him," Thomas continued. "That tells me everything I need to know."

"What do you know?" Hetty faced him, anger thrumming through her, and she remembered he was the reason she was out here in the first place. Because Thomas wouldn't give up on his silly business, she had to see a ghost of her past that she had not wanted to see ever again.

"That man couldn't have noticed you. The distance was great and he was busy hawking his wares." Thomas's words were gentle, as if she were a scared little bird. "He wouldn't expect to see you at all—"

"And if he did?"

"Haven't you dealt with him before?"

Quite easily, in fact.

Several times, and the first had been in an effort to stop—

Hetty's thoughts crashed together. Her first encounter with Nathan Payne would not have happened if they had not been bringing Sarah Jacobs's children to safety.

An event that was even stronger in Hetty's mind because Valentine Duval asked about that adventure earlier that day.

Hetty didn't believe in coincidences, but she did know when she found a puzzle piece that would slot in perfectly into the section she had toiled over.

With purpose and sudden clarity, Hetty climbed off the roof.

Thomas scrambled to keep up with her, but she left him behind with swift strides.

The match was over by the time Hetty stepped inside.

All it took was a glance. Her eye caught Benjy's across the room and he went from toying with the Wildcat to striking.

He hit three times.

First to break the hold, second to stun, and third to ensure that the Wildcat would wake up with a splitting headache.

The thump echoed in the room, and while people around her expressed little surprise at the outcome, there was excitement in their faces as they went to collect bets.

Benjy never failed to put on a good show.

Despite the concerns pulsing through her, Hetty felt the corners of her mouth lift as Benjy waved to the crowd. Then he blew what remained of the violet magic around his hands. It drifted in the air as it sought her out. The light swirled around her before fading against her skin.

By the time it did, Benjy had bounded out of the ring to meet her. He held out his hand, ignoring the voices calling for his attention.

The moment Hetty placed her hand in his, he whisked her away to the back room in the saloon.

It was a closet of a room and stank of cigar smoke, but it had a door that could lock.

Hetty sat down on a bench and picked up Benjy's neatly folded clothes. Tucked away in a pocket was a small jar of healing salve. She uncapped it, easily falling into this routine.

"You missed the match." Benjy sat next to her. He didn't quite pout, but there was disappointment lurking underneath the sheen of sweat glistening on his skin. "One moment you were there, the next you were gone."

"I saw the most important bits." Hetty took his hands and slowly began to rub the salve into his skin, taking special care around his knuckles. He did so many things with his hands, it was hard to say what would be the greatest loss if he ruined them. "I would have watched the whole thing if Thomas hadn't dragged me to see if these white men were buying stolen magic or not."

A muscle in her husband's cheek twitched. "I knew there was something bothering him. What happened?"

"A man was selling a few things. Nathan Payne."

Benjy's hand jerked under her hands, and she realized she was rubbing too hard. Releasing him, Hetty dropped her hands into her lap.

"Nathan Payne is—" she began, but Benjy spoke first:

"You saw him too." Benjy spoke softly, with equal parts worry and relief filling his features. "I guess I was wrong. I suppose ghosts do exist."

DRAGON

INTERLUDE

March 1861

TATE FAMILY FARM, TENNESSEE

I<small>T WAS AFTER DARK</small> when Hetty woke, curled up against the basket's side. She supposed it was the cold that woke her, for spring nights up this high were downright wintry.

Silhouetted by the dim lantern light, Benjy sat across from her, bent over the map spread out over the basket floor.

It was a sight that was hardly different from what she saw before she shut her eyes, the only change being the lit lantern by his elbow.

"You didn't wake me up," Hetty muttered to Benjy. "You said you would."

"There's no use in both of us being short on sleep." Benjy shrugged. "You were yawning."

She had, although Hetty would never admit it. She made a spell up to hide the air balloon from sight, and maintaining the spell was much harder than she had thought. Especially over the many hours she had to keep it up until true dark fell. An air balloon was hard to miss in the sky. And it took only one look over the basket rim to know that if someone shot at them, death was a likely outcome.

But that was the risk they took, because timing was that important. Benjy's estimates of travel by balloon, buoyed by the modifications he made that allowed the balloon to be steered at a controlled pace, had them arriving just as they planned. That they hadn't gotten lost was the work of small miracles. Although Bernice Tanner told them that she would send news ahead to the other agents of the Vigilance Society scattered in their path, Hetty and Benjy didn't bother to make contact. Given their speed it was nearly certain they had surpassed even the quickest telegram. And the time they would waste explaining things would be time they could not afford to lose.

Through a mix of luck, the use of the stars to guide them, and the modifications made to the air balloon, they arrived exactly as planned to a tree that towered majestically above its neighbors. A tree that, according to Sarah Jacobs, was the site of funerals, for it was near enough to the farms in the area for people to travel, meet, and mourn.

While Sarah was utterly confused about their plan with the balloon, she was able to describe everything about the tree, including the good luck charm tied to the topmost branches that let Hetty and Benjy know they were right where they needed to be.

There was no place to land the balloon—the trees were too close. Instead, Benjy anchored the balloon to the top branches and Hetty set spells to conceal them until nightfall. It was a bit risky, but it would do.

Because getting here was the easy part. Leaving was going to be a bit more tricky.

"We need to start now, to make use of full dark," Hetty said, stretching out her back.

"Wait." Benjy pointed to the instruments above their heads. "How does this work again?"

This was the third time he'd done it, and it irritated her even more now that they were on the cusp of the task at hand.

"I don't need to know how it works," Hetty said. "You know how to do it. It's enough."

"And if it's not?"

Hetty turned away and swung up on top of the basket, one foot ready to land on a nearby tree branch. "It's not going to be a problem."

She dared him to argue it wasn't. Part of Hetty was even curious what he'd say. She never met someone who didn't fight her every single step. He stood his ground on things that were important. But even when he didn't protest, his opinion was clear.

Benjy wasn't pleased about her refusing to learn how to work the balloon. But he didn't understand. Her learning how to fly the balloon meant he'd try to stay behind if things went poorly. She wasn't going to let that happen. She was in the business of finding people. She refused to lose any more.

"Do you still have the knife I gave you?" Benjy asked instead.

Still sitting on the basket's rim, Hetty lifted up her skirt to reveal the top of her boot. The hilt of the knife he gave her before leaving Philadelphia stuck out, ready to be grabbed at a moment's notice.

Hetty didn't know why he gave it to her, knowing she was likely to stab him as well, but it made him feel better and she liked having the knife with her.

It was over a mile to the farm, and the darkness made it feel longer. They had only what Sarah Jacobs told them of the area, and she had only walked to this place in the daylight so a number of the things she told them to look for were swallowed up by shadows.

Yet they arrived at the right place, guided by the flickering fire-light on the grounds before them.

Candles lit up a few windows in the big house that loomed on the slight hill ahead. And down near the cabins there was light too, a small communal fire which several people sat around. Although the air around wasn't exactly cheerful, there was a shared spirit of relief about.

Crouched on the boundaries of the farm, Hetty stared at the fire, wondering if this complicated things or not.

That was when Benjy tapped her arm.

Hetty reached for her knife, but stopped when she noticed the beads around her wrist were glowing.

The sigils carved into the bracelet weren't brighter than the glow of a firefly. But the light had a twin.

From the group around the fire, a woman abruptly moved back to the cabins, her cupped hand not fully hiding the glowing beads around her wrist as well.

She walked back to the cabin and lifted the sheet to slip through.

Perhaps luck was still at their side, because this cabin faced away from the fire, so the way toward it remained in the deepest shadows.

Over the fence they went, going the way Sarah had advised them to. The weakest part of the fence moved at their touch, and they walked as swiftly toward the cabin as they could without drawing attention.

The cloth moved aside and a young boy only a couple years younger than Hetty stepped out. His feet were bare and he looked as if he had been stirred from sleep.

He woke up completely when he saw them.

Benjy grabbed the boy, slapping a hand over his mouth and firmly trapping him before he could make a sound.

The boy struggled for just a moment, before he went limp.

"Let him go right now."

The woman had stepped back into view.

"Let him go." The woman held a mason jar aloft. The jar didn't glow with magic, but the fury in her eyes told Hetty the contents inside held a promise of great harm.

"We aren't here to hurt him," Hetty said.

"I don't know who you are." The woman still held the jar, but her eyes were locked on the glowing beads at Hetty's wrist. "But you are not Sarah. How do you have that?"

"Sarah gave this to us. We are the conductors she sent from Philadelphia to bring her children to her," Hetty said.

"I'm supposed to believe you?"

"You're Anna, right? She gave me the beads because Jim carved them. Sixteen beads for the star sigils they know and will teach their children."

The jar lowered, and Anna stared at Hetty. "She really did send you."

Hetty nodded. "We're here to steal the children to safety."

"You can come with us." Benjy let go of the boy. "And anyone else who wishes."

"Such big talk. How can you manage that?"

"We fly," Hetty said.

Anna stared at her, her next words lost in her surprise.

"Can you give us wings?" the boy asked in awe.

"In a way," Hetty said. "How many are here, and how many are willing?"

"I don't, I can't possibly—" Anna began. "You hear stories and people talk. But—"

"It's a simple question. Are you willing?" Hetty asked.

"Yes." Anna looked at the boy. "I wanted to run ever since this one grew like a weed. The master has debts, and a sale will happen soon. But this isn't a big place. There's six of us, not counting the babes. Anyone missing will be noted. Tomorrow might be Sunday, but—"

"Then we shouldn't waste time," Benjy said.

Anna turned to her boy. "Go tell Zipporah. She should be resting in her cabin. Find out what she thinks. The others will say yes. I'm sure of it."

He nodded and slipped away to a nearby cabin.

Anna led the way inside her cabin and knelt by the pallets on the floor. Nestled together were two small children, the oldest five and the younger perhaps two. While they were certainly quite young, they were not the babies Hetty hoped they would be, if only because tiny babies would be easy to carry away.

Hetty knelt down and lifted the oldest's arm, and inside along the forearm was a small circle with a line etched across like Sarah said would be there. Its twin was on the other child in a similar spot.

Anna watched all this in silence, but her expression grew less grave, as if this confirmed Hetty truly was who she claimed to be.

The oldest stirred then, her eyes opening wide when she saw the bracelet.

"You're not Mama," the girl whispered. The little girl looked at Anna. "Anna, where is Mama?"

"Emily, this woman's going to take you to your mother. She's a friend."

Hetty held up her wrist to show Emily the beads. "She gave this to me. And I will give it to your mother when you are with her again."

Emily looked on suspiciously but nodded in the end. "Okay."

"I'll carry the bigger one," Benjy said. "You take the other."

They did just that, the younger daughter staying sound asleep as Hetty picked her up.

That's when Anna's son ran back into the cabin.

"The lights are on in the field!" he cried.

Anna gasped. "That's the alarms! They know and will be here shortly, but how? Were you seen?"

Hetty hesitated. She had not seen anyone on their way here. Nor had Benjy. But that didn't mean they weren't seen, or maybe there were quieter spells.

Or maybe someone was watching.

Hetty looked down at the child in her arms. Sarah Jacobs was so important that Bernice Tanner insisted on getting her out, and that when Hetty told her that Sarah would only leave with her children at her side, Bernice gave them money, a list of contacts, and everything they wished for before they left. Something more was going on, but there was no time to find out what it was.

This lurch in their plans wasn't going to change their goals.

"They were watching for anyone," Hetty said finally. "Doesn't matter. All it means is that I need to make a distraction." Hetty placed the younger daughter into Anna's arms.

"What are you about to do?" Benjy asked.

"Set something on fire."

"I'll help," Anna said.

"No, you go with him. You get everyone willing out, and I'll grab anyone who takes their time."

"But you can't," Anna protested.

But Hetty wasn't listening to the protest. There was only one person whose protests she'd listen to at the moment, and he interrupted Anna.

"Trust her," Benjy said. "We need the distraction she'll make. The alternate is we leave you behind and take the children. Your choice."

What choice was that? Anna took one look at her son, and nodded. She held out the mason jar to Hetty, placing it in her hand.

"Use this as part of your distraction."

"I will."

Hetty left the cabin then, striding for the farmhouse.

It was still quiet, but a tense sort of quiet.

The light that Anna's son had mentioned created a brightness that left few places to hide. It wasn't bright as day, but the light had the strength of several campfires.

A few of the cabins were open, and the people called out to Hetty.

But Hetty ignored them all. Her eyes were on the house. It sat on a slight hill, where movement and shadows stirred like ghouls. Ghouls they were, and she was going to do her part in getting rid of them.

Three years ago Hetty ran from a place not much bigger than this. She had only thoughts of escape back then as she hadn't known the magic she knew now.

Calmly, Hetty drew arrow star sigils in the air, and launched them in all directions like she was throwing darts. Some hit buildings, some hit the ground, and others hit places she wasn't aiming for at all but would work just the same.

Then she took Anna's mason jar and dug a shallow hole. She buried the jar and placed more spells around it to make sure the jar broke at the right moment.

Distantly Hetty could hear the ring of alarms. But she ignored them. She had more spells to cast. Sagittarius came to her fingers next; it was a complicated star sigil, but she managed it all the same, bringing it in an almost lifelike form next to her. She nodded at the star sigil and urged it forward to charge at the big house. Its hooves sparked flames as it ran, which spread across the ground and didn't stop until it hit the building.

Then she summoned the wind.

Slowly Hetty moved the flames along the house so that by the time an alarm came from within, it was already surrounded.

She saw windows open, but she didn't stay around to see who got out.

Hetty ran.

Hetty ran across the now empty ground, priming her spells to react at the next burst of movement that passed over them.

She ran and ran, until she reached the edge of the farm, where another man had stopped at the edge.

His eyes were wide as he stared at the flames.

"What is this?" he whispered.

"A way of escape," Hetty said, guessing he was another one of the people in the cabins, the only one left, it seemed, who might have been skeptical of escape being possible.

"Are you willing to come with me?"

"Come with you?" The man stared at her. "Did you do this?"

"I'm just helping things along. If you don't want to come, stay here, but I don't think you want to."

Something boomed like thunder back on the farm. One of the arrow traps she'd set had gone off.

An explosion of air to send whoever disturbed it flying backwards.

"No, I don't," the man said.

They ran down the path Hetty had carefully crouched along earlier. The light from the flames trickled through the trees. But it was still dark, and she wasn't too surprised when the man tripped, stumbling over the uneven terrain.

Hetty stopped when he did not jump up right away.

"Need help?" she gasped, holding out a hand.

"Yes, I do."

He grabbed her hand, but instead of pulling himself up, he twisted her wrist as if to snap her bones.

Pain dazzled Hetty for a moment, but being used to pain, she fought through it and jerked her hand away from him.

She shook her wrist to make sure it wasn't broken, but something worse had happened to it. The Canis Minor star sigil glowed on the back of her right hand. As the glow grew brighter, she found she couldn't move her fingers. "Why, what—"

The man stood up, and in that moment Hetty realized she was wrong to mistake him for a runaway.

Her eyes had adjusted a bit to the darkness and she could see his clothes were much nicer than anything that Anna or her son wore.

But more than that, there was something unkind in the way he held himself.

"Let's make this easy, shall we? Give me the children you took and you can go on your merry way."

"Why would I do that?"

"Because it's the only option that lets you walk free."

Hetty didn't bother answering. She drew the first star sigil that came to mind. But the spell was too quickly done, and it fell apart in a flash of light.

The man howled in laughter, and then waved his hand forward.

The sigil on Hetty's right hand lit up and dragged her toward him.

Hetty kicked and swiped at him with her good hand, but he evaded her. The man grabbed her, and wrenched her arm back so hard that this time Hetty couldn't power through the pain. "Don't make this hard. They just want the children. Give them to me and you won't be hurt."

"I can't. I don't have them." Hetty tried to wiggle out of the grip, stomp her foot on the man's heel, to do anything that could get him to let go. But he yanked her back, so her gaze swung skyward to where the stars should have been.

"Lead me to them. I know they went somewhere. You don't have time to play games. If you don't take me, my employers will force you. I can't say what they'll do, but you will not like it."

Trapped as she was, Hetty wasn't frozen in fear yet. For whatever reason the man was holding back from hurting her too much. She could use this. He clearly thought he was presenting the kinder option and that she would consider it. If she played along with this assumption, she might be able to cut her way out of this trap.

"I will," Hetty stammered then. "I have something that will let them know where I am. Let me go and I can get it."

To her surprise, he let go without a word.

But her surprise was not so great to stop her from ramming her shoulder into his chest.

Hetty bent over, grabbing the knife from her boot.

When he reached for her again, Hetty spun around, sweeping the knife like a scythe.

Her knife slipped across a surface, and warm blood splattered against her face and hands.

The man reached out to her at first, but then he staggered, falling to the ground clutching his face. More blood spilled, pooling around him.

Hetty stood over him, clutching the knife.

He was still moving. He was still alive.

At first she was glad. She had not killed a man this night. But that gladness turned to fear.

She had not killed him, but should she?

He was after these children, he had threatened her. He still could follow them and get the upper hand.

A bird's whistle caught her ear.

Hetty looked up and realized why there were no stars.

The stars were still out, but they were blocked by the expansive canopy of the air balloon.

A rope ladder fell down before her within easy reach.

Hetty shook herself, and shoved her knife back into her boot.

Wiping the blood on her skirts, Hetty grabbed ahold of the ladder. As she climbed, the balloon began its ascent. Soon Hetty was surrounded by stars, the gentle night breeze taking her far away from the fire and the yelling below.

Hetty hadn't even reached the basket's rim before Anna appeared, with her hand outstretched. Hetty grabbed it, the glowing bracelets becoming even brighter as they came into contact. Anna's son came to the other side, and helped haul her over the rim.

The balloon, which had felt so spacious before, was crowded with Anna, her son, an old woman, and a young man missing part of his left foot. A young woman held Emily Jacobs in her lap, while Emily's sister slept on peacefully in the middle of the basket.

All of them were staring at Hetty, none more than Emily, whose eyes were the widest and struck with amazement.

But Hetty ignored the stares to look for Benjy. He was well occupied with getting the balloon and its occupants far away from here at a reasonable height and speed. Yet busy as he was, Hetty didn't miss the relief on his face.

"I told you," Hetty called to Benjy. "I don't need to know how to work the balloon!"

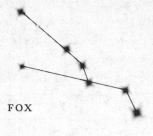

FOX

8

THEY SAY WHEN FACED with impossibly difficult circumstances, people turn to words or actions.

So when Benjy denied Hetty the chance of going after Nathan Payne to prove that the ghost could bleed, she turned angry words on him the moment they were inside their home.

"I'm not being unreasonable—you said you saw him too! Why aren't we doing anything about him?"

Benjy stepped around her to lock the door, magic wisping from his fingers as he set a number of wards in place. "What would that change?" he said in a measured tone that told her that he'd spent the walk back home preparing a number of arguments.

It made her want to shake him. It made her want to scream and yell at him. But it mostly made her realize she had made the wrong move, that she should have gone after Payne the moment she saw him, consequences be damned.

"Nathan Payne chased after us long before the price on our heads was enough to make it worthwhile. He sent dogs chasing after us! He crossed a battlefield just for a chance to put a knife to our throats! How can you not want to do anything?"

"Well, if you'd killed him when you had the chance, you

wouldn't be worried about him now." Benjy sat at the foot of the stairs. He pulled out the wad of winnings from the match. He didn't count them or take them apart, just turned the rolled bills over in his hands as he spoke. "You let Payne live. With any choice comes a stream of consequences."

"I don't care. I want him out of our city! Why is he here? Is he after us again?"

"He might not be." Benjy tucked the money back into his pocket. "A few months ago the *Eventide Observer* had an article about One-Eyed Jack."

"I didn't hear about this."

Hetty had noticed he'd suddenly gotten interested in purchasing the newspaper when previously he had been content with stealing it from their friends. She figured it was an indulgence that came with the rise of their fortunes, but clearly she was wrong about that.

"He was not mentioned with that name, of course. But reading between the lines, I knew who it was. It wasn't too exciting, mostly tales of misadventures with the opinions of the reporter peppered through. But then again, I already heard some of the tales with a different ending."

"Do we need to worry about this ghost, too?" Hetty asked.

"No. I saw a notice for One-Eyed Jack's funeral this morning. Reports of his death could have brought Payne into town."

"I doubt it. You should have seen the operation Payne had going on in the alley. He must have been here for a while. When was this article? Why didn't you tell me?"

Benjy held up his hands as if to shield himself from her words. "You'd only needlessly worry about an old slave catcher living on the outskirts of town."

"Like I am about Payne?"

"Payne was never a slave catcher. Just someone who cared for nothing but himself." At Hetty's huff, Benjy retorted, his patience finally snapping. "Why are you worried about him? Nothing's going to happen to you as long as I'm around."

"You can't promise that."

His eyes caught hers, and the intensity there stole her breath.

"I'll make that promise."

He'd keep it, too. He didn't have to say that for her to know.

She knew, because that's what he always did. Looked after her and made sure she was safe. It was the only thing that hadn't changed in the years she'd known him, and the only thing that never would.

"I'm sorry," Hetty admitted. "It's just one more alarming thing to face today, and it's by far the biggest one. I can handle strange fires set on purpose by Beatty Hose. I can deal with secret tunnels. I can even cope with magical objects being sold in back alleys. But Payne is different. There are a lot of things that want to kill us, but he's the only thing that wants to do it personally."

Against these words, Benjy still shook his head. "We can't do anything about him unless he makes a move first. Anything more is a waste of effort."

"Everything feels like a waste if we don't!"

"Then why didn't you follow him when you had your chance?" Benjy asked.

"Because I learned my lesson about plunging into things without support."

"Thomas would be upset to hear that," Benjy said. His words were light, but there was a different story in his eyes. His left hand ran along his right arm, resting right along where the bone had been broken back in May.

And just like that, all of Hetty's boiling anger vanished.

The case that got his arm broken was extraordinary in one fashion—the victim, the suspects, and the motives were all personal. It showed them the things they were willing to overlook and revealed that they were more vulnerable than they would like to admit.

"You're right," Hetty admitted softly. "Going after Payne like this isn't wise. But we aren't courting danger. After all, there's two of us against him, and we have one thing he doesn't have."

"What's that?"

Hetty didn't even blink. "Everything to protect."

In answer, Benjy held out his hand to her.

Hetty took it, the calluses on both their hands brushing against each other for just a moment before Benjy pulled her toward him.

She placed her free hand against his face, and let it rest there as she stared down at him.

He captured that hand too, but instead of pulling her down toward him, he stood, slowly and with care.

He kissed one of her hands and let it fall. While still holding the other, he led the way upstairs until it was necessary to let go of that hand as well.

"It doesn't look like there's a deeper connection."

The next morning, Hetty reclined inside her tub, and because she was fully dressed for the day, the fabric of her clothes gave her enough cushion that it was nearly comfortable as long as she didn't bump her elbow on the water taps nearby.

Hetty jiggled her leg as she flipped through the *Eventide Observer*, reading once again the obituary for the friend Jay had mentioned the previous night.

"Billy Yates. A former teacher at Olmstead. He taught roughly the same years that Jay did. No mention of the Vigilance Society."

"There wouldn't be." Benjy rolled up his shirtsleeves with care before he lathered shaving cream on his face.

"There would be a hint." Hetty turned a page. "A mention of a familiar name or two."

"The pastor just wants us to do something."

Because he had picked up a blade and had it against his neck to shave, Hetty didn't say what she really was thinking.

Jay didn't care about what they did—he just wanted them to share the same impossible hope that he had. A hope that all the strange things around Raimond Duval's death meant something. There were too many questions that had been neatly given answers, and part of Jay's anger had been how easy it seemed . . . and that Hetty and Benjy had accepted it.

Hetty understood that anger.

For little over a decade she held a similar impossible hope about her lost sister. A hope of being reunited one day, even as the years went by and the dream became less likely. By the time Hetty had finally gotten news about Esther, every one of her friends had told her to stop looking, except for Benjy.

Even then, it wasn't enough at times.

"Will you be fine looking after things later today?" Benjy said as he patted his face dry. "I'm going to give Thomas back the fiddle and an earful. I know he didn't want Oliver to worry about his troubles, but hasn't he learned, such things always come out in the end? I might be gone for a while."

"Take your time," Hetty grumbled. "It's not like we have any clients anyway."

Benjy knelt down next to the tub so his face was nearly even with hers.

There was a bit of shaving cream he had missed, and Hetty absently rubbed it off his face.

Benjy caught her hand and held it in place with his own. His skin was slightly damp, and cool to the touch.

"It's not a bad thing, to not be busy," he said softly.

"You won't say that in a few months."

"In a few months things will have improved."

Benjy settled gingerly on the stool they kept nearby. Just as easily, he took the newspaper from her and slid on the glasses he'd left near the sink.

The thin wire frames were a new addition and a reluctant purchase—Benjy had insisted he didn't need them. But oddly enough, a few comments about how much Hetty liked them had quelled any further complaints.

"Did you notice anything interesting in this?" Benjy asked.

Hetty shook her head. "Nothing much today. Although Miss Carole had a particularly cutting response to the fool who asked why there is little support for temperance."

"I see it." Benjy cleared his throat. "'I stand against banning alcohol, because the law will be twisted to enforce things that had nothing to do with it. It'll become an excuse to arrest people and snatch babies from their mothers. But it's mostly a sneaky way to ban brewed magic. White alchemists can't replicate even the simplest of potions. If the white man can't take it or make it, they destroy it.'"

"That column is the only reason to buy the paper," Hetty declared. "Whoever owns it surely knows it."

"Miss Carole gives sound advice in most cases," her husband agreed and turned to a different section.

"I'm curious about who she is."

Benjy shrugged. "That's easy to guess. It's someone well connected in the city who wishes to remain anonymous. Which suggests they are someone active in the community. A teacher, an organizer, or even someone prominently placed in church."

"You know that much," Hetty exclaimed, "but you can't tell me a name?"

"The name is just a detail."

Hetty snorted. "That means you don't know!"

He looked over the rim of his glasses at her, a smile playing at his lips. "I never said that."

Hetty huffed and lightly kicked him.

He caught her foot easily, and his fingers tapped against her stocking foot.

She wasn't ticklish there, but her breath caught all the same as she stilled, images of the previous night washing over her.

"It's my turn to make breakfast, isn't it?" Benjy asked as Hetty gently pulled her foot away, sinking into the tub.

Hetty nodded instead of answering aloud, and he left then, allowing her to soak in her thoughts a bit longer.

After breakfast, Benjy disappeared into the study to finish reading the newspaper. But Hetty had other mouths to feed.

"You're early," Hetty said as she carried out a bowl of seeds and a boiled egg for the five birds neatly lined up outside the kitchen door. "Or maybe it's me that's late."

The birds only watched her as she walked toward the bench. But the moment she sat down, they flew to rest around her, waiting for her to scatter the seeds.

A crow and her mate had built a nest on the rooftop, which made them neighbors in a sense. Hetty had found the nest when setting up her telescope and crows came rushing at her. Only when Hetty stayed a good distance away from the nest and offered food did the crows leave her alone. Providing these meals slowly gained her their trust, and hopefully their affections. With the eggs hatched and the baby birds fending for themselves, Hetty was seldom bothered these days. She wasn't sure if they'd taken a liking to her, but they clearly didn't mind her being around.

Hetty sat there watching the birds until a shadow fell over her.

"Did you want to help—" Hetty stopped midsentence, realizing the shadow had split into two.

She spun around, alert and ready to attack, only to see two of Penelope's cousins behind her.

Sy and Rosabelle looked at Hetty nervously, and it was only then that she realized her hand was already shaping a spell.

She relaxed and the magic faded as she stood to greet them properly.

Before the war, the Caldwells had been a family with five daughters, scattered forcibly across several states. After the war, the Caldwells had several grandchildren, a newly discovered niece, and four daughters and a son. That son was Sy, who had run away to fight for the Union. He found that what had been a disguise turned into a revelation answering the unease he'd felt about his life before the war. The rest of the Caldwells accepted that change without a hint of fuss, as they saw it as gaining a son instead of losing a daughter, and when someone in their old town tried to make Sy's past into a scandal and ruin the family's business, the entire Caldwell clan used the excuse of learning Penelope's whereabouts to move to Philadelphia.

This move benefited the youngest Caldwell sibling, Rosabelle, the most. The baby of the family, Rosie was a recent graduate of Olmstead Secondary. But her mother's dream of Rosie's being the first to attend college in the family was cut short by a mysterious illness that had left Rosie bedridden for several months. Rosie was painfully thin and had a delicate look of spun sugar at times. But there was no sign of illness today. Rosie carried a box of books under one arm, and her eyes danced with mirth as her brother took a hasty step away from the crows, who were watching Sy rather closely.

"It's fine," Hetty said to the birds. "They're friends."

As if to acknowledge her words, the birds flew onto the roof. The lead crow and her mate peered down, still holding watch as if they doubted Hetty's judgment.

One raised its wings when Sy stepped forward, and when he stumbled back, the bird's beak fell open in a way that looked like silent laughter.

"Sorry that we came early, but Penelope told me you wanted

to come as soon as possible. She gave me her key in case you were gone," Sy said. "I came because I started a new job—"

"*We* started a new job," Rosie added in a rush. "Sy is working at the Chiron Bookshop and he can't do it without my help."

"No wonder you turned down working for us! When did this happen?" Hetty asked.

"Just last week," Sy said with a tinge of pride. "But it's mostly inventory. There are so many books to organize."

"It doesn't sound like a well-run bookshop."

"It's not," Rosie jumped in. "I never heard about it before Sy got the job, and I know all the best places to get books from."

"So do I." Benjy stood in the doorway behind them. "I got a list of books that I want to purchase, and shelves to fill."

They all froze at his sudden appearance. Even Hetty was at a loss to explain why the siblings were here this early in the day.

"And I'm here to help!" Rosie thrust the box of books at Benjy. Her voice became rather high pitched and breathless as she rattled on like an oncoming train. "I found the book you were talking about since last Christmas! And an older translated copy!"

"In the original Greek?" Benjy took the box from the girl, tilting it toward him as he did. "I see you brought back the copy of *Willows at Dawn* that you borrowed. Clever sneaking it in with these. Have you read the latest serial?"

"Not yet!" Rosie dashed inside. "Do you think D. R. Vanders survived the plunge off the mountain? I don't think it's possible!"

Benjy was already debating this point as they returned to the house, and it wasn't entirely clear if Rosie was seriously arguing with him or just being a distraction.

"This worked better than I planned," Sy said with clear pleasure.

"You could have dropped books like breadcrumbs in the house and it would have worked just as well."

Sy gave her a curious look. "Have you done that?"

"No, but I might one day."

Sy had left a wagon around the corner, with a restless horse, waiting for them. Both wagon and horse belonged to one of his older sisters, Clarabelle most likely. The horse was certainly distempered like the woman, snapping its teeth as Hetty set a spell of invisibility over the beast.

With the wagon and horse hidden from sight, they brought in and began to unload the equipment and tools that she still didn't know the names of. But that was what Sy was there for. He hadn't been present when she bought it, but he had confirmed she made the right choices. With Sy's help and a bit of magic to lighten the load, they moved everything that was on the wagon into the shack.

Hetty had already put the table that had been in the cellar inside. While she wanted to put hooks in and shelves for the tools, she resisted the urge.

She had gotten one of their previous clients to build the shack. It looked perfectly fine to her, but given Benjy's exacting standards it'd probably be down and rebuilt within a few weeks. Or days, if they didn't get any other work soon.

"You should be pleased," Sy said as he rearranged the last of the tools onto the table. "You got everything in without him knowing."

"I am." Hetty patted the table. "Thank you for your help with this."

"I'm always happy to help. Penelope considers you family, so you're also my family. Between you and me, I'd take you and Ben over Clara and Adam any day."

Hetty was laughing over this as they stepped out of the shack. So she was still smiling when she looked back at the house and saw Benjy standing in front of the window in the study, staring right at her.

He had a book in his hand, which meant he had his glasses on. Because he was wearing those glasses, she knew there was no way he'd miss the shack behind her, absent of the many layers of spells that kept it hidden from him the entire time.

The shock that splashed across his face was worth every moment she'd spent planning over the past couple of weeks.

When she borrowed some money from Oliver, he'd teased that Hetty was giving Benjy his own personal forge so he could make things for the house. Which she admitted, to the laughter of her friends. But in private it was a gift. She could spin stories around the drops of starlight and whispers from the moon, but words eluded her when speaking of her true feelings, even to those closest to her.

So she used a gift to say all she wanted to say. That she loved him, that she hoped this would make him happy, and that this gift marked a new beginning for them.

Still smiling, Hetty waved at her husband.

Rosie suddenly jumped into view, thrusting a book in Benjy's direction, but what would have been a good distraction any other time failed miserably.

Benjy vanished from the window and moments later reappeared at the back door, waving his glasses at the shack.

"This wasn't here before! It's too big to come by wagon!"

"It was already here." Hetty's face felt like it was going to split into two as he stammered and stared.

"But I checked," he moaned. "I knew there was something going on back here, but I looked and I didn't find anything."

"Benjy, Benjy," Hetty said, hooking her arm into his. "How many times must I tell you? I'm better at magic than you!"

He swung his head around at her, but said nothing. "What's inside?"

"A surprise. Close your eyes." Hetty gestured to Sy to open

the shack's door. The young man sprang to action, and Hetty led Benjy inside.

At her direction, Benjy opened his eyes.

Hetty clasped her hands together, anticipating his reaction as he looked around.

He took in the entire shack and shook his head with a laugh. "I wondered what happened to all the tools! I went around asking Amos about these things, but he just yelled at me."

"You didn't realize I bought everything?"

"I didn't think you would," he said softly, running his hand along the tools laid out before him. "The cost—"

"Was of no concern." Hetty assured him. "I haggled with Amos, and Oliver and Thomas provided some funds. As you can guess, Penelope's work with the garden was an excuse to get all this in place. And Sy insisted on helping once he heard. We all could tell you missed the forge."

"It's about creation and transformation." Benjy's arm went around her shoulders, squeezing her for a moment. "How did you get the birds to not sit on this?"

"I have my ways."

With a cough, Sy poked his head in. "We're off." His cheeky grin said he wanted to say more but knew better. He and Rosie left, although if they stayed any longer or not, Hetty didn't really care.

She was reveling in the fruits of her labor as Benjy rearranged things to his liking.

"You hired someone to make this shack," Benjy said as his magic turned equipment around and sent tools rearranging themselves. "It's not bad, so you hired someone who wasn't boasting about their skill. Do I know who they were?"

"Violet Morrow helped me with this. Her brother was the man we found with a glass bottle shoved down his throat."

Benjy grimaced as they left the shack. "That was a nasty one."

"The body? We've seen worse."

"No, all the fuss with people afterward. The secret lovers and children. It was messy."

"You're going to knock the shack down?"

"No—why would I ruin what was very cleverly done?" Benjy pulled her toward him, so his words were whispered into her hair. "What spells did you use?"

Hetty smiled. "I won't tell you, but I can show you."

"Excuse me!" cried a voice on the other side of the fence.

Hetty looked around Benjy to see a familiar pair of eyes glaring at them over the fence.

Blythe Holloway lived next door, having moved there not long after they did due to the small windfall her dead husband had left her. Despite the permanent scowl fixed on her face, she was not an old woman, only a bit older than Oliver and Thomas. Her pronounced disappointment in the world just aged her prematurely. Like a ghost she popped in whenever they least expected it, complaining about issues with her house that only Benjy could fix, chiding Hetty about the magic that went on, and stealing their mail. Blythe even tapped on the shared wall in the dining room whenever the gatherings with their friends got too loud.

Every time Hetty saw those glaring eyes, she was reminded why she was content to keep their bedroom in the attic.

"Mrs. Holloway," Benjy said politely, "is something the matter?"

"There was too much noise going on yesterday," Blythe bristled. "I don't know what you young people get up to, but I could hear it in my house and it's unacceptable!"

"We're so sorry about that. We'll do better."

"You will! I'd move, but this is the best neighborhood for Colored folks in the city. No strange fires have started here. I suppose it's the eyes of a finch and sparrow helping to keep it that way."

Blythe huffed and swept back into her house, slamming the door for good measure.

"How can she be so rude?" Hetty grumbled. "She knows who we are and what we do!"

Benjy pressed a kiss to her forehead. "Some people simply aren't easily impressed."

That sentiment, it seemed, extended to their fledgling funeral business.

Having done a few funerals with Oliver in the past with moderate success, Hetty thought running an official business would be easy. They weren't exactly famous in the city, but most people knew who they were. Yet other than some small amount of interest, some polite smiles, and vague promises, their client list was very short.

It wasn't because of the location, either.

When people found their loved ones dead due to mysterious circumstances, people knocked away at their door. There had been no shortage of cases, major or minor.

Just no funerals.

Hetty knew they had just opened their doors, yet she spent the bulk of every day within earshot of the door, hoping to hear the doorbell. It was becoming less about the work and more to prove she'd made the right choice.

That giving up sewing dresses and tailoring clothes was the right choice for her future. She could snap her fingers and find work as a dressmaker. She was the best around—few could challenge her skill with the needle.

But she wanted the funeral home to work. She had been sewing nearly all her life. She enjoyed it, yes, but it was a skill she'd learned to survive. And she didn't want to just survive anymore.

She wanted to live.

CROW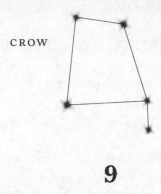

9

Morning slowly turned into afternoon.

Benjy left with the fiddle and returned with a bag of groceries and not once did visitors darken their doorstep. This wasn't the first time such a thing had happened, and most days it was just an annoyance Hetty fumed over. Today it was agonizing. Because bereft of anything to do, she was left there alone with her thoughts, and they kept turning to Nathan Payne.

About all the things she could be doing to quell the threat he represented. About what Payne was doing in Philadelphia. Or what would happen if she did seek him out without Benjy knowing. Although she was tempted to confront Payne, she had to admit Benjy was right. Going after him out of the blue would be like kicking a hornet's nest. She just needed to have a plan that was more detailed than making sure Payne never darkened her doorway.

Eventually Hetty got up and flipped through the mail they received yesterday but had never gotten around to looking through. Most of it wasn't noteworthy, but one small envelope in the stack sent her looking for Benjy.

She found him in the cellar. A mix of magic and gas lamps brightened the place enough to banish the gloom. A new door led directly into the yard so the bodies of the deceased wouldn't have to go through the house. Tucked in the corners were a few crates and supplies. And a punching bag dangled from the rafters, stuffed full with a number of rags and discarded clothes. Benjy used it for boxing practice, and made particularly good use of it after his broken arm had mended.

But a large portion of the room gave a few tables focus. Long tables that could hold the bodies that Oliver embalmed and worked on. There were three tables, but two were pushed to the side, as they never had more than one body in the cellar these days. At this table, Benjy sat on a stool, adding the finishing touches for another casket. Since they had no funerals to work on, it was simply another one to put on display. Custom caskets hadn't been on their list of services to provide, but Benjy saw it as something to keep busy with while practicing his woodworking skills. Like anything he worked on, they were beautiful, and casket sales made up what little business they had recently.

"Look at what was in the post!" Hetty tossed the envelope onto the table.

Benjy snapped his fingers, and the envelope floated into the air before him. "An invitation from Bernice Tanner," he said. The envelope turned over, and he studied the seal on the back. "She has a new assistant. Much better than the last one. Look how everything is perfectly done. Even the words are crisp." He plucked it from the air and ripped open the envelope. "We've been invited to a ball."

"A ball?" Hetty snatched the card from him.

In elegant handwriting that must belong to Bernice's new assistant was the announcement for a ball to be held in the Peabody Hotel this Saturday night, and hopes that both Hetty and Benjy would attend. The only explanation for why it was being held was at the end. The money raised would go to Olmstead Secondary.

This was about Raimond Duval.

Olmstead was the school he'd taught at, and Bernice had known him through her work with the Vigilance Society.

Another link to Duval in so few days, and it came from Bernice Tanner, the woman who knew all the rumors in town before they were even whispered in discreet corners.

This was not by chance.

"It's a charity ball." Hetty dropped the card onto the table. She strode right to the punching bag and swung a fist at it.

The bag didn't move, but that didn't stop her from hitting it again and again.

Benjy watched her, letting her swing at the bag.

"Are we going?" he asked when there was a break in the punching. "There should be good food there."

Good food at these types of gatherings was the only reason they went, besides murder.

"That's one reason. I do have an old dress I can alter for the ball. The gold one."

"It's not old if you never wore it out of the house."

Hetty dropped her hands to the side and turned away from the bag, rubbing her slightly sore knuckles. "We should go. It'll be a way to gather some customers if we make some polite conversation."

Benjy raised one eyebrow. "Of course that's the plan."

"What other plan is there? I'm not going to slip poison into the punch bowl."

"That would be a terrible idea," Benjy said. "You can't control the spread and who it affects. A dusting around the rim of a glass would be better."

"And doing it repeatedly is not a good way to keep business," Hetty added. But she shook herself before she accidentally got wrapped up into another conversation about murder methods. "I'll leave the poison at home and send a response saying yes."

Benjy leaned back on the stool, watching her as he clearly sought the right thing to say. "Do you really want to go?"

"Of course I do. Why do you ask?"

"It's a *ball*," Benjy said, as if the word was more than adequate to explain things. "It's not a dinner party with close friends. The room will be filled with all the high society people you hate and I barely tolerate, and we'll be stuck in dreadful conversations about the same topics that have been circulating for weeks on end."

"The food will be good," Hetty said, echoing his earlier sentiment.

"It will be excellent. So will the drinks Bernice will offer to us when she draws us aside for a private conversation."

"A private conversation?" Hetty echoed.

"She'll be in a small room at the hotel and will provide liquor from her private stash. There's something she wants to talk about, but it's not urgent enough to talk about sooner. Just vague concerns."

"Trouble for tomorrow?"

A shadow crossed Benjy's face. And the name of Payne hung between them, unspoken. "There's always trouble for tomorrow."

The doorbell rang just then.

Hetty clapped her hands together. "A customer!"

"Maybe I should open the door," Benjy called as Hetty hurried to the stairs. "You look too pleased to greet someone who is in mourning!"

She scoffed at this, but when Hetty reached the door, she did take a calming breath.

Standing on the steps, however, was only their neighbor.

"A package was delivered to my house again." Blythe's eyes narrowed as she attempted to peer into the hallway behind Hetty. "I almost tripped over the box. It's placed in such a bad spot."

"I'll take care of it."

As Hetty shut the door behind her, the funeral home sign slipped off its post.

"I'd get a new sign if I were you," Blythe sniffed. "It's not very helpful. People might think it's a place for birds."

Hetty waved a hand and the sign flew back to its previous spot. She had painted it herself and she thought it rather straightforward about all the funeral home offered. While it could be bigger, she doubted it was the only factor in their trouble. People die all the time. A tiny sign couldn't be the only reason they were being overlooked.

"Maybe you can drum up some business for us, Mrs. Holloway? I'm sure if you put out a call, people will come."

"Maybe. You won't forget to ask your husband to look into my cellar door? It's been quite loose lately. I don't want any intruders sneaking into my house."

With assurances, false and otherwise, on her lips, Hetty stepped up to Blythe's half of the joint steps.

At first glance, she couldn't blame Blythe for her complaints. It was a rather large crate, and thankfully it was still tightly sealed. Not that Hetty doubted her neighbor would sneak a look if she could. Hetty reached over to pick it up to determine if she should help it along with magic, and stopped dead over the box.

While the name of the sender was familiar, it was the last one she ever expected to see:

Esther Beale
342 Cherrywood Road
Savannah, Georgia

"Esther," Hetty whispered. Her breath came up short and her heart raced, as her vision narrowed to the label.

Esther was dead. It was not possible for this to be sent by her. How was this here?

Unless the news she received had been about a different Esther. People often had the same names ... Maybe her sister was still alive.

For a moment Hetty considered that seductive idea, letting it bloom in her mind about what it might mean. But then she shoved the thought aside.

Her sister was gone, and her wishes otherwise would not change things.

Hetty carried the box inside and brought it upstairs into the spare bedroom.

She dropped down next to the crate and placed her hand on the lid. Opening this alone was a poor idea.

There should be someone with her. Benjy or Cora. Penelope and Darlene. Even Thomas and Oliver would be good choices. She shouldn't do this alone.

But she couldn't bring herself to leave this box unopened, not even for one more minute. She had to see what was inside.

Hetty took a deep breath and drew the lines that made up the Crow sigil. The lines and vertices glowed purple, and the nails in the crate popped out as the lid lifted upward and fell to the side.

A letter rested on top of the various items tucked in the box:

To Mrs. Henrietta Rhodes,

Your sister was a dear friend of mine. I apologize for the delay in this letter. After Esther passed on, I had taken a trip that kept me out of the country for many months. The instructions I left behind to send this crate and the letter formally telling you of her passing had gotten buried under a number of papers. If that was not enough to spur me to correct this mistake, it was learning that you heard of the news secondhand, which having had similar news delivered to myself in such a fashion, I had hoped to spare you the same.

When Esther realized she was sick, she directed me to put all this aside for you. I think she knew she wasn't going to regain her health.

Her only true regret was not leaving town sooner to see you. In this box is everything she wanted you to have and remember her by. If you have any questions for me, you need only to write.

 Best wishes,
 Kit Wright

Hetty read the letter a few more times, as in the first attempts she didn't fully comprehend every word. When she finally finished, Hetty put the letter aside, feeling the warm sentiments of the writer and a tinge of sadness for the fleeting hope that had seized her for a few moments.

Her sister had sent several somethings for her to have. What could they be?

Inside were things she expected to see. Packets of seeds and gardening tools. Small mementos of Esther's life in Savannah in the form of notes and stamps. There were bundles of the letters that Hetty had sent. A wooden box filled with jewelry. A few dusty vials of brewed magic, neatly labeled. And there were several books, mostly cheap sensational tales.

But a large leather-bound book caught her attention. Her sister's handwriting covered every page, broken up by sketches of plants, animals, even a few people. Words made up recipes, observations, and ingredients for potions. It was not a journal—it was too disorganized to be that—but there were small wry remarks on some pages that lifted a smile to Hetty's face. Soon she sought these pages out, hearing Esther's voice in her ear as she read them. Then Hetty got to the middle of the book and there was a bookmark. A scrap of fabric made from the quilt Hetty sewed a lifetime ago.

How did she know?

At her touch, the stitches lit with one last burst of dormant magic before it faded away for the last time.

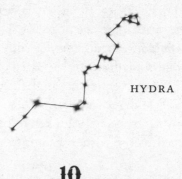

HYDRA

10

Wᴉɴᴅ ᴄʟᴀᴡᴇᴅ ᴀᴛ ʜᴇᴛᴛʏ as she hurried along the street. She barely remembered stumbling out the house, even the excuse she called out to Benjy when she left. She just knew she needed to get away from the box and from the room it was in.

She was trying to move toward the future, but that box dragged her back to the past.

Back to wondering what could have been.

Back to thinking what should have happened.

She thought she could have handled it. She should have been able to handle it. But maybe she only convinced herself she had. It made a good story. After years of searching, she finally found out the truth, and with the love of the family she built around her she had the support to let the past go. It was a story Hetty wanted to be true, because she knew how much she had failed everyone in her life due to her focus on finding Esther. She ruined friendships, lost time and opportunities, all just to be ready to chase after a fallen star.

Maybe that's why the funeral home wasn't working. She wasn't used to staying in one place.

No, that was wrong.

She had stayed in Philadelphia all these years. For her friends.

For Cora and Jay. For Benjy. Benjy had stayed here with her, even throughout the years their marriage was just a formal arrangement so they could investigate murder without gossip spreading.

She had done something right to have all these wonderful people in her life, who wanted her in their lives.

And she wasn't going to let this box send her spiraling.

This box was a gift, after all, a token of her sister's love.

Hetty stopped at the corner, feeling a weight lift from her shoulders.

Even in death, her sister's love was still around her.

Now, that's a better story.

Cora's home wasn't on the way back to Juniper Street, but Hetty found herself walking there anyway, drawn to the possibility of comforting words and sound advice.

After knocking without getting an answer, Hetty was just about to leave when the door snapped open.

"I thought you might have gone out," Hetty began, only to stop when she saw the frantic expression on Cora's face. "What's the matter?"

"I've never been so glad to see you in my life! Come in, come in, I need your help!"

Alarmed by these words, Hetty followed Cora down the hallway into the back room. Once upon a time a bookcase hid the doorway, as this room had been a place for runaways to stay and rest as they figured out what they would do next. That bookcase now sat inside the room properly, although the rest of the room was little changed. There was a cot, some chairs, and small tables for a lantern and water bowl to rest on. Although there was talk about Benjy cutting a window into the room, in the end it never happened, as Cora thought this room would be used for storage one day. But that day might not come as long as this room kept performing its original function.

"Is my assistant back already? I know the girl's good, but this is short of miracles!"

Hetty stopped at the doorway, recognizing the voice of the last person she wanted to see on any given day.

Bernice Tanner.

Hetty shouldn't have been surprised. Cora and Bernice were old friends, but for her to be here to help was unexpected. Bernice did not get her hands dirty—she employed others for that.

But there Bernice sat in a chair, gripping her cane in hand. Although Bernice was around the same age as Cora and Jay, she appeared decades older. That could be blamed on her perpetually pursed lips, a mane of pure white, and large round glasses that gleamed in the light. The dark lenses gave her an air of mystery, and few people ever realized she was blind. Bernice used her glasses to great effect, leaning forward so your reflection peered back at you. Despite being born into privilege and wealth, she had devoted her life to the cause of freedom and had been highly placed in the Vigilance Society, commanding information that went in and out of the city regarding Underground Railroad activities. There was nothing that occurred without Bernice knowing first. She handed out assignments, gave orders, and ensured people arrived where they needed to be, whole and well. But if you wanted something from her, even just information, there was a price. A price Hetty had paid many times before, but she never got her just rewards.

"Not your assistant," Cora said. "It's Henrietta."

Bernice nodded at this. "That might be better. She's always willing to help."

"Bernice found him," Cora explained as she gestured to the man lying on the cot. "She brought him here because it was closest. Thought I could help for some reason, but this is nothing like I'd seen before."

"I don't know if there's anything I can do." Hetty tried not to glare at Bernice, resentment outweighing her desire to lend Cora any help.

"I'm sure you can think of something," Bernice said.

A loud moan from the cot brought Hetty's attention away from Bernice.

On the cot, the man twisted in pain. There was magic around his wrists and ankles, tying him down to the bedposts. Cora's spells, Hetty determined as she noted how the sigils were on the bedposts themselves.

The reason for this was clear. Throbbing red magic on his torso set the man thrashing about. When the light on his chest faded, he slacked against his bounds. As his face relaxed, Hetty recognized him.

"Wise Sammy!" Hetty exclaimed.

Bernice's head swung in Hetty's direction. "You know this man?"

"More like encountered many times." Hetty went to the other side of the cot. "He gets into a number of unsavory things that often have us crossing paths."

Wise Sammy had fought for the Union during the war, one of the first volunteers that signed up after Black men were allowed to serve. While he came out of the war unharmed physically, his unseen scars led him to an addiction of a potion called Narcisse. As a result, he moved from place to place, and got himself tangled in quite a few things he shouldn't. Although he was only a handful of years older than Hetty, from the deep wrinkles and shock of white through his hair, you wouldn't know it.

At the sound of his name, Wise Sammy's eyes flickered open and focused on Hetty. His voice was hoarse as he spoke. "Well, well, Miz Sparrow. Come to terrorize me. I don't think you can manage it on your own."

Hetty leaned in. "I can dangle you off the side of a building without my husband, thank you very much. What happened to you?"

"A spell," Wise Sammy grunted.

He jerked backwards then, and his body arched forward against his bounds. Bernice and Cora both recoiled at the yell that ripped itself from his lungs, but Hetty didn't budge. Wise Sammy's eyes were wide open in pain, and there was something glowing at his throat.

Hetty had no idea what sort of sigils were used. Sigils rarely revealed what the intent was, but that didn't matter when it came to breaking them apart.

With a flick of her fingers, the mythical beast of Hydra appeared before her.

As it glided across Wise Sammy, the sigils across his body lit up. Hetty waved her arms like a music conductor. She directed the Hydra's head to attack the spell. She aimed widely at first, trying to destroy the toughest part of the spell. The hex fought her, attacking her own spell, but Hetty pressed on, chipping away until the hex faded and Wise Sammy's breathing returned to normal.

"Oh, dear stars above." Cora had a hand pressed to her chest. "To think I thought herbs would do the trick!"

"That is a strange sort of magic," Hetty said. "However did he encounter it?"

"Don't know," Bernice said. "My nephew bought some dodgy potions the other day and I had my assistant tracking down the source. She was led to this 'Wise Sammy,' as you call him. And this."

Bernice tapped her cane against a filthy and patched bag that lay next to the cot.

Hetty brought the bag over to her side. Inside were wrapped packages and potions. Picking up one of the packages, she got a strong smell of herbs, and although she didn't know the name, she'd bet everything they were magical instead of mundane. But her guess rested mostly on the packaging. There were a handful of herbal shops in the city, and they all stamped their packaging. Penelope's shop, for example, stamped an acorn. Hetty knew the others by sight. This package of herbs had no stamps, just a number scrawled onto the paper. The potion bottles, however, were labeled. None were poisons or deadly potions that Hetty recognized, and a few even had Penelope's handwriting on the labels, but they were all from different shops. Hetty tapped the cork. This proved it wasn't fraudulent potions flooding the streets, but this felt much worse in a way. Less worrisome were a few amulets tucked into the bag, and a coin purse bulging to the point of the seams splitting.

"Should have let me die, if you're trying to steal from me," Wise Sammy muttered.

"You weren't going to die," Hetty said. The man's voice was strained, but his eyes were open and alert. "If you did, be happy to know you would have a properly attended funeral."

A raspy laugh escaped Wise Sammy. "With all the people I owe money to in attendance."

"Most likely." Hetty glanced up at Cora and Bernice. "Can I talk to him alone? I don't think he'll talk freely with you here."

"He's talked freely enough," Bernice grumbled.

Cora just tapped Bernice's shoulder. "Leave her alone. She seems to got a good handle on things."

Either because she agreed or because she'd rather not sit around listening anymore, Bernice got up and followed Cora to the back room, leaving Hetty alone with Wise Sammy.

Hetty tucked the bottles she thought might be poison into her pocket and then drew the Arrow star sigil. Gently, she sent the spell at the bounds that kept Wise Sammy tied to the bed.

He drew his arms back down to his side but folded them over his chest and let them rest there.

"They're gone. Tell me what happened," Hetty said.

"Told you. Got caught up in a bad spell. Thought it wasn't so bad. Guess I was wrong."

"Quite wrong. But that's not the whole story."

Wise Sammy licked his lips. "You know my woes, Miz Sparrow. My bad luck is worse than a two-headed frog. I got to talking to somebody who was selling potions and magical trinkets. Said I could do the same. I get a crate every week or so and told to sell them. And it's been a good thing."

"Who gives you the stuff to sell?" Hetty prompted.

"A fella," Wise Sammy said. "I meet him at different places. Last time was two nights ago. I got the goods, but the fella told me I couldn't walk the streets. That the police had things set up to find us out. And he said not to worry, there's a shortcut. Well, it was no shortcut I'd ever seen! It took me underground, into a tunnel."

Hetty sat forward at these last words.

"Where did you enter?" Hetty interrupted.

"The Greek church—"

"St. Gregorious?" Hetty finished for him.

Wise Sammy nodded.

Hetty sat back. He was talking about the tunnel she'd visited on Barclay Street. Did this mean that whatever Wise Sammy had gotten tangled up in, it had to do with the fire or even the hex she found? Hetty didn't believe in coincidences, but this was an unexpected twist.

"When you were in this tunnel, that's when you got caught up in the spell?"

He nodded. "Lit up everything around me like all the stars coming home. I didn't feel nothing that night, but the pain started yesterday afternoon."

"A delayed reaction," Hetty said softly, as she thought back to when she'd set that hex off in Valentine Duval's home. Could it be related? It seemed like it could be. "Is there anything else you can tell me? What's the man's name? What does he look like?"

Wise Sammy opened his mouth but stopped. "I don't know what he looks like. I saw him with my own two eyes. But I can't tell you if he was a tall man, a skinny man, or even if he was missing an eye. The words aren't coming to me."

"That's a cloaking spell," Hetty said, after giving it some thought. "Done so you can't betray this man."

A very well-done spell too, which annoyed Hetty. She hated it when they were clever.

Wise Sammy was also annoyed, but for different reasons. "Why would I betray him? He's helping me make money!"

"I wonder that as well," Hetty remarked.

She brought the bag over to him. "You can sell the rest of these. But that's it. Don't get any more things from this man. You go rent a room at the Goode House and get yourself a hot meal. I'll send your brother to check on you, and if you're not there the next time our paths cross, you're going to dangle off a building. You understand?"

Wise Sammy smiled. "Understood, Miz Sparrow. You be careful too, looking for this man. I got a feeling he's not so nice to people messing with his business."

"Most aren't, but that's no surprise."

Wise Sammy leaned back. "Can you send me off to sleep? I'm beat."

"I will, but you got to promise me, when you wake up you leave here with nothing else in your bag. Mrs. Evans and the pastor are like kin to me, so you hurting them is hurting me."

"Ah, what do you take me for?"

"Somebody I can't trust even with my eye on him," Hetty said.

With a wave of her fingers, Hetty set a sleep spell on him. Then she went in search of Cora and Bernice.

They were in the kitchen, holding a private conference.

"How's the man?" Cora asked.

"Sleeping. He'll wake up in a few hours and be on his way."

Cora's eyes narrowed. "Did you spell him asleep?"

"Yes, but he asked for it."

"How lucky for you to drop by and take care of things." Bernice cackled. "I always knew you could be relied upon!"

"What's his story?" Cora asked.

"Bad luck and poor judgment. He's selling stolen magic to make money. Somebody gives him a crate and he sells what's inside. I spotted a few potions from Penelope's shop and there's bound to be others in there," Hetty said.

"Has Penelope told you about any thefts?" Cora asked.

Hetty shook her head. "She says there's always been some petty theft, but she overlooks it as long as it's not poisons—but she wouldn't know about the other shops."

"Sounds like you should ask around," Bernice pointed out.

"Yes," Hetty reluctantly agreed, "you're right."

Bernice smiled at these words, stealing the rest of Hetty's goodwill toward the woman. "Well, this is something I'll keep an ear out to. And if my assistant finds any more people caught up in some hex, I'll make sure to send them your way. All in all, this was quite an exciting afternoon. I thought I wouldn't be seeing you until my ball," Bernice said. "Did you get my invitation? My assistant posted things somewhat late. I was awaiting news from Valentine Duval, and he has only just returned to Philadelphia."

Hetty nearly had whiplash at the sudden lurch of the conversation.

She wasn't the only one. Cora's eyebrows raised in surprise at the subject change.

"Is having a ball a good idea?" Hetty managed to say. "Mr. Raimond Duval was just buried."

"I arranged this with Raimond long before his death," Bernice replied rather mildly. "He wouldn't want to call it off, especially when it's for the school.

"I hope that you will be there, Henrietta. Whenever you're around, it means there shall be some interesting conversations."

Benjy's words about Bernice pulling them away to ply them with good wine came to mind.

Hetty gritted her teeth, and said as pleasantly as she could, "We'll be there. I always love an excuse to wear a pretty dress. Perhaps we can talk more there."

The doorbell rang.

"Ah, that'll be my assistant. Don't bother, Cora, I'll see myself out. It looks like I have overstayed my welcome." Bernice stood up and left the room, slumping more than usual with her cane, as if the sight would make Hetty feel guilty.

"Henrietta, you're skating on a fine edge," Cora reproved.

"You know I don't like her!"

"But you should respect her. She has that right, no matter what you think personally."

Hetty shook her head. "She dangled information about my sister for years to get me to do what she wanted. I did what she asked, but she never held up her end of the deal. I was her puppet then, and she still thinks I am now. How can you be friends with her?"

"Bernice has her good qualities. Her methods might not be what you or I would do, but she means well in the end. She'll look into any reports of missing brewed magic and even keep an eye on the man she brought here."

"She's still a liar!" Hetty huffed.

Cora turned, and in the shadows of the kitchen she looked older than usual. "I swear, you are so much like Jay, both stubborn and steadfast about silly things."

"Is that a bad thing?"

"It depends." Cora picked up her kettle and set it on the stove.

"While your timely arrival was perfection, you never said why you showed up here. And don't lie and say it was just to see my face. You are quite often busy, my dear."

"I just got a box of Esther's things today. Items she put aside for me when she knew she was dying," Hetty said. "Most of it looks like her notes for brewed magic, herbs, and other tonics. Harmless things."

Cora's face softened, as understanding filled her eyes. "Still, they are haunted. Did you go through it?"

"I started, but I couldn't."

"You need to. You won't move past her death if you don't. I'll go through it with you if need me there."

"I can't ask that of you."

"You're not—I'm offering. Also, you own a funeral home, Henrietta. You can't let it be occupied by a ghost!"

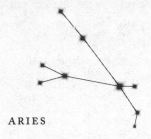

ARIES

11

WHEN HETTY RETURNED HOME, the sign had fallen again. Spying it lying in the bushes, she was tempted to leave it there.

Hetty almost did, but at the last moment she picked it up.

She was never one to give up on anything in her life, and she wasn't about to start now.

She *would* make this funeral home successful. She'd be so busy with it that the ghosts of her past, either in the form of Esther or Nathan Payne, would never have a chance to haunt her.

The lid for the postbox was askew, and grimly Hetty wondered if her neighbor had come back and stuck something in there. Blythe never opened their letters, but Hetty more than once had noticed that letters suddenly appeared in the box long after the mail courier had come and gone.

Leaning the sign against the door, she checked it and found that tucked inside was this month's *Amateur Star Seeker*.

"Finally!"

Hetty flipped through the pages. With each page turn she sought her name and the title of her essay. She hadn't gotten a rejection letter from the magazine. That meant only one thing. Her article about using the stars to navigate across land had made it in.

However, neither her name nor her article appeared.

She turned the pages more slowly a second time when someone approached her.

A woman stood on the neighbor's side of the steps. She blew her nose into her handkerchief very loudly, although her eyes were quite dry.

When the woman blew her nose again, Hetty lowered the magazine.

"Can I help you?" Hetty asked.

"Is this the funeral home?" The woman's eyes drifted toward Hetty, the magazine clutched in her hands and the letters threatening to spill onto the ground. "Or am I at the wrong place?"

"You're at the right place." Hetty extended her hand only to realize she still held the magazine. "Is there something you need?"

"My uncle has passed away. I'm looking for the funeral home. I heard there is a new one?"

Eagerly, Hetty pointed to the sign lying against the wall. "Yes, this is the Rhodes Family Funeral Parlor, a Place of Celebration of Life, History, and Tradition."

"That's quite a mouthful." The woman sniffed, and there was no sorrow in the gesture this time. "You might want to look into changing that."

"Why don't you come inside?" This was the first person to come to them for a funeral in weeks. She could endure this woman's sour attitude as long as she needed to. "We can discuss matters far better that way."

"I'd rather speak to your employer."

"I run the funeral parlor with my husband."

"That's quite a bit of work for two people."

"Not at all—it's just a matter of setting the proper spells."

"Spells?" A rather magnificent sneer filled the woman's face. "You use *magic?*"

"For preservation—"

"Why not embalming? I want the very best for my uncle."

"That's very different," Hetty protested. "Embalming is what I meant—"

"You're putting words in my mouth."

"Of course not—I only meant that it's a separate thing that we do—"

The woman shook her head. "Why offer it as a separate service, then?"

The question caught her off-guard, as it was intended, but Hetty had a great deal of practice in keeping her features bland and smooth.

"I only wish to point it out," Hetty said finally.

"What other things are separate?" the woman demanded.

Hetty started to list them. She got halfway through that list before a crow and his three babies dropped onto a nearby ledge.

They looked at her rather sternly, and in that moment Hetty realized she was wasting her time.

She was never going to get this client. This woman had come eager to pick and prod as if this were a jumble sale at church. Even if she wasn't, the woman's words had been clear from the start: They weren't her first choice. They were only a last resort.

"There is something else I need to show you. Wait here." Hetty picked up the fallen sign. "It's part of a special service. It's a ceremonial aspect. It allows us to highlight the passing of one soul leaving this world for the next."

Hetty opened her front door and then slammed it shut behind her. There was a moment of stillness before the woman began banging on the door.

"You won't be burying my uncle!" the woman yelled.

"Go on," Hetty yelled right back. "You were considering other places anyway!"

"And I will!" The muffled voice came through the door, shoving its way through the cracks. "Some business you have. You'll be closing if I have anything to do with it!"

"Don't flatter yourself!"

Hetty slid backwards against the door, and pressed her hands against her face. The sign clattered onto the floor, and her mail tumbled about like fallen leaves. She fell with them, sinking to the floor with her skirts pooled around her.

She wasn't sitting there for long before she heard footsteps.

"In the history of terrible ideas," Benjy's voice floated above her, "there is Napoleon's march into Russia, books on phrenology, and the interaction you just had."

Hetty lowered her hands to find her husband crouched before her, equal parts amused and sympathetic.

"I tried."

"I heard." Benjy picked up the fallen sign. "Why don't I make a new one? I can even change the name."

"What's wrong with this one? Rhodes Family Funeral Parlor also implies we are a family-run place, which makes us appear nice and friendly."

"As opposed to what? That we aren't?"

"You make fun, but sometimes people need a reminder."

"There are better names." Benjy placed the sign out of the way. "Now, besides the third most disastrous thing in the world, what have you been up to? I went looking for you earlier, but you were gone."

"I took a walk and found a person tied to the hex in the tunnel we found."

Benjy blinked. "How did you manage that?"

"Wise Sammy told me all about it," Hetty said.

"Wise Sammy?" Benjy scoffed. "You know better to trust anything he says, especially after he had one too many sips of Narcisse."

"The proof of his words was the hex on his person. He was down there the night of the Barclay Street fire and got caught in a hex. But the most interesting part is that he was guided by a stranger. A stranger that he could not describe in any manner."

"We're talking about Wise Sammy," Benjy said again.

"I trust he was telling the truth. The way he described it, it sounds like a rather intricate spell. Wise Sammy could tell me nothing about the man. The words weren't coming to him."

Benjy sighed. "A spell like that is nothing but trouble. Why was Wise Sammy in the tunnel anyway?"

"He was selling stolen magical goods. He had things from Penelope's shop and probably others."

Her husband grimaced. "I guess we'll have to find out, then. This makes it a case. Anything else I should know?"

Hetty thought of the crate upstairs in their spare room, but she didn't want to talk about it now, so she grabbed a suitable substitute off the floor.

"The *Star Seeker* came today."

"Really?" Benjy sat down on the floor next to her. "Is your article in it?"

Hetty shook her head. "I was so hopeful I would be accepted this time. I should have known better. I read that article to everyone, and they didn't like it much. I shouldn't have sent it."

"You really can't be that upset about it." Benjy flipped through the magazine. "This is just the first one you sent. Maybe the next one will do better."

"Maybe?" Hetty sat up at hearing that. "You're supposed to be more encouraging than that!"

"Is that a rule?" Benjy asked, still flipping through the pages, but the twitch of his lips betrayed that his word choice was on purpose.

"It is, or do I need to remind you of the story about the husband who lost the keys to his home?"

"I think I can guess the end. But I have another story for you." From his pocket Benjy pulled out a pamphlet and held it for her to read.

"'Authentic Statements Regarding Buried Treasure in the Delaware Valley,'" Hetty read aloud. "What is this?"

"Something from Rosie to make me forget about the books she borrowed from me. It was tucked in the box she brought. The Clarke Papers."

"I heard about this." Hetty nodded. "It's all people could talk about lately. I thought someone had published a book with secret love letters."

"And that didn't interest you enough to find out what it was!" Benjy exclaimed.

Hetty shrugged. "I'm only interested in one love story. Everything else just pales in comparison."

"In your humble opinion." The gentle smile on his face undermined the rebuff in his words.

Hetty tapped the pamphlet. "Tell me the story behind this. I can tell it's not about love letters, but it has to be something interesting for you to bring it to my attention."

"It's five printed pages of an extraordinary tale. You can read it later, but the main points are the following: A white man digs up sapphires and precious jewels in North Carolina and comes up here to bury it before joining the Lost Cause. The writer claims it's real, told to them by someone who had been there that night. It's only being printed now, since all parties are long dead. The writer has tried to find it over the years, but admits defeat and hopes others will have better luck finding the treasure."

"It's a good story." Hetty nodded. "But I'm not sure I can believe in treasure buried somewhere outside the city. Wouldn't someone have found it by now?"

"As far as I know they haven't. It's protected by something stronger than any magic." Benjy turned the page.

Instead of words, numbers filled the page that made no more sense to her than ancient Greek. But still, Hetty smiled.

She understood his interest now. Ciphers, codes, and other puzzles always drew his curiosity. The treasure could very well be pieces of glass painted blue and he'd still be happy.

Unable to hide his excitement, Benjy continued, "According to the pamphlet, the location can only be found once the cipher is solved."

"This looks like your area of expertise," Hetty said to her husband. "How soon do you think you'll solve it?"

"Me, solve a complex cipher that has gone unsolved for years, for a treasure that may or may not be real?" Benjy exclaimed. Then he shrugged, turning back to the pamphlet. "I just need a day or two."

"Is that all?"

The doorbell rang above their heads.

They jumped up, Benjy quickly picking up and moving the sign, their mail, and anything that could be in the way.

"Don't look *too* pleased," Benjy whispered as he left the hallway. "It could be a client."

Hetty stuck out her tongue at his retreating back. Then, smoothing her skirts, Hetty opened the door.

But the moment she did, she knew it wasn't a customer.

A young woman stood on the doorstep. Her hair was neatly tucked into a bun, and golden tan skin was flush with a bit of pink from the walk in the summer heat. She was very short, with the grace of a dancer. In a light green pinstriped dress, she might have been mistaken for being much younger than she truly was, if it were not for her sorrowful brown eyes.

But this was no stranger. This was Evelyn Wong.

Last month, someone had pushed a laundry worker into a steaming vat of wash water. It was a common accident in such places, but the man had fallen in with a knife in his back. The death was clearly murder. But the police didn't care, not even when more deaths started occurring, because the dead were all Chinese. Hetty and Benjy only heard of it by chance because one of Penelope's cousins, Jobelle, ran a laundry business of her own. When an employee of hers died, she went to Hetty and Benjy, and their questions led them to a little restaurant where Evie, eager for excitement since moving here from California, was happy to assist them in finding answers.

But that was a story for another day.

Hetty was more interested in the story Evie had for them now.

Evie tucked the card in her hand into her pocket and bowed her head slightly in greeting. "I'm glad I had the right address. I thought I was lost, but then I saw the birds roosting on your roof. There are quite a few."

"I make sure they're welcomed. Come inside so we can talk."

Hetty was about to call for Benjy, but he stood behind them already.

"Greetings," Evie said to Benjy. "I'm pleased to see your broken arm has healed nicely since I last saw you. It's not good to break bones so close together."

Benjy absently rubbed his arm. "Luckily it was the same spot. What brings you here? Murder or death?"

"Neither, but there is a mystery for you to consider," Evie said.

As this was a conversation better had when comfortably seated, they settled in the parlor.

"Something odd is going on on Race Street," Evie began. "You know how my Uncle Bobby is experimenting with Sorcery?"

Hetty nodded. Evie had introduced them to several uncles, older men that weren't necessarily related to her but were friends of Evie's older brother. Of the group, the man they were told to call Uncle Bobby had been in Philadelphia the longest.

"He's been purchasing things. Wands, spellbooks, and the like. The law doesn't prevent the Chinese from practicing Sorcery, but given certain attitudes I can't say it's a good thing he is."

"We sympathize," Benjy said. "But we can't do anything about that."

"It's not that he's buying these things, it's *what* he bought. I don't have it with me, but he's got in his possession a spellbook about Celestial magic."

"No such thing exists," Hetty said as Benjy added:

"Maybe you're confusing it with an astronomy textbook. There's been cases in which white scholars tried to use star charts to attempt our spellcraft."

Evie shook her head. "I looked through it. They weren't star maps. And there were instructions. How to form the sigil, what it will do, and the effects."

"It's fake," Hetty said, stubbornly refusing to engage with the idea. "Someone made it all up."

"A book is a book, and that can't be faked." Benjy leaned forward, his eyes locked on the span of wall before him. "But the ideas inside. They can be dangerous. That's why you are here, isn't it? The spells described in the book, they are mostly spells to harm others?"

"Every spell listed," Evie said softly. "Every spell listed in the book leads to pain. Some of the body. Some of the soul. Uncle Bobby saw them and right away he started talking about how terrible Celestial magic was—and other things."

Evie cleared her throat, her face growing a bit pink over the things she wouldn't say outright.

"He didn't call it Celestial magic, did he?" Hetty asked, noticing the hesitation that ran through the other woman.

"He called it something I won't repeat. But it worries me, because Uncle Bobby never said such things before. Should I have brought it with me so you could see it for yourself?"

"No, it's fine. You said enough. I believe this book exists," Benjy said. "I have no doubts there will be a spellbook made of star sigils someday, but this is not the book. No one who knows a thing about our magic would make a spellbook like this, unless their aim isn't to teach magic but to malign it."

"Done on purpose?" Hetty asked. Then hearing the sound of her own words, she shook her head. "Of course done on purpose! Evie, where did your uncle purchase this?"

"Not at a shop. He gets his things from vendors who travel through. I don't know more than that. Or even how long the book's been around."

"It can't have been for long. I would have heard about it." Benjy turned to Hetty, and there were concerns in his eyes that he wasn't voicing, to keep from distressing Evie.

Going around town were rumors of a forthcoming magic ban. Philadelphia had a large Black population, which made the visibility of Celestial magic commonplace in the streets. It was not a coincidence that the expansion of voting rights brought on talk of magic bans. Voting, just like magic, held prestige. The latest bans talked about restricting public displays of magic, limited the sale of brewed magic, and required any magic lessons being taught in schools to have the approval of the city council. The proposed ban, even if enacted, wouldn't change much. But such bans were never about the actual rule of law but about the symbols they evoked.

This spellbook passing itself as a source of Celestial magic was certainly related. Something false to stir up fears that the spells being worked in the street were dangerous. Even though star sigils, just like any sort of magic, could be used for any purpose.

"I'll bring it to you next chance I get," Evie said. "I can ask Uncle Bobby, or maybe take it when he's not around."

"It's not that book alone that's the problem." Benjy shook his head. "It's others like it."

Evie's face fell a bit, and Hetty hastened to add, "He means we were going to look for other books. That copy alone won't be enough. But you described it very well. And we'll certainly be able to find more thanks to you."

"I'm always happy to help," Evie said.

"This mystery-solving business is rather fun, even if it's a bit dangerous at times. Come around the restaurant whenever you can. My brother has a few new recipes he'd like for you to try."

"How can we say no to that!" Hetty replied.

Although Hetty saw the younger woman off in high spirits, when Hetty returned to the parlor Benjy was still staring at the wall rather pensively.

"How do we stop people from printing such books?" he lamented.

"The same way we do anything," Hetty replied, "with stubbornness."

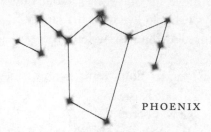

PHOENIX

12

WHEN HETTY WENT TO FEED the crows the next morning, she found Penelope already in the garden, digging a hole and muttering angry words.

So engrossed was she that Hetty was able to get right behind her friend without being noticed.

"Good morning," Hetty said rather loudly.

Penelope sprang to her feet, dirt flying everywhere as she spun around, and she waved the tiny shovel in her hand at Hetty.

"Don't scare me like that!"

Amused, Hetty merely replied, "That's what you get! I didn't give you a key so you could sneak in."

"I didn't!" Penelope dropped the clumps of grass in her hand back to the ground. "Benjy let me in. We crossed paths when he went to get a newspaper."

As if to prove the truth of this statement, Benjy passed by with his tool bag as he crossed the yard to enter the shack. He nodded at Hetty, but said nothing as he disappeared inside.

Hetty sat down on the bench as Penelope knelt back on the ground.

"Why were you up so early, then?" Hetty asked.

"Dinner with my cousins went terribly last night. My aunt

asked me to move in. She heard about how Darlene plans to move and says I should live with her family."

Hetty glanced at the new hole in the garden. "And you don't want that?"

"I never did, and I don't want it now, since it'll be because they're fretting about Rosie."

"I thought she was better?"

"She is, but the worry remains that she'll get sick again. Not to mention they're pulling out the old argument that it's silly for me to live on my own when I'm not managing a household."

"That's just silly. Tending to all your plants is so much work."

"I know, but no one believes me." Penelope sighed. "But I might have to consider it. I can't afford rent in most places, and the ones I can won't be good for my plants."

"There's an easy solution. Stay here. There's a bedroom, and you can stay as long as you need. You'll just have to take your turn cooking every so often."

Penelope's smile was guarded. "I'll think about it."

"What is there to think about?" Hetty laughed. "You're here all the time!"

Penelope did not share in Hetty's laughter. "It's too far from the herbal shop. Speaking of which, I should head out there now—"

"Wait!" Hetty cried. "There's something I need to show you. Follow me."

Hetty hadn't been back in the room since she'd run out of it. The crate and its contents were left where she had dropped them, scattered in a few places.

"This came yesterday," Hetty said as she picked up Esther's book. "It's from my sister. She put it aside for me when she got sick, with instructions for her friend to send it. Apparently this friend just had a chance to send it here. They were out of the country for business, and I'm not sure—"

Hetty's rambling came to a stop as Penelope crouched down next to the box, her face quite sad.

"You opened this by yourself?"

Hetty turned back to the box. "I wanted to see what was inside. There's so much tucked away in here."

"Her whole life, or the one she wanted to share with you." Penelope held up one of the vials.

"Everything in the box is something she wanted me to have. Although, I'm not sure how to best use all these herbs. But you might."

The vial slipped in Penelope's hand. "Me?"

"Yes, you. You're an expert in all this! You know what to do with all this stuff, and could use it easier than Benjy or I could. And look."

Hetty pulled out the book, flipping through it so Penelope could see the notes and drawings. "This is brimming with knowledge, so much you can start your own shop with it. Don't argue with me—just take it."

Penelope backed away. "I can't. It's the only one."

"Then I'll make a copy. Darlene can draw the pictures and I can type it up on a typewriter. I want you to take this. I want you to have all of this. You're just like my sister, after all. Take the book and make magic with it."

Hetty held it out once again, but Penelope shut her eyes. "Why do you always do this? You get bad news about your sister and you turn to me? I can't replace your sister. We're entirely different people."

"You think I don't know that?"

Penelope took a deep breath, and she exhaled so strongly that some of the dust in the room stirred. "Sometimes I don't think you do. I have to go to work now. I'll come around later."

Without waiting for Hetty's reply, Penelope left the room.

Hetty didn't follow.

She lay down on the floor with Esther's book clasped to her chest. She turned over the conversation in her mind to see exactly where she went wrong. Although given the pinched lines of pain in Penelope's face, the problem went further than that.

It wasn't long before she heard Benjy's footsteps in the hallway. The door was already open, so she saw him when he appeared, illuminated by the light. While he could have told her to get off the dusty floor, he just lay next to her, shoulder to shoulder, staring up with her at the invisible cracks in the ceiling.

He smelled of soot, fire, and sweat. Hetty lay there breathing in the familiar scent as she dabbed the corner of her eyes with her sleeve.

"You should have asked her about the stolen potions," Benjy said after a while.

"She would have told me if it was trouble."

"Like Thomas did? Our friends have gotten into the bad habit of only telling us things that are dire. They think they're being kind, but it's just trouble that crops up far worse than it started."

"Then you talk to Penelope about the missing potions, if you care so much about it!"

"Hetty," Benjy gently chided, "you should know by now that never ends well."

Hetty couldn't help it, she snorted, barely suppressing a laugh. Without a moderator Benjy and Penelope's conversations about brewed magic tended to shift to experiments, even if they didn't start that way.

"What do you think about her staying?"

"I'm hardly surprised, as she's taken over the yard for her garden."

Benjy got to his feet then, and held out his hand to Hetty. She took it, allowing herself to be pulled up.

"What shall we do now?" Benjy asked. "According to the map

in the study there are few things we can look into. I wouldn't call it a case . . ."

"The tunnels are a case." Hetty dropped Esther's book back into the crate. "Strange fires were around both. Plus with Wise Sammy and the stolen magic it's clear something is going on."

"I'm more interested in the fraudulent spellbook," Benjy admitted. "We have more leads there."

"We're likely to hear more about it too," Hetty agreed. "If it's as bad as Evie says. Let's look into the spellbook, then. If I'm lucky I might even get to stab someone with a hairpin."

That simple plan fell apart even before they got a chance to lock up the house.

Coming up the street, somber as a slowly approaching storm, was Jay.

This was not a social visit.

The sadness in his eyes said it. As well as the regrets that weighed down his shoulders.

"What happened?" Hetty whispered, bracing herself for the worst.

"Something terrible." The pause Jay left after those words only increased Hetty's fears. "Valentine Duval died last night."

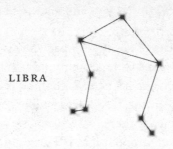

LIBRA

13

In the kitchen, Jay sat at their table, staring out the window. He might have been staring at the garden or the birds flitting around—either way, it was more to have something to look at than to give his full attention.

Hetty took a seat across from the pastor, but Benjy remained standing, his hands braced against the back of a nearby chair.

For all his talk about not holding grudges, Benjy appeared to be determined to cling to this one. Sparks from the clash of wills from the other night still stretched between him and Jay. But as much as Hetty loved and respected Jay, she would not let things simmer further. He had come here not as the surrogate father with some odd tidbit of news. He was here as a client, and he would not have shown up so quickly if Valentine Duval had simply died in a sudden accident.

Silence hung in the air a bit longer before Hetty cleared her throat and spoke. "You said Valentine Duval is dead. How did you find this out?"

This question was a bit bolder than what she usually asked people who came to them in this slightly shocked state. But this was Jay, who was accustomed to such questions, was accustomed to sometimes even asking them, so these blunt words stirred him to speak.

"I visited the house this morning. We were set to meet, to talk about old days and stories I had about Raimond and a few of my friends. The household was in a bit of uproar when I arrived. There is a cousin"—Jay frowned here—"who did something upsetting. Adelaide was yelling at him about it when I arrived. The maid went to see if Valentine was awake, to break things up, and she started screaming. We all went to see what happened, and there he was."

"In what room? What was the position of the body?" Benjy interrupted.

"His bedchamber. He was in bed, but slumped over to the side, one hand over his chest."

"A heart attack?" Hetty asked.

"It looked like it," Jay said.

"But you think it's murder." Like dropping a card in a game of noughts, Benjy placed these words down to see the reaction he would get.

Jay's eyes flashed with irritation. "I wouldn't have come here straightaway if I didn't think it was a possibility. They're going to attempt to work with Brown's, but if you take on funeral preparations . . ."

"We can see if there's a case," Hetty said, quickly catching on.

"How presumptuous of you." Benjy's hands tightened on the back of the chair. "All we have at the moment is your word. While I respect and trust it in all other matters, frankly, sir, this is not your area of expertise."

"Benjy," Hetty hissed.

Jay held up a hand. "No, he's got the right of it. This is not my area of expertise. It's yours." He pulled out a card with a sun and a crescent moon sketched on it. Jay waved it at them, his eyebrow cocked as if he knew they could hardly refuse him now. "The least you can do is look into it. Have Oliver examine the body for foul play, pace about the room, speak to the family, and prove it's more than what it seems."

"We'll look into it," Hetty assured the pastor, before Benjy could say a word more. "That's all we can promise at the moment."

Jay grunted and rose from the table. "I see. Tell me what you find, the moment you do."

With a nod to Hetty, Jay left, letting himself out.

The moment the door swung shut, Hetty pinned Benjy back with a glare. "There's no need to be rude!"

"Actually, there was." Benjy pointed to the closed door. "He didn't come here to tell us about a murder. He came here to tell about another murder within the same family. He hasn't been shy about wanting us to renew our previous investigation, and this is just an excuse."

"It might not be that," Hetty protested.

When Benjy scoffed, she stepped right in front of him, placed so that he had to physically move her if he wanted to pass. He didn't, and she stared up at him until the anger boiling in his eyes cooled. "Valentine is dead. At the very least we have a funeral to put together, which is more than we've had in some time. But if you don't want to be involved, I'll take this case on myself."

"Don't be ridiculous," Benjy said flatly, with none of the bite the words could have had.

"Then don't be so hard-headed! I know you don't want to look at the Duvals again, but you have to admit it is curious."

"And you see this as a chance to make amends with the pastor."

Hetty took his hands into hers and squeezed. "I don't like you fighting. If we look into Valentine Duval's death, maybe we'll settle the lingering questions about Raimond that Jay wants us to find out about. Once we do, he'll let things go."

"What if we find answers he likes even less?" Benjy countered. The bullish question had enough merit that Hetty couldn't brush him off.

"I don't think he's afraid of that. He doesn't want us to give up. He thinks we haven't tried hard enough. And I don't mind."

Benjy, who started to speak, suddenly shut his mouth, startled by this admission.

"You don't mind?" he repeated rather gently.

"How could I? We stopped looking because Beatty Hose was a dead end. But what if it's not?"

"And if it is, then we'd know for certain this time." Benjy ran his thumb along the back of Hetty's hand. Although he sighed, he didn't look as grim as before. "You're stubborn as the fixed stars, you know. But you're right. It wouldn't hurt to look into things. But if we're going to go, there's one place we need to go first."

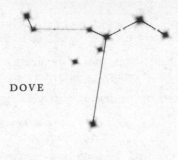

DOVE

14

WHEN OLIVER AND THOMAS moved into their new home, they only moved a few streets away, but at a distance far enough that when it rained Hetty was inclined to wait out the downpour. Although the pair had lived there for a very short time, they had settled in so quickly that it felt like they had always been there. The size probably helped. It was smaller than the house on Juniper Street, with fewer rooms. Only two bedrooms were on the second floor: their room and a guest room. The kitchen was a generous size, which was a good thing, because the rest of the house had been taken over by Thomas's fledgling mail-order business.

That morning Oliver sat on his front steps reading a newspaper with an unlit pipe clenched between his teeth. Next to him, in an old picnic basket and chewing on a wooden block, was Lorene.

The baby's eyes darted right to Hetty and Benjy, and she gurgled in delight, causing the block to fall into her lap.

"I wouldn't go inside if I were you," Oliver said as he turned a page. "There's a storm brewing."

"You mean he's hard at work?" Hetty asked. "That's not a bad thing."

"It is for me. We're supposed to be watching the baby together. I don't like doing it on my own."

"You're doing well," Benjy remarked.

Oliver snorted and continued his overblown grumbling. "I have plenty of practice looking after this little one. With George now working at Olmstead and Darlene at her fancy painting job, Lorene ends up here quite often."

"Why not with Darlene's mother?" Hetty asked.

"Not anymore." Oliver laughed. "Darlene's mother arranged for someone from an asylum to take a look at Lorene. It was quite shocking. I always knew Darlene's mother was a bit disappointed to learn that Lorene was Deaf, not that she would try to get rid of — Ah." Oliver lowered the newspaper, and looked at them with surprise. "You haven't heard about this?"

"No." Hetty got that word out as calmly as possible. How she managed, she hadn't a clue. "Nobody told me a thing."

Oliver shrugged. "Probably didn't want to worry about you."

"Did it happen back in May?" Hetty asked testily. "Lately I've been finding out all sorts of things happened that month that I wasn't aware of."

"A few weeks ago. Don't get mad at me—I'm not the one keeping secrets from you." He folded his newspaper. "You didn't come here to chat, did you? Did someone die last night?"

"Valentine Duval," Benjy said.

"Funeral or murder investigation?"

"We're not sure yet."

"And you need my help?"

"Your assistance would be greatly appreciated," Hetty said.

Oliver lifted his eyes to the sky. "I'm going to regret this, aren't I? But I have nothing to do other than play babysitter, so I might as well help you."

"You're right about that," Benjy said in a deceptively generous tone. "You'll be with us as my assistant."

"Your assistant!" Oliver cried.

"Having one more pair of eyes will be helpful, although we're hoping to have one less." Hetty pointed to the baby, who had been watching their conversation with rapt interest. "We can't bring her with us."

"Thomas will be happy to look after Lorene. If not, he'll have something to truly complain about."

Oliver picked up the picnic basket and opened the door.

Last month this room had been a sitting room, with slightly uncomfortable chairs and an unsteady table where they played cards. All traces of the room were gone, and in their place was the business that had engulfed Thomas's life. There were boxes everywhere, all ready to either be shipped, packed, or put aside.

"Careful," Thomas called as he guided another box across the room, Leo and Leo Minor shimmering in the air next to him. Hetty took a generous step out of the way as the boxes flew past.

"What's all this for? This can't be the things you're sending out," Benjy said.

"If only," Thomas replied quite cheerfully. "There was a fire in the building that prints the *Weekly Sentinel*."

"Never heard of it," Hetty said.

"And no one else will. They're ruined!"

"Don't sound so cheerful," Hetty remarked.

"Can't help it." The last of the crates moved onto the shelf. Thomas dropped his hands, his spellwork fading as he did. "What survived was given to me, so I have the opportunity to sell what I can. That was a stroke of luck."

"I've told more believable stories spun out of whimsy and whispers!"

"But haven't you always said, 'In every story is a bit of truth'?"

Oliver stuck out the basket for Thomas to hold. "Since you have all this to sort through, can you spare a moment to look after the baby while we go collect a dead body?"

"I can spare a bit more than that." Thomas took the basket automatically, and looked on in dismay at the baby sitting up in it. "Why did you put Lorene in my picnic basket!"

"It's the old one. I got you a new one."

Thomas clicked his tongue. "I like this one! I can get four sandwiches, a soup canteen, assorted side dishes, and a bottle of wine in it! And you stuck the baby in here!"

"If it can carry your precious soufflés in it," Oliver retorted, "why not something equally dear?"

"I don't see what's the problem," Hetty said. "The last time we watched Lorene we left her in one of the coffins."

Oliver and Thomas both stared at her.

"That's terrible," Oliver said. "Tell me you're joking."

"It was a new one, so it was just on display," Benjy added.

"At least it's cushioned," Thomas groused.

As Oliver turned to him, Benjy interjected, "Can we borrow the wagon from your neighbor? We'll need it."

Thomas nodded. "Go ahead. Just don't tell Joseph you're using it to carry a dead body."

"For some reason it bothers him," Oliver said. "People are so strange."

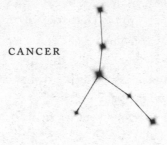

CANCER

15

THE DUVAL HOME WAS a squat house with the dignity of a matriarch who buried two husbands and nearly all her children yet still went on with life. This street was solidly middle class, and took pride in it, from the clean sidewalks to the shiny lampposts.

Black didn't drape the door, but mourners had already come to visit. As the wagon drew to a stop, the front door opened. A woman clung to a man's hand, her face buried in her handkerchief. But when she lowered it, her face was dry, and she sniffed as she adjusted her clothes. Both overlooked the three of them even as they walked past the wagon.

"Rude or suspicious?" Hetty asked Benjy.

"Rude," Benjy said as he got up from the driver's seat, looping the horses' reins together. "And looking for money they don't need."

"Dry eyes with hysterics." Hetty nodded. "Pure theater. Probably not the only one."

"I thought we are here about the body?" Oliver asked as he hopped off the wagon. He took care to brush invisible dust off his sleeve. "These people are hardly our concern."

"Wrong," Benjy said. "Everything in that house is worthy of our concern until we discover what we need to focus on."

Oliver sighed. "Why did I think coming here would be interesting?"

Despite his grumblings, Oliver followed after them, taking on the role of a humble assistant.

When Benjy knocked on the front door, an older woman peered out. Her neat appearance and dress had marked her as the cook, but she clearly didn't often greet guests. Her eyes swept over them with clear bafflement.

"Are you teachers at Mr. Valentine's school? Miss Adelaide wasn't expecting anyone from Olmstead until tomorrow."

"We're not teachers," Hetty said. "We're from the funeral home."

The woman nodded. "No one told me a thing, but then, I don't pay much attention other than what requests are for dinner. Come around to the back. I can't let you in through here; you don't want to talk to any of these people in here."

They walked around the house, entering through a small gate in the back. Once inside the yard, they passed a small kitchen garden ripe with summer vegetables and greens. It would have attracted a great deal of scrutiny from Penelope, because it was overgrown in a few places. A well was in the corner, and a path made of bricks weaved its way around, leading to the back door.

The cook from the front door stood there, looking at them with more scrutiny than she had previously. "You're not from Brown's, are you?" the cook asked.

"No," Hetty replied.

"Good. They were terrible with Mr. Raimond before. If you aren't from Brown's Funeral Parlor, who are you?"

"We're from the Rhodes Family Funeral Parlor, and here to take care of Valentine Duval. A friend of the family invited us."

"Which ones? It's a full house."

"Full house?" Hetty echoed.

Smugly, the cook pulled open the door. The sight nearly rocked

Hetty back on her heels. She had expected a handful of visitors, but this was much more than that. People were everywhere, and at first glance it was hard to say who were relatives, who were friends, and who were merely curious.

Then she saw someone who didn't neatly fit into any group: Eudora Mason, the medium from New Jersey.

Of the list of people Hetty expected to see, Eudora never crossed her mind. But it clearly was the medium. Her brightly colored shawl and turban stood out against the crowd of mourners, but her features were schooled into a suitably somber expression.

Standing next to her was Horace Duval. While he certainly belonged there, he looked upon the crowd with suppressed glee, rubbing his hands together in an eagerness most unbecoming. Although Hetty recognized him at once, he didn't seem to notice her at all. Which was fine by Hetty.

"All these people in this house," Oliver said. "Didn't he die last night? How can they all be here already?"

"Because they weren't here for Mr. Valentine," the cook said rather helpfully. "There was supposed to be a séance to speak with Mr. Raimond's ghost. Plans changed, of course. Not that I thought Miss Adelaide would let a séance occur in the first place. But the cousin pulled a sly one."

"Is that so," Benjy said. "Where is the deceased?"

"In the back room. Miss Adelaide said no one was to come in. Doesn't want anyone to see her brother like this. Can't blame her. Such a sad thing."

It was.

With no visible marks of injury, Valentine Duval looked like he was merely sleeping. Stretched out on the cot, years weighing heavily on now careworn features. A sight so different from their vibrant conversation. Jay had come to them clearly believing that Valentine was murdered, but this sight had Hetty hesitating. People did drop dead, after all, and it wasn't always foul play. Maybe Benjy was right about Jay's intentions and reasoning?

Benjy and Oliver went straight to the body, but Hetty's attention fixed on something else that nearly had her scrambling backwards out of the room.

"Benjy," she murmured, "there's a mirror in here."

"What mirror?" Benjy turned around, looking for it, only to stop when he found the small disk against the wall. His reflection looked back, rather bewildered. "Is a mirror important?"

"It should never be uncovered around a dead body or it'll collect the soul and hang on to it." Hetty picked up the mirror and turned it around. Uncertain if she needed to do more, she patted it uneasily. "Don't you remember Roger Cummings?"

Whatever protest might have been on her husband's lips died at the mention of the name.

Even Benjy, adamant as he was about ghosts not being real, could not deny that among the many things that had gone wrong during the Cummings funeral, some went beyond understanding. A casket had popped open. Voices drifted in the room. It went bitterly cold without a clear reason. And the only explanation for it was a mirror left naked and facing the body.

"Although it might not be entirely bad if his spirit got trapped in the mirror," Benjy said. "He could tell us who poisoned him."

"Poisoned?"

"Why do you have to spoil everything," Oliver growled. With a flick of Oliver's wrist, Duval's right hand lifted into the air. Oliver twisted his own hand and a sphere of light appeared in his palm. He passed it over the dead man's hand, revealing shiny patches of green.

"What poison is that?" Hetty asked.

"Jaley." Oliver grunted. "It's not a particularly dangerous one on its own—it's used to accentuate the potency of certain potions. But it is the easiest magical poison to get on short notice.

Without looking too closely, I'd say it's likely a larger dosage than usual did him in."

"He died last night." Hetty glanced around the room, neat and orderly to show to guests if they dared come in. "It could still be in the house. I wonder if I can find it."

"Wouldn't hurt to try," Benjy said. "Check for something he might have touched. Meanwhile, I'll talk to those gathered here. We need to eliminate suspects."

Hetty nodded. She brushed her fingers along her choker.

The Swan star sigil expanded around her, cloaking her from sight.

"After you," she said to Benjy.

Bemused, Benjy led the way out into the crowd. Striding forward, he walked right up to the nearest group of people. As he struck up conversation, Hetty drifted around the room, making her way to the door.

The spell may have hidden her from sight, but it didn't mean it was easy to move through the group, especially when people clustered in tight knots.

Hetty found herself wishing she'd suggested that Benjy clear the way for her, but in the end she decided that drifting like a ghost allowed her to pick up traces of interesting conversations. Like the one between Horace Duval and the medium.

"I'm sorry about my cousin," Horace said to Eudora Mason. "I thought she would be fine, given her frayed relationship with her brother. But I suppose a loss is a loss."

"I have faced my fair share of difficulties," Eudora assured him. "You can bring me to her later. In the meantime, tell me more about your other cousin. It'll help me contact him from the great beyond."

"And my uncle?"

"The recently dead is more receptive to the living. I know you cannot take me to his room, but perhaps a place where his spirit dwelled?"

"I think I might know such a spot," Horace said.

They moved away, and Hetty was glad for it.

The only thing she would learn from them was just how good a liar the medium was. Because while it wasn't obvious to Horace, Eudora Mason was clearly here to swindle him, and if he didn't realize that now, Hetty wasn't about to inform him otherwise.

Deciding that was enough gossip, Hetty worked her way around the room, heading for the doorway. It led into the hallway. A few folk lingered at the foot of the stairs. Careful to make as little noise as possible, Hetty squeezed her way through the gaps and headed upstairs. She wasn't afraid of being caught as much as she didn't want to attract attention.

No sounds reached her ears, and no voices, for that matter.

Just silence all around.

The second level had four bedrooms. The first had a suitcase open on a bed and men's clothing piled on a chair. The other room had a battered and worn trunk, closed but not securely. That room smelled of flowery perfume with a touch of musk. Was this Adelaide Duval's room? And did the other belong to her horrid cousin?

It seemed so.

The next door opened to a room shrouded in darkness. The curtains were tightly drawn, and old cigar smoke and aged whiskey clashed with a scent that reminded Hetty of the shaving cream Jay favored. Books crowded and overspilled from a nightstand by the bed, and a writing table was pushed in a far corner. But the thing that drew Hetty's attention the most was the striped dressing gown hanging from a wardrobe's door with slippers resting right below. It made an odd sight. One in which it seemed an invisible man stood, ready to ask why a stranger entered this room.

The more she looked around, the more it became clear. This room was Raimond Duval's.

Raimond Duval did not die in this room, but that didn't mean there wasn't information to be had.

Hetty stepped inside, feeling as if she were crossing hallowed ground in a sense, disturbing a place she should not be in.

However, this was not the first time she'd entered a space where it wasn't polite to be.

A poke inside the wardrobe showed Raimond had a simple and frugal taste, as the clothing there was sparse and was all geared to comfort. The table had a small lamp, and an inkwell with some pens nearby. An old copy of the *Eventide Observer* was on the table as well, folded over so the Miss Carole column could be seen. Hetty skimmed the words, and had only a vague memory of the letter in question. There were a few alchemistry books on his table, either for his classes or personal study. There were letters from old students, both in town and as far away as Toronto, plus an unfinished letter to Octavius Catto with advice for some matter that would never get resolved. And on the corner of the table was a scribbled note to Bernice about the ball.

After making sure everything was as she'd found it, Hetty left the room and went back into the hallway to check the last door.

This last room was the one Valentine stayed in.

It wasn't an idle guess.

Not only was the process of elimination in her favor, but the door was covered in wards. Showy wards, in her opinion, made with boldly drawn magic.

Ursa Major and Orion pulsed as she drew near, the combined spells forcing her back with a firm but gentle push.

But like any obvious star sigil, they were easy to dismantle.

Hetty drew out her first spells to pull the wards away from the door, allowing the spells to remain intact when she put them back when she left.

With the collection of spells hovering in the hallway, Hetty slipped inside the room.

A large bed took up a corner of the room, with pillows stacked to the side. There was a book on the table next to the bed, a slim volume of *The Wild Escapes of Peale Straits*, a book Hetty knew was also on their shelves at home.

A small chalkboard slate lay there on the table as well, nestled against a tin of chalk. All the pieces were broken little stubs. Numbers were written on the chalkboard, although it didn't appear to be an equation. They looked like they were written at random.

She ignored it at first, but her eyes kept returning to the chalk.

When Oliver had pointed out the poison, he'd lifted up Valentine's hand, splotched with revealing magic.

Could the chalk have traces of poison on it?

It was worth finding out.

The tin went into her pocket, but the chalkboard she left behind. She studied the numbers until she knew she could replicate them later.

She rifled through the drawers, but there was little left that was as interesting as what she'd already found.

Except the folded-up note on the table.

On it, Valentine had written a short list of tasks, with the following at the top:

Check and secure the well to make sure no one can come through.

LEO MINOR

16

Hᴇᴛᴛʏ ʜᴀᴅ ᴛᴏ ʀᴇᴀᴅ that note several times before she understood the full weight of the words.

To check and secure the well seemed sensible enough, but the last bit ... As far as Hetty knew, only water came out of wells. Anything else, such as a talking frog, was the stuff of stories.

Unless of course the well was not *just* a well.

In Cora and Jay's living room there was a very beautiful fireplace that was only there for show. Push back a brick in the right place and it swung open, revealing a tunnel that connected to a street a few blocks away.

Raimond Duval and his son had worked with the Vigilance Society, so there were plenty of reasons for them to have a tunnel near the house. Having it in the well made a great deal of sense, and less of a worry in one way. Intruders would have a much harder time climbing up a well.

But that didn't mean it wouldn't be easy to get in.

Hetty headed back downstairs and slipped through the kitchen. The cook, grumbling as she put together refreshments, didn't even so much as glance up, even when Hetty left through the back door.

The well was still in use. There was an upturned bucket hanging on the side, and the mechanism to draw it up still appeared well oiled.

There was also no magic.

Her touch didn't stir up any sigils, nor did the protections sewn into her clothing react in any way.

This was good, but also a bit sad. Magic faded for three reasons: interactions from other spells, the natural decay of time, or the death of the practitioner.

Hetty climbed up onto the well's rim. Once seated, she considered using the rope to help her descent. But then, just as quickly, she put the thought aside.

There was an easier way to get down the well.

Hetty dropped over the side, clinging to the edge. The moment she was inside, she let the concealment charm fade. She ran her finger along the stone in front of her, drawing the Capricorn star sigil. The lights from the lines and vertices pulsed for a moment before a gentle coil of air surrounded Hetty.

It encircled her protectively, one part shield and another a rustling wind tickling against her face.

Then she let go.

In the center of the well Hetty floated slowly down, the light of her magic illuminating the way. As her eyes adjusted to the dimness, she spotted evenly spaced handholds carved into the well across from her.

She followed those handholds down to a ledge big enough for a grown man to stand on. With a sweep of her hand, Hetty urged the wind to push her forward. She placed one foot on the ledge and then another before gripping the slimy wall. With care, she walked along the ledge, her footsteps becoming farther and farther apart until they became strides and she was no longer hugging a ledge but moving through a passageway.

With her magic turned into a light fluttering above her palm, Hetty walked on.

The passageway widened into a tunnel. As Hetty crept along it, she swept her light about for signs that people had been down here. But there was nothing. Not even a marker.

It was likely she was the first person down here in a very long time. This ruined her theory that a murderer might have come through, but a part of her was glad. This was the last place she wanted to run into trouble.

Why hadn't the Duvals closed it up? Especially with the entrance on their grounds. Was there no fear of further trouble, or did they expect wards to protect them?

The path widened to a fork. The left-hand path was the only way passable. The other path was a solid wall of packed rocks and dirt. Hoping an exit still remained at the end of the left-hand path, Hetty continued along it.

As she walked, she heard the rumbling of wagon wheels and streetcars on the streets above. There was also scuttling. Rats, by the sound of clicking toes. The sound of dripping water. But nothing that told her where she was or even where she was headed.

Which was a problem since the tunnel stopped at a dead end.

The buzzing of panic filled her ears, but Hetty pushed it firmly down. She could always walk back the way she came, or punch a hole above her. Idly she looked upward, and spotted a worn door handle dangling in arm's reach.

"Thank the stars," she muttered, and grabbed it. The first tug opened the door. Sunlight and debris rained on Hetty as she climbed out of the hole.

Catching sight of the grave markers around her and the building nearby, she knew where she was: behind Perdition Baptist. This put her around eight blocks away from the Duval home, although given how long she was walking, the tunnel wasn't in a straight line.

Not that it mattered.

Her greater concern was if someone came through.

The doorway in the grave marker was already closed. It was also for a person that never existed. The name etched into the stone was Eula Rivers, the code name used in Vigilance Society for various things of importance. Hetty pressed on the stone in an attempt to open a door, only to stop when she saw a crow land on top.

This was no ordinary crow. It was midnight blue and speckled with stars.

Slowly, Hetty turned around. Behind her, Benjy sat on the stone bench, reclined as if he had been sitting there for ages.

Smirking, her husband waved at her.

Words were lost to Hetty for several moments before she managed: "How are you here?"

"I knew about this grave marker being a tunnel entrance. It's the closest thing around here to the Duval home. I would have told you about it if I'd known you were going to jump down a well."

Hetty had the grace to be a little chagrined. "I forgot to tell you," she said. "I found a note in Valentine's room about the well and I was so curious about it that I rushed to investigate."

"I know."

"Wish you'd come with me?" Hetty plopped down on the bench next to him.

"Just a bit. The conversations I had with the relatives proved that most had no motive, no opportunity, or were simply at the house because Horace Duval had brought in a medium. The family's convinced he's after an inheritance, although opinion is mixed on whether or not there was really any money. But people were curious about what the medium would say."

"Lies, perhaps. She's the one I saw in New Jersey."

He blinked. "The same one?"

Hetty nodded.

"Well, isn't *that* curious," Benjy remarked. "Did you find the poison?"

"I can't say for sure. I did find some chalk." She patted her pocket. "We can test it later for traces. Valentine was writing something before he died. A bunch of numbers. Six, eight, nine, one, two, five . . ." Hetty repeated, only for Benjy to laugh and finish the sequence for her.

"That's the Clarke Cipher," he said before Hetty could ask, brimming with delight. "He must have been looking into it before he died."

"Don't get too excited. It just means someone knew him enough to know that this would be the best way to deliver the poison. Besides, I thought this wasn't a case." She eyed him closely. "I thought Jay just jumped to murder because he wanted us to look at Raimond's death again."

"Poison changes that," Benjy said. "And there are other factors at play."

"Like what? Valentine's cousin plotting for an inheritance that might not exist?"

"The timing," Benjy said softly. "Valentine just returned to the city. It was under ten days according to the cook. Plenty of time for a slow-acting poison."

Hetty scowled. "It's almost like the murderer realized the wrong Duval was dead and scrambled to correct the error."

"That is the most convoluted thing I have ever heard! The wrong Duval killed!" Benjy paused and repeated himself very slowly, as if taken by surprise. "The wrong Duval killed. What if the wrong Duval died first?"

It didn't seem like a question he meant for her to answer, but she did so anyway. Because while she hadn't been serious when she'd first said it, this reaction had her reconsidering her words and their implications. "It could mean that Raimond Duval wasn't killed by someone at Beatty Hose," Hetty said slowly. "And that the murderer might still be around."

"And killed Valentine—but why?"

"An old enemy?" Hetty suggested. "Someone Valentine clashed with in the past? There was a fire near his home, and it had so much magic in it."

"And a tunnel underneath," Benjy said absently. "It's too bad that the tunnel—"Mid-thought, he slammed a fist on the bench's armrest as he started to swear. "Tunnels!" he declared. "They're connected to places the Duvals were known to have been!"

Hetty stared at him blankly, lost at this abrupt leap. "What do you mean?"

"That's the pattern. You've found multiple tunnels this week, and the Duvals have a history with them! What if there were more? Is it really just chance that Wise Sammy was moving stolen magic under Valentine's house? Or that there was a fire on Stars Haven?"

"Or that Valentine made a note about closing up the well's tunnel? At this rate, we'll have to look at all the tunnels still open in the city just to make sure this is all related."

Benjy's enthusiasm dimmed quite a bit. "It'll take time to look through them—not to mention, we don't know their locations."

Hetty grinned. "But we do know someone who does!"

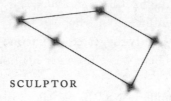

SCULPTOR

17

THERE ARE TWO STORIES Hetty told when people wondered how Darlene got the job as an artist's assistant. The first involved chasing after a jewel thief, a gust of wind that knocked everything into the street including Darlene's sketchbook, and Hetty jumping from a streetcar, tackling the would-be thief to the ground. The second involved Darlene sketching Hetty feeding birds on the banks of the Schuylkill, and Darlene's sketchbook falling into the hands of her future employer and mentor.

The first tale was the truth, but no one believed Hetty. Then again, few believed Darlene had gotten the job in the first place.

The Academy of Fine Arts was currently on Chestnut Street, but plans were in the works for it to move to a new location. Construction on the new building on Cherry Street was under way, and already parts of the school were closed off. All of which made it easy for Hetty and Benjy to slip in, attracting little notice.

Hetty had visited once before with Darlene, and it had been a hurried affair, with both of them uncertain of where exactly to go. Hetty was still uncertain even now, but with Benjy watching, she pretended she wasn't as she strode through. At the end of the hall, Hetty glanced between the door before her and the door on the far left before choosing the latter to knock on.

It opened at her touch, and she pushed further into the room. Everything was covered in fine white powder. And the places that weren't held chunks of white stone.

Most were just shapeless lumps of rock, but some looked as if they were part of something larger. Fingers? A face? A claw?

"Well, would you look at that," Benjy whistled. "It's *Winged Victory.*"

He could only mean the marble statue of a woman with out-stretched wings flowing from her back. It was breathtaking in both scale and detail, and the woman made of stone looked ready to launch herself into the air.

"That is lovely," Hetty said.

"But not Darlene's work," Benjy said, moving between the other statues that were arranged. Not all were completely done as the first, but she could see the statues emerging from the stone, even half finished as they were. "This artist has recently arrived to town." Benjy stopped in front of a deer emerging from a block of stone. "From Vienna, although a considerable time has been spent in Greece."

"You don't know which city," Hetty teased. "Why, dear husband, you're losing your touch!"

Hetty lost sight of Benjy as he disappeared behind a statue, but his voice still rang clear.

"There isn't much trace here. This is a person who spends all their time working. All I can tell are simple details. She's shorter than you, has a wealthy patron allowing her to live in style, lost her parents at a young age. Her mother was Chippewa, her father was born a slave, and she has few living relatives."

Hetty laughed, impressed despite herself. "Only that? I could have guessed all that myself!"

She expected to hear protests on this fact, but heard nothing.

Hetty walked around the statues and found Benjy in the very back of the room gazing up at a statue that made all the others look like a child had made them.

Unlike the rest of the stone around the room, this was black rather than white. It wasn't shiny like the pieces of jet Hetty had seen used in jewelry, but it still had a polished finish. The figure carved in stone was no Greek goddess. It was a mother gazing adoringly at the lump in her arms that was the size and shape of a young child. Every line and curve of the stone was so true to life that Hetty almost expected the stone woman to lift up her head and ask why she was being stared at.

"What stone is this?" Hetty whispered reverently.

"Basalt," Benjy supplied. "I cannot imagine all the logistics involved getting it here."

"It pays to have patrons who support my work," said a voice seething with acid.

Hetty swung around and came face-to-face with Adelaide Duval.

She was clearly the artist, dusted as she was in white powder from head to foot. She wore a thick leather apron with a few tools sticking out of the pockets over her dress, and a scarf protected her hair. She also pointed her chisel directly at Benjy.

While this was a rather interesting sight, it baffled Hetty to see Adelaide in the first place.

The woman's brother was dead. Jay had told them that Adelaide was there when Valentine was found. So what exactly was she doing here in this art studio instead of being back home mourning this great loss?

"What are you doing here?" Adelaide demanded. "Don't think I shall be fooled with your 'we're lost' gambit. I have seen too many cunning thieves who run off with my work."

Privately, Hetty found herself impressed that anyone could steal a statue.

Something of this must have shown in Hetty's face, for Adelaide wagged the chisel with the promise of violence.

"Miss Duval, we met the other day at—"

"I know who you are," Adelaide interrupted. "It doesn't change my question. Why are you here? There's no fire for you busybodies to poke your noses in or anyone to make excuses for you."

The chisel had lowered, but the older woman's voice shook with suppressed emotion.

"I'm sorry," Hetty said, the picture of contriteness. "We opened the wrong door. We're looking for Darlene Needham."

"And did not expect to see me," Adelaide remarked.

"I did not know you are an artist," Hetty said quite honestly.

"You are quite talented," Benjy added.

Adelaide's twisted scowl untangled itself into a smug smile. "I am an artist of many talents. These days I sculpt mostly. But my paintings grace the halls of kings, dukes, and an exiled queen. Would still do so if claims of forgery did not follow at my heels at every step."

"But sculptures can be forged as well," Benjy said, studying the nearest statue.

With a growl, Adelaide flicked her fingers to draw Ursa Minor into the air. The star sigil flashed and a sheet threw itself over the statue. "Go. I will throw you out!"

"Miss Duval," Benjy interjected. "We've heard about your brother."

Adelaide did not react at these words. "What have you heard?"

"Only that he unexpectedly passed last night," Hetty said. "Pastor Evans told us what happened. Because he knew your father and your brother quite well, he hoped that we could do Valentine's funeral, if that suits you."

"That's right, you own a funeral home." Adelaide squinted. "Bernice Tanner says you're still figuring out how to run the place. She said that's why she went with Brown's for my father's funeral. I didn't get here in time for it. But it was all done in a way I knew he would not have wanted. Will you be better?"

"We aim to be."

"Good." Adelaide grunted. "You have my permission to do what you wish with my brother. Your usual work—no, the best work you have. The funeral will be Monday. That's all I can decide right now. We can talk later."

"Here?"

"No, at my father's grave, over in Elmhurst. I'll be in better sorts to talk then, and I'd rather speak of the dead around the dead."

There was clear dismissal there, and one that Hetty was inclined to take. They'd gotten their funeral, and confirmed they would have the body as long as they needed. After setting a time to meet in the morning, they went to finally seek out Darlene.

In contrast to the studio next door, this room was rather bare. There were sketches pinned to the wall—of coastlines, and ancient buildings, old towns with rustic charms, and interesting animals that Hetty had never seen before. At first glance Hetty knew this was not Darlene's work. The sketches didn't have Darlene's keen attention to detail in them. But the pages drying on a nearby table held the vibrant colorings Darlene was known for.

With her back facing the door, Darlene worked in the middle of the room. Light from the wide windows streamed around her, leaving little shadow to interfere with her work.

Perched on a stool in front of her easel, Darlene hummed to herself. A few sketches bobbing around her head, jockeying into view with the slightest twitch of her finger. She dabbed paint to the foliage around a crumbling European castle.

So intent was she in her work, Benjy managed to get right be-hind Darlene without being noticed. "Now, this is quite lovely."

The papers fell to the floor as Darlene let out a small squeak. She nearly fell off the stool, but Benjy put out a steadying hand to keep her from toppling over.

Darlene looked up at him, then across the room at Hetty.

"You both are here. I feel as if I should be worried." Darlene flicked her fingers and a small star sigil flashed in the air. The sketches lifted from the floor and settled on the nearby table. Darlene picked up her paintbrush again, but instead of turning back to the canvas, she twirled it over and over in her hand as she watched them very closely. "Nothing's happened? At least noth-ing that directly concerns me, right?"

"You needn't worry. We came about the map," Hetty said. "I know you said you were going to draw one, but could you get us a list of names—"

A withering glare cut off her words. "Who do you take me for?" Darlene asked. "I said I was going to draw a map, and draw it I did."

"Good. We came here because we found another tunnel," Hetty said.

"*Another* tunnel?" Darlene asked.

"Yes," Hetty said. "And we have a new case. Valentine Duval died last night. Oliver thinks Valentine was poisoned, and we're trying to piece together what else might be going on."

Darlene's gaze darted to the next room. "Does she know?"

"We spoke to her," Hetty said. "If she says anything interest-ing . . . or incriminating, do let me know."

"Of course." Darlene nodded.

"What an interesting thing to say," Benjy remarked. "You should be insulted that we consider your employer a suspect."

"Why? You consider everyone a suspect." Darlene stuck her paintbrush in the jar of water next to her and jumped off the stool. From the nearby table she went to her satchel and pulled out a long tube. She popped it open and a tightly rolled piece of parchment fell into her hand.

Darlene drew the Libra star sigil. The constellation flashed for a moment in the air before washing over the table. The items there arranged themselves on the side, leaving enough space for her to spread out the map.

Darlene had actually drawn out a full map, though it wasn't highly detailed. She had drawn the key landmarks of the city, but marked only the major streets' names. There was more detail on the southern and eastern parts of the city compared to the rest. But that was more than fine considering the most important bits were the trails of bright paint that showed the locations of the different tunnels.

"Blue is for tunnels used by the Vigilance Society," Darlene said as she pointed to each line. "Yellow for shops, gray for tunnels known to be used by various gangs in the area. Red for places that are no longer in friendly territory. Slashes mark places that I know to be closed."

Hetty traced the lines with the tip of her finger. She had hoped to find some answers, but what she found were not the ones she needed. "So many of these tunnels are localized. I was hoping for more connections."

"It's all about getting in and out of certain places without being seen." Darlene nudged up her glasses. "I hope this isn't an excuse to go exploring. Some of the tunnels are sure to be falling to ruin. You don't know what lies in wait."

"Traps wouldn't be surprising," Benjy murmured. "Even after all these years."

"I'm more interested in where they go," Hetty said. Her eyes went to Barclay Street. There was no line for a tunnel there, although she'd expected that.

"If you do go into the tunnels, be wary of those marked with an anchor," Darlene said.

"Aren't those just shipping routes to the river?" Hetty asked.

Darlene shook her head, and while her expression remained pleasant, worry shot through her eyes. "Those are marked territory. There is no magic in the marks, but it's a warning."

"I'll be careful."

Benjy cleared his throat, and Hetty smiled.

"*We* will be careful," she corrected. She gave the map another look and frowned, as she glanced at the lines. "So where do we begin?"

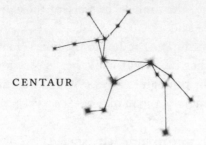

CENTAUR

18

Despite their great hopes, their search turned up very little. The tunnels that Darlene had marked were there — it's just that they weren't useful. Two were collapsed and closed off. One was around a very busy corner. And the last one they tried presented a number of issues that neither felt like dealing with.

"I feared this might happen," Benjy said as they turned away from the Italian bakery, where the baker glared at them as she put out the day-old bread for sale. The map marked the tunnel as being inside the building, and it was clear they weren't going to get inside. "It's been several years. It's no wonder a few things are wrong."

"Are you saying Darlene's memory is bad?" Hetty asked.

Benjy sighed. "This is the problem with biases. It makes you overlook more important factors."

"Such as?"

"I mean," Benjy said, backing away as if he realized the carelessness of his words, "that the Vigilance Society worked like a puzzle. What we knew, what Darlene knew, and even what Thomas knew at times were all different, but when we came together we got the full picture. The tunnels are no different."

"So we are no better than where we started?" Hetty asked.

"No, we're better. We have a list now to check odd things against."

"I suppose that is a relief."

"Shall we try for one tunnel while we're in this part of town?"

Hetty studied the map, but instead of a tunnel she noticed something else they were close to.

"What do you think of heading over to Race Street instead?"

Though it was only a few blocks away, the moment they crossed over to Race Street, it was like arriving in a different city entirely. The street brimmed with an energy that was missing in the nearby neighborhoods: warm conversation drifting from buildings, laughter at street corners from people leaving work, and wafting spices that spoke of the world beyond Philadelphia. Yet there were many familiar sights. People haggled with shopkeepers as they made their purchases for dinner. Children ran around in the midst of some game. Abandoned newspapers in a variety of languages were posted on a wall for all to read. And on the fringes an unscrupulous vendor hawked wares of dubious quality.

This vendor in question was a German man who stacked on his cart a vast array of items, although if they were magical Hetty and Benjy weren't about to find out.

"He looks ready to spit on us," Hetty said to Benjy as they walked right past the vendor.

"Spit out a hex, you mean," Benjy said. He grinned right at the man.

The vendor sneered and jerked his cart in the opposite direction.

"I don't think that's the person Miss Wong mentioned. The man had illegal goods, but nothing of particular magical quality."

"Or nothing he would sell to us."

"Don't be so sure. Green is one color no one has trouble with."

The restaurant that Evie's brother owned was mostly empty at this hour. There were a few diners, quietly eating at their tables, and in a corner was a trio of men arguing over cards. The same three men were always there whenever Hetty and Benjy visited. As usual, the trio didn't notice them, as they were too busy insulting each other in Cantonese.

Evie, sitting in a corner doodling on a napkin, noticed them right away, and rose to greet them.

"I was just thinking I should call on you again," Evie said. "I couldn't get copies of the spellbook, but there is something else I wanted to talk about."

"Then we shall talk," Hetty said.

Evie led them to a table tucked into the back corner. With a flick of her hand, she lit the candle in the center. "The usual? Or today's special?"

Hetty glanced at Benjy. He shrugged.

"You choose," Hetty said. "But make sure it's enough for three."

Evie disappeared into the kitchen, and in no time at all returned with a teapot and a collection of steaming baskets stuffed with an assortment of dumplings and steamed buns.

Benjy asked for the proper names of everything, and Evie repeated them in Cantonese as she pointed out each one, describing the either sweet or savory flavors tucked inside. Some were things Hetty had had on previous visits, but the dim sum, as Evie called it, contained many things Hetty had never tasted before.

As they ate, Evie mentioned a few more tidbits of news she thought worthy of their attention. "There's been a number of thefts going around," she said. "Uncle Bobby's apartment was the last. Nearly every magical item he owned, except his pendulum and bells, was stolen. After what happened to his shop in Sacramento, any theft has him spooked. The old store had seen many smaller break-ins before it was utterly destroyed. He's convinced history will repeat itself."

"I don't think this is the case." Using her chopsticks, Hetty pulled the basket with the last sweet bun toward her before Benjy could grab it. "If a thief took only the magical items and nothing else, that's all they were looking for."

Hetty waved the bun at Benjy before popping it into her mouth. Benjy made a face and turned to one of the side dishes.

"Is your uncle the only person dabbling with Sorcery around here?" Benjy asked.

"That I know of," Evie said. "But if they were after magic, why not take his pendulum?" As she spoke, Evie pulled out her own. An antique silver chain, it was weighed down by a sapphire the size of an acorn cut specifically to amplify and focus her magic. There were symbols engraved on the band holding the gemstone. Used for what Evie called the Five Pathways, this brand of magic manipulated the elements of the world. A novice could light candles and make windows rattle. But an expert could blend the elements together to craft illusions of both sight and sound. This magic had been a great help during the laundry case, but despite Hetty's curiosity, Evie had carefully avoided explaining exactly how it worked.

"The thief clearly doesn't care about your magical traditions," Benjy said.

"Or," Hetty pointed out, "whatever your uncle had, he wasn't supposed to have it in the first place."

"The spellbook!" Evie cried.

Hetty nodded. "That would be my guess."

Benjy placed his chopsticks down next to his empty bowl. "Which magical items were taken?"

Evie listed a few magical herbs, but most of what she mentioned were tools—candles, flasks, even a small hand mirror.

"That wasn't even enchanted. But these thefts are pushing my brother to return to Guangdong, despite protests from me and my sister." She looked down at her teacup, her fingers tapping along the delicate porcelain. "It's mostly why I'm telling you about this. I'm just getting to like Philadelphia. I don't want to move again."

"When we find the root of the thefts, that'll put the end to that worry. Have thefts only been here?" Hetty asked.

The younger woman shook her head. "A Greek bakery. A stationery shop. A tavern on the docks. A glassmaker's shop."

"Where exactly?" Benjy pressed.

Evie named streets and locations that all fell along places with notable immigrant populations: Greeks, Germans, Italians, Russians, and even the Irish.

"These are all places where a report of theft will pass unnoticed," Hetty said. "What's the latest one you heard about?"

"A wand shop," Evie supplied. "The owner is Jewish. He comes here regularly with his son. I heard them talking about the theft, and concerns about telling the police. Apparently there are fines when wands go missing."

Despite her distaste for Sorcery, Hetty found her interest piqued at hearing about stolen wands. If there was a premium magical item to be sold in the back alleys it would be wands. For the skill in making them, as well as the law forbidding someone like her from buying them in a proper shop, made wands a desirable good.

"Which shop?"

"I'll give you the address."

The wand shop was on Washington Avenue, which wasn't far. But from the clipped words Benjy gave as they said goodbye to Evie, she knew he wasn't keen on going.

"I don't plan to go in," Hetty said as they headed south. "I just want to pass by."

"It's enough to know about the thefts. There are other places we should look at."

Hetty paused, recognizing that he was trying to sway her mind, and trying very hard at that.

"What sort of place?" Hetty asked.

"Still-Bowers."

The Still-Bowers Library Company was one of the many places Benjy frequently sniffed around for books. Founded way back in 1833, it started as a private collection with a membership fee required for access. A fee that was well worth it, since the collection housed the few rare magical artifacts in the city, a rather robust seed library of magical herbs, and oral histories from Lenape elders who wanted to preserve their tribe's history of magical practices.

"I wanted to check if they knew anything about the false spellbook," Benjy continued.

"You just want to go to the library," Hetty accused. But she couldn't blame him. This thing with the spellbook was becoming more and more interesting as new information arose. And more pressing, too. While Valentine's death was sudden and alarming, it didn't have the sweeping reach this spellbook might.

"The librarian there might know enough to help us, and we can lay one question to bed while we focus on the Duval case," Benjy said, with enough confidence that Hetty decided this slight detour wouldn't be so terrible.

Housed in a building in great need of repair, Still-Bowers didn't look remarkable. Once the home of a generous donor and patron, after her passing the library's collections moved here from its original quarters. It still felt too small to Hetty as she followed her husband. Chairs and tables were squashed together in the main room, shoved between heavy bookcases.

A handful of people were settled in plush armchairs or seated at a table. Nearly all looked in Hetty and Benjy's direction, as if they were a curiosity of sorts. But the onlookers turned back to a person who was leading a discussion on something to do with gemstones.

Benjy of course didn't notice. Drawn as he always was by the siren call of new books, Benjy left Hetty on her lonesome to scour a shelf under the hand-painted sign labeling new acquisitions.

Not wanting to wait, Hetty wandered through the nearest shelf, idly letting her eyes slide along the dusty books in front of her. She never had much luck with books, but maybe there was something here that could be useful.

"Can I help you?"

The whisper near Hetty's ear was like a shout in the quiet room. It took an effort not to jump, and an even greater one to not whirl around at the speaker. Hetty managed a slow turn in the end and came face-to-face with a dainty woman with gray-streaked hair and brown skin the color of parchment.

"I'm here with my husband." Hetty looked around for Benjy, who of course was out of sight. "He's looking for a book."

The librarian peered at Hetty over her small wire-framed glasses, sternly frowning. "I'm not asking about him. I'm curious about you. What interests you?"

Taken aback at the expectantly polite words, Hetty blurted out: "Astronomy."

The librarian nodded. "We have quite a good assortment of titles on that subject. Are you more interested in star charts or the journals of astronomers?"

Before she knew it, Hetty was steered up a short set of stairs that led into a room that, while still quiet, did not seem to begrudge a small amount of noise.

"There are a few writings from travelers. Some very old and out of date. Our collection is mostly donations, but generous patrons provided funding so we can make our own purchases. I'll need to check the records. We limit the number of books households can have out on loan." She looked on expectantly at Hetty.

"Rhodes," Hetty said. "I'm—"

"Henrietta." A true smile filled the librarian's face. "I should have known the moment you mentioned astronomy! Benjamin always makes an excuse to talk about his wife and her interest with the mysteries of the stars. And quite a few other stories, too. I've been wanting to meet you for a long while. How do you like the telescope? He found it in the archives and kept complaining about it collecting dust when it could be put to better use, until I gave it to him to shut him up."

The telescope currently perched on their rooftop had been a gift. It appeared with little fanfare last month, hidden in her wardrobe with a bow tied around it. Hetty could tell it was old, with owls and the phases of the moon engraved along the gold tube. Although it looked very expensive, Hetty had been too de-lighted to ask for any more details. To hear the full story now only increased her fondness for the thoughtful gift.

"I like it very much," Hetty said. "It came from this library?"

"From the donations we got a long time ago." The librarian went to a shelf and started to pull out a series of books. "You should find these interesting."

"These are very nice," Hetty said, glancing at the covers. "But there is one thing I'm particularly interested in: magic. I wasn't sure if you had anything related, Celestial or otherwise."

For a moment Hetty thought she'd miscalculated. Silence stretched for several long moments without seeming to come near an end.

But then the librarian reached into her pocket and drew out a small brass key.

"I think you'll be interested in this particular collection."

The key unlocked a small circular room. Bookshelves lined ev-ery wall, even the one with the door—a shorter shelf just started above the door frame. A ladder was hooked onto the bookshelves with wheels to allow it to move as needed. A thick rug covered the entire floor, and there was a small round table in the center surrounded by a few comfortable armchairs. The only flaw Hetty could see in the room was that there were no windows—the only light source came from a large glass orb flickering with magic overhead.

"We are the only Negro library on the East Coast with books about magic. And the rarest of materials are contained here," the librarian declared happily.

"Even spellbooks about Sorcery?"

The librarian pointed to a shelf at eye level. "Are you looking for the origins with the Greeks, what came out of the Crusades, or how Darwin's theories about the human capacity for magic made a lot of white folk angry? There are of course some spellbooks," she continued, "mostly school primers and elementary lessons. Though there are some battered copies that were liberated when freedom came. People train from them, but they're hardly successful."

"They tell you that?"

"I watch them. The spellbooks can't leave the grounds — there is a stamp on the inside of the cover to ensure that. There's a room on this floor where we allow the interested to practice. If they are going to learn, it needs to be in a safe and controlled environment."

"Why would anyone want to learn Sorcery?"

"I don't ask," the librarian said. "I'm here to provide knowledge and answer questions best I can."

"Do you also acquire the books?"

"Not by myself." The librarian's open curiosity seemed to intensify as she studied Hetty. "What book are you really looking for?"

"A spellbook about Celestial magic."

Whatever the librarian had been expecting, it was not that. "Where would you have heard of such a thing?"

Hetty let her fingers trail along a bookshelf. "A friend who I trust has seen it. It's fake, and it's meant to be propaganda. The spells inside show Celestial magic in the worst light."

"Why do you think we would have such a copy here?"

"Because you know where all the books are, Mrs. Saunders." Benjy stepped into the room. Surprisingly, he did not carry any books with him, although his eyes did wander to the shelves behind Hetty.

"You are attempting to flatter me," the librarian protested, but didn't hide her smile. "I might not know where that book is, but I have an idea of who might. I know someone else who has a collection to rival this." She waved a hand at the shelves behind them. "But it's in an odd sort of place."

"We've been to a great many odd places," Hetty assured her. "This will not be a problem."

"Then you will be fine going to Fool's Moon?" the librarian asked.

Recognizing that name, Hetty could only stare at the librarian, unable to imagine the prim old woman seated at a table in the smoky and magic-filled saloon below Eighth Street.

"We'll be more than fine," Benjy said. "Who do we talk to there?"

"I only have the name, Lou Notts. The leader of the Magnolia Muses."

"That name is plenty," Benjy said, far too enthusiastically. Enough that Hetty was left pondering if she should have recognized the name as well. "Thank you, we'll be heading out."

"No books today?" the librarian teased.

"Not today. I was looking for books on ciphers, but they all have been lent out."

"Of course they have!" the librarian said gleefully. "Out for weeks! That little pamphlet about the Clarke Cipher has been quite good for us here! Although, there are a few books that should have been returned by now. I'm going to have to place another one of my stamps in them. I've tried reaching out to the person who has them. But maybe you'll have better luck. Let me get you their address, and the next three books you borrow, I won't ask for their speedy return."

She bustled out of the room before Benjy could even agree. But she probably didn't need to wait for that. The smile on Benjy's face was all the answer required.

"You've helped her before?" Hetty asked, unsurprised that Benjy would make himself quite useful to any place with books around.

"Knocked on a few doors, threatened a few people," he admitted. "It's becoming less often since the people are better at returning books."

Instead of waiting for the librarian to return, they went back downstairs to a large desk on the main floor. With great relish, the librarian handed Benjy a card.

"You don't have to take care of it right away, but any help you can provide will be appreciated."

Benjy tucked the card away, and he and Hetty departed, leaving behind the library and all the secrets yet to be found.

"Shall we go to this saloon?" Hetty asked.

"It's not open at this hour."

"When has that stopped us before? Unless you'd rather go shake down a poor man for books."

"He lives a fair distance away. But it's not urgent. The books are just on linguistics."

"You should go take care of it. I think the tip we got about the spellbook is the best we've had so far. Which is impressive, given the hundred tiny things we've been focused on."

"It likely has nothing to do with either Duval."

"Doesn't matter," Hetty said. "This spellbook is trouble."

"Which makes me wonder what sort of people might have the book."

"Doesn't matter." Hetty shrugged. "As long as we get our hands on it, we can figure out where it came from."

"We already know where. It fits a pattern of previous behavior." He stopped. "Beatty Hose."

"You think they're behind it?" Hetty asked. "I know they've done nasty things, but making a false spellbook is a bit—"

Benjy shushed her.

At the far end of the street was a white man wearing a bowler hat. His beard was neatly trimmed and his nose was squashed as if an elbow had rammed into it in the past. Although dressed shabbily, he wore his clothes rather proudly, and people moved away as he walked, as if he were visiting royalty.

"That's the alderman. Ed Anderson," Benjy whispered. "The man who tried to kick me out of line in last year's election."

Tried was scarcely an apt word.

Anderson's attempt ended with him lying on the ground with a bruise starting to blossom on his face. With a small riot going in the Fourth Ward around that time, the police weren't on hand to do much of anything. But Anderson had laughed it off, even offering to shake Benjy's hand, saying it was an honor to meet the "bravest Negro in the city." The words were outwardly polite, but that man's eyes had held a chill in them that promised nothing but future trouble. Which was especially true, since the alderman practically ran Beatty Hose, and when he wasn't messing about with fires, he was doing his part in suppressing the vote.

"What's he doing here?" Hetty said.

"Wrong question," Benjy replied softly.

Hetty didn't even have a chance to ask a better one, because stepping into view at that very moment was Nathan Payne.

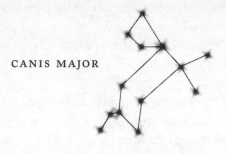

CANIS MAJOR

19

THAT PAIR IS CLEARLY up to trouble," Benjy grumbled as they watched Nathan Payne and the alderman head down an alley.

"Which means we have to follow them," Hetty said.

Benjy was clearly troubled by this odd pairing, because instead of dissuading her, he held out his arm for Hetty to take.

With her arm hooked into Benjy's, Hetty set a spell similar to what she had done at the Duval home earlier, but this time to cover him as well. As they walked, Hetty kept her spells going with ease. This was mostly because Payne and Anderson were in no great hurry, and soon enough they all arrived at an old ware-house. With the boarded-up windows and fading paint, it had the look of being abandoned, but this was obviously a façade.

Anderson and Payne went right to it and stepped inside.

Hetty and Benjy stayed outside, going around the perimeter until they spotted an open window. They crouched by it to eaves-drop on the conversation inside.

"Where is it?" Anderson was saying. "You were supposed to have it."

Payne smirked and walked around the room, moving out of frame for a moment before stepping back in. "I got the goods.

The potions you wanted, plus that little spellbook of yours. I got them set aside some ways back, if you want a look."

"Then show us." Anderson whistled. A few burly white men came around the corner, all falling in line behind Anderson.

Payne's composure slipped for a moment, but he quickly flashed a smug smile.

"Follow me, gentlemen."

The group left the building and headed down the street.

The moment they were out of sight, Benjy let go of Hetty's hand.

"Keep watch." He pulled the window open wider and climbed inside. "I'll be right back."

Hetty didn't waste her breath trying to stop him. Instead, she caught the bottom of the window before he shut it. She met and held Benjy's gaze until he lifted the window back up and helped her climb through.

They found themselves in a corner that was the sort of space where things just ended up instead of being purposely placed. A few broken chairs, a long table covered with empty bottles and a few cups. The air was heavy from the summer heat, unbearably sticky and reeking of sweat. All things that made it the perfect place to hide things that shouldn't be there and do things no one should do.

Stairs looked to lead to a loft. Benjy climbed up, leaving Hetty to check the crates in the corners. The first boxes held ordinary goods—kettles, silverware, and the like. Nothing that looked like it was made of magic. But Benjy had crafted and mended magical objects before, so there was still a possibility. She let her spells slide around the room, trying to stir up something with her spell. Nothing happened, though, and she wasn't sure if she was disappointed or not.

Hetty shut the lid and moved on to the next box.

Inside was nearly every item that Evie had told them about, plus a few things that weren't mentioned at all. And in a long narrow box inside, she found a cache of finely crafted wands.

Never had Hetty seen so many wands in one place. Carved from a variety of woods, they ranged in colors from a pale brown to so light it was almost white, to a deep, dark brown of teak and mahogany. She didn't recognize the types of all the woods used. She suspected they had to be from local trees in the area, though she couldn't know for sure. The lore of wand-making was a shut door to her, and one she'd never had any desire to unlock. She was able to tell, however, that they were all made by the same person. On the end of each handle was the same insignia.

A familiar low whistle came from up in the loft.

After shutting the box, Hetty joined Benjy upstairs. She found him leaning over a table, flipping through a set of papers. There were more scattered papers on the table, and Benjy turned to those as he absently handed Hetty a page.

"This is just a set of numbers," Hetty said.

"It's a list to go along with this."

He handed her another page. It was a listing of all the neighborhoods in Philadelphia, plus a few outlying places. Each one had a number that corresponded with the first list. But there was another column on the far right on the same page that immediately caught her interest. "Are these dates?"

Benjy ran a finger along the list. "They're keeping track of the places they're doing things. Could be fire, could be planting magic, could be other trouble."

"Why write it all down?"

"Why *not* write it all down? It makes sure everything is going where it needs to go."

Hetty grunted. "Is there a list of devious plans here too? That would be more helpful."

"This isn't a headquarters, but it is an important spot." He pointed to the far wall. On it, painted in white, was an anchor.

Beware of the anchor, Darlene had said.

Hetty had thought it a mere warning at the time, but she should have known. Her friend was clever enough to warn about Beatty Hose but to do it in a way so as not to draw attention. She knew exactly what Hetty would do with such information.

A star-speckled crow landed on the table in front of them. It hopped around in a circle before disappearing in a soft pop of light. "Time to go, they're coming back," Benjy whispered.

Hastily they replaced all the papers they had picked up. Hetty started for the stairs, but it was too late.

The door had opened. Men filed inside, and in front was Nathan Payne. He rubbed his arm, his nose twitching as if he could smell magic in the air. He stopped and peered up into the loft.

His jaw visibly slacked when his eyes found them—but only for a moment. With a growl, he flicked his fingers and sent a blast of magic up into the loft. "Get your men to go around," Payne called to Anderson. "You got some vermin poking about!"

More magic flew in their direction, preceded by muttered incantations. This time the magic was strong enough to take out a chunk of wood. But that was typical of Sorcery. It was stronger in raw power but weaker in range.

Up close, though, it would cause trouble.

Hetty wasn't about to confirm this if she didn't have to. Just as she prepared to run to the nearest window, Benjy strode forward and sent Taurus charging down into the group below.

Not to counteract any magic headed their way. No, he was foolishly attacking Payne, Anderson, and whoever else was down there.

Hetty watched in horror. This is how people got trapped!

She drew the Phoenix star sigil in the air. The mythical being made of stars and flames shimmered before her, filling with the potential of her magic. Clapping her hands, she sent it diving into the table. The spell ignited the list these terrible men had created to destroy her city, and ate away at everything else. The spark of flame quickly spread, filling the room with fire.

One look at the flames had Benjy running back toward her and the only exit available to them.

A burst of her magic shattered the glass of a window. She jumped out, twisting her spells to slow her landing.

Benjy landed harder on the ground next to her, but was already on his feet and running down the alley, leading the way out. Hetty ran after him, her boots pounding on the ground, the map Darlene made of the tunnels rustling in her pocket.

Alarm clamored in the air, as voices cried out for firemen.

Hetty wasn't familiar with these streets in the daylight. At night, there were more places to hide and deeper shadows to give a person sanctuary.

Daylight was a different matter. In daylight, eyes turned to the street. Windows opened and people peered out, watching the ruckus as it unfolded.

And the faces that looked out were not friendly. There wasn't any safe place in sight, not for a comfortable distance. Soon they would have to choose between fighting and attempting to escape.

But then a third choice descended upon them.

They had just turned a corner when the ground underneath them started shuddering.

Earthquake! Hetty thought, and grabbed for Benjy just as he grabbed for her. In the fleeting moments Hetty saw the wide-eyed surprise in his face. She was surprised too—Philadelphia was not known for earthquakes.

But this was no earthquake. The very ground they stood upon moved upward as if they were in a well, being drawn up in a bucket. Except instead of a slow and steady rise, they ascended rapidly until they were level with a roof.

"In here!" called a heavily accented voice. "This way!"

Hetty found she couldn't move, couldn't make the leap from the earth platform to the roof.

"Quickly!" the voice said.

Benjy swung her into his arms and carried her onto the roof and through a small door. The door shut behind them, muffling the yells from below on the street, some strangled swears, and the angry footsteps of people keen on finding their prey.

Benjy set Hetty back down on her feet, and they braced themselves for anything that might break through the closed door.

But then the voices retreated, the sound faded away, and the only magic around Hetty was her own.

"You are glowing," said the white man who stood by the door they had come through. "How marvelous!"

There was such delight at seeing Hetty's magic, her worries eased quite a bit.

The man's hair and beard were two fluffy clouds of white, although his other features did not seem so old. His eyes were merry behind a small pair of spectacles perched on his nose, and as he spoke there was an uneven rhythm to his words, of an accent that was unfamiliar to Hetty's ears.

"Who are you?" Benjy demanded.

"Someone who doesn't like the fuss people make," the man said. "Grigory Feinberg is my name." He might have said more, but a trapdoor in the floor opened up, sending up more light and the sound of a young man's voice.

"Father, those men are gone!"

"In that case, I will come downstairs with our guests." He looked over at Hetty and Benjy. "You'll be comfortable in the shop. Don't say that you will hide up here. It is nonsense. The air is too heavy this time of year."

Having little choice, they followed the man down into the shop, where Grigory's son hastily closed the curtains.

Names were exchanged, but the son grunted and did not offer his hand to shake.

Turning back to Grigory, Benjy said politely, "We thank you for your help, but I wonder—"

"Why help?" Grigory asked. "I heard the noise and knew I should."

"Maybe we should have ignored it," his son spat, glaring at Benjy. "This will bring those men to our door next."

"You said nothing when I told you to help them," Grigory replied as he sat on a bench.

"I cared only about fooling our heartless neighbors. I did not notice they were—"

"Enough!" Grigory slapped the wall, rattling the toys resting on a nearby shelf. He said more, a stream of words in another language that turned the anger in his son's face to shame. The young man muttered an apology to Hetty and Benjy before he stomped out of the room and back to the apartment above the shop.

The old man leaned back, pressing his fingers against his nose.

"Do not mind him," Grigory said finally. "He thinks the Americans will like him if he does as they do. Bad thoughts and all. He will not bother us. Any trouble he brings to you will come to him too. Stay." He gestured for them to take a seat. "Please. Those people will be out hunting for some time. Do not become their prey."

"We know all about that," Benjy said. He remained standing, positioned so his back was toward a wall, leaving him a clear view of both the windows and the closest door.

If their host noticed, he did not appear to care.

"I can tell," Grigory said. "You ran, but not like rabbits. You weren't afraid of the trouble."

"Should we be afraid?" Hetty asked.

"I do not know. Unless you are thieves. But if you were thieves, help would not have worked."

He pointed to a collection of tiny clay figures on a shelf.

What Hetty mistook for toys were clearly something more. Something far more powerful, with ancient traditions that traveled across a vast ocean and a cold, unforgiving land. Could such magic weigh a person's soul to see if they were worthy of help? Anything was possible, she supposed. There were many traditions of magic in the world, many more than Hetty could ever possibly learn.

"Your magic is the stars," Grigory said, interrupting her thoughts. "What can you do?"

At such a simple question, Hetty could only laugh. "I can do anything I wish!"

Grigory sat forward, and if she had any worries about his intentions, they faded as she recognized the curiosity in his brown eyes. "Tell me. Can you find things?"

"What do you wish to find?" Hetty asked.

"A thing. Several things, stolen from me." Grigory stood up then, and walked around the counter.

He shuffled behind it for a bit and then returned with a box in hand. Once he was in front of them, he gently lifted the lid.

Inside was a wand.

"You can touch it," Grigory said to them. "If it will help."

Benjy picked up the wand, turning it over, but Hetty ran her gaze around the room, realizing what the dim lighting had initially hid from her.

This was a wand shop, and likely the very wand shop Evie had told them about.

"You're a wandmaker."

"Mender, maker, and seller." Grigory bowed his head. "Fifth generation. For many years in my country, Christians did not make wands. They came to us for the mending and making. But here in America it is different. I make, I mend, but I cannot sell to certain people because of their color. I also have thieves."

"You are not the only one," Hetty said. "Magical items are being stolen all over the city."

"Who does this?"

"No one knows for certain, but others have stories much like yours."

Grigory shook his head. "No, not like mine. These wands are dangerous in certain hands. Some were not even complete when they were taken."

"That's the thief's problem," Hetty said.

"What of the innocent who bought them from this thief?"

Hetty felt the old scars around her neck prickle from an even older memory. "People always know what they are buying."

"Yes," Grigory said, looking her full in the face, his eyes sad. "That is a truth."

"Did you mark the stolen wands?" Benjy asked, interrupting them. With care, he balanced the wand on the tip of his index finger. It teetered like a seesaw, gently moving up and down, but never falling.

"Not always. But I started when the thefts began. Why?"

Hetty glanced at the wand's handle and recognized the mark there. "Because we know where your wands ended up!"

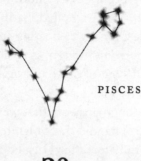

PISCES

20

THE WANDMAKER WAS INFURIATED to hear the details about what happened at the warehouse, and not just because of the wands that had been stolen. A few of the pilfered items that they told him about matched accounts of associates of his who'd had run-ins with thieves as well. When the question of getting the goods back to the rightful owners arose, Hetty sheepishly admitted to starting a fire at the warehouse in question and being unsure how much damage occurred in its wake.

But that didn't appear to concern Grigory. He even suggested that the fire was a good excuse to go back and poke around to see what was salvageable. Something about the glint in his eyes told Hetty that might not be the only thing he would do.

"Maybe we should have gone with him," Hetty remarked as she pushed a pin in the map for the wandmaker's shop.

They had a few hours to wait before Fool's Moon opened its doors, and the time was better spent on a few things they'd neglected to work on so far. Which was why Hetty adjusted her ball gown on the dress form, intent on finishing the alterations for the event. But her thoughts kept returning to the conversation with the wandmaker.

"We would have been a distraction. Besides, the wandmaker can handle himself," Benjy replied, hardly bothered. The pamphlet for the Clarke Cipher was floating around him as he worked at the desk. He ignored it, though, as he absently tapped his pencil against paper. "It's out of our hands now."

"Is it really?" Hetty asked.

"It is. We got enough answers that we can put this aside. Let him and his contacts handle the stolen magical items, especially as it doesn't relate fully to either Duval death."

"That we know of." Hetty turned back to the gold dress, resuming her sewing. "You just want to work on that cipher for a bit."

"We have more proof it's connected," he said, not hiding his grin, and turned back to it. "Why are you sewing in here? Aren't you going to use one of the rooms upstairs as your sewing room? You had to drag Beatrice Jane downstairs."

Hetty rolled her eyes. "I wish you would stop naming these things. They're just dress forms."

"It helps tell them apart. And you didn't answer the question."

With her scissors, Hetty started snipping away at the dress, using the activity to delay answering. When they'd first moved in, she had set up one of the spare rooms to be her sewing room. She had sewn in there for half a day, not making as much progress as she liked until she sat out on the stairs with the dress in her lap while Benjy painted the main hallway.

She and Benjy had previously lived together in a room that was barely bigger than this study. While this house offered ample space, she was still accustomed to looking up from her work to find Benjy on the other side of the room. And if she had to guess, Benjy felt similarly. For all his teasing, Benjy had been more than happy to help her drag the dress form into the study.

"I'm working in here because there's another conversation we need to have," Hetty said.

"About what?"

"About you insisting that we leave Nathan Payne alone until he bothers us." She tucked her scissors into her pocket and pulled out a needle. "Yet from what I saw today, the opposite happened."

Benjy spun around in his chair. "He attacked first!"

"You didn't have to strike back."

"I only did it to give us time to escape!"

Hetty snorted. "If I didn't set a fire, you would have jumped off the loft and fought, with or without magic. Don't argue with me, I know your temper." Hetty saw the stubborn set in his face and a hundred excuses he could make that could have her seeing things his way. But she was in no mood to be placated. "It's not fair. You can't tell me one thing and then do something else. If you're just stubbornly trying to protect me, let me remind you *I'm* the reason he has that scar!"

"I know," her husband said. "I haven't forgotten. But that's exactly why you shouldn't confront him."

"So you're saying it's my fault we have a ghost haunting us? I didn't kill him when I had the chance, and so whatever happens next comes from that mistake?"

"I never said that."

Hetty huffed as she started sewing again, rapidly jabbing the needle through the cloth. She kept sewing for a bit longer, her anger and distress causing her to go faster and faster until she nearly sewed her sleeve to the dress. As she was plucking out the stitches, Benjy spoke up again:

"Whatever Payne does, it's not your fault," he said, in a much kinder and softer tone than he'd used just a moment earlier.

"It is if we don't do something about it," Hetty grumbled.

"We will. Especially as it seems he's part of this scheme of stealing magical items. This impacts not just Thomas's business but Penelope's shop as well." Hetty looked up to see the rather sincere expression on Benjy's face. "Once he messes with our friends, it becomes something we need to look into."

"Yes." Hetty felt a smile lift the corners of her mouth. "Yes, it does."

With that, they settled into a companionable silence for some time. Hetty finished her alterations for the gown while Benjy toiled away at the mysterious Clarke Cipher.

It was hard to say how long they had been at this work when the study's door swung open and Penelope walked right in carrying a watering can.

Penelope took a half step out the door. "Oliver said you jumped down a well. You're not supposed to be here."

Reminded of their argument that morning, Hetty snapped, "Or otherwise you wouldn't have come?"

Penelope swallowed rather guiltily. "Oliver visited my shop. He needed a poison detection potion. I brought it here and—" She stopped and then lifted her chin stubbornly. "I'm sorry about earlier, but I don't have time for this back and forth. I have magic to brew, plants to water, and—oh my stars, whose dress is that?"

"Mine. It's for Bernice Tanner's ball."

"You really are going?" An odd sort of disbelief filled Penelope's face, but when it resolved itself, Penelope was back to her usual cheerful self. "Well, it's a lovely color for you."

"All colors look nice on her," Benjy said absently.

As Hetty feigned modesty at these words, Benjy tossed his glasses onto the desk. "Penelope, when was the last time you've been to Fool's Moon?"

"I don't know what you're talking about. I've never been there before." Spoken firmly and without a trace of a quiver, this might have been convincing—to anyone else. But looking for the obvious lie in the face of truth was what Hetty and Benjy did all the time. Plus, they knew Penelope too well.

"I thought you've been there with the Magnolia Muses," Benjy said with a small shrug. "Even though it's not the singing group you led me to believe."

Penelope bit her lip, and her eyes darted around, scrambling for a way out of this conversation. But in the end, she sighed. "It's not that I lied. I did think they were a singing group when they first invited me out, but I quickly realized that they were only interested in my potions. How do you know about them?"

"We're told they have a collection of spellbooks that might be of interest," Benjy said.

"I wouldn't know." Penelope tapped her chin. "Although, I never really paid much attention when I was there."

"That's fine," Hetty laughed. "We'll see for ourselves when we go there tonight."

"They're not going to talk to you." Penelope was quite firm as she said this, although a bit apologetic. "They're very careful about who they speak to."

Benjy smiled at her then. "Which is why you're going to introduce us."

LYRA

21

Fool's moon had not changed since Hetty had last been there. The smell of tobacco hung in the air even when the only smoke tendrils were tinged with blue, green, or orange. Tables were sparse and were moved often to allow for dancing, fighting, and more. Several webs of fine netting hung from the ceiling to keep magic to a minimum in the saloon. Hetty suspected a previous fight or two was the reason for their presence. It vexed Hetty to see them. If there was trouble, she couldn't fully rely on her magic to face it head-on.

Penelope suggested they wait until nightfall before arriving, and the three of them queued behind another group made up of folks a bit younger than them in body, but older in spirit.

Because it was below Eighth Street it was easy to imagine that no one but hardened criminals, gamblers, and two-bit thieves frequented the tables. There was some of that, including people selling star-dusted herbs that were banned in seven different states. But the caliber of most of the people here was the sort you can find in any saloon uptown. As long as you didn't poke your nose in their business, you'd be left alone.

Piano music and laughter grew louder the deeper they went

into the saloon. Though judging by Benjy's scowl, the piano player was not very good.

They found the piano in the center of the room placed back to back with a second one, although only one was being played at the moment. The sloppy playing was likely due to a lack of skill as much as the empty whiskey bottles lined up on the piano's top.

"They let anyone play, don't they?" Benjy growled.

"Sometimes, but it's a way to get entry to the back of the house." Penelope pointed to the piano. "See those glasses on top of the piano? When one's turned over like that it means the player is trying to get an audience with the Magnolias."

"Why go through all that trouble?" Benjy asked.

"It's mostly because of all the magic ban talk and the fires. People want either to help or to get answers," Penelope said.

"Is that man trying to get answers?" Hetty asked as the drunk man was finally pulled away from the piano by jeering spectators. A woman took his place and began to play.

"They have competitions, too. Anyone who can make the keys sing goes home with a heavy purse," Penelope said.

"Penelope," Benjy said, his eyes locked on the pianos, "you're saying a lot of things, but not telling me what I need to know. Who do I have to talk to to play?"

Penelope laughed. "I'll introduce you." She grabbed his arm. "Hetty, mind if I steal your husband?"

"As long as you bring him back in one piece."

Penelope winked. "Oh, I can't promise that!"

Hetty watched them make their way through the crowd. Penelope was not shy or one to linger in the corner by any means, but she seemed positively effervescent as she interacted with the people here. Stopping every few steps to talk to someone for a few moments and introducing Benjy as if this was the thing that came most naturally to her. Benjy, like the great actor he was, echoed Penelope's energy.

"What shall you be drinking tonight?" a voice asked.

Hetty spun around on the stool to face the bartender. The only thing interesting about him was an impressive handlebar mustache and beard. While he wasn't exactly looking at her all friendly-like, the lines of his face did a downward turn the more he looked at her.

"I've seen you before," he grumbled. "You order drinks you don't touch, and your husband does an impressive job of becoming drunk on watered-down whiskey."

"Who says it's watered down?" Hetty asked.

"I do," the bartender said, "because I don't sell the good stuff to people who aren't looking for a drink."

"Then let's forget all about drinks. I'm looking for someone. Lou Notts. Know anything?"

The bartender grunted. "Can't say if Lou is around, but playing some music usually settles the matter. Looks like your husband has the right idea."

He pointed back into the saloon, and Hetty obligingly turned her head. The woman was still playing, but the attention in the room had shifted a bit as Benjy sat down in front of the other piano.

"You should give your man a kiss for luck."

"Trust me, he doesn't need luck."

The bartender grunted and moved to fill the glass of a patron looking to wet their lips with drink.

Someone from the crowd got up and turned over a glass, saying something that Hetty couldn't make out, but the watching crowd cheered.

The music that the woman was playing suddenly changed, veering into a popular piece that people were humming at the last carnival in town. The sort of music that got toes tapping.

Then Benjy began to play—simple notes at first to test the instrument, then easing into a song. He took what his opponent already played and turned it on its head.

This was what Benjy did while he played, because that's how he'd learned the piano in the first place. By listening and repeating it, and then changing what parts he could. It was very good so far, but Hetty suspected he'd have to make more of a showing if he was going to draw Lou Notts out.

Hetty leaned back on her stool, looking at the faces visible to her in the crowd. She imagined Lou as someone like Benjy, who was very quick to pass judgment and very slow to show approval. So far the faces scattered around seemed quite pleased with what they were hearing.

Benjy played a little faster, making the music a little more up-tempo, and creating a sound unlike anything Hetty had ever heard. The entire room was paying attention to Benjy then. Even his opponent had long since stopped playing.

There was magic in music.

Hetty had seen it with her own eyes, as a very small child watching her father play the fiddle. He would play, and things happened around them. A little gust of wind that tugged at her clothes, stirring the dangling dried herbs in their cabin. Magic that made her mother laugh, and made her sister frown as she tried to figure where the wind came from.

Magic was the world, and the world was magic.

While Hetty knew there were many ways to channel magic, she was reminded every time Benjy played how music really could be the perfect conduit for it.

Sometimes she saw flashes of spells when he played. A few were on purpose, usually spells to draw attention or distract. Everything else was just the product of his playing and where his thoughts were at the moment.

Which was now becoming a big problem.

The net overhead, designed to hold back magic, had that bright look that reminded Hetty of the last time one of Penelope's experiments had blown up in Hetty's kitchen. A dangerously bright light that had Hetty concerned. But the net held.

Or it did until a knife skimmed across the surface, ripping the net in half.

At first nothing happened.

Just tendrils of magic falling like stars.

But these were not clumps of meteorite—they were *magic,* and when they struck, the mark they left created chaos.

First through the gathered crowd, who reacted to the impending danger. And second when the magic hit and rattled the saloon to its very foundation. A mote fell near her and Hetty was thrown backwards off her stool into the bar. The bartender broke her fall. He clearly intended to catch her but failed as the shaking threw him back as well. She scrambled up with a quick mutter of thanks, and surveyed the damage.

The people who could manage it were hurrying out of the saloon, survival instincts kicking in. With big magic it was best to get out of sight before the police showed up.

Benjy had climbed up onto a table, manipulating the magic flying about the room to counter some of the harmful effects. Others did the same, and Hetty saw someone attempting to regain command of the magic net. In all of the chaos, Hetty was having trouble finding Penelope in the crowd. But as she surveyed the scene, she caught a flash of purple similar to the dress that Penelope wore that evening. But it wasn't Penelope. Not only was the figure slenderer, but the woman was older, too, with a fair amount of gray in her hair. And when she turned, Hetty realized it was someone she knew.

Adelaide Duval.

What was Adelaide doing here? Had she simply come for a drink, or was she one of the many petitioners looking to talk to the Magnolias? It didn't seem likely. Hetty was still considering other possibilities when Adelaide suddenly darted out of sight. Not toward the exit, as many folk were doing, but deeper inside the saloon, toward the back room.

Without a moment's hesitation, Hetty followed Adelaide.

The bright-colored dress made it easy to keep track of Adelaide, and the many obstacles — overturned tables, chairs, and the still-fleeing crowd — allowed Hetty to quickly catch up to the older woman while remaining out of sight.

That is, until a boom crackled in the air.

Hetty spun back, fearing the worst. But no disaster lurked behind her. Nor in front, though Adelaide had managed to disappear in those brief seconds Hetty had turned away. Figuring that the woman could have only gone through the hallway, Hetty hurried on before she stopped at the threshold.

Unwillingly stopped.

Something had shifted in the air, pressing her back.

A ward to keep people away.

If it was meant to block passage, it would need to be much stronger. At the moment, it functioned as a camouflaging charm, to keep eyes turned away from it. Which would work on most folks . . .

Not so much on Hetty.

Drawing out the Arrow star sigil, she hurled it forward, sending it ripping through the spell. When the effect was dispelled, a burst of pressure pushed Hetty back as the spell faded away. A bit of grit blew into her eye as the air swirled around her. She wiped it out of the corner of her eye and continued down the hall.

At the very end of the hall she saw what the ward must have been set against. The wall at the end of the corridor was black with soot. Hard to say what caused the charring, but Hetty's first guess was some spell gone awry.

Hetty tapped her boots along the floorboards, looking for any sort of resistance. Knowing there was likely magic residue nearby, she ran a finger along her choker, drawing the Herdsman from her stitches.

The star-speckled woman appeared and swung her staff around the hallway. Dazzling splotches of different colors highlighted the remnant magical energies left in the small space. While it covered most surfaces, the largest concentration was not far from Hetty's feet.

She stepped around the splotch of pink. She held her foot in the air for a moment before she stomped down hard on the mark.

Nothing happened at first, but then the floor under her foot buckled and swung open, revealing itself to be a trapdoor. Through that trapdoor was a set of stairs leading down into yet another tunnel.

How many did that make so far? Hetty hadn't brought Darlene's map with her, but she knew that this tunnel certainly wasn't on it.

Of the tunnels she walked through just this week, this one was the least surprising find. Given what she'd learned about the Magnolias, it would have been more surprising if they *hadn't* had a secret tunnel. Her only question was if they'd known about it before they moved into this location or if its being on-site was a happy accident. What she did know was that it was in constant use. Glass orbs were placed at regular intervals and light flickered on as she came near and turned off once she passed. The air was fresh, the dirt under her feet hard packed, and wooden beams supported the tunnel here and there.

These were all such pleasant things to see that when Hetty turned the bend and found her way blocked by an angry red ball of magic, she was greatly disappointed.

Encased in glass, the magic pulsed like a barely contained

storm, lightning flashing inside, sending a soft glow in all directions.

"I wouldn't mess with that if I were you."

With the floating orb between them, the haze of magic steaming off it left the stranger looking like he had walked through a cloud of rouge. A short but round man, he would have appeared intimidating even without the star sigils glimmering at his side.

"Nothing but poison in there. So you stay right there if you got any sense left to you, unless you can pay the toll to pass."

Of course there's a toll. "How much?" Hetty asked.

"Not in coin," the man said. "Music is the traditional fare."

"I don't think you want me to sing to you," Hetty said. "I'm awfully terrible at it."

"Then tell me a story. Any would do."

"Ah," Hetty laughed, "that's the sort of thinking that got an old man to lose everything he had of value and gain nothing in return. You see, he was traveling after the war ended with a surrender. The old man wasn't sure what it meant for him, since talk of war wasn't for the likes of him. But it changed things. Changed things so much that he and a few others thought it was best to leave, before change turned into something bad. Lots of people went up north, seeing and doing things that aren't important to tell right now. But the old man in this story went west, looking for gold. Not because anybody told him about it, but because he had a dream.

"Now see here," Hetty continued, watching the star sigils fade around the guard as the man grew enthralled by her tale. She slowly edged herself around the man and the floating orb of poison. "Dreams are curious things. Usually they can give warning of the things to come, but most times they can drag you to your doom. And this was the case for the old man of this story. The person who told him of the treasure was a ghost eager to lure a fresh sacrifice to the grave. Soon the man learned the lesson, though a bit too late," Hetty added as she discreetly let loose a spell of her own. "Don't trust people telling you tales."

The guard blinked, but he moved too slowly. Hetty had already dropped a veil of magic between them. It solidified as he rushed toward her, and he slammed into the magical barrier Hetty had thrown up. Soundlessly, the man yelled at her, striking at it with his fists, but Hetty just waved at him before dashing off.

Ahead, the tunnel slowly widened, the space growing to the size of a small room.

It had seen better days. As if a giant had rampaged about, glass, stone, and wood were strewn all around, much of it stacked in an untidy heap.

And Hetty could sense the magic left there.

She was still pondering what it might be when a baseball bat swung in her direction.

Lightning fast, she pivoted, catching and yanking both the bat and the person wielding it forward. Sticking out her boot, Hetty sent her attacker stumbling to the ground. By the time the young man staggered back to his feet, Hetty had the bat in her hands and swung it over her shoulder.

"Are you going to be trouble?" she asked.

In lieu of a proper answer, a star-speckled lion lunged forth from the boy, crashing right into Hetty's protective spells. The clash filled the tunnel with dazzling light for a brief moment.

When it faded, the boy, instead of doing the reasonable thing and giving up, simply started a new spell.

Hetty sighed. Why couldn't this tunnel be empty like the others?

Swinging the bat around with only a fraction of the force she could muster, she tapped the boy's arm, aiming to distract instead of harm.

She shouldn't have bothered.

He deftly jumped aside and started drawing the Arrow star sigil, targeting another spell at her.

Hetty tapped the band at her neck. Sagittarius leapt forward, snatching those magical arrows out of the air and loading them in her own bow. With a smooth gesture the centaur fired back at the boy's poorly drawn spells, before vanishing in a pop of light.

This should have been enough to deter him from attacking further. But he was stubborn. He grabbed a loose rock and flung it at Hetty.

Hetty didn't bother with magic this time.

The bat cracked as Hetty struck the rock and it whizzed through the air with such speed, it sent the boy lunging to the ground.

Hetty drew her own arrows now. And by the time the boy was on his feet once again, dozens of arrows made of stars floated in the air between them.

The arrows dove at him before he could even work his next spell. They lifted him up as they hit, pinning him to the wall.

"You should have done that from the start."

Still wielding the bat, Hetty turned to find her husband and her best friend watching her from the doorway on the other side of the room.

Both were uninjured, unconcerned, and more bemused than anything. Benjy even clutched a book in his hand, while Penelope sipped from a cup of tea.

"Did you come to rescue us?" Penelope asked rather cheerfully. "That's awfully nice of you."

"She didn't know we were down here," Benjy said as he struggled to keep a straight face. "Did you follow— Ah, you hanging up there, what's your name again?"

"Peter," called the young man. He had stopped struggling against the arrows as he gaped down at them all.

"Oh yes," Benjy continued with a nod. "Did you follow Peter down here?"

"No," Hetty said, her hand tightening on the baseball bat. "I didn't know you were down here, because I thought you were caught up in the chaos you created when your magic piano playing ripped apart the net! If I knew you were having a tea party, I wouldn't have come all this way. I was chasing after a murder suspect!"

Benjy's amusement vanished at these words, but Penelope was unmoved.

"No murderers down here," she said. "As for chaos, the Magnolias brought us here. We're waiting for Lou Notts now. Come in and wait with us, and let poor Peter down. Gently," Penelope added as Hetty lifted a clenched hand.

Hetty released the young man with great reluctance. He slid down the wall. Not meeting anyone's eye, he said, "I'll go tell them you're here, if they don't know already. Can I have my bat back?"

Hetty handed it to him and the boy ran as quick as he could to get away from her.

The room in which Benjy and Penelope waited was everything Hetty expected of the hidden headquarters of a magic rights group. Several chairs around a circular table covered with papers, and a tea tray. A bookshelf stuffed with books both magical and mundane. There were quite a few lanterns scattered about; some were lit while others remained unused. And on the wall was a painting brought in to brighten things up.

It was a painting of the Delaware River. The sort of painting that tourists bought all the time because it depicted ships. But this was from no market stall. Hetty had seen it as it was sketched, seen it in various stages being painted, and Hetty herself had picked out the wooden frame so she could give it as a gift.

And so when the door opened once again and someone entered the room, Hetty was the only one unsurprised to see Cora Evans standing in the doorway.

"I had wondered," Hetty said, pointing to the painting, "why this wasn't in your home."

"No space there," Cora said easily, as if they had planned to meet all along, instead of this being an unexpected turn of events.

Benjy was clearly shocked, speechless for a change. But Penelope wasn't just shocked—her face showed betrayal at the sight of the older woman.

"*You're* Lou Notts?" Penelope's voice shook, caught as it was between two very different emotions. "No wonder we never met! No wonder nobody questioned my knowledge in plants or potions. You told them about me?"

"Just a few things to get their interest," Cora said serenely. "Sit down, you three. This day has been tiring enough without all the ruckus you caused upstairs."

"An easily avoidable ruckus at that," Benjy retorted.

Cora glanced his way, but Benjy said no more.

They all sat at the round table, Hetty sandwiched between Benjy and Penelope. Cora took a seat on the opposite side, and she sat there alone, without Peter or any other Magnolias at her side.

"I heard you were looking for me, so why don't we start there. Since you went through all this trouble."

It was all too reasonable a tone to take, and it jabbed at the wound of betrayal even more. While it was only Hetty's own preconceived notions that led her to believe Cora's activities these days were limited to charity work and being a pastor's wife, there had been plenty of chances for Cora to inform her otherwise. And not once had Cora taken them.

After the silence had gone on long enough, Benjy spoke:

"We're looking for a spellbook on Celestial magic. We heard you might have a copy."

"Why would you care for something like that?" Cora asked.

"You've seen it?" Hetty asked.

"We have it. Why should I give it to you? Don't you have a case you should be working on?"

Benjy's expression, already carefully neutral, turned to stone. "Not you too."

"Raimond was my friend as well, and the death of his son is devastating to me. But that's beside the point," Cora replied. "You handle murders and strange deaths. This false spellbook is not something you should concern yourselves with right now."

"It could be tied to Valentine's death," Hetty said. "Both he and his father were concerned about issues of magic rights."

"All the more reason the spellbook will be safest with me." Before Hetty could say more, Cora added, "You're not the first to ask about this. A stranger already came here earlier this evening asking for the book."

"What sort of stranger?" Hetty asked.

"I don't know exactly. My guard outside, the one you bamboozled with a ghost story, told me this. Roberts saw a strange woman at the mill next door. She asked all about the book. Although why she wanted it she wouldn't say. The whole thing is grotesque. Trust me when I tell you the fake spells aren't the worst part. There are illustrations that are practically minstrel show advertisements. No one should see such a thing. I shouldn't have even looked at it, because all it did was make me wonder why we're even bothering with any of this if someone could make something so hateful."

"We don't run," Hetty said softly, repeating words told to her a long time ago. "We don't run, because there are much worse options."

Cora's voice regained its earlier crispness. "You wanted to

know about the book. Now you do. And I daresay you've learned more than what you came to find to begin with."

"Still, I could stand to learn a great deal more," Benjy started.

The door flung open and Peter ran in, shaking and trembling and trying to hold back tears. "Lou," he cried. "Come quick, it's horrible! You have to see!"

Words delivered in such a way only meant one thing.

So Hetty knew what to expect as they followed Peter back through the tunnel.

The barrier Hetty had thrown up was gone. The orb of poisoned smoke was still there. But the guard who had demanded a story from Hetty for safe passage was lying on the ground in a way that did not look natural.

The bartender from upstairs was crouched by his side, and moved to speak to Cora the moment he saw her. As he passed her, Hetty stepped toward the guard and bent down to press her fingers against his pulse that she knew would not be there.

Benjy knelt next to her. He did not touch the body, but his eyes traveled along the dead man's still form.

"This just happened," Hetty said. "I just saw him, spoke to him. Do you think he was poisoned by the gas?"

"No." Benjy pulled back the dead man's collar. A jagged cut ran along the man's neck, with a trail of slowly drying blood alongside it. "He wasn't surprised. His features were too neutral. This happened quick. Might even be magic."

"Any residue would be hard to see. I cast some spells earlier, it'll mess with whatever we find," Hetty said.

"And you were not the only one to do so."

Cora stood behind them, looking very tired and sad at the man on the ground.

"Does he have family?" Benjy asked.

Cora shook her head. "Only us. We'll have to figure out what to do with him."

"Let us help," Hetty said, and for the benefit of Peter and the bartender, she added, "We own a funeral home."

Cora smiled, as if she knew these words were coming. "As generous as that offer is, that won't be necessary. He was part of the Southgate Mutual Aid Society. Arrangements for his funeral and last rites have long been in place. He will be buried at Lebanon. Though we will need help to get the body to the cemetery."

"That we can help with. We'll come with a wagon to meet you," Benjy said.

This settled the matter.

With care, the men brought the body up to the main level, where the dead man could rest in peace for the night. Penelope went with them, one of the vials she had to test for poison cupped in her hand.

Hetty and Cora took their time following, mostly because Hetty was dealing with the poison ball. With care, she spun and turned the orb of foul magic, shrinking it down to size as she led it out of the tunnel and into a bottle Cora had found for her.

Hetty squeezed it inside, releasing the magic once the gas was sealed in the bottle.

"I forget sometimes that you do not exaggerate all the stories you tell," Cora said as she locked the bottle away.

"All stories have some truth to them. It just depends on what people say."

Cora sighed. "I would have told you eventually."

"I doubt that. You had plenty of time to do so earlier!"

"You were too preoccupied with the death of your sister to be of any help. And quite frankly, you'd have been a distraction to this work. What you do is small, individual efforts. I'm working toward something bigger, and you're not ready for it."

"I have a great interest in magic. Doesn't my skill grant me entrance?"

Cora looked at her sharply, with a gaze that usually sent Hetty crawling from the disappointment that radiated from her. "And who taught you magic?"

"My mother. My father taught me some before he was taken from us, but she taught me everything else I know."

"Not everything," Cora said.

"Maybe not, but what I learned from her can never be overshadowed by anything else."

They weren't talking about magic anymore. And Cora knew it. Hetty could see the moment that realization occurred, because the serene air that Cora had been projecting withered away, and only hurt filled her features.

"I don't think we'll be over for dinner this week," Hetty said rather stiffly. "We're looking to be quite busy."

Cora nodded. "I understand. Maybe next week."

"We'll see."

Hetty went in search of her husband. Surprisingly, he wasn't in the back room with Peter, the bartender, and the dead man. Penelope was there, though, studying the odd coloring of the vapor that hovered over the body.

The vapor turned the color of limes when poison was around, but because the vapor was still yellow, Hetty didn't even step into the room like she would have done otherwise, and kept on with her search.

She found Benjy in the main room of the saloon. It was still being cleaned up. Diligent workers put tables back into place while someone restored the magical net.

"Who was the murder suspect you ran after?" Benjy asked as Hetty stopped at his side.

"Adelaide Duval," Hetty whispered. "I saw her when the chaos broke lose."

"I figured it was her."

"Do you think she was the woman after the spellbook?"

"It's possible. But if it was her, I wonder why she wanted it so badly."

"Why do you say that?"

Benjy pointed at the net. "That net can withstand a lot of magic. I didn't break it when I was playing the piano. Any magic that occurs when I play are merely illusions. They wouldn't have ever overwhelmed the net. Whoever did it, did it with a lot of force. The question is, why go through all the effort."

"To cause confusion to steal the spellbook," Hetty said, thinking of the poison orb, the guards, and even the spell that forced her back from the tunnel's entrance.

Benjy grimaced. "Or to get rid of a witness."

WOLF

INTERLUDE

May 1863

IT CAN'T BE COINCIDENCE," Benjy said once again.

"Oh no, it's much worse than that, it's bad luck." Hetty grunted as she stared at the chess set before her.

They sat in the shade of a Bottle Tree, on the grounds of what had once been known as the Biddle Manor. The tree, like the grand house, had been transformed lately, and like everything else on the island, it was for the best. Glass bottles of every possible color dangled from the limbs. When the sun shone through them at the right angle, rainbows danced along the ground. The bottles glowed at night as well, because they were charmed with powerful protective magics to capture bad spirits to keep them from causing harm.

Hearing the news Benjy had brought, Hetty hoped that magic could go a bit further.

"Doesn't make it less real. A man with a scar on his face, caught somewhere he isn't supposed to be—it means Nathan Payne didn't drown like we hoped he did," Benjy said.

"If he's locked up and out of the way," Hetty asked as Benjy moved his remaining knight along the board, "why should it be our problem?"

"Because if he's here, it's because he's looking for us after what happened in Charleston."

"The money people want for us isn't that much." Hetty reached for her bishop.

Benjy tapped the board. "I don't think he cares about the money. And that's check if you move a few more spaces down."

"Why are you helping me win?" Hetty asked, her hand frozen over the piece.

"Because I'm going to see Payne and you need to stay here and out of trouble."

Hetty sucked her teeth, taking offense at that last bit. "I'm not the one that was shot last month when we were in that swamp. Maybe you need my help keeping out of trouble."

"Hetty," he began, only to stop short because their hostess was approaching.

Pearl was born on this island, according to her. Her family and the others were used to white folks leaving them on their own during the summer, as the storms and heat spurred on a seasonal migration to the mainland. But with war and the Union army in and around Charleston, every slaveowner had packed and fled the island, leaving the lands in the hands of the people who knew it the best. Pearl and everyone who spent their lives on Teach Island didn't consider themselves emancipated as much as claiming rights to what was theirs. They moved into their former masters' homes, choosing with their pleasure from the large and spacious rooms, and built new structures on the island for a proper schoolhouse and a church. They even purchased acres of land through the new redistribution policies, in an effort to keep unscrupulous outsiders from staking claim on their homes. Out in Washington this was called the Port Royal Experiment, but as far as

Hetty could see it was just people living the lives they were always meant to have in the first place.

"How are you two faring?" Pearl asked. She grinned at the chessboard, which, like everything else in the grand house behind them, once belonged to the absent Biddles. "Or did you lose again?"

"I don't think I can lose as badly as to your grandfather," Benjy laughed.

"You're not alone there! He gives everyone quite a thrashing, though he does think you made a half-decent opponent. I came to tell you that Clare is back home. You said you wanted to see the doctor?"

Hetty looked over at Benjy. "We did."

Ignoring Hetty's pointed look, Benjy said to Pearl, "I heard about the person that was locked up. I think I know who he is and might be able to take care of him for you, if you like."

Pearl nodded, not hiding her relief. "Can't speak for Abner, but I think he'd be happy to hear that. People are worried about so many strangers just showing up here, in a short amount of time."

That certainly was true. Hetty had spun a masterful tale of her and Benjy's being shipwrecked in a recent storm. They even took care to wash up on a beach, timing it so some children could stumble across them. While Pearl, her family, and a few others questioned them little, others were a bit more wary.

For good reason.

Their whole story was a ruse. Tucked and hidden in a shallow inlet was their rowboat, and the coded messages that Bernice Tanner had given them were hidden away in a panel in Hetty's bodice. After escaping the swamps in Virginia, they'd contacted the Vigilance Society and gotten this task from Bernice. Because it had been the closest they had ever been to finding Hetty's sister before losing their lead, Hetty had been eager to take on this mission even if she was now regretting that choice.

The flight of the landowning whites left the homes they'd once occupied empty. But they also left caches behind. Caches not of gold or jewels but of information. Records regarding the domestic trafficking of human cargo since 1853 were supposed to be locked up in the study. Copies were kept in an office in Charleston, but they lacked the details of greatest importance, such as names and other crucial information that could be checked against papers collected elsewhere.

The contact who would help Hetty and Benjy find these records was Clare, a doctor who lent her skills not just on Teach Island but on all the other islands in the area. She had been called away not long after they first arrived, due to a difficult pregnancy on a nearby island, but now with her return, this task of theirs would soon be over.

Because Benjy was going to see what he could do about Payne, Hetty visited the doctor alone. Although she was irked at him, once she was headed on her way, Hetty found she didn't mind. They had been too often in the other's company of late, playing being a couple for the benefit of the islanders. To be on her own for a few moments was nice.

The doctor's house sat overlooking the sea. A boat, still drying in the sun, was tied down next to the house. A wind chime of tarnished brass hung from the roof and a few chairs were placed on the porch, and there were bright blue flowers in pots with bees cheerfully buzzing around the petals.

Hetty went to knock on the door, but it was already partially open.

"Hello?" she called as she pushed the door wider. "I'm sorry if you're busy, but I needed to talk to you." Not hearing an answer, Hetty stepped inside, and into something soft that wasn't a rug. Dirt moved through the hall. If there had been a plant that had been knocked over, she might not have worried. But the dirt continued into the hall, footprints leading to a broken pot.

Hetty stepped around it and the forlorn plant lying there, looking for any further signs of damage or signs of struggle in the house.

The doors along the hall were shut tightly, but before Hetty went to try to open them, she saw one open farther down the hall.

This was the door Hetty went through.

No more dirt trickled into the room. Although there was a body sprawled facedown on the ground.

A woman of middling years, with her blouse smudged with dirt.

Hetty placed a hand on the shoulder, rocking the woman back and forth.

"Are you dead?"

"Not quite," a voice grumbled.

She rolled over and blinked up at Hetty. "But can't say the same for you."

She jerked her hand, the light of a spell flashed, and something jammed itself into Hetty's neck.

Hetty gasped, staggering against a wall. She yanked out a syringe, and a few drops of yellowish liquid splattered onto the floor. The tiny spot at Hetty's neck burned like hot coal had been placed on it.

Clare stood, brushing off her clothes, and calmly yanked the syringe out of Hetty's hand. Hetty could only stare up at the doctor.

"Why would you do this? I came looking for your help!"

"Yes, I heard you were looking for me," Clare remarked. "You were about to bring trouble."

"I wasn't." Hetty fought the urge to rub her neck. She was still on her feet, although her vision was brightening around the edges. "I'm trying to help."

"Your type of help isn't wanted."

Air hissed between Hetty's lips, and she started to draw a sigil into the air. But the focus she required wasn't coming to her, and her attempts to grab on to magical energies fell apart.

"I wouldn't do that, it'll increase the poison," Clare said.

"What kind of doctor are you!" Hetty's arm twitched on its own accord. Grabbing it sent her sliding down the wall.

"I help people," Clare said. "I just make sure it's for the right reasons."

A shadow walked into Hetty's vision.

"Give me the antidote and I promise I won't hurt you," Hetty said.

"Threatening people is not how you get help."

The shadow that stepped forward had a face, a very familiar face. One she knew would be around, but not the one she expected to see.

Nathan Payne.

"What forsaken stars brought you here!" Hetty spat. "You're supposed to be in jail."

"They caught the wrong man." Payne knelt down to be level with her face. He was inordinately pleased with himself, which was worse than any leer he might have thrown in her direction. "And quite lucky it was. I was able to speak with the good doctor and tell her all about the villain who did this to my face." He lightly traced the jagged diagonal cut. "The night you did this, you sentenced my son to death. My punishment for failing. But you won't win this time."

"How did you find us?" Hetty asked.

"Oh, you're easy to find. My employer is very interested in the ledger, just like you. Although not nearly as much. After all, the ledger is the only way you're going to see your sister again!"

Hetty fought through the poison's grasp and drew the first star sigil that came to mind, the Crow, and flung it at Payne. But instead of a bird pecking his eyes out, the magic exploded in her face and rebounded back on her, destroying what sense of self Hetty still had left.

Payne said something. His lips were moving, but somewhere along the way, Hetty lost the thread of it. Her thoughts kept returning to a cemetery, a hand pushing out of the grave. Her sister's hand. Benjy's hand. Hetty's own hand.

Dead and buried, and Payne standing on top, grinning in triumph.

Hetty's vision began to narrow. The only thing she could see was Payne before her. Still talking. He kept talking. Using words to threaten, to promise, to hurt, to confuse.

But around him, around Hetty, shapes stepped out of the shadows, tall and spindly. They were solid enough to touch, yet they floated back in the space they occupied, slowly gathering like ghosts until they came to rest behind Payne. Their mouths were sewn together, the straggling ends of cords flopping about as they moved. Brown skin once dark in life, now ashen gray. Then there were their eyes. Eyes that were gold and flickered like flames.

Payne didn't react. He couldn't see like Hetty could see.

She was going to point it out. But one ghost shook its head, urging Hetty to stay still. To wait. To watch.

So she did.

And suddenly Payne was in pain, howling and crying out in a scream that Hetty could hear like a distant cry of a wolf at night.

The ghosts had grabbed Payne and held his arms and hands as he fought them.

The blood fell onto the floor like rain.

Hetty watched it fall and fall and fall . . .

Then she was falling and falling and falling . . .

She tried to scream. Tried to yell. But if she managed it, she heard nothing.

No sound, no voices.

Just her falling and falling.

Then she stopped.

Hetty lay on her back, staring up into nothingness, and saw things clearly for the first time in her life.

Death encircled her.

No, not death. The ghosts that cling to the world.

They were real and they were here.

And they were here to tell her all about her failures. About the people she hurt on the way, and the people she left to die.

So many people. So many . . .

Then she smelled flowers, as bright and crisp as the promise of spring.

Something, somebody, shook her by the shoulders. She could hear muffled voices as if she were underwater.

Then more shaking, and a voice that she knew as well as her own.

"Stay with me. Tell me a story. Tell me any story. Just stay awake."

The simple words caught her and wouldn't let go, and soon she forced out the first words that came to mind.

"There was a woman who got lost on the way home and she heard a voice," Hetty said, each word bringing her out of the strange darkness that had grabbed ahold of her. "When the old lady turned around, no one stood there. She was in a swamp and it was a lost spirit sent to guide her home." Hetty coughed. "She didn't know it was a bad spirit because she didn't have a lantern with her."

Hetty coughed again. She was still on the floor on the doctor's room, held up by the wall. Except instead of Payne in front of her, Benjy was at her side, and on the other was Thomas.

"What are you doing here?" Hetty asked, staring at Thomas. His face was a bit bruised, and his eyes were rimmed with what could have been tears.

"Is that part of the story?" Benjy asked calmly, as he always did, sounding unbothered even as his eyes glittered with concern.

"I haven't got to that part yet," Hetty admitted. Then she remembered everything. "Where is—"

"That lying bastard?" Clare said. She had a cut on her forehead, and a scowl that wasn't meant for Hetty anymore. "Unfortunately, he's not dead. He escaped on my boat. If he stays around the islands we'll find him. I'm sorry I let myself be tricked and attacked you like that. He had a convincing tale."

Hetty shook her head, even if it hurt a bit. She knew Payne wouldn't be found that easily.

"Why are you here?" Hetty asked Thomas again, because she truly was confused by his appearance on the island.

"I'm here to help about this ledger," Thomas said. "If I hadn't come, I wouldn't have caused all this confusion, and you wouldn't have been—"

"It's fine." Hetty patted Thomas's hand. "Payne's the only person to blame. Good thing he ran with a tail between his legs. He knew death was coming for him if he stayed."

Thomas forced out a laugh.

Benjy didn't, however.

"The next time he shows up, he won't get away," Benjy said. He absently rubbed a thumb over his bloodied knuckles.

"That might be sooner than we think," Hetty remarked. "He said he's after the ledger too."

"Then this time we'll be prepared for whatever he's going to throw at us."

AQUARIUS

22

Wʜᴇɴ ʜᴇᴛᴛʏ sᴛʀᴜᴄᴋ the punching bag and it moved, it meant one of two things. Either she'd used magic to strike it, or she'd hit it hard enough to hurt herself.

In this case it was the latter—a broken hand that had her curled up on the kitchen floor, bottles and canisters scattered around her. The throbbing pain in her fingers moved to her head when Benjy crouched next to her. "Do you need help?"

"Go away," Hetty growled.

"You don't want that." Benjy picked up a potion jar from the floor.

Hetty glared at him. "I do."

Instead of leaving her alone to wallow in her mistakes and poor judgments, Benjy scooped her into his arms, so quickly she didn't even get a chance to react. He carried her out of the kitchen, cheerfully ignoring Hetty's continued grumblings. Instead of taking her to the study like she expected, he took her into the backyard.

The sun was out, but it was early enough in the morning that the heat was not as strong as it would be a few hours hence. Benjy's sketchbook was on the bench, a pencil holding down a page with a rough design for a new funeral home sign. After setting her on the bench, Benjy sat on the other end, uncapped the potion jar, and took her injured right hand into his.

Gingerly he spread the creamy blue poultice across the broken ridge of her hand, smoothing both the cream and her hand out as he worked. The poultice was cold at first, but warmed up as it knitted together the fragile bones in her hand.

"If you want to hit something, sparring with me is the better idea," Benjy said, massaging the poultice in small circles. "You won't get hurt."

"Just my pride," Hetty groaned. "I still can't knock you down without resorting to magic."

"You should resort to magic first—that's your best talent. Although, you aren't completely terrible. You took down that fellow very easily with a bat."

"That *boy*," Hetty scoffed, even as she glowed with the compliment, "could have been taken down by Penelope just as easily. What I did was nothing special."

"Your opinion, not mine." The bit of a teasing smile he had faded as he asked: "Feel any better?"

Hetty pulled away from Benjy's grasp, pretending to be focused on flexing her newly healed hand. She had said very little to him about her argument with Cora. Although he knew she was upset, he wasn't going to press. Mainly because talking about Cora meant also talking about him and Jay. While the arguments were different, the root cause was eerily similar.

"I do. I feel much better. I'm starting to understand why you became interested in boxing." She looked around the yard, remembering that the reason she had gone into the cellar in the first place was to do something about her restless energy. "Do you think Sy will show up soon? Penelope said she'd send him over with a wagon."

Benjy grunted as he picked up his sketch pad. "I'm thinking I should have walked over this morning and got him myself."

"Why didn't you?"

"I had a few distractions. Mostly trying to figure out when Mrs. Evans started the Magnolia Muses. I figure a year and three months ago."

"Try further back than that. It might have even bloomed out of whatever work she was doing before with the Vigilance Society." Hetty sat back on the bench, absently tapping her foot against the grass. "I can't believe she never told me. I can understand Penelope not saying anything at first. She thought they were a singing group. But Cora. She knows all about my interest in magic."

"But not magic rights."

"I care very much about that!"

"On a personal level," Benjy said, without a hint of judgment. "There have been other groups you could have taken part in that are less secretive than the Magnolias."

Hetty squinted. "Did Darlene or Penelope say something to you about holding the E. W. Harper meeting here?"

"I'm not surprised, given the space here, that they're interested in having you host. Plus, you're their friend and likely to make good conversation." Each word was carefully said so it could still be true even if it wasn't all the truth. It was as impressive as it was annoying.

"Well, maybe I will reconsider it," Hetty said loftily. "But not until after this case is settled."

"And there's much to settle. Do you agree that Adelaide Duval is our top suspect at the moment?"

Hetty nodded. A number of things had helped Adelaide rise to the top of that short list. All the events that happened at Fool's Moon the previous night. The dead man's testimony of a strange woman lurking around. Even how Adelaide disappeared into her artist's studio the same day her brother was found dead. All these facts were circumstantial, but compared to the only other real suspect—her cousin Horace—she was the more likely candidate. Horace Duval's main crime was being odious enough to bring a medium into the family home hours after his cousin's body was discovered just to ask questions of inheritance. Adelaide had a closer relationship to Raimond and Valentine, possible knowledge of tunnels, and ample opportunity to kill her brother slowly through poison.

It all made sense.

But it had made just as much sense that Beatty Hose was the cause of Raimond Duval's death.

"It doesn't quite feel right to me," Hetty said. "It's a bit too perfect."

Their crows had fluttered down to the ground before them, forming a semicircle, looking up at Hetty rather impatiently. They weren't alone, either—they were joined by other crows that were either friends or extended members of the family. Hetty made to get up, but Benjy pulled out a small bag of seeds. He held it so Hetty could reach inside. She sprinkled some seeds onto the ground, and almost immediately the birds began to feast.

"She *is* a bit too perfect," Benjy agreed. "If Raimond Duval was poisoned instead of stabbed, I would be convinced. Poison is a woman's weapon."

Hetty knocked him in the arm. "That's just leaping to conclusions! He's an old man, and if he wasn't expecting it, Adelaide could have easily stabbed him."

"If our theory that the wrong Duval was killed first is true, then why such an impersonal death for Valentine? And what of Roberts? I thought at first he might be dead because he was an eyewitness. But you remember how the librarian at Still-Bowers asked me to inquire about an overdue book?"

"Yes, but surely that can wait— No, it can't be." Hetty gasped.

"Yes," Benjy said rather grimly. "She gave me the address for Johnathon Roberts."

"So whoever killed him was looking for the spellbook?"

"Or something else. Mrs. Evans is convinced the spellbook is irrelevant to the case. While I disagree with much she said last night, on this I must begrudgingly agree. The spellbook doesn't matter with the Duvals. It's a detail, but only a small one."

They sat in silence as the crows ate.

Drawing the links between Valentine's and Raimond's deaths was never going to be easy, but Hetty had thought there would be fewer complications than this.

"I think I'll pay Olmstead a visit this morning," Hetty said. "Both Duvals taught there. It's one of their connections that we haven't given much attention to. It's not a terrible idea," she added after spotting Benjy's frown.

"I spoke to his students when we first looked at Raimond's death. Nothing they said back then stood out."

"George's been teaching there these past few weeks. He might have stumbled across something."

"Chances are not high either way," Benjy muttered. "It's not a good use of time."

Hetty's gaze fell to the shack, their sign lying abandoned against it. The wooden sign looked even worse than before, and not just because it had a long scrape through the painted words.

"Better use than usual," Hetty said. "I have to meet Adelaide Duval at Elmhurst to talk about her brother's funeral. Unless you don't think I should go, given she's now under suspicion."

"No, keep the appointment. She'll know something is wrong if you don't. Just be careful."

"I'll try to be," Hetty said.

"Before you meet with her, can you go to the bookshop and check in with Sy? If he's there, tell him I'm headed to Fool's Moon."

Although it was a little strange to not start her day with funeral home business, Hetty had to admit it was a relief to have a morning without having to worry about clients—or the lack thereof.

Hetty rode her bicycle over to the bookshop. Along the way, she hoped to cross paths with Sy on his way to Juniper Street, but she arrived at the shop without seeing him.

Leaving her bicycle outside, she headed into the shop, and found Sy in the middle of arguing with Rosie over a stack of books.

The siblings were shouting at each other at such a volume that neither noticed Hetty until she cleared her throat.

"I see you're busy," she said.

"Hardly." Sy glared at his little sister. "This one is making a mess of my shop!"

"It was already a mess, with all the new books you ordered coming in on top of all the old books we still have to sort," Rosie declared. "I was trying to make things better."

"All you're doing is creating chaos!"

"What's with all this?" Hetty pointed at one of the open boxes. As expected, inside was a jumble of books, but they had weathered covers and split spines.

"Books we can't sell. They're from a private collection," Sy said, fixing his sister with another glare. "I only took them on because I got them sight unseen. I can't return them, either—I got them from Mr. Duval."

Hetty stopped reaching for the closest book. "Duval? Which one?"

"Valentine," Sy said, with little concern. "When Rosie graduated, we got to talking after the commencement. I told him I was looking for work and he told me he needed someone to run this shop."

So that was how Sy got the job at this shop.

"I forgot you were at Olmstead," Hetty said to Rosie. "You knew Valentine Duval? What about his father?"

Rosie nodded. "A bit. Mr. Raimond taught alchemistry, which

I didn't need to graduate, so I never had a class with him. But Mr. Valentine taught the mathematics course, which was my favorite class. He was always very good at allowing me to make up the exams I missed when I was sick. I paid him a visit recently. I'd been helping him try to solve the Clarke Cipher."

"Isn't it the other way around?" Sy grumbled.

"How recent was your visit?" Hetty asked. Because there was no easy way to say it, Hetty added rather bluntly, "I'm sorry to have to tell you this, but Valentine Duval is dead."

Rosie didn't sway, but it was a near thing as the shock settled on her. Her brother came over, swinging an arm around her shoulder, squeezing slightly.

"Dead?" Rosie asked. "How? When? We just saw him!"

"He came around to talk business and brought his father's books over," Sy added.

"He was so very sad about it," Rosie said.

"—a great deal of books, but he looked well—"

"—so very sad, we were going to meet later—"

"—we talked about—"

Quickly the siblings were talking over each other. At first Hetty could follow, but soon enough their voices ran into each other's and not a word could be pulled out of the tangle.

Eventually Hetty clapped her hands. "Quiet!"

The siblings stopped talking.

"You visited Valentine Duval about the cipher?" Hetty asked Rosie.

"He hadn't solved it. But he was working very hard. He was happy to have help, said it was more difficult than he had thought at first."

Hetty turned to Sy. "All these books belonged to Raimond Duval?"

"Yes, but we don't have the space to keep them," Rosie added. "Do you want them?"

"I'll have to take a look." Then, remembering why she had come here in the first place, she added, "You should ask Benjy what he thinks when you meet him at Fool's Moon."

Embarrassment flooded Sy's face. "I forgot all about meeting him. I'll head out right away!"

"Don't forget to bring that box back to Clarabelle! She won't let you get the wagon again if you don't," Rosie called as her brother ran out.

Sy spun on his heel, smoothly turning without losing his stride.

He disappeared into the tiny apartment, leaving Hetty and Rosie alone in the shop.

"I think my brother agrees to things before realizing how much work it might involve," Rosie grumbled. "It's mostly why I'm helping him. He needs me."

Hetty pointed to the box before her. "Are these all the books Valentine brought?"

"That's just a few of them. I stuck the rest on a bookshelf in the back."

"There's that many? I suppose it wouldn't hurt to take a look."

If the main shop was a mess, the back room was even more so, where instead of empty shelves, crates of books were everywhere, like great stacked piles of coins. The arrangement made it something like a hedge maze, though Hetty needed no ball of yarn to make her way through. It was a straight path to a far wall with a bookcase crammed between towers of boxes. Even more boxes were under the table next to it. On the table was a small printing press, rust spotting its frame, that looked to be just the right size to print small books or pamphlets.

Hetty ran her fingers along the spines of the books on the shelf. They had a well-loved quality to them with their cracked spines and peeling titles. As she stood before them, there was a peculiar smell, something perfumy that was familiar, but the name wouldn't come to her lips.

More importantly, no magic stirred no matter what book she touched. Not even when she pulled a book off the shelf.

How disappointing.

Hearing that Valentine had brought these books here with such haste, she'd thought it might have been for safekeeping. That someone wanted his father's books and he'd needed to hide them. But if no magic was present in them, perhaps she was wrong. Maybe Valentine simply brought the books here to get rid of them.

While most of the books had their titles printed on the spine, Hetty noticed one did not. She pulled it down off the shelf and opened it. Inside she was pleasantly surprised to see the hand-written lines:

Some Thoughts on Celestial Magics and Its Uses
by Raimond C. Duval

That was enough to encourage her to start reading. She knew no one who studied Celestial magic. Not like this. It was clear, even from the first few pages, that Raimond approached the history, the rise, and the practice in a way Hetty had never seen before. When Hetty thought of studying magic, she pictured trying out spells with Benjy. Dazzling her friends with the different sigils she used for spells, and carefully weaving star sigils into her stitches. She never thought too hard about what she was doing.

The last few pages talked about the applications of magic, and how music and magic in harmony became what he termed "the unknowable knowns of Celestial magic."

She smiled, thinking of last night at the Fool's Moon. Maybe it wasn't too unknowable after all.

A door creaked open.

Hetty looked up, expecting to see Rosie, who would be perhaps wondering if Hetty had gotten lost in the maze of books. But the door opening was the door that led outside.

And the person stepping into the back room was a stranger.

Hetty tapped the band at her neck, drawing on an invisibility spell, just as the woman shut the door behind her.

Her face was too angular to be called pretty, and it was a tad stern. Her russet-brown dress was too plain to tell Hetty who made it, but it was good quality, with a very practical tailored cut that allowed an ease of movement.

The stranger looked around the room, and walked toward the bookshelf, not seeming to notice Hetty at all.

Still gripping the book on magical theory, Hetty watched as the woman pulled and pushed aside books along the shelf. Thieves were always interesting people, Hetty found, because what they targeted spoke about their priorities.

In this case it was how the woman searched the bookshelf, desperately and frantically. She searched from top to bottom, moving and shifting books around. She even bent down to the bottom shelf and touched the tightly packed books there.

"Where is it?" the woman whispered. "Is it up there, down here . . . or in your hands?"

She stood up then, pointing a pistol at Hetty.

The woman stood in a relaxed stance, her finger resting on the trigger, and her eyes locked on Hetty.

The woman wouldn't shoot. Not yet.

This was a warning.

The only warning Hetty was likely to get.

Hetty eyed the weapon and its owner.

"Don't do anything foolish," Hetty advised.

"Foolish?" The woman's hand shifted on the pistol, but her eyes never moved from Hetty. "Like what, shoot you?"

"Attempt to."

Hetty snapped her fingers.

Like a tree with roosting crows stirred awake, the books on the shelf launched themselves at the imprudent woman.

The gun fired.

It missed Hetty by a wide margin, striking the ceiling.

Hetty didn't waste a moment more. She elbowed the woman and knocked her into the wall.

The pistol fell to the ground. Hetty kicked it out of the way.

The stranger hissed and drew Canis Minor along the nearest crate. The simple spell exploded in Hetty's face, more of an idea than a tightly woven spell, but it did the trick.

Hetty jumped out of the way and the stranger slipped past her.

"Hetty!" Rosie's voice sailed over the crates. "Are you okay?"

"I'm fine," Hetty called as she drew the Leo star sigil in the air next to her. "There's a thief in here!"

Hetty launched the star-speckled lion at the stranger, but the woman lunged out of the way just in time. The spell charged through the towering crates. They swayed, but didn't fall.

Using that moment of distraction, the woman darted toward Hetty, wildly grabbing for the book in her hand.

Without time for magic, Hetty switched tactics. She yanked one of her hairpins out and jammed it into the woman's arm.

The stranger didn't howl or yell. She grunted and swung out her leg, hooking her foot around Hetty's. A sharp tug knocked Hetty off-balance, but she didn't fall. Landing on her other foot, Hetty spun around and kicked the stranger in the chest. The kick wasn't a powerful blow, but it knocked the woman back far enough.

"You're a very bad thief, you know?" Hetty said, bracing for another attack.

The woman smirked. "Only because I didn't expect *the Sparrow* to be here."

Before Hetty could react, a potion bottle flew over the crates.

It crashed onto the floor between them. Recognizing the potion in question, Hetty twirled her fingers around, drawing up a simple wind spell to send the resulting fumes flowing at the woman instead.

But Hetty underestimated the stranger.

The crates rattled suddenly as the woman, impossibly, jumped up on top of them. With a handkerchief placed over her face, she ran along the top, sending books flying as she headed for the back door. Once she got close, the stranger jumped off, kicking the door off its hinges on her way out.

Hetty followed, but came to a sliding halt as a lash of magic sparked in the air to her side. Hetty jumped, half spinning to get out of the way.

"Watch it!" Hetty yelled. "You almost hit me!"

Sy stopped in the narrow corridor, and Rosie bumped into his back.

"Sorry!" Sy sputtered as his sister peered around him.

"It's okay." Hetty sprang for the door.

The thief was long gone now, with only a scattering of trash showing the aftermath of her departure. "I should have stopped her when I had the chance. But I wanted to see what she was here to steal." Hetty turned to Sy. "The thief went directly to the bookshelf. Have you made a list of the books?"

Sy shook his head. "No, not yet."

"Make it. Or better yet, bring them all to Juniper Street. This thief came here for a reason, and it must be in one of these books!"

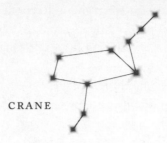

CRANE

23

ONCE AGAIN ON HER BICYCLE, Hetty headed for Elmhurst Cemetery. As the morning grew old, the streets became crowded with people, and she bobbed and weaved to avoid them all. Most people ignored her, but there were some grumbles from those who took offense at the close passing of a bicycle. One little girl, though, clutching her mother's hand, stared openly as Hetty rolled past her. Hetty waved and the girl waved back before her mother pulled her along.

Before long, Hetty caught sight of the cemetery gates and went around to find a tree to leave her bicycle against. As she was hiding it with a spell, she heard the door to the caretaker's cottage open. She tensed, readying herself for a possible argument.

Hetty did not get along well with the current caretaker, as they'd met in the worst way possible—due to the discovery of his murdered brother. Thankfully the person who stepped out of the cottage instead was Gabe Lewis.

Although he was a nephew to both Rosie and Sy, he was practically another sibling, as he was several years older than Rosie and a year younger than Sy. Though his mother and stepfather owned a shoe shop, Gabe had been too restless to work on shoes and had taken on a number of odd jobs. Hospital porter was one of them, and a worker at Elmhurst was another.

"Miz Hetty, shouldn't you be around back?" Gabe asked.

"Is there a funeral going on?"

Gabe nodded. "Pastor Evans is here, but not officiating. Thought you'd be there as support."

This must be the funeral for Jay's friend that recently died, Hetty surmised, and said as much to Gabe.

"So if you're not here for the funeral, what brings you here to-day?" Gabe asked.

"A different funeral. The one we're putting on on Monday."

"You are?"

Hetty clicked her tongue. "Don't sound so surprised, Gabriel Lewis! We've gotten work before."

"But not recently. Thought you got out of the business. Aunt Clarabelle and Auntie Jo both think you should. The uncles got a bet going on when you'll quit. And Granny Caldwell said it's better to start a business after you have children."

"Well." Hetty blinked, not sure what part she should take of-fense to first, and decided there was no need to play favorites. "Let them all know we're doing Valentine Duval's funeral, and it's going to outshine what Brown's Funeral Parlor ever did!"

"Won't be too hard. Brown's been busy lately, and I do say they'd probably love to give you some of their business." The young man rubbed his shoulder. "We've been having a lot of ser-vices due to all the fires. I don't mind the work, but I wouldn't mind if things slowed down some."

"Something will be done about the fires soon," Hetty prom-ised.

"I sure hope so."

Hetty walked out to the cemetery grounds. The morning sun beat against her skin, making her wish for a gentle breeze. From a distance she saw the funeral in the works. A sizable cluster of people were in attendance, though she was too far away to truly tell which was Jay.

Easier to discern at this distance was Adelaide Duval, standing in front of her father's grave.

The older woman had traded her artist's smock for a gray dress so dark that it looked black. The color aged her as much as her grief, and the silver in her hair appeared much more prominent than it had been in their previous encounters.

Hetty approached her. The headstone was a simple one, with Raimond's name carved on it and below: DEVOTED FATHER, TRUSTED FRIEND, AND TEACHER TO ALL.

"We were here the other day when this was installed," Adelaide said to Hetty. "My brother and I. He stood where you did, and reminded me it was nearly two years since I last saw Father, and that I chose to stay away and not visit even when I had the means. That all my letters meant nothing. I said hurtful things to my brother and we parted in anger. That's the worst thing about the dead. You apologize afterward, but you'll never know if they truly hear you." Adelaide's eyes were dry as she turned to an undeveloped corner of the cemetery. "My father bought us lots here. He loved Philadelphia, said it was home in a way New Orleans never was to him." She said "New Orleans" the way they did it down there, with a sweet tang and a gentle roughness of a city that knew it was one of a kind. "This was my home too. No matter how far or how long I went away, I always came back. It's not the best city I lived in. Over in Europe I could forget every limit that defined me in the past and become whoever I wished to be. But I always felt like a visitor there. The ball Bernice Tanner and my father worked on was my idea. I wrote to him last winter, joking I'd only visit if there was an event showcasing my statues. But he wrote back saying he was going to make arrangements. I envisioned him making a deal with a museum to temporarily allow us to take up space. Instead I find that the space is a hall owned by a friend of his, and that I could have a permanent exhibit there on display. This city never fails to surprise me."

"I can agree with that," Hetty said.

Adelaide turned over her hand, and the Dove star sigil flashed in the air for a brief moment.

"I realized I forgot about Valentine's suit." A satchel that lay on the ground lifted into the air. Absently, Adelaide brushed the dirt away before handing it to Hetty. "This is what he'll need to wear. I'm not sure if it's a proper suit, but it will have to do, since my brother's house burned down."

Long practice at hearing such remarkable things kept the surprise out of her face as Hetty gripped the satchel by its strap. She had hoped to visit Valentine's home again, and now it seemed she had missed that chance. "It burned down? How terrible!"

"But not surprising. I assumed his neighbors did it because they thought his house cursed. I certainly did when I came upon it with him. As much as he claimed it was his spells that protected the place, I had my doubts. But with him gone . . ."

"His magic is no longer active."

"Precisely." Adelaide nodded. "Now I have nothing of him, and worse, his last prank on our cousin will not be as effective as we'd have liked."

"Prank?"

"Oh, yes." Adelaide's dour features turned cheerful for a moment. "Horace has been asking about Father's will for ages, so Valentine put together these stones that he claimed would tell who the true heir of the family was. He explained the magic involved, even got me to carve a few small pieces—" She shook her head. "The prank won't work now."

"Why would you pull a trick on your cousin?" Hetty asked.

"Pardon?"

Hetty chose her next words carefully. "I remember seeing him. I thought you were close."

"Oh no!" Adelaide exclaimed. "Horace is the only son of my father's brothers that survived the war. He accomplished that mostly because he was in England, up to no good. He stayed a bit in Philadelphia in between his travels. Although never for a long period. I can't say we're close, but we know him better than the rest. But that just means he has the greatest claim on my father's house. The Duvals are old-fashioned. They determine family by blood. In their eyes, because my brother and I were adopted, we don't count."

The longer Hetty stood there, the less certain she became that Adelaide was the murderer. Nothing she told Hetty spoke of a strong motive. The deaths of father and brother were both severe losses to her. In fact, the only advantage Adelaide might have gotten would have occurred if her *cousin* had died instead. But even then, it would be a small change at best.

"I wouldn't worry about your other relatives. Sometimes family chooses you, other times you choose family. It might even be better to be lonely than to surround yourself with people who have no love for you."

"Make no mistake, my dear," Adelaide remarked. "I claim none of those people as family. Neither did my brother, although he was more forgiving. I won't have them at the funeral. Can you and your husband bar them from entering? You have my permission to use any means necessary."

"With ease and pleasure," Hetty replied gleefully, because there was nothing she loved more in this world than to make the lives of snobs just the tiniest bit inconvenienced.

"I cannot offer more than your fees, but maybe I could make a statue with you as a model?"

"That's completely unnecessary," Hetty replied.

"It is. You have a very interesting face. But I like to get permission from people I plan on seeing again. I won't give you the statue, but you can have the miniature I'll make."

As Hetty was protesting both the statue and the compliment, she realized someone had stepped up to join them.

"Miss Duval," Jay said rather coolly. "I see you have met Mrs. Rhodes."

If Hetty had any doubts Cora hadn't told Jay about the events of the previous night, they were squashed with his words just then. Jay always addressed her with great warmth and familiarity. None of this was evident in his words this morning, as he spoke as if he only knew her in passing.

"This is not the first time we met," Adelaide said, unaware of the turmoil before her. "We spoke before about my brother's funeral, and she will be very helpful for what needs to be done, much more than Brown's. They are quite old-fashioned and I'm looking for a more personal touch."

"I hope things go well for you," Jay said stiffly. "If you need to talk, either as a pastor or a friend, I am here for you. Your father was a dear friend of mine, after all."

"I appreciate that. In fact, can I take up that offer right now?" Adelaide said. "My heart is heavy this morning."

"Then I shall be the one to leave you," Hetty said quickly. "Send any further instructions to my home directly."

Without a word more, she left, pretending she wasn't fleeing or dabbing at the tears that prickled her eyes.

Hetty rode back to Juniper Street as if carried by winds. But no matter how quickly she rode her bike, she couldn't escape the dual regrets she had from her recent encounters with Cora and Jay, and the slight fear that she had ruined things with them beyond repair.

Back home, lost in her thoughts, she rolled the bicycle back through the yard, only to see Oliver sitting in the long shadow that appeared next to the shack.

Over his clothes he wore the heavy apron he used while embalming, with his gloves resting on his knees. He leaned back, smoking a pipe, staring up at the back of the house, or perhaps it was the sky. But the former was more likely. Oliver was not a cloud gazer.

Hetty sat down on the grass next to him, placing the satchel in her lap, and only then did he appear to have noticed her.

Oliver turned his head toward her, his eyes flicking to the bag she carried. "What do you got there?"

"A dead man's clothes."

"Belonging to the one in your cellar?"

Hetty nodded.

"Good, I was wondering if he was going to go into the ground as he came into the world."

"Find anything interesting?" Hetty asked.

"Nothing so far. I'm waiting for the results of the poison test to come back." Oliver made a face as he added, "Your husband says to meet him at Olmstead."

Hetty scoffed. "Oh, he's being funny! I told him to meet me there earlier. He must have changed his mind about it being a bad idea!"

"Well, I don't find it funny at all. I don't work for the Western Union."

"If you're going to work here, you might as well learn to take messages."

"I'm not your assistant, either. I'll pretend as needed, but this is not a fact. I work when you need my help, or when I want to make sure you're not in deep trouble."

"Or when you want a favor?" Hetty asked.

Oliver's lack of surprise confirmed he knew he was being transparent. He tapped his pipe against his knee, scattering ash about.

"I'm worried about Thomas. He doesn't deal in magical items as a rule. But all this stuff going on has me worried that he's about to be caught up in more trouble than any of us can handle."

"Then tell him to find something new," Hetty said. "He's never settled on anything for long before."

"This is different. He believes that ordering select goods from a catalog and having it delivered to your home instead of going to a store is a revolutionary idea that will change life as we know it. This isn't a barbershop."

"That's when you convince him it's a poor idea. You turn on the charm, and flattery, and ..." Hetty started laughing mid-sentence, mostly from the idea, and the rest from Oliver's scornful expression. "Oh, I'm sorry, I just can't see it."

"I'm perfectly charming!" Oliver protested.

"In whose opinion?"

Oliver smiled. "The only one that matters."

That was a statement Hetty could not argue with. She playfully patted his shoulder, letting his word be the last on the subject. "Well, I'm off to see my own husband, whose opinion on certain matters I need to learn. I leave this with you." She dropped the satchel at his feet. "And don't smoke around the shack. Benjy hasn't started using it yet, but someday something might go boom in there."

SCORPIO

24

Olmstead secondary was not a place Hetty had visited before, despite hearing so much about it. Unlike other schools that started in a basement, Olmstead always owned its building and enjoyed healthy donations and patronage since its opening.

In the foyer, an abundance of sunlight streamed in through the window. It was a very plain space. The walls held no decorations save a small portrait of the school's namesake, James Olmstead, a double agent during the Revolutionary War, whose talent with Celestial magic made it easy to obscure messages from the British army.

Next to the principal's office, a woman sat at a desk. By the twisting of her mouth, she looked ready to set the typewriter in front of her on fire. Having used a typewriter herself, Hetty sympathized. These newfangled machines were just so difficult.

"May I help you?" the poor woman asked, clearly eager to have a distraction.

"What classes are in session? I'm looking to meet with one of the students."

The interest in the woman's face faded right away. "Literature and alchemistry should almost be over. Literature to the left, alchemistry opposite."

Hetty didn't need much more direction than that. For while each door had nothing to mark it as different from the others, only one had George Needham standing outside of it, his foot tapping against the floorboards as he peered through the open doorway.

Inside the classroom, Benjy explained the alchemy that would be used in a steam propulsion system for a streetcar, and related alchemical concepts. He rattled off the terms as he drew along the board, with confidence and complete obliviousness to the students staring up at him from their desks. Benjy, flushed with the excitement of explaining the alchemistry at work, commanded their attention easily, his intensity spilling freely throughout the room.

Hetty wasn't surprised to see many entranced faces. She would be among them if George weren't quietly seething next to her as he watched.

Darlene's husband was far from Hetty's favorite person. He was a stubborn mule of a man with a mouth that always managed to say the wrong thing, and half the time Hetty spoke with him, they argued. But George had a kind heart, best seen in the way he rearranged his life so Darlene could paint without worries. So Hetty tolerated him, although sometimes he wasn't the easiest person to abide.

"I see your husband has come to take my job," George bristled.

"He doesn't want a teaching post."

"Are you sure?" George jabbed a hand at the room. Benjy had stopped the lecture long enough to take questions. There were several hands raised, all with enthusiastic faces. "He seems to be enjoying this an awful lot."

"He likes people paying attention to his words."

George pulled the door shut. "I hesitate for a single moment on a tough question, and there he is with all the answers."

"Why are you so upset? Alchemistry was never one of your favorite subjects."

"Math would be my favorite subject if it got me the post." George sighed.

"Why did you take it then?" Hetty asked, carefully neutral.

He gave her an odd look. "Raimond Duval died, and suddenly there was a spot to fill. And it looks like it's a good thing that I took the job in the first place."

"Darlene told you about Valentine's death?"

"Of course she did. We talk about everything. She didn't mention you would be coming here too, but with both of you here, I think I can guess why." He gave her a smug grin. "You need my help!"

"Don't make me jab you with a hairpin."

"I'm right, aren't I?"

"You are," Hetty reluctantly admitted. "You've been here for the past few weeks. Have you seen anything that could be related to either Raimond's or his son's death?"

"Certainly not. But there are a few things Raimond left in his desk you might find interesting."

George took her into a large room that served as the office for the teachers. Luckily, there was no one else besides them in the room. One bookshelf crammed with books lined the room, and a narrow window let in a surprising amount of light. Six desks were squeezed into the room, and Hetty knew all the teachers didn't regularly go about in skirts, for she had a bit of a struggle as she walked between them to meet George in the back corner of the room.

George opened a drawer and took out a worn leather-bound book. Without a word, he handed it over to Hetty. Raimond's journal, Hetty realized as she flipped through the pages.

"Why is this still here?"

George shrugged. "No one wanted to touch anything. His son was supposed to come around, but he never found the time."

"But isn't this your desk? Why are things still in here as if it was Raimond rather than his son who died yesterday?"

George's shoulders sagged. "I saw no reason to make the effort. I don't think I'll be here for the new school year. Things have not been good, even without me having such big shoes to fill."

"What will you do, then? Start your own school again?"

"I don't think I could. I couldn't keep it up the first time. To be frank, it was only floating along because I was getting money from Charlie and Clarence."

He said the names a bit awkwardly. As he should, given that Charlie was dead and that it was Clarence who had done the deed and attempted to do worse to Hetty and Benjy back in May. These days Charlie and Clarence were ghosts. None of Hetty's friends spoke about them anymore, except for George. While everyone else treated it as a delicate matter, he wasn't afraid to mention the names of their lost friends and he generally refused to pretend the incident hadn't occurred.

Hetty appreciated that even when it was the last thing she wanted to hear.

"Then you made changes for the best. Darlene is happier these days," Hetty said crisply.

"And I'm happy that she is happy," George replied.

"Does Valentine Duval have a desk here?"

"No, someone took it over a while back. He hasn't taught classes since last term. Nothing of his is here."

Hetty reached into a drawer in Raimond's desk and pulled out several flat disks. Checker pieces, she realized as she ran her finger along them. She dug around a bit more and pulled out a small bag, which she upended onto the desk.

Red and black checker pieces rolled in every direction. As she separated them by color, she picked each one up and very gently tapped it against the table.

"What did you expect to happen? That they'll glow or something?" George asked.

"It doesn't hurt to check." Hetty finished her sorting. A few pieces were missing. Two red and one black.

"I thought you were supposed to be looking for clues, not playing with game pieces."

"I can't do either of those if you keep bothering me," Hetty said without looking up.

"No need to be rude."

"No more than you." Hetty dropped the checkers back into the bag and picked up the journal. "I'm taking these."

"What do you think is in there," George scoffed, "some idea that got him killed?"

"Ideas don't kill. At least not with such power," Benjy called from the doorway. He smiled at them, although George grunted as he turned away.

"I could tell you ten different ways you're wrong," Hetty countered, "but I think that'll just start you lecturing again."

"That was not a lecture. Just a conversation. Those students are rather bright, with ideas for improvements. Flawed, mostly, but in the right direction."

Holding himself stiffly, George said, "You can have further conversations with them if you like. The class meets three days a week."

Benjy blinked. "I didn't mean to interrupt the class. I've just been thinking about this topic for some time, and there was a chalkboard in there."

George covered his face with his hands, groaning as he sank into a chair. "Stars save me! How are you content with your life? You could go much further than where you are!"

"And go where? I'm exactly where I want to be. I don't want

your job, Needham," Benjy said. "You're not in danger of losing it. Those students wouldn't be able to ask as many questions as they did without you teaching them."

"Raimond Duval had them first."

"Yet they're still here," Benjy observed quietly. "And they're waiting for you to return."

With a jaunty step and improved spirits, George went back to his classroom, leaving Hetty and Benjy to finish their searching without further interruptions.

"Did you ask the students questions or just lecture them about your theories?" Hetty asked.

"I did both. But they told me nothing of interest about either Duval." Left unsaid was a comment about his questioning being a waste of time, which Hetty was grateful for.

"Did Sy finally show up?" she asked.

"He did. Everything went as well as could be expected given the circumstances. The Magnolias wanted to keep it quiet."

"Did Cora tell you that?"

"She wasn't there. You should go talk to her."

"I don't think she has anything to say to me." Hetty tapped the desk, a bit of the despair that had driven her to spar with the punching bag returning. "I saw Jay at Elmhurst, and he was cool toward me. Cora must have told him what I said last night."

"Hetty." Benjy placed his hands on her shoulders, so she had no choice but to look at him. "There is nothing you can say that neither of them won't forgive."

"You didn't hear what I told her."

"Doesn't matter." He looked at her again, and frowned. "Who did you fight?"

"No one." Hetty fought the urge to touch her face, afraid some scratch or bruise was there, although she didn't remember taking any hits.

Would Sy have said anything to Benjy about the thief? Sy's

loyalties were skewed in Benjy's favor, but at the same time, he knew better than to stoke Hetty's wrath.

"Something happened at the bookshop?" Benjy pressed on, a hair away from asking a question Hetty would need a gentle lie for.

"Did you know that Valentine Duval gave Sy the bookshop?" Hetty blurted out.

The distraction worked. "No, I didn't. Is this important?"

"Very much so!" Hetty said, with a bit more enthusiasm than what was warranted. "Valentine brought over his father's books. I encountered a thief when I was looking at them."

"Someone else was after the books too. Hmm," Benjy said. "What could be so interesting about them?"

"We'll find out soon enough. Sy and Rosie said they'll bring the books over later. But for now, I got Raimond's journal right here. It was in the desk." Hetty held it out.

Benjy took the journal from her. "How do you feel about re-counting Raimond Duval's last day?"

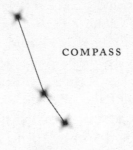

COMPASS

25

RECOUNTING A VICTIM'S LAST STEPS was typically largely guesswork, even when you were doing so within days of their death. Even then, it wasn't always particularly useful.

"It's like making tea after the water has cooled," Hetty complained to Benjy as they stood on the corner of the street that led to the Duval home. "There's too little to follow."

"It all flows backwards in the end." He paused, giving her one of those particular looks when he thought he was being funny. "You can always go home without me."

"If that was the case, I wouldn't be here in the first place." Hetty hooked her arm through his. "Lead on!"

They headed west as Benjy flipped through the journal. "According to his last entry, Duval left his home bright and early the day he died. He dropped by his usual spot to get coffee. Collected a newspaper and noted with amusement the day's letters in the Miss Carole column. Then he went to Olmstead. He doesn't mention the classes by name, but we have his schedule. Three alchemistry classes, plus one at an advanced level. There was a test that day he surprised students with. He also writes about preparing to have a conversation with a student about a project. The entry ends with him going to the meeting. We know from other accounts he talked with this student for some time. You remember the one. We spoke to him after the funeral."

The funeral had been a bit chaotic. People from all walks of life had come to mourn the beloved teacher. Hetty remembered it had been by sheer luck that she and Benjy had even been able to find the last student Raimond spoke with the day he died.

"He said Raimond went down this street."

"Which wasn't in the papers," Benjy said.

"Neither were a number of things," Hetty reminded him. "The things we found out, what wasn't deemed important, and what we don't know."

"The last of which is the largest," Benjy replied, although his soft murmur did not seem meant for her ears.

"From here to where he was found on Powell Street is quite a distance," Hetty said. "There's nothing that tells us he did anything more than take a long walk."

"There's a dozen reasons that could explain that, starting with he ran there on foot to he was placed there."

"And the other ten?"

"Involve magic." Benjy ran his fingers against the wall, drawing the star sigil Pyxis, the mariner's compass.

The spell glowed silver against the brick, and the needle spun around, seeking north.

"There won't be enough magic traces to point the way," Hetty scoffed. "You've tried this trick before, and it never works!"

"Never works the way I want it to," he corrected.

"Too much time has passed. Too much magic has been cast about since then. Plus, you don't even know if magic was used in the first place."

"There was magic residue near where he was found. Some of it had to come off his body."

"That's speculation," Hetty said. "And it's quite unlike you to suggest something so far-fetched that—"

The needle inside the compass sigil stopped, pointing to the east. The stars that made it glowed even brighter until a ball of light shot from it. It sped down the street, leaving in its wake a path of starlight.

"Not a word." Hetty waggled her finger at Benjy, who smirked at her. "Not a single one!"

They ran after it. The pulse of magic darted along the street, disappearing like ice in the summer sun.

Down the streets they went, pushing past pedestrians and carts as they chased after the spell, which kept increasing in speed. Benjy had clearly messed up the spell, because even if Raimond Duval had been chased by the murderer there was no way he—

Benjy stopped suddenly in the middle of the street. Hetty ended up spinning on the ball of her foot to avoid colliding with him. As she regained her balance, she demanded, "Why did you stop? We're losing it!"

"We know where it leads. But we just found something else that's even more important."

"What?" Hetty asked, but as she turned to look in the direction he faced, the scowl on her face went away.

Across the street was the old boardinghouse they used to call home. It had hardly been a few months since they had moved away, yet it looked very different to her eyes. Older, and more worn down. It hadn't exactly been the finest accommodations while they'd been living there, but Hetty supposed she'd gotten used to it over time, so much that now it was shocking to think she'd ever tolerated it in the first place.

"I think I know why the pastor is upset with us," Benjy said softly. "Raimond told him about a problem, and Jay told him to go see us, but forgot to mention our change of address. Raimond came here and couldn't find us."

The night Raimond Duval died they had been at their new home on Juniper Street, having a rare night to themselves not occupied with their friends or murder. Hetty remembered being on the roof with her telescope, working on her star map. Benjy had sat out with her for a bit, and they talked about nothing in particular.

If Raimond Duval had come there that night instead of their old address, they would have seen him and certainly would have listened to what he had to say. Perhaps then his death might not have occurred.

"Powell Street isn't that far from here," Hetty reminded him, as if that detail could ease the guilt rising in her chest. "He could have been passing through. It's only a coincidence."

"Maybe," Benjy said, but he was only humoring her. "Let's see where the trace continues to go."

The magic they had followed was long gone now, but Benjy had clearly seen enough of it to know where to go next—something he proved when he started up the same spell once more, although with much less fanfare.

While it moved just as quickly as before, they didn't have to chase after it for long. After a few turns, the magic stopped.

But it didn't disappear.

Benjy's magic swirled along the wall, creating an outline of a doorway on a wall.

"That can't be," she murmured as Darlene's map fluttered into her thoughts. In her mind's eye, she traced the blue lines on the map that made up the confirmed tunnels, recalling the nearby street names. "But there's no tunnel here."

"That we know of." Benjy strode to the wall and kicked where the wall met the ground.

The slab of stone fell backwards, revealing the tunnel's entrance. With a quick flick of his fingers, Benjy summoned Canis Major. The star-speckled dog dashed forward, showing the way.

After being in so many tunnels recently, Hetty didn't find anything particularly special about this one. The walls were smooth.

The tunnel had been carefully dug with magic during its construction. This observation had a familiar ring to it . . . No, it was an echo of what Benjy had said before. He'd told her this very recently, when they were in the tunnel under—

"Barclay Street!" Hetty exclaimed. "We're under Barclay!"

As she turned to her husband, he grinned, as he must have known this from the start. "We're in the same tunnel of the first one we found, just on the other side of the collapsed portion," Benjy said with great relish. "Raimond Duval must have thought he could escape his murderer by going through here."

"To Valentine's house. It's just above us!" Hetty recalled.

"That's what he was doing down here. But his luck ran out." Benjy pointed out the signs of a struggle in the dirt before them. "Look. He tried to fight off his attacker. Duval was not just a scholar of magic. He was a skilled practitioner."

"And his murderer?"

"Must have been better."

Hetty frowned. "But why not leave him down here? Why take him to a building streets away and start a fire there?"

"His death was a warning."

"But to who?" Hetty asked.

She really shouldn't have asked the question. She knew what the answer would be. Even if she didn't want to admit it after staring it in the face. But like most things, it didn't feel real until Benjy put the words out into the air.

He seemed to know that, because he paused before speaking. "Us."

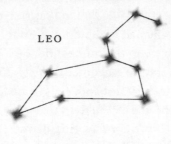

LEO

26

W<small>HILE HETTY COULD SEE</small> a number of connections coming out of the revelation that the deaths were staged as a message for them, she found fault with the crux of Benjy's argument.

"You told me earlier going to Olmstead was a waste of time," Hetty said as they approached the old boardinghouse. "This is a greater one. Six weeks have passed. We don't know if Raimond was seen by anyone other than his murderer, and even if that isn't true, people might not want to talk to us."

"I was wrong about Olmstead," Benjy countered. "And people will answer our questions."

"You don't sound confident," Hetty accused.

Her husband tapped his fingers against Raimond's journal. "Well, I'd probably have more luck without you with me."

Hetty fixed a rather stern glare at him that remained even when he hastily moved to correct himself. But before he could formulate an apology, a voice called out to them:

"I thought for a moment I was seeing ghosts! But here you are!" The careworn but friendly face of their old neighbor appeared behind them. Willa was in her maid's uniform, though it hung looser off her frame than it had when Hetty had seen her last, and there were dark circles under her eyes. But she was not faking her pleasure at seeing them. "What are you two doing back here?"

"Why else? Murder," Hetty said.

"No one's died recently."

"No, this was several weeks ago," Hetty clarified.

"An older man who might have come here looking for us," Benjy added.

"Who didn't know you moved!" Willa added slyly. "I think I know who you're talking about. A few people come looking for you every so often, but they usually scuttle off when someone pokes out their head and looks at them funny. But this man, he asked for you by name."

"Did you see him or hear about him?" Hetty asked. Of her old neighbors, Hetty trusted Willa the most to tell them the straight truth, but she still needed specifics. The difference in hearing gossip and seeing things with your eyes could alter a case drastically.

"I spoke to him," Willa said. "My baby was fussy, so I took her out so the older ones could do their schoolwork in peace. When I came back in, I saw the old man. He was knocking on your door, getting no answer. Then he saw me and asked about you. I told him you moved, but I didn't say where. I might have. He was a nice-looking old man. Worried, of course, but polite enough to me when we talked. Even when I pretended to not know where you'd moved to."

"Why didn't you tell him?" Hetty asked.

Willa shifted a bit, screwing up her face as she thought back to the day. "Well. There was this other man in the hall. Younger and lingering at the other end. I didn't know him. Wasn't anybody new in the building. The last people who moved in were the folks that got your old room. And this man, he didn't have a good look to him. He was staring our way and pretending he wasn't."

"Maybe he was a friend of the old man," Hetty suggested, just to see what Willa would say.

As Hetty hoped, Willa shook her head vigorously. "I doubt it. The old man left, and the other man didn't."

"He didn't follow the old man?"

"I can't remember exactly," Willa said. "My little one was making a fuss then. But I know he left. I'm sorry I can't tell you more."

"You've been more than helpful," Hetty assured her.

"What did the man look like?" Benjy asked suddenly. "The one that was watching?"

"I—" Willa started. She squinted, and a frown tugged on her features. "I don't remember. I can see his face, but I can't describe what it looks like!"

This was not the first time Hetty had heard this, and she glanced over at her husband, realizing right away why he'd asked this question.

The person who murdered Raimond Duval and quite likely his son was the same man who was selling stolen magical items!

Spells to hide a person's face were so unusual that no other conclusion made sense.

Hetty excitedly explained all this to Benjy on the long walk back to Juniper Street. "It's got to be the same person killed them both," she said. "I know it!"

"You're right." Benjy nodded. "I just want to know why Nathan Payne killed the Duvals."

"What!" Hetty's voice echoed in the mostly empty street. A window opened above their heads, but she barely heard an annoyed grumble before the window shut again. Barely heard it because she was reeling from Benjy's words. "What do you mean, *Nathan Payne* murdered them?" Hetty said in a measured whisper.

Her husband blinked, and then Benjy said the words she absolutely loathed to hear him utter: "Isn't it obvious?"

"To you it is!"

He had the grace to look chagrined. For this was not the first time he'd leapt to a conclusion without even telling her the way to get there first.

"Nathan Payne," Benjy said carefully, "is dealing with stolen magical objects, something we know for certain, between what you saw with Thomas the other night and what we found at that warehouse. He moves about in a few tunnels, gets the goods using people like Wise Sammy, and has the blessing of men like the alderman to sell his purloined goods. He uses a spell to make it hard for people to remember his face since his scar makes him so memorable."

"Which is how you linked this all together."

Benjy nodded. "This might be me forcing the connection, but the pieces fit well enough. Payne worked for One-Eyed Jack. And if he could work for a bounty hunter, it's not a long road from there to becoming a hired killer."

"I'm not going to say I dislike the idea," Hetty said. "But it doesn't change much. We still don't know who orchestrated all of this. And our list of suspects isn't very long. There's Adelaide, who is suspicious-looking on the outside for small things but without true motivation. Then there's Horace, who is after an inheritance and is easy to dislike because he's so loathsome. After that, there are no real suspects, just profiles of them. Ambitious teachers like George who might bump off his betters for a spot. A rogue member of Beatty Hose striking out on his own. A person who might have had a personal grievance with the Duvals, for their past work in the Vigilance Society, their present work with magic rights, and their future work they might offer the city. Do any of them strike you as someone who'd hire someone else to kill for them? And to do it in vastly different ways?"

"Not different," Benjy corrected softly. "The deaths weren't different."

"Raimond was found after a fire and Valentine in his bed."

"The *outcomes* were different, but they were designed to be taken at face value. These weren't hastily done crimes — they were meticulously planned. The work was just sloppy with Valentine."

"How was it sloppy?"

"The timing," Benjy said.

Which wasn't much of an answer, but it was hardly a poor answer. But she would have to ask what he meant later, because Darlene stood on their front steps.

"Oh, there you are. I was just about to leave." Darlene shifted her baby to her hip. "Is my mentor still a murder suspect? I can spy on her if you need me to."

"No need. You'd be looking for proof of her innocence. Which isn't helpful," Benjy said.

Hetty hastily interrupted, "Have you come for a visit? How long have you been here?"

"Long enough. I wanted to talk to you about something. Although I suspect I might have to wait a bit, since I was the last to arrive."

"Those are ominous words," Benjy remarked dryly. "Who else is here?"

"Oliver and Thomas are in the cellar," Darlene said. "Penelope is in the garden, and her cousins are in the study. They came in with boxes of books. I'd go talk to them first if I were you, because neither Sy nor Rosabelle was keen on telling me the truth."

"Don't know why, it's just books," Hetty said.

"Exactly," Darlene said mysteriously as she went inside.

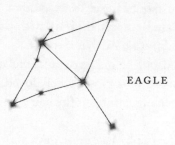

EAGLE

27

W‌HEN HETTY MADE HER way up to the study, she found several new boxes of books crowding the space. Sy was busy unpacking and stacking books on the bookshelf. Rosie, instead of helping, was sprawled out on their couch with a tidy pile of tomes at her elbow.

Benjy looked past Hetty's shoulder into the room and called loudly: "What are you doing?"

Sy startled and stumbled into the bookshelf, causing a few books to fall onto the floor. Rosie didn't move, though she lowered her book, as if suddenly afraid she'd done something wrong.

But Benjy wasn't glaring at either one of them. As he approached the crates, he favored them with a bemused smile. "I appreciate the bounty of books, but I like to know what they are before they go on my shelves. What did you bring?"

Sy swallowed, and his eyes darted to Hetty for a moment. "Didn't Hetty tell you? These are from Mr. Raimond's collection. All his books, papers, and journals, brought here for safekeeping."

"Probably the only place they'd be safe," Rosie piped up. "Since a thief was after them."

"A thief?" Benjy asked as he moved to his precious bookshelf.

"She tried to shoot Hetty!" Rosie added.

The stern glare Benjy fixed Hetty with was worse than she had imagined. "I did not know that part."

Hetty moved out of his gaze, and picked up a book at random. It was small and clearly well loved, as she could barely make out the peeling letters on the spine to read: *By the Archway's Light.*

"Are these the books Valentine gave you?" Hetty asked.

Sy nodded, just as eager to move on from the subject of thieves and pistols. "This is all of them. Plus a few other books we were given that looked too worn to sell."

"They'll have some value," Benjy said. "If not, there will be libraries that'll take them in. I'll help you check."

Realizing he meant to do so right then, Hetty quietly put the book back and slipped out of the room, not wanting to get ensnarled in this project.

Her first thought upon leaving was to go speak with Penelope in the garden, but the cellar door was open and Oliver's voice drifted up: "What would you do if they said no?"

"You know they won't," Thomas replied.

"But if they did, it'll be trouble you can't get out of."

"You wouldn't help me?"

Oliver sighed. "It depends."

Intrigued, Hetty headed down the stairs.

A light bobbed over Oliver's shoulder as he sewed up Valentine Duval. A cloth covered the dead man's face, with a larger sheet covering everything below the torso. The satchel that Adelaide had given Hetty sat on the nearby table. Hetty shook her head at the sight. Oliver had not taken the funeral suit out and hung it up. Everything would surely be dreadfully wrinkled by now.

Thomas sat on the stool next to the table, his back facing his partner. Which meant he saw Hetty first.

"There you are—I was hoping you'd be back soon!" Thomas said, a bit too eagerly.

"How long were you waiting?" Hetty asked.

"He got here an hour ago," Oliver said as he snipped the thread held taut in his hand. "And has been nothing but a distraction." He might have scowled at the back of Thomas's head, but it was a scowl with only a fraction of his usual temper.

Hetty looked down at the body, then up at Oliver. "What have you learned?"

Oliver pointed to an open notebook on the end of the table, where he kept all his observations. "The chalk and the residue on the body are a match, as expected. This poison kills gradually in small doses, quickly in large—which is what killed this man. I had Penelope look at it and she agrees with my assessment."

"The death was meant to look natural." Hetty peered down at the body again. With most of Valentine hidden under the sheet, it was easy to see only a puzzle and not a once vibrant, living man. "You examined him thoroughly? For bruising, wounds, and the like?" Hetty asked.

"I know how to do my job," Oliver said. "You keep me well trained. I even learned to jab a spike into a foot to make sure they're really dead."

"Did you?"

"Of course! Once you've had someone's eyes snap open and scream to make the stars fall when you cut into them, you never want that to happen again."

"Or hear that story again." Thomas winced.

"So, are we ready for the funeral then?" Hetty asked.

"I'm finishing with him as we speak. I only need to dress him and renew the preservation spells before the funeral on Monday. Will there be a wake?"

Hetty stared, stunned both by the efficiency of his words and the fact that an answer to such a simple question did not come to her lips right away.

This was the problem when clients were also murder suspects. Some questions got asked, others got forgotten.

"There is no wake," Hetty said finally. "At least, I don't know if there is."

Oliver looked over his glasses at her and Hetty found herself wanting to melt into the shadows. "You should find out. Sooner rather than later."

"I will."

Oliver griped, "Sometimes I'm not sure why I agreed to do this for you. Unpaid, by the way."

"Think of it as trading favors."

But as much as she thought the comment was in jest, the smile on Thomas's face vanished, and Oliver's frown deepened.

"Don't tell me," Hetty said when neither spoke, "you're helping because you want me to do something for you."

"I would like your help," Thomas said to his hands. "It's the only way I can save the Pony Post. But I don't think I can ask that of you. Things are much more complicated than I thought previously."

"How complicated?" Hetty asked.

"He's been accused of selling illegal goods." Each word out of Oliver's mouth was like a hammer driving down a nail. But behind the veneer, Hetty sensed great fear.

Earlier that day, Oliver said he worried about Thomas, and she hadn't thought much of it then, as it had been just a vague sentiment. But now she could see the stress not just in his face, but also in how little work he'd gotten done on Valentine Duval's body.

"Blackmail?" Hetty said.

"If being forced to tell lies about printing spellbooks and selling wands is blackmail, then yes," Thomas said.

Hetty rocked back on her heels as she connected with his words. "Did the alderman of the Fourth Ward threaten you? The one that works with Beatty Hose?"

Thomas nodded.

Hetty swore vividly and creatively.

"I'm pleased to see you so upset on my account," Thomas remarked. "I thought you disliked the Pony Post."

"I do, but *we're* the only ones that should be trying to force you to quit, not the alderman."

"I'm touched," Thomas said. Hetty had to look at him intently to know if he was joking or not, but no—he was completely serious. "Perhaps it was best I stop anyway," he continued. "When I was looking for a space to work from, I found a building that would make a great place for selling furniture. Imagine if I ran a company like that? I can hire carpenters and sell custom pieces."

Thomas went into great detail about both the place and his idea for a new business. Usually, this was the part where Hetty made a joke about him once again dropping one idea for a new one, but this time she refrained.

Thomas had bounced from one thing to the next in all the years Hetty had known him, and she always thought it was just him being drawn to the newer idea. But given how Oliver listened with patience, she wondered if she had only seen that because that's what she wanted to see: the flightiness of a person unable to make up his mind instead of how hard it was in this world to build and maintain a business for long.

Hetty left the cellar, choosing to go through the door that led directly to the yard. She stepped out expecting to see Penelope and Darlene sitting near the garden. Instead, all she found were a few crows poking around at a spot near the kitchen door.

A spot that didn't just smell like magic but reeked of it.

It was a curious sight, made alarming by the fact that Penelope, who had just been coming outside with a cauldron, suddenly backed into the kitchen, shut the door, and locked it.

Hetty snapped her fingers and the door jerked open at the slightest touch of her magic.

Penelope stood there half hiding behind the cauldron.

"Did you really think that was going to work?" Hetty asked.

Penelope attempted to grin. "I wasn't thinking clearly."

"That's obvious." She glanced around the kitchen, looking for what would have caused Penelope to react so. There were no cauldrons bubbling with Penelope's latest concoctions, nor plants scattered on the table. Darlene only sat there, somewhat stiffly, as she fed her baby.

Something about the scene was odd, and it wasn't Lorene attempting to grab the bottle from her mother. It took a moment, but eventually it clicked in Hetty's mind: Darlene was sitting in a chair, yet all six of the kitchen chairs Hetty owned remained unoccupied.

Without a word, Hetty drew a star sigil next to her and lifted the table into the air.

With the table floating above their heads, it was easy to see that instead of one of Hetty's chairs, Darlene sat on a wooden crate . . . the crate Hetty's sister had sent to Juniper Street.

"I told you it wasn't going to work." Darlene stood up and moved aside, throwing Penelope a distasteful look. Still holding on to her baby, Darlene pointed a foot at the crate. "Penelope wanted to hide this from you, and I don't understand why."

Hetty lowered her hand, bringing the table back to the floor. "Because I tried to give it to her and she refused to hear it."

"Well, she seems to have changed her mind." Darlene flicked a few spells into the air, and brought the crate on top of the table. "When I got here, she was messing with things in there. It all looks very interesting. I think I might start seriously working with brewed magic again. I want to make magical paint."

"Why?" Hetty asked.

Darlene pulled out a vial, giving it a look. "Why *not?*"

There was no real answer to that, so Hetty turned her attention back to Penelope. "Why did you hide the crate? I told you you could have it."

Penelope placed the cauldron onto the table and sighed. "I was trying to stabilize another one of the elemental pistols. Thought there might be an answer in the box since your sister also studied herbs. Well, what I tried didn't quite work, and I had to dump it outside. I was embarrassed. I'd made such a fuss about not taking the crate, and then I used the herbs anyway and just made a mess of things."

"That's what happens with magic," Hetty said. "You make mistakes. Over time you get good at hiding them. But if you want the crate, it's fine."

"But it's from your sister!"

"From her ghost," Hetty corrected. "I would have never gotten this box if she still lived. Having it here reminds me that she's gone."

"Oh, I bet that's just because it's in the crate," Darlene said. "Let's take it all out and scatter things into drawers and baskets."

Before Hetty could approve, Darlene did just that, pulling various items out and setting them on the table. Soon the surface was covered in little piles of items grouped together. Books and papers. Vials, both empty and full, seed packets, bundles of dried herbs. Candles, and pens, and inkwells. And some items that Hetty had previously missed entirely, like spools of thread, buttons, and a large jeweled butterfly brooch.

Lorene actually saw the butterfly first. The baby's tiny hands reached out for it, making cooing sounds, unaware of the despair blooming in Penelope's face.

"I suppose she and I were quite alike. I have one just like that." Penelope absently brushed a finger against the brooch. At her touch it split in half and a long thin needle emerged from its center, making it appear less like a butterfly and more like a bee.

"Or maybe not." Darlene pulled her daughter well out of range, just as Sleeping Beauty's mother should have done when faced with a spindle. "She is Hetty's sister, after all."

"Now what do you mean by that?" Hetty demanded.

"If that isn't poisonous," Darlene said quite reasonably, "then it does something worse."

With a twist of a spell, Hetty lifted the brooch into the air. Holding it aloft, Hetty noticed for the first time a tiny flask attached to the back of it connected to the needle. "I hate to say it, but I think you're right, Darlene," Hetty said. "Are there any other vials like this?"

Penelope picked up a tiny little vial that seemed to be a good fit. "These all look like they were used for— Sweet galloping stars! Do you know *anything* about your sister in her last years?"

"She was a healer," Hetty said.

"She must have been more than that." Penelope gulped as she turned the tiny vial around so they could see the label. "This is Cassandra plant!"

"Is it poisonous?" Darlene asked.

"Not at all." Although Hetty was speaking to Darlene, she watched Penelope grow more and more agitated as she looked at the tiny vials. "Penelope gave me a tin that I could slip into tea. It loosens the tongue and makes a person more willing to let secrets slip between their lips. It's harmless."

Penelope put the vials aside. "As a tea it's harmless. Not when it's injected into a person. I don't know the full effects, but it's not good."

"What's in the vial attached to the brooch?" Darlene asked.

Penelope reached for the brooch, but Hetty pulled it away.

Hetty had already seen the label on the back. While the liquid inside was dried up, she knew the name of the notorious poison would only send Penelope into hysterics.

"I can't believe I didn't go through this box," Hetty said brightly, determined to drag the conversation in a new direction. "I'm glad you made me. And you're right: I shouldn't give this away without taking a closer look. There's all sorts of interesting things in here."

"And this crate is something you shouldn't look through alone," Darlene said. "Especially given some of these unmarked bottles."

Of which there were quite a few. Dark, opaque bottles that were nothing but a mere curiosity until moments ago. More jewelry, too: not just brooches, but rings that had a hidden hollow cache, and hairpins with enviable sharpened points.

Penelope eyed them now, her anxieties clear across her face.

"You've given me poisons before," Hetty reminded her friend.

"Nothing like *this*." Penelope gulped. "And not in such clever ways. I feel like I'm looking at the works of a master. Here I am jumping from one thing to the next, like a rabbit. Making elemental pistols, exploding orbs, sleep-inducing lip paint, and bone-mending tonics . . . But your sister had a singular focus that brought a real eloquence to her work."

"Are you saying," Darlene remarked rather dryly, "that you're ashamed for not being a better poison maker?"

"I'm just supposed to be better!"

"You are—don't sell yourself short. Do you see any bone-mending salve in this box?" Hetty asked as she patted Penelope on the shoulder.

"Anyone can make a healing salve. You could too if you tried!" Penelope's words ended with great gulping sobs.

Darlene looked on, startled at the sight of it, but Hetty saw the ring that Penelope had picked up. The blue gemstone embedded in the center was glowing softly.

Carefully, Hetty reached over to uncurl Penelope's hand. A

strong wave of sadness washed over Hetty, unmoored by any particular moment, but it prickled her heart with a loss she could not name.

The gesture was not lost on Darlene. Genuine curiosity and interest withered away as Darlene clutched her baby even more protectively. "I think you might want to put this all back and read the journal your sister left you. It might tell you exactly what she left," she said.

"I think so too," Hetty said. She eyed the items again then, and instead of growing alarmed, Hetty grew excited at the possibilities. She tapped the hollow ring used perhaps to carry poison. "These would pair well with a few of my dresses."

"Are you going to show up to Bernice Tanner's ball with the butterfly brooch pinned to your chest?" Darlene asked.

"Not that one, it won't match. I'm wearing gold."

Darlene smirked. "That'll make you easy to find."

"Why do you say that? Wait, are you going to the ball too?"

Darlene nodded. "That's what I came to talk to you about. I got the invitation today. I thought it funny, because I remember you telling me you were going. But when I mentioned it to Thomas, he said he and Oliver were invited, and Penelope got an invitation too. It's all very odd, and I think Miss Tanner wanted to make sure you're there."

"She certainly does," Hetty muttered.

"Why so worried?" Penelope asked then. She dabbed at her tear-streaked face. She did so with a curious air as if she were surprised by the tears. "I know you don't like her, and you can refuse."

"I could," Hetty admitted. "But I hate to pass up an excuse to wear a pretty dress."

Just as she wanted, they both laughed at her words. But as a sign of how tense the contents of the crate had made them, they quickly moved on to talking about dresses and expectations for the ball.

They were debating who they might expect to see at the ball when Benjy entered the kitchen.

He made a quick study of the contents on the table and glanced at Hetty with mild confusion.

"Your sister had a brooch that you can poison someone with?" he asked.

Hetty ignored her friends, who were suppressing their giggles. "Yes, and a few other pieces that could maybe do worse," Hetty said.

"How interesting," Benjy said. "I could make you a better one that's not as obvious."

"I'm sure you can. Did you want me for something?"

"Actually, I'm here for Darlene," Benjy said. "Can you settle an argument about poetry? Once I admitted I have little interest in such things, I lost all ground with Rosie."

"That's your own fault, you know." Darlene stood up from the table and handed her baby over to him. She rubbed her shoulder absently as if gearing up for battle as she led the way out. "These young folk think they know everything!"

"Poetry?" Penelope asked once they were gone.

Hetty shrugged. "It's probably about the cipher Benjy's been working on."

Penelope blinked.

"It leads to buried treasure nearby."

"Ah, I heard a bit about that! Maybelle's son and a few of his friends went around digging. They weren't going to bother with the puzzle part."

"Isn't that dangerous? There are parts of the Delaware Valley where it isn't safe to show our faces."

"Which is why my uncle was very cross with them." Penelope rapped her fingers on the table. "But I don't think you're concerned about them running amuck looking for buried treasure."

"There's a loose connection to Valentine Duval's death," Hetty said with some hesitation. "Valentine was working feverishly on the cipher before he died. Poison was even dusted on the chalk he was using."

"Poison." Penelope sighed. "Some poisonous herbs have gone missing from the shop. They're not the most dangerous, but my employer was quite upset. She's afraid of it happening again with something more valuable."

"Not dangerous?" Hetty asked.

Penelope gave a wan smile. "It's all the same to her. Also my employer expects better from me. I expected better of myself too, because I know how often common herbs are stolen."

"It's not your fault. You were targeted by a man who has an elaborate scheme involving a number of magical items."

"Still, to think such poisons are out in the street. Dodgy potions are one thing, but this . . . I worry that Valentine Duval might not be the only victim."

"Poisons exist everywhere; it's only how they're used that matters."

"That's not making me feel any better."

"Maybe this will, then. I'm sorry that I forced this crate on you. I just wanted to get rid of it."

"I don't blame you for that."

"You know, after I showed it to you, I forget all about it. Granted, Jay did show up to tell us Valentine Duval was dead soon after. But I shouldn't have. It's odd, isn't it? I spent so many years with Esther in the forefront of my mind. So much I neglected everything else, but when I got a collection of all her things and memories, I could put it aside."

"I won't say it's a terrible thing," Penelope said very carefully. "You suffered a great loss, and how you recover from that loss is a path you must take alone. But know that if you want company for such a journey, you need only to ask."

That took a lot for Penelope to say. Penelope always came to Hetty's aid, and even her playful threat to poison Benjy if he ever hurt Hetty was sincere. But Penelope was afraid that she was only a replacement for the sister that Hetty had lost, not realizing that she was the sister that Hetty had found.

"I'd be careful with such promises." Hetty adopted a lofty tone. "You know firsthand that all my travels deal with the dead and stranger mysteries."

"Yes, quite strange, and some more avoidable than not." Penelope grew quiet as she studied the crate before them. "Does the offer still stand about staying here for a time?" Penelope asked, avoiding Hetty's eye.

"Why would you think I changed my mind? You know how stubborn I am."

"*Everyone* knows that," Thomas called as he swept into the kitchen.

"You don't even know what we're talking about," Hetty said.

"Whatever it is"—Thomas winked as he opened the pantry—"it's true for anything. Tell me I'm lying."

He wasn't, so Hetty remained quiet as Thomas gathered ingredients, opening cabinets and closing doors with the slightest twitch of his hand.

"Is it safe to cook in here?" he said as he got out an onion.

"I wasn't brewing any potions," Penelope said.

"I meant . . . Hetty didn't attempt to cook something?"

Hetty sniffed. "If you weren't about to make dinner, I would have some very nasty things to say."

"But would I deserve them?"

"Yes," Hetty said, even as she knew it wasn't true. There were many nights when they were busy with cases when they had a hot meal only because Thomas had made something, reminded them it was there, and sometimes cooked it while they argued over the finer points of a case in this very kitchen. This was what he always did for them, and something that Hetty took particular notice of now upon his return to Philadelphia after many months away.

"I keep trying to remember why the Duval name is familiar to me," Thomas said as he chopped away. "I just have this feeling I've seen it before."

"Valentine's father died last month," Hetty said. "Raimond Duval. We took on his case briefly."

"It's not that," Thomas said.

"Maybe it's because of the school. Both of them worked at Olmstead," Penelope said. "Rosie had them as teachers, and George took Raimond's vacant teaching post."

Thomas squinted. "Not that, either."

"Maybe you just remember it from conversations Hetty and Benjy been having," Penelope suggested.

But even Hetty knew that one was wrong. Thomas had been too distracted by the problems plaguing his mail-order business to really get involved in this case.

"Maybe Valentine Duval bought something from you. You didn't happen to sell him any chalk?"

"No." Thomas shook his head. "Definitely not that. I haven't shipped anything that small. Why can't I remember?"

Penelope laughed. "Why do you care so much?"

"You never know what sort of information might be useful." Thomas moved to the icebox and took out a piece of meat Hetty knew hadn't been bought by either her or Benjy. "And sharing that information is how I'm useful to you."

"You're very useful now," Hetty said. "If you weren't here I have no idea what I would've done about dinner."

"And it'll be a very good dinner, no matter what you make," Penelope added. "Sometimes I think it's a shame you don't get paid to cook."

"Well, the days of the Dandy of Honey Hill County are over," Thomas said, looking squarely at Hetty as he did.

Hetty only batted her eyes. "If you don't want me to tell stories about you, don't lead an interesting life."

Thomas snorted and Penelope frowned. "What do the Dandy stories have to do with Thomas?"

"They were inspired by his life before he met us." Encouraged by Penelope's curiosity, Hetty eased into storytelling mode. "They called him the Dandy then. The finest cook all around, who strutted about in fine leather shoes and a tailored coat that made him the envy of all. He wore one silk cravat as he cooked and a different one when he presented the meal. And he had everything he wanted except for the one thing most dear—his freedom. So he made a bet with his old master. He'd make a meal for the most disagreeable, most cantankerous, most bitterly sour old woman in the county . . . and the meal would be so divine that she'd weep tears of joy as she ate. And when those tears ran, he and his would be free. All the arrangements were made. The finest and most high-quality meats, cheeses, and more were ordered. Lace tablecloths said to grace the tables of royalty were brought out, and cups said to be used by the Sun King were ready to have wine poured in them. Everyone in the county had gathered at the farm. But the Dandy never showed, having used the preparations to lend him cover to make his escape. Him dressed in rags, and his wife and daughter hidden in a wine barrel. They left aboard a wagon and they were never seen on the plantation again."

Penelope turned around in her chair, rather aghast. "Do you really let her tell that story about you?"

"It's all true," Thomas said calmly. "She stops it before it gets to the part I don't want told."

"Because that's only the beginning of the tales of the Dandy," Hetty teased. "His story gets more exciting when a very talented dressmaker shows up."

"Wait a moment. I've heard stories about the Dandy before, like the one about him stealing a ledger with the names of lost families from a pirate? That was *Thomas?* All those Dandy stories?" Penelope gasped at a sudden thought. "Do you tell stories about all of us and just hide us under different names?"

In her sweetest and most innocent tone, Hetty replied, "I don't know what you're talking about."

Thomas coughed. "The Gardener of the Glass Palace, and her friend the Painter of the Seas."

Penelope's mouth fell open. "Henrietta! I can't believe you'd do such a thing!"

Hetty just grinned. "Don't lead such interesting lives."

Penelope was beside herself as she recounted the little tales Hetty had made up on the spot over the years, and there were quite a few. "I always knew when you talked about a blacksmith you meant Benjy, and anyone ill-tempered was Oliver or George, depending on the tale," Penelope grumbled. "Do you tell stories about Cora and Jay?"

"A few," Hetty admitted. "But I don't feel like telling them now."

Penelope stopped fuming as her ear perked up over this slip of the tongue. "Is this about what happened with Cora last night?"

"What happened with Cora?" Thomas moved over so he stood behind Penelope, mixing bowl in hand. "Is this related to your argument with Jay?"

"How do you know about that?" Hetty demanded.

Thomas just kept mixing the biscuit batter. "I overheard you the night I brought the fiddle. I went looking for you."

"You shouldn't be eavesdropping."

"It's hard not to listen when voices are raised. You shouldn't argue with them."

"Benjy gave me that same advice, and I didn't listen to him. Why should I listen to you?"

"Because I'm more sensible than him," Thomas said. "It comes with age and wisdom."

"You're not all that old," Hetty said.

Ignoring her, he added most sincerely, "Take my advice, Hetty. No matter what case you're elbow-deep in, having regrets is the last thing you need."

He said it with a jaunty enough air that Penelope giggled.

But Hetty knew better.

Thomas had heard more than just a simple argument. He had heard, he had observed, and had understood what was really going on. Maybe he was the only one who'd noticed. In gatherings, Oliver and Thomas often drifted over for conversation with the much older couple, wearied of "young people problems" as they liked to say, although Oliver and Thomas were no more than fifteen years older than Hetty. While that didn't seem like much at times, those years carried a weight that became significant every so often. Perhaps it wasn't wisdom coming from Thomas, but it was certainly experience and a reminder that she should know better than to let arguments fester.

Life was so unpredictable that you couldn't put off things. The apologies that you said you'd make soon might not ever get said. And all you'd be left with were regrets. She'd had that with Esther, but wasn't going to allow that to happen with anyone else.

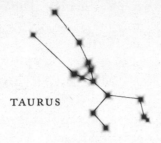

TAURUS

28

THOUGH THOMAS HAD COOKED DINNER, his doing so did not make it a dinner party, or even a sit-down meal. Upon smelling food people came in and out, taking plates and returning with empty ones later. Even Oliver ate, though to Rosie's disgust he returned to the cellar with his plate and made little conversation with anyone else.

Benjy, however, did not get a plate. At some point in the evening he'd started working on the cipher. According to Darlene, who was the first to emerge from the study, it was not going well. This fact was supported by Rosie and Sy, who escaped soon after, both with accounts of Benjy threatening to toss a book at them for some innocent remark.

Rosie had been driven nearly to tears, as she'd never seen Benjy like this before. Hetty took a moment to assure the girl she had done nothing wrong.

Sy, however, looked thoughtfully at the closed door.

"How does he know the cipher isn't a fake? Or that all of it isn't a story?"

"That's not the part he cares about," Hetty said. "He'd be working on it anyway, but it seems to be tied to the case, so he's trying harder, which means all the little frustrations become much bigger."

Sy nodded, understanding. "You want me to ask around to see who else was working on it? With all the chatter around there's sure to be news. Or maybe someone was killed for nearly solving it."

"That's a terrible thing to say," Rosie said.

"But not entirely unlikely," Hetty mused. "Maybe you two should ask around."

Although she didn't think they would find a connection, seeing how Sy's face lit up, she wasn't going to say otherwise. Who knows, maybe there was a connection.

The siblings were the first to leave, but they were not the last. Darlene, Penelope, and Thomas soon followed one by one, once the sun started to set.

It was only then that Hetty found the time to pile what was left of dinner into a bowl to force Benjy to eat something.

As she headed to the study, Oliver emerged from the cellar, yawning and spotted with ink.

"You were down there for a while. Thomas already went home," Hetty said. "Is everything done?"

"Yes. Everything's ready for the funeral." Oliver started to say more, but he saw the bowl in her hands.

"This is for Benjy," Hetty explained. "He's in one of his moods."

"I see," Oliver said. "Maybe then you can look at my notes later. I found something interesting."

"No hints?" Hetty called as he headed out.

"My notes will be enough," he said, waving a hand over his shoulder. "Good night."

Hetty almost went to see what these vague words were in reference to, but decided against it as she opened the study's door.

Hetty half expected a storm of books and papers flying around in the room. But none of that was there.

The boxes that Sy and his sister had brought were gone, but the books remained. They were stacked in three towering piles against the wall, squeezed between the bookshelf and the window.

The map of the tunnels Darlene had made was pinned next to their map of the city. No pins were stuck in this map, but there were circles drawn in a few spots. Most were on the tunnels they had gone through, but there were others that weren't.

Raimond Duval's set of checkers were scattered across the surface of the desk, arranged in small piles that probably only made sense to Benjy.

As for her husband, while he was nowhere to be seen, he had left a trail of papers floating in the air from the desk through the window.

The papers continued up to the roof, and Hetty followed, one hand weaving a spell to gently lift her skyward as she clutched the bowl to her chest.

Hetty's telescope was turned toward the horizon instead of skyward, but he wasn't looking into the scope. Instead, Benjy sat on the roof surrounded by more floating papers, muttering under his breath.

At first she thought he was rambling to himself, but he was addressing the trio of fledgling crows perched on the roof next to him. They had their heads tilted toward Benjy as if they were sincerely listening. But they must have only been indulging him, for the moment Hetty's feet landed on the roof, the birds jumped up and flew to her, going for the bowl in her arm.

"This is not for you." She shook a finger at them. "Go find your own dinner."

The crows flew off then, leaving them alone.

The papers swirling around Benjy dropped to the roof then, stacking themselves into a tidy pile.

"Were the crows helpful?" Hetty asked as she sat down next to him.

"I just needed someone willing to listen to me without interruption." Benjy eyed the bowl Hetty held. "Is it that late?"

"You didn't notice the sun setting?"

Benjy just blinked at her, and Hetty firmly placed the bowl into his hands.

Sluggishly, he moved to eat, as Hetty picked up one of the papers scattered on the roof. It was a copy of the cipher that Benjy had written out, with letters placed on top as if he was figuring out the message.

Hetty only knew the simplest and most common ways to unravel ciphers, so anything she could suggest had been long considered by many other minds.

Still she wanted to help, if only because it was alarming that Benjy was having a hard time with it. He had brute forced codes before, but this just seemed to send him around in circles.

"Why are you out here on the roof?" Hetty asked.

"I thought maybe I could see something through the telescope that would help." He scraped at his bowl. "It didn't help, of course. I think I just came up here because it's so calming. I always forget how much of the city you can see from here."

He gazed off at the distance for a bit, before he continued:

"I can't organize my mind. I was trying to connect it all together, to see if there's something we missed. I know we have. There are so many small parts to this case. But I don't know what it is."

There was that strained note in his voice again. Fear that he had about missing something obvious when it could lead to their deaths or worse. This was, Hetty recalled, their first major case in a while, and with so many different moving pieces, it was no wonder that he'd sought the comforting quietness of the roof.

Very gently, Hetty said, "You don't have to worry about connecting everything together. If you miss something, it's fine. No matter what happens."

"You don't know that."

"I'll make that promise."

Benjy blinked, recognizing his own words thrown back at him. "One thing at a time," he said softly.

"Yes. Shall we look at the books? Rosie and Sy did go through all that trouble to bring them here."

Returning to the study, they settled in for the evening. Hetty brought an armful of books to the couch, while Benjy set up at the window seat with several books floating around him.

After flipping through dozens of books, Hetty lost interest in reading more than a few words until she found a leather-bound book without a title printed on it. The fine handwriting inside told her it was the old man's journal, but not the one they had taken from Olmstead. She flipped through the pages, looking for dates, but her eye caught an odd scribble of a bird in a corner of one, and the words next to it:

With a single letter that horrible night comes back to me. What was V thinking?

The obvious answer was sometimes the best one. There was only one possibility about who V was. He was talking about Valentine.

Hetty flicked back for a date on the entry. April.

What happened then to cause such an entry? The entries ahead were from February and early March, and contained nothing of great importance. Once April started, Valentine's name appeared constantly. And that abbreviation was not the only one. Many shortened versions of names and places peppered the pages. Hetty shouldn't be surprised—Raimond's journals were not meant to be read by anyone but him, but it made for slow reading. But eventually Hetty understood enough to recognize most of the references Raimond made.

V says no harm will come from the pamphlet's printing. I'm amazed after all this time he fails to understand the powers of the written word. Men killed for that treasure, and they will do so again. Both mortal men and ghosts taunt with ciphers. I thought he understood what happened back in '53, but it's clear I was wrong. Did I fail him?

Ciphers and pamphlets. That could mean only one thing. The Clarke Cipher. But what about it made Raimond so mad?

And 1853? What happened then?

Hetty reached over to the stack she'd pulled this book from. It was too far away to comfortably reach, so she snapped her fingers, sending the book through the air. It flew into her grasp, but not without first dropping a thick packet of papers.

Hetty picked them up only to find it was a bundle of letters.

The oldest letter was a response from someone named Dora Reynolds, from the middle of March. It looked like something an old student sent, so Hetty put it aside.

The next letter underneath it was dated around the same time, and the sender's name made her forget everything else.

The letter was signed by Emily Jacobs.

Not Sarah Jacobs, but *Emily*, her daughter.

Hetty remembered the little girl who they'd rescued all those years ago. Emily must be close to Rosie's age now, or a bit younger.

Why was Emily writing instead of her mother? Had something happened?

It didn't seem like it. The letter consisted of simple pleasantries, nothing that spoke of anything of interest.

But that name was all that mattered.

"Benjy!" Hetty spun around on the couch to face him, but she only thrust the letter at empty air.

Her husband had moved to the bookshelf, the journal floating next to him.

"Benjy," she repeated. "This letter is from Emily! Sarah Jacobs's daughter. She wrote to Raimond!"

Expecting him to be taken aback, he merely shrugged. "I'm not surprised. I have a letter here from Sarah dated five years ago, thanking him for making some arrangements."

"Have you found any others?" Hetty asked.

"No, because I picked it up by chance. I don't want to blame Sy, but everything's out of order. The journals I can arrange easily. But the letters. So many people and so many dates."

"But it explains why Valentine asked us about Sarah Jacobs. He must have known about these letters. Valentine did drop all these things off at the bookshop. Wait, do you think Emily wrote to him as well?"

"There's a question we never had answered." Benjy leaned over the back of the couch, peering down at her. "The reason a bounty hunter was chasing after Sarah Jacobs all those years ago. We never found out why. But does it connect to the deaths of father and son?"

"Maybe Sarah and her daughter killed them for revenge?" Hetty suggested.

"That doesn't make any sense," Benjy said as he stared at the map on the wall.

"I'm just tossing out the idea. Everyone's a suspect, right? Valentine asked us about Sarah Jacobs," Hetty said, circling back to what she felt was a key. "Why he did is something we don't know yet. Could it be in one of Raimond's journals?"

Benjy shook his head. "Not in what I read so far. He kept mentioning ghosts. It's hard to say if they're another code, or references to what he saw in the living flesh."

The doorbell rang.

Hetty jumped at the sound, and from the way Benjy grabbed on to the couch, she was not alone in being startled.

"Shall I get the door?" Hetty asked.

"I'll get it." Benjy straightened up, casting a wary eye about. "It can't be anything good at this hour."

It wasn't.

Their neighbor stood on the front steps, clutching a beaded shawl around her shoulders as she complained about noises coming outside her windows.

"At this time of night I know it has to do with you." Blythe glared in particular at Hetty, who made the mistake of lingering in the hall. "Your friends are always coming around through my yard, and don't forget the miscreants that come to you about murders and terrible things!"

"Mrs. Holloway," Benjy interrupted her. "Why don't I take a look? It might be an animal." With such soothing assurances, he gently guided their neighbor back into her own home.

Having wisely decided against following, Hetty shut the door and she headed back to the study.

Settled as she was on the couch, it was in this silence that made the thump beneath her feet seem even louder.

No, *thump* was the wrong word. It was a *bang*. A bang that rattled against a door. A bang that sounded like a person trying to get in.

Even if Benjy had locked himself out, he would have rung the doorbell first. But Hetty's racing heart told her it wasn't him.

That bang had come from the cellar.

Her protection spells had not activated. But when she'd touched that desk at Valentine's home, her spells hadn't reacted then, either.

Preferring to face trouble head-on instead of waiting for it to find her, Hetty slipped out of the room. As she walked into the dark hallway, she removed the sharpest of her hairpins and clutched it between her fingers. Although this was a reliable weapon, she wished she had something a bit better. Both the spare elemental pistols, along with all the knives, were in the kitchen. While the curtains were closed, the light she needed to see would alert whoever was still in the yard.

No, the hairpin would have to do, and of course her magic. But it would have been nice to have a knife in hand too.

Hetty opened the cellar door and descended the stairs. She summoned a small ball of light to float near her head, and carefully crept down, avoiding the spots where the wood was known to creak. No more strange thumps greeted her as she entered the cellar.

Outside her little light, it was still completely dark downstairs. The familiar lumps and shapes in the corners greeted her. The only person down here was Valentine Duval, lying in an open casket.

Although her light didn't reveal everything in the room, she could tell Oliver had finished his work. Valentine had been dressed in his suit, and a thick layer of preservation spells surrounded him, keeping the body frozen in its current state for the funeral in three days' time.

The more interesting sight was the mess Oliver had left behind. On the nearby table was a stack of papers and newspapers, and the satchel that Adelaide had given Hetty was half hanging off the table.

This was unlike Oliver. He was very neat when it came to his work.

Hetty was just reaching for it when something banged against the cellar door.

Not just banged. It sounded like something was dropped. Like a massive stone against the wood, attempting to break it. And then a faint green light ran along the door, starting from the top and working its way down like scissors. But the moment it touched the bottom of the door, the star sigil Benjy had carved into the wood lit up.

Orion stepped out from the door, drew his sword, and then charged through the door into the yard.

She expected to hear a yell or an outraged cry, but Hetty didn't hear anything.

All she felt was the pressure from magic clashing around her, and faintly, very faintly, she heard a voice.

Knowing for certain meant opening the cellar door. While she was brave enough for the task, caution stayed her hand.

Still, she approached the cellar door, pressing a hand along the wood.

It was warm from the magic, and it thumped like a heartbeat under her palm. Hetty breathed in time with this gentle thump, her worries floating away.

All the doors and windows in their home had protection spells. Spells of protections done in the way only Benjy could have done, resolutely, sternly stubborn, and with a promise to remain as long as he still breathed.

Hetty liked to think that last bit was just a boast, although she knew it was the truth. She just didn't want to think of the day she'd place her hand against a door and find no magic brimming under the surface.

The cellar's lights turned on, and her husband's voice carried down into the cellar before his footsteps.

"Hetty, are you down here?"

Hetty turned away from the door, going to the side table where Oliver had left his notebook.

"Yes, I heard strange noises. Were you out in the backyard?"

Benjy said yes, and started to explain, but even before he did, Hetty had stopped paying attention.

The papers scattered on the table were copies of inquest paperwork. They weren't recent, but they were all under six months old. Raimond Duval's name was on one. So were a few other names that Hetty recognized parts of. Sullivan. Yates. Sam. Roderick. John Roberts. Names of the people who'd worked with the Vigilance Society. Some had not been active when Hetty had worked with the group, but they were all friends of Jay and Cora.

Then there were the newspapers: obituaries or articles with each name circled.

But it was the topmost paper, placed prominently so it couldn't be overlooked, that caused Hetty to stop paying attention to anything else, including Benjy coming to her side.

It was a short note, written quickly and clearly in Oliver's handwriting:

Check on Pastor Evans — he might be the next victim!

LITTLE HORSE

29

Panic over the unexplained noises and visions of a nightmare come to life propelled Hetty along the streets, so much so that she felt like she was flying on her bicycle. Benjy trailed behind her. She stopped for nothing and no one, veering around any hapless person foolish enough to be out in the streets and in the shadows.

She almost threw her bicycle down to run up the steps to the door. She knocked first, forgetting the doorbell, forgetting her manners, aware only of Oliver's note clutched in her hand.

She kept knocking even when the door opened and Jay himself stood there, lit up by his own magic that he had summoned around him.

"Henrietta, Benjamin," the pastor asked. "What's wrong?"

Hetty held up Oliver's note. "You said your friends were dying. You neglected to say there was a connection or voice concerns about yourself!"

Jay studied the note calmly before he handed it back. "I only just realized things myself as I started to think over recent events and saw the link was in the past. Come inside. Cora is asleep, but we shouldn't be heard in the kitchen."

The light was already on in there, as he had been in the middle of enjoying a late-night cup of tea. He pushed aside his mug as Hetty and Benjy sat down.

"I have not always been a station master," Jay began. "In my youth I worked the Road back before anything was organized. Just a few brave souls eager to do all they could. I came to Philadelphia as a young man in the late thirties, but after the 'forty-three riots I spent years doing what I could, mostly as far west as Ohio and south as Maryland. I traveled further as needed, and when the Fugitive Slave Act went into effect our little vigilance group came into being. We did targeted retrievals of persons known to us. You did a few of those yourself, so I think you understand how those went. It was fairly simple, but there were also some interesting cases. And none more than the one that began in 1840 when a young man I knew as Alvin Jacobs went to get a drink one night, in a little town not far from Boston. His company for drinking were strangers, and they were the wrong sort of company. They drugged him and tossed him into a wagon, and he ended up on a trader's block in Virginia. Jacobs was a freeborn man, but without his papers, without people willing to give value to his words, he was enslaved.

"His wife of course tried to fix this. She petitioned the courts to overturn things, but it never went anywhere. By then Jacobs's attempted flight to freedom caused enough damage and loss that the judge ruled against him. The family went around looking for anyone who could help, and the news reached Bernice in 1853. Bernice made arrangements for a group of us — myself, Raimond, Valentine, John Roberts, and a few others — to head down and bring Jacobs back home. The plan fell apart right away. I blamed Bernice at the time, but that was wrong of me. She didn't know all the details."

"What details?" Benjy asked.

Jay looked them both in the eye. "That in 1848 Alvin Jacobs dug the hole in which Vernon Clarke found his sapphires."

"Stars above," Hetty whispered. "Are you saying that—"

"This is about the Clarke Cipher!" Benjy exclaimed.

"Sadly, yes," Jay said. "Rich folk are paranoid people. They find treasure and instead of sharing it, they hide it away. In this case, Clarke traveled to hide his treasure, hoping to keep it hidden longer. He created the ciphers to hide the location and other information, even if it fell into the wrong hands. I know all this because when we rescued Alvin Jacobs, he told us. Even as he escaped he had snatched those papers from Clarke's study, fully intending to claim the treasure for himself since he'd dug it. It wasn't greed, though. During the time of his bondage, he had adopted a young girl named Sarah. The girl had reminded him of the daughter he had been torn away from. The treasure would go to Sarah. We had even rescued her along with him that night. I wish this story could end happily. Or that I could say we took extra care as we headed back north. But I didn't realize that Clarke, in addition to being paranoid, was like a dog with a bone. No—much worse. When he couldn't get everything he wanted, he decided instead to destroy everything."

"He caught up with you," Hetty guessed.

Jay nodded. "Sent bounty hunters after us. Surrounded us, forced us on the run. Raimond got hurt, a few others were wounded in the fighting, and we all got separated. Then the bounty hunters grabbed Sarah. The ciphers or the girl's life, they said. It was no choice for Alvin Jacobs. He gave himself up. They shot him even before the papers were in Clarke's greasy hands. Sarah was taken away screaming. I tried to see if there was anything I could do, but there was never a chance. We could do no more."

Jay tapped his fingers on the table, lost in his memories of the night and the regrets he'd carried since.

"If Jacobs gave the papers back, why is there a pamphlet?" Benjy asked.

"Jacobs was a clever man. He had the foresight to create a fake set of ciphers. Those were what he gave up while he passed the real ciphers to someone else."

"To Valentine," Hetty guessed. "The bookshop he owned has a printing press. It would have been an easy thing for him to make a pamphlet."

"No one knew he had the ciphers until the pamphlet started making rounds. Raimond was so angry about it, but Valentine didn't seem worried, or that's the impression I got. I'm not sure why Valentine printed them in the end. Maybe he wanted to see if someone else could solve it. Maybe he wanted the money that came from selling a fantastical story like that. Maybe he thought enough time had passed that everyone who knew anything about it was dead or wouldn't be bothered. Either way, he should have known better."

"What about 'sixty-one? How do our travels with Sarah Jacobs fit into all of this?" Benjy asked.

"Clarke died in the previous winter rather suddenly, and his brother-in-law inherited his estate. He learned about the treasure, and from what I gathered, Sarah knew about a key that would aid in solving the ciphers. She was kept close and never let out of sight."

"She was so closely watched the whole time, why go through all the effort?" It had been a great deal of effort, even before Hetty had made things tricker with a plot to rescue Sarah's children. But even then Bernice did not balk at the change of plans.

"Bernice saw this as atonement. For what we should have done before." Jay sighed. "She wasn't alone in that. Getting Sarah to freedom was an attempt to fulfill what we failed to do with her father. That's why you had so much help on your journey to Toronto. Although, we didn't realize you would need it so badly. Or that the ciphers would still be that important."

"They still are," Hetty said. "Has anyone else contacted Sarah Jacobs? Has Bernice?"

"Bernice hasn't told me so. But I wouldn't be surprised if she had."

"Or she's waiting for the right moment," Benjy remarked.

Hetty and Jay shared a look. "The ball!"

"Yes, the ball." Benjy folded his hands under his chin, deep in thought. "It's important to make sure we can talk. But not important enough to tell us right away."

"That woman," Jay grumbled. "She takes on too much, keeps too many secrets. What if it's too late?"

Benjy only shook his head. "We would have heard, we would have known."

"I beg to differ," Jay said. "Six of my friends are dead, some very recently!"

"Which is why," Benjy said, "Bernice didn't say anything right away. The connection wasn't clear. And now that it is, she's going to try to protect you. Since it's clear the murderer is after everyone connected to the Clarke Cipher."

"How do you know that's why she's doing it?" Jay demanded.

Benjy's gaze drifted over in Hetty's direction. "I recognize that behavior."

The insult was a gentle one, but it still stung even if she knew it was true.

"I promise, you'll get a note saying not to go to the ball. Ignore it," Benjy said.

"I would have anyway." Jay struggled to smile. "If you two plan to go, it promises to be very interesting."

"I think we can all agree on that."

Cora entered the kitchen. She had been asleep, just like Jay had said. A scarf was still tight around her hair, and as she belted her dressing gown she floated like a queen into the room, stirred from her rest.

"Jay, why didn't you wake me?" Cora asked as she stopped by the chair to Hetty's left. She smiled at Hetty, as if they had never exchanged bitter words. "I know they didn't come here at this hour to talk about a ball."

"It's about Valentine Duval," Jay said when no one else spoke up. "It turns out what happened to him relates to what happened with Alvin Jacobs all those years ago."

"That was when you, Raimond, John, and ..." She blinked, catching on rather quickly, as she looked at him, horrified. "Sweet stars above! Don't tell me this is all because of that silly little cipher?"

"Who told you it was a silly little cipher, again?" Jay asked tersely.

"Bernice." Cora shook a finger at him, before he could interrupt her. "That's because the idea of treasure is as fantastical as one as Henrietta's stories."

"My stories always have a bit of truth in them," Hetty reminded her. "And there's more. Valentine asked us about Sarah Jacobs before he died, and Emily, Sarah's daughter, had written to Raimond very recently."

"If you look into the past two months, nearly everyone that was there that night has died," Benjy said. "Mostly in a manner that didn't attract attention."

"Nearly everyone," Cora echoed. "Old man," she said, looking intently at her husband, "you're in trouble."

Jay turned to each of them. "I'm perfectly fine. I have all of you looking out for me. I've noticed nothing odd."

Cora tapped the chair's back, unswayed by his words. "There was that fire on Carver Street."

"Where your tunnel used to lead out," Hetty said with a nod to the fireplace in the living room.

"Which Benjamin swung a hammer around and collapsed for us so no one can come through!" Jay gestured to Benjy.

Benjy only raised an eyebrow. "You had reason to doubt my work before."

"I have never doubted you," Jay retorted. He coughed, seeing the disbelief on Hetty's face. "I mean, I was only pressing because you are a stubborn man, Benjamin Rhodes. It takes a strong wind to get you to pay attention!"

"A strong windbag, you mean," Cora muttered under her breath, just loud enough for Hetty to hear. Louder, she continued, "Old man, you could have saved us some heartbreak if you'd said something earlier!"

Jay sucked in a breath. "I didn't realize it. All that business with Jacobs was so long ago, and Raimond never said much about it."

"Because he blamed himself for what happened," Cora said.

"And because Valentine printed the pamphlet. He felt responsible for all the trouble that came from it," Hetty said.

Benjy spread his hands across the table. "We have a handful of possible suspects, but we're certain about two things. One, the murderer hired a man to kill people with ties to the Clarke Cipher. Two, Bernice Tanner will relate many things to us at the ball, and not a moment sooner."

"Not sooner?" Jay asked.

"She wouldn't have invited us to the ball if the timing wasn't right," Benjy said. "There's something she's waiting for."

Cora grunted. "Well, it's a good thing we'll be there to help. If the worst comes, Jay can be a distraction."

"Absolutely not!" Hetty exploded, her nerves getting the best of her. "You will do no such a thing!"

The older couple only laughed. "We can handle ourselves, thank you very much, missy," Jay said, with a bit of a twinkle in his eye. "We know quite a few spells. The world didn't sit around and wait for you to invent magic!"

Jay projected it the way he spoke from the pulpit, with that particular cadence all preachers used, and Benjy started to laugh.

When they all looked at him, he continued in earnest.

"That's exactly what she thinks!" Benjy cried between breaths.

Jay chortled. "You should have seen her when she first came here. Doing spells all over the place and seemed to think we didn't even notice!"

Hetty was ready to defend herself when Cora tapped her on the shoulder.

"Let them talk," she mouthed. She urged Hetty to follow her and led the way out of the kitchen and into the small study down the hall.

Cora turned on the lights and went around to the large desk that filled the room. The desk was mostly clear except for a stack of letters, a Bible, and a basket with balls of yarn.

"We both married rather stubborn men who need to be certain they are right in what they say or do," Cora said as she sat down at the desk. "Let them talk about silly things. I'd rather that than play messenger between them. But I also wanted to talk to you. To apologize, mostly. I made the error in listening to Jay first instead of you. Mostly because I saw fear in you and thought it came from the wrong place."

"I should be the one to apologize. You were right to say what you did. Every lesson you taught, I carry with me always."

"Which is why I apologize for what I said in turn." Cora opened a drawer and pulled out an envelope. "Just because I have gray hair and wrinkles, it doesn't mean I know everything. Nor do I always make the best choices. I should have told you about the Magnolia Muses earlier and should have given you the choice to take part or not."

"I probably would have said no," Hetty admitted.

"What about now? Consider this an official invitation to the group." Cora held out the envelope.

Hetty took it, expecting a key at the very least, or some sort of magical token. But instead it was tickets to a baseball game between the Independents and the Pythons.

"Baseball?" Hetty asked.

"A group of Magnolias are meeting tomorrow. It's more of a general meeting to talk about things. Someone who worked with Valentine will be there. Oh, and Henrietta, there are enough tickets for you and your friends—don't go alone. Sometimes these meetings get interrupted by the police."

"You're not going?"

Cora smiled. "That's the benefit of working with young people. I don't have to do everything."

Hetty nodded, putting the tickets away. "One question: Is Bernice Tanner involved with the Magnolia Muses?"

"Bernice knows about my work, but she's not involved." Cora leaned back in the chair, her hands folded across her chest and her expression devoid of anything that gave away her innermost thoughts. "Why do you think she would be?"

This reaction, even more than Cora's question, took Hetty by surprise. "I thought you were good friends."

"We are. I daresay I may be her *only* good friend," Cora said. "But that doesn't mean we have the same goals. For example, if I knew my friend's husband was in grave peril and had information I could give someone to stop it, I wouldn't wait until a ball to tell it."

Cora did not raise her voice, nor do anything more than sit there as if she were pondering what book to pull from the bookshelf behind her. But Hetty knew she had asked the wrong question and it was better she leave now before she made things worse.

"Have a good night under happy stars," Hetty said.

"And to you, my dear, and to you."

Hetty collected Benjy from Jay, the latter in the middle of a story about the time Hetty accidentally had shot a hole into the dining room wall. She used that story as an excuse to walk around outside so she and Benjy could add protective spells to the house. It wouldn't do much, just add another layer, but it was the peace of mind Hetty wanted.

The ride home was sedate in comparison to the frantic flight there, as they pedaled along quiet and mostly empty streets. Hetty remained lost in her thoughts, going over all she learned from both Cora and Jay. She had known in some fashion that the ball was important, but that it might provide answers to her last lingering questions was something she never would have guessed.

It was only when she heard Benjy swear under his breath that Hetty drew back out to the world around her.

There were flames flickering in the distance.

Blythe Holloway had not been rambling about their neighborhood being protected from flames. When the fires started occurring with alarming frequency, Hetty and Benjy had set a wide perimeter of protections on the streets closest to their home. The spells covered all the residential homes, homes of people who might never know they were being protected. But the spells only went so far, stopping where the street turned to shops.

The place on fire was a tiny little trinket store that Hetty had never gone inside of. It wasn't a big fire, and it already seemed to be under control. The owner and nearby neighbors were working away at the water pump, tossing over buckets of water, and in some cases guiding water with magic to douse the flames.

But still Hetty and Benjy stopped. Not to see what could be done, but because on a distant street corner a man stood illuminated by a flickering streetlamp.

His white skin, more than his bowler hat, gave him away.

Alderman Anderson, watching them from the corner, puffs of cigar smoke drifting lazily into the air around him.

When he saw them noticing him, he smirked, tipped his hat, then turned to disappear into the night.

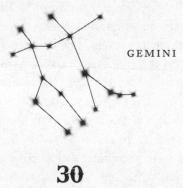

30

THEY FOUND MARKS ON the cellar door and a dusting of magical residue that didn't tell them much beyond the fact that someone had tried to use magic on it. Their own wards had countered whatever spell had been thrown at them. And not even a half-hearted joke from Benjy about the efficacy of his wards made it better.

That this had been done by the alderman was the unspoken worry between them. That he had found where they lived and, unable to set their home on fire, instead chose a building that could take the flames. A scenario so plausible that to speak it risked making it a reality. This meant of course neither Hetty nor Benjy would rest easy, so they spent the night reading through the journals and notes. While Benjy read through them in order, Hetty started jumping around, looking for dates, events, and recognizable names. Eventually when the words started to blur in front of her, she put the book away and lay down on the floor.

The last thing she remembered before she fell asleep was Benjy reading aloud a passage to her. It must not have been very interesting. For despite reading the many adventures of Raimond Duval in the prime of his life, her dreams were a blur of colors and sounds that seemed so important to her while she slept but were long forgotten when she awoke.

Hetty lay there a moment, slowly realizing that instead of the floor she was on the couch, with her feet resting in Benjy's lap.

Sunlight trickled in through the curtains, and judging by where the light fell, it wasn't too late in the morning.

"Are you awake?" Benjy asked, barely looking up from his book.

Hetty sat up, stretching out her back. "I am now."

She should have pretended to still be asleep. Because the moment she spoke, Benjy put the book aside and got up from the couch.

Within seconds, music started to pour into the air.

Not one of the complicated pieces he played for fun, but a simple melody. The one he played when he was stuck on a problem. The music flowed around her, the notes crystal clear, even though Hetty's ears barely could tell one from another.

While Benjy waited for her to wake up, he had been busy organizing the journals and papers. A deceptively simple process where there was a large pile of everything not useful, and one very small pile with all the things that were.

The books and papers Benjy deemed useful were not unexpected. There were the two journals that spanned the last year of Raimond's life, with slips of paper marking relevant places. The letters that Raimond received, all dated from the past six months. Surprisingly there were even newspaper clippings. Oliver had marked places where poison or something else might have a role in the deaths, just using the scarce details in the articles. Although he might be guessing, it was his way of connecting the deaths.

Hetty picked up the article about Billy Yates, the first death that Jay had mentioned, although others had died in the weeks following Raimond's demise. Would she had heard about this earlier if things hadn't gotten icy between the pastor and Benjy?

"Why do you think the murderer targeted everyone that took part in the events of that night?" Hetty asked.

Although the piano playing didn't stop, the music slowed as Benjy replied, "The reason matters very little."

"It certainly does matter! It says how likely Jay will be next, and how deliberately he'll be targeted."

"He's always been on the list."

Hetty's head snapped up at this decisive statement. She could hear the guilt in his voice as much as she recalled his many protests each time Jay insisted they look into Raimond Duval's death. If they had looked sooner, if they had not given up, could several lives have been spared?

"If the murderer knew about the Duvals, the pastor would have certainly known. He was no small player. Just think of how he told us about his involvement. He was in the thick of things, just like Raimond and Valentine."

"But surely," Hetty started to protest, unsure why she was arguing. Nothing had happened to Jay. He had not been harmed in any strange fashion in the past weeks. Nor had there been a whiff of trouble around him. In fact, the only trouble was the fire on Carver Street, and that could be a coincidence. There was no sign someone attempted to get into the blocked tunnel. Yet Hetty worried all the same, unable to let go of her fears. "But surely something could have happened?"

Benjy turned around then to face her, holding up his arm, angled to show off the fine stitchwork on his sleeve. "He's been protected by your magic. I think you underestimate the strength of the spells. For they are as enduring as the love you sew them with."

He met her eyes then. Instantly, Hetty recalled incidents where her spells were the literal last line of defense from the worst occurring. The magic wasn't perfect, but it did exactly what it needed to do.

"I hope that is true," Hetty said. "I don't think Jay will like to be wrapped up in protective spells until we do something about Nathan Payne and his employer. This isn't going to stop otherwise."

"I'm afraid you're right." Benjy went back to the piano and started a rather energetic piece. "There's a list that is being worked through. With the easy-to-reach targets marked off first. But we don't know who else is still on the list."

"Everyone involved with Sarah Jacobs and her father," Hetty murmured. "We are certainly on it."

"Was it any doubt, with Payne involved?" Benjy asked.

"Then isn't it Payne we should focus on instead?"

Her answer was more piano playing, with a flurry of notes that Hetty couldn't follow, but they were a decisive rebuttal to this plan.

There was a bump on the dividing wall. Hetty nearly jumped up before she realized it was only their neighbor voicing her displeasure.

A giggle escaped Hetty as Benjy slowed the music, playing something softer.

Something that was familiar, too.

She came up behind him, looping her arms loosely around him. Not enough to disturb his playing, but enough so he'd pay attention to her.

"What's the piece you're playing?" Hetty asked.

"I'm trying to turn *L'Amant Anonyme* into a solo piece. It was meant for a full orchestra."

There were a few pieces of sheet music resting on the piano. Some were songs he and Penelope worked on together. But the piece he played had been composed by someone named Joseph Bologne, whose importance to Hetty was more about him being a champion fencer than being a musician of some note.

She listened for a bit. "I like it. What's it about?"

"A widow who claimed she'll never fall in love again, and the anonymous gifts from a suitor that appear to challenge that claim."

"Sounds like a curse. Is it a tragedy?"

"What does it sound like to you?" he asked.

"Noise in the background." She moved to kiss him, but Benjy's hand slammed down on the keys, filling the air with the discordant notes.

"What's wrong?" Hetty asked.

"You're brilliant!" He kissed her instead, hard enough she forgot her next question. "I have to go. There's one more thing I need to look into before the ball tonight."

"Which is?" Hetty asked as he bounded around the room.

"Everyone's been talking about the ciphers, but I want to know where the interest started from and how far it spread. Do you want to come with me?"

Hetty shook her head. "Can't. I have a few things I need to take care of too. Questions to ask of a certain embalmer we know. Although talk to Sy. He said he was going to look for information about the pamphlet's printing."

"You still could come along."

"Cora gave me tickets to a baseball game. Apparently the Magnolias will meet after the game. I'm going to ask Penelope and Darlene, if she'd be interested, to come with me."

"Oh, I imagine Darlene will be," Benjy chuckled. "Then I'll see you when I come home."

After a bit of breakfast and freshening up, Hetty walked the few streets to Oliver and Thomas's home. When her knocks didn't get a prompt reply, she slipped in a little magic to get attention.

"Good morning to you too," Oliver said, yawning, when he opened his door.

Hetty stormed into the house, barely acknowledging Oliver was still in his dressing gown.

Oliver drifted into his kitchen, fixing himself tea as Hetty railed at him for several minutes.

"Why didn't you tell me Jay might be a target for the murder! You had several opportunities! But you just left a note! A note, of all things! Which you left for us to find! Explain yourself!"

Oliver sat there at the table, uncharacteristically quiet as he stirred his tea. "Shouldn't you have known without me telling you? The number of his friends dying strangely wasn't enough?"

Hetty almost strangled him.

"How would I know about all that!"

"Because this is what you do?" Oliver said. "I mean, it's all you do. If you actually wanted to focus on funerals, you would have taken up my offer for embalming lessons. Which you haven't, by the way."

"This is the first funeral we had in weeks."

"And it's tied to a murder investigation. I wouldn't recommend doing that all the time. It'll muddy your reputation in both lines of work."

Hetty slumped then, leaning against a chair. "We might have no choice."

Oliver put his cup on the table, giving her his full attention. "It'll pick up," he said, a bit more kindly. "Just be patient. Although, I wonder how serious you are about running a funeral home?"

"I'm very serious. I wouldn't be bothered otherwise."

"Then why didn't you open the satchel? You don't know how to embalm, but you could have cleaned and dressed the body."

"You were busy taking care of it," Hetty said quickly.

"And because I was, I opened the satchel and found all the newspaper clippings and papers tucked away, plus a card with a moon on one side and a sun on the other."

Their calling card. What people left when they wanted help.

Adelaide Duval had left it in the satchel with her brother's clothes.

She *wasn't* the murderer then!

"She left that in there," Hetty whispered. "Why didn't Adelaide say anything earlier?"

"Maybe she did but you weren't listening," Oliver suggested.

Hetty didn't get a chance to respond.

The kitchen door opened and Thomas poked his head in. He was also in his dressing gown, and for a moment Hetty thought he was about to shoo her out of the house. But he had some papers in hand.

"I hate to interrupt," Thomas said, "but I heard your voice, Hetty, and I couldn't miss the chance to avoid paying you a call later today." Thomas brandished the papers. "I was going over the list of the goods that had gone missing, and guess who engaged me to sell them?"

Rather than bother with guesses, Hetty snatched the papers from him. Horace Duval's name was circled in several places.

Thomas had said the name had seemed familiar, and this appeared to be the reason why.

"He's a relation?" Thomas asked, quite merrily.

"He's a suspect!" Hetty replied.

"Wonderful." Thomas leaned over and pressed a kiss to Oliver's cheek. "You owe me ten dollars."

Oliver huffed. "You knew the odds were in your favor!"

"You didn't have to take the bet." Thomas drifted away to pour himself his own cup of tea.

Ignoring them, Hetty turned her attention to the list. Horace had been buying up the stolen goods and selling them again, for several months. And if he was dealing with stolen goods, he likely met Nathan Payne, exchanged stories, and things progressed from there.

Hetty handed the papers back to Thomas. "I could kiss you right now," she declared. "But I'll leave that task to Oliver. You helped more than you could possibly imagine!"

"Oh, I very much doubt that," Thomas drawled, but there was a note of pride in his voice. "But we're always here to help. Remember that when you go plunging into a mystery."

"It could be coincidence." Oliver frowned.

"I'll take a coincidence, because enough of them together create an undeniable pattern!"

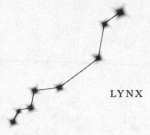

LYNX

31

As DARLENE SPENT MOST Saturdays at the art school Hetty went there directly, hoping her friend was not too busy.

She went to the right door this time, but voices from Adelaide's studio led Hetty through that door instead.

During Hetty's last visit she'd had the impression of a grand mess of a mind in the middle of several ideas at once. But the mess that greeted her today was vastly different. It looked like a powerful storm had blown through. Statues had been knocked over, tools lay on the floor, and a table had been flung against a wall.

"None of it can be fixed," Adelaide wailed. "Can't you see! I can't even get the marble replaced!"

Hetty followed the voice to the back.

Adelaide was sitting on a cot. Darlene was sitting next to her, twisting her paint-smeared fingers around in worry. Penelope sat on a stool nearby, rather awkwardly holding the head of a stone cat in her arms. "And you went and ruined the painting. I might as well pack up and leave!"

"That can be fixed," Penelope said. "I told you there are potions and powders that—"

"Your silly potions can't fix my statue!"

"There might be a way to re-form the marble into one piece again," Hetty said.

All three turned her way.

The sculptor blew her nose. "You can do that?"

"I can't promise anything—"

Adelaide wasn't listening anymore. She'd recovered at once, jumping up from the cot, filled with new energy. "I'll try anything! Theory or not. I cannot afford to lose this commission."

"How did this happen?" Hetty asked.

"I had someone meet me here. I needed some magical tools I couldn't get easily in town. I knew not to trust him, but Valentine had bought some things from him. I don't know what happened. We were talking money, then he was throwing things, asking about birds."

"Birds?" Hetty echoed. "Which kind?"

But Adelaide was back to dwelling on the ruin of her studio. "He knocked aside a piece I had just started and once it fell everything else followed."

She pointed to the statue lying on the floor.

Hetty glanced at it mostly because it seemed the best way to deal with the artist, but she nearly staggered backwards once she realized what it was.

There was a chisel rammed into the statue on the floor. A statue with a face that was unmistakably Hetty's.

"Sparrow," Hetty whispered. "That's the bird he was asking about."

"Why, you're right!" Adelaide replied, her cheery voice a contrast to the rushing wind in Hetty's ears. "You are awfully clever. What else can you guess?"

"The man who sold you magic had an unsightly scar across his face," Hetty said.

"I don't remember a scar." Adelaide's gaze grew distant as she turned to her memories. "I don't remember his face at all."

"But I know who he is. A very dangerous man who in the past expressed great displeasure at me and my husband meddling with his affairs."

"Must be a great deal of displeasure," Adelaide said.

"It certainly sounds like it," Darlene added.

She and Penelope stood side by side now with matching scowls. They might not know everything, but they'd pieced together enough. And they liked none of it.

"Do you need help cleaning up?" Hetty asked, hoping that Adelaide would say yes.

"No, I can manage on my own." Adelaide pulled herself together. "You have plenty to do with the funeral. Tell me — did the clothes fit?"

Reminded that it was more than just Valentine's clothes in the bag, Hetty nodded. "They did. And I found a few extra things. Papers and newspaper clippings. You could have just asked me outright to look closer into your brother's death. You heard about the investigations we do."

"I did. I had concerns, but I couldn't bring myself to ask. Because if he was murdered, that meant it could have been prevented," Adelaide said.

"It often feels like that," Hetty said. "But you must not think so, or you'll never have peace. And your brother wouldn't want that."

"You'll find out who did it?" Adelaide asked.

"That's what we do."

Adelaide wouldn't let them help clean up. She shooed them out, saying it was better for her to deal with it. Left with no choice, Hetty and her friends retreated to Darlene's studio.

This room was a mess as well, but on a smaller scale. A chair was knocked over. And an arch of blue paint had dried on the painting set on Darlene's easel, ruining the castle she'd been painstakingly working on.

If this troubled Darlene, she had yet to show it. Instead, the moment the door shut, she spun on Hetty. "What did you do to make a man so angry he attacked a statue of your likeness?"

"He used to work for a bounty hunter a long time ago."

"This is Nathan Payne we're talking about, isn't it?" Penelope asked.

Hetty nodded.

Darlene sighed. "You certainly have your list of enemies, don't you?"

"I try to keep it short."

Darlene's response to that was not quite sensible. In fact, it was more of her kicking a table and glaring at Hetty.

"I certainly picked an interesting day to come visit," Penelope said.

"Why *are* you here?" Hetty asked. "I thought you'd be at the herbal shop."

Penelope pointed to a jar sitting on the table. "I brought some paint pigment from the shop. Darlene wasn't joking about the magical paint."

This seemed truthful, but Penelope had avoided Hetty's eye when she said it. But her friend's usual nervous tics weren't present, so Hetty wasn't too curious at the moment.

"What brought you here?" Penelope asked.

"A simple question," Hetty said. Darlene had calmed down enough that she turned back to listen to them. "Would either of you like to go to a baseball game?"

VIRGO

32

League baseball games were played in a number of different locations. Mainly because it was hard to convince the city to grant permits on a regular basis. Which meant in order to avoid having games disrupted, the games were held over in Camden, mostly in a small park with trees tall enough to hide all the action.

Hetty had seen many baseball games over the years. Some were played between battles during the war, as soldiers channeled energy into quick games. There were also the semiprofessional teams that played in Fairmount Park. But the most interesting games were within the small league that Octavius Catto and his buddies created. It was doing surprisingly well and had even drawn players and interest from New York City, D.C., and Chicago.

Because Benjy didn't play, Hetty had little interest in watching baseball. But going to the games was less about the sport and more about gathering in a high-spirited crowd.

Out above the field, players stood on broomsticks waiting for a chance to catch a baseball as it flew past. One person was high enough to nearly block out the sun, a daring but rather risky move. The broomsticks didn't have the best enchantments on them. Casting spells on wood was a hair too close to wands, as a broomstick needed only one end to be broken off before it became a staff. So there were strict regulations on broomsticks that kept the magic on them at the barest amounts. It wasn't unusual for games to be paused when players fell out of the sky. And while this should have been a reason to have different rules for the game, it was just one more thing that made it all very exciting.

"The Independents were never contenders after they lost Watkins," Darlene said as they took their seats in the stands. "Although they did have a few good games last season. But the Pythons are better overall."

"Probably because a few of the Magnolia Muses are on the team," Penelope remarked.

Which was why the Magnolia meeting would take place after the game ended. A quite unfortunate thing in Hetty's opinion, since it meant she had to suffer through the game first.

"I hope this doesn't go for too long," Hetty grumbled. The ferry to Camden had been delayed, and part of her hoped it meant missing the game entirely. But alas, the game was nowhere near being over by the time they arrived.

"It shouldn't." Penelope pointed to the floating scoreboard. Held up by various spells, the chalkboards displayed the points earned already by the teams. "Try to have fun, Hetty. We don't get to do that often enough."

A player picked up a bat and waited for the pitcher to toss the ball. It struck on the first try with a resounding crack. The ball arched upward into the sky. The player on the ground threw the bat away, jumped on a waiting broomstick, and flew up to the floating marker that was first base.

Unluckily for him, a member of the opposing team caught the ball. He swooped down, waving the ball at his opponent.

Boos filled the air as the player flew back to the ground. Darlene's voice was the loudest among them.

"So that's the team we're rooting for?" Hetty asked as the player went to bat once more.

Darlene shot her a glare. "Yes, we are cheering on the Pythons. And don't start rooting for the other team. That's what Benjy does!"

Darlene turned back as the ball was pitched again, and Hetty was free to ignore the game once more.

"It's not true that we don't spend time together," Hetty said to Penelope, who thankfully wasn't watching the game that closely. "You're in my garden all the time."

"Not really. Just a few hours here and there," Penelope said. "I don't count the time I spend helping with your cases and funerals."

"As if you aren't busy yourself! The pair of you going on doing things without me. Leaving me out of everything."

"Left out?" Penelope exclaimed. "When? I tell you everything!"

"Is this about going to see the medium?" Darlene asked.

Hetty was surprised to see they had her attention until Hetty saw the Independents were up to bat. "I honestly thought you wouldn't want to come," Darlene continued.

"It's not just that. Lately I just feel I've been missing out on a lot." Hetty squirmed, feeling a heat that was not from the blazing sun overhead. There was confusion in her friends' faces as well. Confusion that was making her think she had gotten quite a few things wrong. "Secrets you kept from me."

"What secrets? Do you mean about planning to move?" Darlene asked. "That's hardly news, and was decided rather recently. As if we could keep secrets from you for long." Something happened in the sky just then. In a flash, Darlene was on her feet and hollering so loudly, it was hard to tell if what happened was good or bad.

"What Darlene is trying to say is this," Penelope said. "You're being silly."

"Thank you for such wise counsel," Hetty replied, but she sat back and found herself enjoying the game a bit more after that.

She was actually just beginning to follow the course of action in the game, when she noticed Horace Duval.

He stood at the bottom of the stands, at the far edge, near the scoreboard. If Horace looked up he might see nothing but the sun and miss Hetty entirely.

Or maybe not.

Hetty stood up. "I'm going to walk around. I'll be back when this is over."

Darlene nodded, clearly not hearing a word that was said, but Penelope got up and followed Hetty.

"Just watch the game," Hetty said when Penelope caught up to her at the bottom of the stands. "I'll be right back."

"You're doing it again," Penelope said.

"Doing what?"

"This." Penelope waved a hand around Hetty. "Not saying a word about trouble until it's too late."

"This isn't trouble. This is me trying to talk to a suspect. The only real suspect we have left."

"A suspect is here?" Penelope looked about the stands.

"Yes, standing by the goal sign. Now if you'll excuse me—"

"How did he know we'd be here?"

Hetty spun around at Penelope's thoughtful but worried tone. "What do you mean?" Hetty asked.

"That man you said is a suspect. I saw him this morning. He knocked on my door looking for Darlene. Luckily, George wasn't home. He took Lorene for a visit with his parents. That's the real reason I was at the art school. To tell Darlene about it, but I didn't get a chance."

Hetty absorbed this information rather calmly, even as alarms sounded in her ears. "What did the man say?"

"Just that he was looking for her. He asked questions, too, like about how long Darlene had been painting and when did we become neighbors. Seemingly harmless questions, but he asked them with shifting eyes. I'm pretty sure you would have hexed him before he finished speaking."

"You don't think that's concerning enough to mention it earlier?"

"Well, he doesn't look like a murderer. An art thief, maybe."

"He still showed up looking for Darlene. That makes him dangerous, and I think—"

A loud pop shattered the air. People all around her jumped up to yell into the sky and grabbed at others around them.

Hetty darted forward, one hand creeping up toward her choker, ready to face whatever danger that was coming.

But only when she saw Penelope smiling did Hetty realize she assumed wrong.

"The Pythons won!" Penelope cheered. "Darlene is going to be so happy!"

That was an understatement. Up in the stands, the usually composed and demure Darlene was jumping around with her arms around total strangers, celebrating the win.

"Ah, I hoped they would win too." The librarian from Still-Bowers was in front of them, holding a basket with little bags of roasted peanuts. "Here, take these, and don't worry about paying me, I'm trying to get rid of them."

The librarian handed Hetty three packets and then continued on. Although the basket was still more than half full, she didn't stop to hand over peanuts to anyone else.

"Have you met Nora before?" Penelope asked.

"The librarian?" Hetty asked. "She works at Still-Bowers. She's the one that told us to go to Fool's Moon."

"Ah, that's why she knew to give this to you." Penelope picked up a packet, and instead of pulling out a peanut, held a train ticket instead.

"The meeting is on a *train?*" Hetty bemoaned. "Why couldn't we have just met at the station? Is this all just a ploy to get people to watch baseball?"

Penelope blinked, her surprise rather genuine. "You know, you might be right!"

Darlene, of course, was not at all upset about this. "It's perfectly reasonable," she declared when she caught up with them and they began making their way toward the train station. "It gets everyone in one place without notice. It also means that there's less worry about their meeting places being found."

"I could have gotten the train tickets instead," Hetty grumbled.

"But it would have increased our chances of being discovered." The bartender from Fool's Moon stepped up to join their group, giving them a little nod in greeting.

"Is that a problem?" Darlene asked.

"A great one," he said rather solemnly. "A few times fire has even struck places we were known to have met."

He walked with them to the train station. He was also a fan of the Pythons, so he and Darlene chatted a bit as they all went to the train car marked on their tickets. They each handed their tickets to the conductor. The man nodded and opened a door for them.

"I have a question for you," Hetty said, drawing the bartender aside before she took a seat. "Did you work with Valentine Duval? Co— I mean Lou told me there would be someone here that might have."

"That person is me," he said easily. "We worked together on heading off the legal challenges if these magic bans ever come to fruition. I'm a bit of a lawyer on the side."

"A bit?"

His smile was bitter. "I know the stuff, just can't legally practice."

Hetty nodded. "Anything else?"

"A few different things. Valentine was traveling. When he wasn't doing that, he was teaching or working on solving that cipher."

"And what were you doing?"

"Recruiting members," he said. "Or to be frank, determining what prospective members were suitable. There was a concern going around about possible spies."

"That's what happens when you're a secretive lot," Hetty said. "Complicated meeting arrangements, special tasks to gain entry, passwords, and the like."

He laughed. "I suppose so."

The bartender took a seat next to a friend of his. Penelope had found a seat near the back and saved a spot next to her. Hetty looked for Darlene, and found her friend happily chatting away about the baseball game with an older couple.

The Pythons' coach clapped his hands to get everyone's attention.

"Shall we get started? What old business has yet to be discussed?"

Hetty listened closely at first, expecting to hear about fires, or even how the proposed magic bans were going to be a major issue in October's elections. But the conversation that began was about cauldron sizes.

Surely, Cora hadn't given Hetty these tickets for *this?* Cora never had explicitly said anything important was going to be talked about. She just wanted to invite Hetty into the group. This was what being part of an organization like this involved, she supposed. Dealing with both the fun and boring.

Hetty's gaze drifted to the train window. The train was still sitting in the station. The delay was due to some luggage being loaded, and a man arguing with the conductor.

The man turned ever so slightly.

It was Nathan Payne.

Hetty got up. Penelope turned in her direction. Hetty just shook her head as she slipped out the back of the train car.

Hurrying out the vestibule, Hetty jumped back onto the platform.

The luggage was gone and so was Payne.

There was no train on the other side. And no one else on the platform, just a few pigeons. Hetty looked up at them, pondering for a wild moment if they could be some help.

"Hetty!"

Penelope stood in the open door of the train as it slowly started to move.

Hetty picked up her skirts and ran, jumping through the open door before the train cleared the platform completely.

"Who did you see out there?" Penelope asked. "Was it that man we saw before?"

"Someone else," Hetty said. "Why aren't you at the meeting?"

Penelope crossed her arms over her chest. "Because you aren't."

That was an answer Hetty couldn't refute.

"Then let's get back to it, shall we?"

Hetty lifted the handle for the door back to the compartment, but snatched her hand back.

It was as cold as ice.

"What's wrong?" Penelope asked.

"Everything," Hetty grunted. "Step back."

As Penelope did, Hetty tapped the band at her neck. Obediently the Herdsman appeared in a flash of light.

The star-speckled woman lifted her staff and swung it over the door.

Two star sigils marked the door, but it was the thumps and muffled cries beyond that alarmed Hetty more.

Flinging her magic at the door, Hetty broke through the spells and pushed her way back into the compartment.

A haze of dust hung in the air, and figures that were once upright and forward-facing were now slumped over. Some were even lying on the floor. The bats and brooms the players had brought with them had fallen to the floor.

Hetty stepped over all of them, headed for Darlene.

Darlene was standing up, as she was too short to see whatever had happened otherwise. She was slumped forward, her outstretched hand reaching to grab something.

"They're only sleeping." Penelope had bent over a young man in an Independents uniform. She had her fingers pressed to his wrist, even as she peered at his seat companion. "It's a spell." Penelope looked up at Hetty, her eyes widening. "Look out!"

Light flashed to her right as Hetty's protective spells countered the magic lobbed at her.

Through her view of Aries lowering its horns to face her attacker, Hetty saw Nathan Payne standing in the aisle.

Hetty glowered at him, and he snarled back, before summoning the Hydra star sigil.

Arrow star sigils flitted from Hetty's fingers almost before she was even aware of it. The first glittery arrow flew through all the heads of the mythical beast. The second one dove for its center and disrupted the spell. The third went straight for Payne.

It hit. But not flesh. The spell bounced harmlessly off magical shielding.

Hetty ducked as the magic rebounded and fell against the seats, bouncing painfully against a sleeping person.

Slightly dazed, Hetty sat up just in time to see Payne darting for her once again.

Hetty slapped her choker. A spell exploded between them, pushing him away. The force of the magic also knocked Hetty back, pushing the breath out of her lungs. She hissed as she moved to stand up, only to see Payne drawing a knife.

"I had orders to wait, but let's do this now," he said. "One less problem for the future."

Payne raised his arm only to have his hand snapped back by a gust of wind. He dropped the knife with a yell.

Behind Hetty, Penelope banged the back end of the wind pistol, frustration crumpling her face.

Payne started to attack once again, but then ducked to the far side of the train car.

Something whizzed past Hetty's head. As she expected to hear another shot fired from Penelope's elemental pistol, it took her too long to realize what it really was: a gunshot.

A new person had stepped into the train compartment. She swiftly strode forward through the aisle and gently shoved Penelope out of the way into a nearby seat.

One look at the angular face and Hetty recognized the bookshop thief who'd aimed a pistol at her the day before.

The woman grimly unloaded her gun at Payne, firing round after round.

Payne danced like his feet were on fire, ducking and dodging with surprising agility. His attempt to throw back the magic was less successful. His spell fell apart until finally he blasted raw magic into the compartment.

In the haze of burnished orange, Payne turned tail and ran.

Hetty hurried after him, jumping over the rolling broomsticks as she made her way out.

The door to the next compartment was still shut, but the door to the outside was wide open.

Hetty leaned out, grasping the door handle as she did.

The train was at full speed. They'd be passing over the river soon. Right now they were speeding along mostly empty expanse, but there was nowhere safe for anyone to jump off at this height and speed.

Then she heard a thump overhead going in the direction of the cargo car.

Payne was on the roof!

"He's getting away!" Hetty cried.

"Not on my watch." The stranger pointed her gun to the ceiling and fired it. But it only clicked. "Stars shove it," the woman growled. "Empty!"

The car rocked a bit, and one of the broomsticks rolled to Hetty's feet.

Without considering it twice, Hetty grabbed it.

Hetty ran out the door, flung the broom forward, and jumped on.

The jolt into the air nearly knocked her off, but Hetty quickly regained her balance. She had only been on a broom once before, but she had jumped across tree branches before and run across moving trains. She could manage to stay on a broomstick.

Shifting her weight, she tapped her foot on the front of the broom, urging it forward. She flew over the train, looking for a tiny figure running across the top.

Though Payne had a big head start, it didn't matter. With Hetty on the broomstick, she would catch up to him soon enough.

But not to take him by surprise.

Payne must have seen her shadow. As soon as she moved close enough, he sent a burst of magic right at her.

Hetty slid back onto the bristle brush to dodge out of the way as much as possible.

The broom dipped backwards at the shift of weight. Hetty's arms windmilled as she fought to keep her balance. A searing panic gripped her, and for once a spell to get out of this spot of trouble didn't come to her.

But a hand clamped on her shoulder, keeping her steady.

The stranger stood beside her on her own broomstick, the wind whipping at her hair. In her free hand was Penelope's wind pistol.

"Got you," the stranger said. Then she leaned forward and expertly fired the wind pistol.

It struck dead center in Payne's back.

If the pistol had had a full charge, it might have done more than send him staggering back. It might have knocked him fully over. Instead, the pistol could only produce small gusts. Which was how, under his own power, Payne jumped into the Delaware River as the train roared across the bridge.

"Coward," the stranger muttered as they watched tiny ripples on the river's surface as Payne swam toward the nearest shore.

The stranger let go of Hetty.

Hetty gingerly slid her foot along the broom, leveling it so she stood firmly on it once again.

The woman didn't pay her much mind, tapping at the elemental pistol. "Now, this is something truly special." She turned her hand so the barrel was pointed in Hetty's direction. It was coyly done. Just enough to be a threat, but not enough to be overtly so.

"What else can this do?" the woman asked.

"I didn't make it, so I don't know." Hetty crossed her arms over her chest. "Why did you help me?"

The woman gave a small shrug, acting as if they weren't having this conversation standing atop broomsticks. "My employer sent me to make sure you didn't get hurt or worse."

"And that employer is?" Hetty asked.

"Bernice Tanner."

Hetty was too weary to be surprised. She just moved right to annoyance. "You're Bernice Tanner's new assistant?"

"Correct. I'm Temperance Murray. Recent arrival to this lovely city. I take dictation, answer letters, and tend to everything that greatly concerns Miss Tanner. That encompasses a wide variety of things, as you can tell."

"I can," Hetty admitted. "Where did you acquire such a set of skills?"

"I worked for the post office out west."

Temperance tossed Hetty the empty pistol. Hetty caught it by the handle.

Temperance shifted her stance on the broom and darted off, heading down to the other end of the train to see what Payne thought so important to bring here from Camden.

Not caring enough to follow, Hetty tapped her foot on the broom. She flew back to the train, and got close enough to jump back inside.

"Who was that?" Penelope asked, still gazing up at the sky.

Hetty scowled at the dark speck that was becoming smaller and smaller. "She said her name was Temperance Murray. She's Bernice's new assistant."

"Isn't she wonderful?" Penelope had clasped her hands to her chest. "She knew exactly how to fire that pistol without me telling her. And how she rescued you! She's absolutely wonderful!"

"*Wonderful* is a stretch," Hetty grumbled.

"She saved your life!" Penelope insisted. "We must thank her!"

"You'll get your chance," Hetty said. "She'll probably be at the ball tonight."

As Penelope squealed about this, Hetty shifted the elemental pistol in her hand. Doing so, she found a wedge of paper stuck behind the trigger.

It was folded several times over, and once Hetty got it open, she saw a crescent moon on the corner.

Underneath was a short note:

Miss Bernice,
 Emily Jacobs is on her way to Philadelphia, you must protect her. The person I warned you about is after her. — V. Duval

HERO

INTERLUDE

April 1865

SOMEWHERE NEAR FARMVILLE, VIRGINIA

THIS IS THE LAST TIME we trust anything Bernice tells us," Hetty whispered as they watched the fifth wagon of white landowners flee over the rough terrain.

On the tree branch across from her, Benjy placed a finger on his lips, gently chiding her. Hetty ignored him.

Her spells to muffle noise were still well in place, and even if they weren't, no one was likely to even hear her. The white folks below were too busy trying to get away from the war that was swiftly marching its way onto their land. When it wasn't wagonfuls of people carting with them everything they considered precious, it was people making their way on foot, worried about the sounds of gunfire and sight of Sorcery flashing in the air.

Hetty didn't blame them. Armies moved slowly, but when they got moving they trampled over everything in their path, ransacking homes and farmhouses looking for supplies, and always setting up camp in the best home in the area.

With the wagon out of sight, Benjy lifted a small spyglass to his eye. He tapped his shoulder to signal it was clear. Although

Hetty dropped down first, he still landed before she did, making his way to the bushes for cover and protection.

They headed to Petersburg with the information that Hetty's sister was still enslaved on a small farm nearby. However, once they were there, instead of talking about Esther, the contact spoke about Union generals, a riverboat meeting with Lincoln, plans to disrupt Confederate supply lines, and prisoners goaded to use their magic to protect the retreating Confederates.

Information that was the last thing Hetty expected. But not Benjy.

"Bernice is a spy."

Benjy's words came as they crouched in the bushes near a farmhouse.

Hetty, ready to step out of the protective shadows, crouched back down next to him. "A *spy?*" she whispered. "Are you sure?"

"We were always sent places where no one had even heard about your sister, but they were places of some importance to the war."

Hetty grunted. "Why not say anything before?"

"Would you be out here if you knew otherwise?"

Hetty gazed at the sky. Plumes of smoke floated from the fighting several miles away, the same plumes they had been seeing no matter what direction they turned on this trip. Benjy knew her well enough to know her answer. He was asking a different question entirely. "The North Wind wants us here, to do something no one else can."

"Exactly." Benjy pointed to the farmhouse. "This place isn't abandoned."

Hetty had to agree. No signs of a hasty retreat could be seen from a distance. But that wasn't what Benjy noticed. Hetty stared at the home for a bit longer, and then saw the shimmer across the window.

"It's warded," Hetty said.

"Are you willing to bet the magic protections extend further than the home?"

Hetty should have taken that bet, for it turned out to be an easy one. The protections stretched out only as far as the shadows that surrounded the structure. Even those went away the moment Hetty prodded them. So easily were they taken care of that Hetty wasn't expecting any sign of resistance, especially not the woman who stood there at the back door with a rolling pin in her hands.

"Get out of here, if you know what's good for you," growled the woman. "You tell whatever army you're with that nobody's home!"

"We're not with the army," Hetty said, even though they had used that lie more than once to get access to a home. "We're just trying to get out of here, and we're looking for anyone who might want to come along."

The rolling pin lowered a tad bit. "You'd be looking awfully hard. Most folk left with their masters."

"But not you," Benjy said.

The woman lifted up her chin. "Didn't have much of a choice. I go with them, I lose my chance to slip away."

"You left a lot of spells on the house for someone planning to leave," Benjy said.

Hetty could kick him for opening his mouth. Once he started asking questions, people usually stopped being helpful.

This woman, however, looked at them closely. "You two aren't from around here. You talk too easily about magic," she said.

There wasn't a collar around the woman's neck, or any scars for that matter. The woman, noticing Hetty's glance, grunted. "Out here you don't talk about what spells you can do if you don't want to be dragged off. I do what they call kitchen magic. Not useful for fighting, although my man told those soldiers I could do nothing."

"Where is he now?" Hetty asked.

"Took him," the woman said, devoid of any emotion. "After the fighting at the bridge ended, the Grays took Lionel and a few others."

"What bridge?" Benjy asked.

"The only one that'll cross the river. Up top the trains cross, and just below is the one wagons and people can make their way across."

Later that night, it was the second bridge that Hetty and Benjy made their way across under the cover of darkness. The way across was not easy, both sides of the bridges guarded by soldiers.

Not wanting to risk using magic to pass by undetected, they used a favorite mundane trick of Hetty's that involved Benjy throwing a rock to make a noise far from their current position, drawing the soldiers' attention away. They hurried across the bridge to the other side and set about following the remnants of the army.

The army camp was a couple miles out. A little bit of moonlight was the only real illumination, with the exception of a few tiny fires. This made it easy for them to spot the coldest and darkest part of the camp.

There were no guards, as the thick chains kept the group of prisoners linked together, unable to run without making noise.

Benjy moved to the group, then dropped down so he was on level with them and whispered, "Lionel?"

A man across from Benjy lifted up his head. "Who are you?"

"Someone here to help," Benjy whispered. "Is this all of you? The ones that work magic?"

Hetty counted seven people. More than they'd originally expected, and slightly fewer than what the woman at the farmhouse had said.

"Yes," another said. A young woman by the timbre of her voice. "How can you help?"

"We'll get you out of here," Benjy said. "Is there a guard?"

Nobody had seen one so far, and most of the soldiers had ignored them. Even some of the laborers in the camp did as well, since being magic users meant they were marked for death.

Benjy made short work of picking the locks. Once they were freed, Benjy led the group away, retracing their steps back to the bridge.

Hetty stayed behind, crafting shadows that would take the shape of the seven newly freed people. It wouldn't last past dawn, but by then they should be well away.

Hetty pulled out one of the coins Benjy made. The moon being just a sliver in the sky, it wasn't strong enough to fully charge the invisibility charm in the coin. But it could deepen shadows already there. She was still pondering that when she heard footsteps somewhere ahead of her.

"Aren't you coming?" a man asked. It was one of the seven. Hetty relaxed, putting her gun back in its holster.

"I'm the rear guard." She walked past him. "Come, we don't want to fall behind."

"Don't look like much of a soldier to me," the man said.

She stopped, the skin prickling at her neck. There was something familiar about his voice.

"You got good eyes to see in all this darkness."

"Good memory."

Hetty turned with her pistol in hand as she recognized the voice as Nathan Payne's.

The sliver of moonlight illuminated his twisted smile. "We meet again, Sparrow."

"We must stop doing that," she said.

"This was no accident. I made sure the rumors of your sister would bring you in this direction. Why chase after you when I can bring you to me?"

Hetty's hand twitched against the trigger. She should have

known he'd used her sister against her this way. Used those scraps and whispers about Esther's whereabouts to lure Hetty. It was amazing he hadn't done it before or that he hadn't drawn up a better trap. Even now he underestimated her, because for some reason he thought by facing her alone he had an advantage.

Still a fool after all this time.

"Make this easy on yourself and come quietly," Payne demanded.

"Never."

"You won't shoot me, Sparrow. It'll draw too much attention. They might not get you alive, but they'll get your friend, and I know that's the last thing you want."

"What do you want, Payne?"

"The only thing I ever wanted," he said. "Vengeance for the death of my son."

Payne rushed at her.

Hetty dodged, but he was coming at her furiously. Payne was right about one thing. Her gun going off would draw attention. But she had other ways to deal with him.

Exchanging her pistol for the sewing needle in her pocket, she ran the needle through a scrap of cloth, sewing the quickest star sigil she could. She didn't even bother yanking the needle out as she pressed it against Payne's face.

He was still reaching for her throat when the sleep spell went into effect. His arms fell to his side, and he slumped to the ground.

Panting, she looked down at him and felt the weight of the pistol in her pocket.

One shot.

One single shot and she would never have to see his face again. Never fear his whisper finding her when she least expected it. Never worry that he was going to squeeze the life out of her someday.

But if she shot him, she'd wake up the Confederate camp. She might be able to escape, but she might not. There was a river. There were all the people they were attempting to save. They were in an unfamiliar area rife with danger. And there was no one around to save them.

One gunshot now, and it wouldn't be just Payne who died. It would be her. It would be Benjy. It would be the handful of souls trusting them.

She couldn't do it.

She wouldn't do it.

Payne deserved to be shot, but the cost would be too high.

Hetty spat on the ground, cursing Payne's name. Let the stars take this man, because their next meeting will not end well.

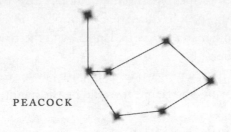

PEACOCK

33

HETTY WAS CURLED UP in the window seat in the study, reading Esther's book, when Benjy entered the study.

"How was the baseball game?"

Hetty shut the book and leaned back against the window with a smile, anticipating how he'd react to her next words. "I nearly fell off a broomstick."

Benjy's eyebrows rose at that, and he sat down on the couch. "Tell me this story."

Leaving off any embellishments for a change, she told him everything, starting with her quick visit to see Oliver and Thomas and ending with the fight on and above the train.

"Adelaide Duval was attacked by Nathan Payne. And her brother bought supplies from him?" Benjy nodded. "You scratched off a suspect and a lingering question in one swoop. Very nice."

"Valentine bought chalk from Payne." Hetty blinked, seeing the connection she had overlooked at first. "If only he hadn't?"

"He'd have met a bad end either way. The murderer has a list to go through, after all."

"Yet Payne has time to transport stolen magical goods."

"He has to, it's his scheme. Although he's working with the alderman, I doubt it's a true partnership. Such things always come at a price."

"Money?" Hetty asked, even though she knew it wasn't the right answer. When they were at the warehouse, Payne had said something about goods. And a spellbook. "Payne gave the alderman some type of magic." Hetty blinked as the pieces fell into place. "Could Payne be giving away a fire-boosting potion?"

"Odds are likely," Benjy replied.

Which meant yes.

Hetty had suspected magic was at the root of the fires, but thought it might have been Sorcery. But if Payne was behind this, it explained a few things, including why the fires had occurred frequently in the past few weeks.

"Now we have another reason to do something about Payne. What did the printers tell you about the ciphers?"

Benjy gave a short laugh. "That the pamphlets sold out quickly. But it was only a short run. The printers were burned down."

"Just that one?"

"Printers, plural," Benjy repeated. "All three places, including their equipment. No more copies to be found anywhere. Which was part of the reason there's such chatter. With only a few copies around, what remains is even more treasured."

Now this was something she didn't expect. "You were looking for other copies?"

"I wanted to compare what I had with another." Benjy shrugged. "Couldn't get my hands on another. Nearly had to fight someone to answer my questions."

Hetty chuckled. "Someone tried to fight *you?*"

"Didn't say they were wise. Speaking of fighting. Anything else I should know about your adventures?"

Hetty plucked the note from her pocket. "I got this from Bernice's assistant. It's a warning from Valentine Duval about the arrival of Emily Jacobs to town. To protect her from danger."

"So this is what Bernice is planning to tell us about."

"I don't think so."

"What do you mean? You got the note from her assistant, didn't you?"

"I don't think she was asked to do that. I was thinking about why she was on the train. Temperance could have been following after Nathan Payne on Bernice's orders. But she only intervened once I was attacked. I think she heard about the meeting and planned to pass this note on to me. She knew who I was. The letter had a crescent moon on it. Maybe Valentine knew about that —Adelaide did, after all. But he wouldn't just draw a moon on it."

"There would be a sun and moon on it." Benjy nodded.

"Exactly. I think Temperance Murray was noticing things and decided to tell us without the approval of Bernice. She faked this note."

"That's a remarkable leap of judgment, given the woman pointed a pistol at you."

"It says more that she didn't pull the trigger," Hetty said. "She never seriously did that, despite her threats. I have a feeling she's keeping several secrets, though. She said nothing really about herself and her place in things. Even this note shows an extraordinary interest."

Benjy shrugged. "If you work for Bernice Tanner, keeping secrets is the way of things. But it's hardly the time to add on yet another mystery."

"No, it's not." Hetty leaned against the window. The crows were flitting about the yard, busy themselves with their own affairs. "What a week this has been. People are dead that should be alive, and we got a number of ghosts haunting us."

"We can't fix the first, but the latter we can."

Hetty turned back to him, quite bemused. "I thought ghosts weren't real."

"Literally they aren't, but metaphorically, yes. Although that's just a turn of phrase to drive a point."

"Never a simple answer from you?" Hetty asked, grinning all the same.

"If it was simple it wouldn't be a question."

Hetty nodded before asking, "How do you suppose I get rid of my sister's ghost?"

Benjy lightly tapped the top of their couch. "You have the right idea of giving items to Penelope. But another part is using the things Esther sent. Otherwise, why would she have bothered in the first place?"

"Use the knowledge?" Hetty glanced at the book in her hand, suddenly struck by something she read. "I thought I was finished with my preparations, but there's one more thing I need to do!"

When they arrived at the hotel hosting Bernice Tanner's ball later that evening, the moon was bright and bold over their heads. Not quite full, but close. Still, it was a bauble as luminous as any decoration that filled the venue.

It seemed a grand palace to Hetty's eyes, though the couple that walked past them grumbled about the small size. The ground floor was for dancing and general merriment. Stairs led up to the next level with the lip of balcony hanging over the room. Around them, windows stretched to the height of eighteen feet tall. Twinkling overhead was the centerpiece of the room, a brilliant chandelier with every orb enchanted with flickering flames.

"This is a brilliant piece of magic," Hetty said. "It should be drawing every single eye."

"There's something else already doing that," Benjy whispered. He ran his fingers along the thin cape she'd attached to her gown.

The same burnished gold as her dress, the cape had a number of embroidered flourishes that hid a dozen star sigils. Hetty's best work was blending the cape's collar with her lace choker, building upon the fabric to hide the scars around her neck. For jewelry, she had the hairpins Benjy had made her, and a ring with a large flower she'd found in Esther's crate. The flower didn't spit out a needle or carry poison, but according to Esther's book it had been imbued with some minor magical abilities that would be perfect for that night.

"You never do anything by half measure, do you? You either disappear into the shadows or steal the glory of the brightest stars around."

Hetty warmed at the compliment and hooked her arm into his. "What fake name do you want to give strangers? I'll let you pick this time."

Benjy was still pondering over names as they made their way across the room. As was their habit, they arrived in a corner of the room with a solid wall at their backs and full view of all the doors that led out of the room.

There were three doors. The one they came in through, another leading to the kitchen, and the last leading to a short hallway the musicians had emerged from.

"For a ball done in the Duvals' honor," Hetty said, "I see less of a tribute to their lives and work, and more rich people talking to each other."

"The Duval name has not been forgotten. Look over there by the buffet. That trio there are patrons for Olmstead, ICY, Vaux, and the other schools. Rich folk who toss their money at the schools in hopes of having a classroom named after them."

"You can stop. I know you aren't enjoying yourself."

"I always enjoy myself in your company," he corrected swiftly.

Hetty suppressed a smile, and looked about once again. "Have you seen anyone? All our friends are supposed to be here."

"Not yet. But it's pretty crowded. They might be here and we wouldn't even know it."

That Hetty could agree with. Even on the edges it was hard to really see people. Most were moving about quickly as they took turns around the room. Hetty thought she might have spotted Cora and Jay in the midst of conversation elsewhere, but it was hard to say for certain.

Then a cluster of people broke away, and one of the reasons they were at the ball at all appeared.

Adelaide Duval glared up at her cousin Horace. And for good reason. At his side was the medium, Eudora Mason.

"Look who it is," Hetty said. "Why do you think *she's* here?"

"Obviously she was invited to put on a show. Expect her to charge money, as all frauds do." Benjy shook his head. "It's poor taste all around."

"She might not be here as a medium," Hetty observed. "Her clothes are not all that fancy, and it's not the costume she normally wears. If I didn't know any better, I'd say she was his guest. Could there be infatuation?"

"For the prospects of imagined riches, maybe. She's using him."

"There are simpler ways, instead of going around announcing herself as Eudora Mason, the great conjurer of spirits and medium extraordinaire. I bet that's not even her real name."

"Eudora," Benjy repeated, but when he said the name he pronounced it as if he were hearing it for the first time. Then said even softer. "Dora."

The name had a familiar ring to Hetty. She pondered for a moment, before a letter floated forward in her memory.

Dora was a name that appeared in one of the letters that Raimond Duval kept. Since it was such a vague letter, Hetty hadn't given it a closer look. There was so much to read, so much to understand, that Hetty hadn't bothered looking for any others.

But Benjy had.

"There were seven letters," Benjy said. "Seven letters that a 'Dora Reynolds' wrote to Raimond Duval after the publishing of the pamphlet. The first few were rather polite. Although rather terse, so it's understandable when later the tone shifts to undisguised anger. The last had open threats about death and violence. Not hints she would do anything herself, but a warning."

"That might all be true, but how do you know it's her? The names are similar, but that's not much—"

"Raimond saw her in Camden," Benjy interrupted. "Three weeks before he died. He didn't mention a séance, but he did mention having to draw Dora aside from a crowd. No details about what they spoke about, but he had a number of concerns, and there was a vague note that didn't make sense then but does now."

"Which was?"

"'The past shows up when you don't stretch out a hand.'"

Hetty wasn't quite sure if this was proof enough. "I want to believe you. I really do. But I can't see how this fits in with the case."

"Then we must talk to her. Even tell her," he said with a shudder, "that we want a private séance."

"Think she'll agree to that?"

Benjy once again plucked at Hetty's gown. "With you dressed like this, she'll be too busy counting her coins to ask questions."

"All we need is a good story," Hetty said.

"Are you going to tell me what it is?" he asked.

"I'll make it up as I go. Just play along."

"Stars above," Benjy muttered.

"We'll be fine." Hetty flashed a dazzling smile up at him. "Trust me!"

The unhappy trio of Adelaide, Horace, and Eudora seemed to be more than glad to have their tense conversation interrupted when Hetty and Benjy approached.

Only Adelaide seemed to recognize them. She opened her

mouth to greet them, but Hetty spoke quickly in a breathy voice: "Are you Eudora Mason? My friends told me you are a medium. I would love for you to do a séance for me. I'm Iris Landry." Hetty made a show of rubbing her hand along Benjy's arm. "And this is my husband, Sylvester."

"I haven't had the pleasure." Eudora's voice was warm as she spoke, but her eyes were coolly calculating. "But I am always happy to speak to those interested in communicating with departed spirits."

"But not at the ball," Horace interjected. His glare was fixed solely on the medium. "Now's not a good time for such things. Even though several people have already voiced interest."

"It wouldn't be proper," Adelaide growled. "Where would you do it?"

"There are rooms upstairs," Horace said. "Plenty of space for a small group."

Adelaide swung around to her cousin. "You will not hold a séance here. I'll have you thrown out! I don't care if you contact the ghost of the Queen of Sheba, I will not have it!"

"Adelaide," Horace cried as he glanced over to Hetty and Benjy. "Calm yourself!"

Adelaide drew back, her hand clenched in a fist. For a moment it truly did seem like she would strike him. Instead, she relaxed, turning her back to him. "You will not get my father's house. I'll burn it down myself before you do!"

She stomped off, into the ballroom.

"Adelaide!" Horace called. His cry attracted some attention, and he grumbled as he followed after his cousin.

"Oh my." Eudora touched her hand to her face, more than a bit embarrassed. "I'm afraid it's all my fault. I'm always looking to help, but didn't realize I stumbled into family trouble."

"Not your fault," Benjy said. "Those lost to us are always a sore subject."

"That is true. I was drawn to this delicate art in the hopes of speaking with my own father," Eudora said. "Cruelly, my gift does not allow me to work on my own behalf. But I do find that speaking with those who've passed on helps people in their grief. Which is why I came here. Miss Adelaide needs a chance to heal."

"She doesn't seem that interested," Hetty said.

"Her grief is too sharp. She very recently lost her brother. It is how these things tend to go." Eudora focused intently on Hetty. For a moment Hetty feared she might have recognized her. "Who have you lost, my dear?"

Benjy took a half step forward, as if placing himself between Hetty and the medium. "My parents. As a very young child."

"And more later, as well," Eudora said softly as she immediately turned to him. "You lost someone recently too, a person you thought a friend. They're gone, but you can't stop thinking about the past."

Hetty could feel Benjy stiffen next to her, but Benjy was too good of an actor to let it show. His hand only tightened around Hetty's.

"You are quite good at this," Benjy said.

"I can't take credit. It's a gift. I would be happy to do a séance for you. At your home, perhaps? Unless you wish to visit me in Camden."

"Such a short distance would not be hard to travel for all that you can do for us," Hetty said.

"Then I look forward to meeting you soon." Eudora nodded at them and drifted away to mingle elsewhere.

Benjy still gripped Hetty's hand, and she wiggled her fingers to get his attention.

"Sorry," he breathed when he finally let go. "Her words cut close. It's like she knew."

"She's good at using vague words once she realizes she's caught your attention. That's how she got me before."

"I can see that. I'm afraid I underestimated her."

"She's still a fraud," Hetty said. "She doesn't speak to ghosts. And what about her wanting to come to our house? I bet you right now, if we go to her tent she'll try to say it'll be better to do a house visit!"

"That might be a good thing if she did," Benjy said.

Hetty was just about to ask what he meant by that when Temperance Murray emerged from the crowd and approached them. Although she did not wear the crisp burgundy uniform the servers were wearing, the muted sable coloring of her dress and its neat practical lines placed her a world apart from the gathered guests.

"You look lovely," Temperance observed. "Miss Tanner will be glad of that. She worried you'd come in disguised as servants. She wants to talk to you."

This was expected, but much sooner than they had planned. Hetty glanced up at her husband, who only nodded.

"Take us to her, then."

Temperance led them from the ballroom into the short hallway. She opened one of the four doors that lined the hall, gesturing for them to enter. Temperance did not follow them inside. Instead, she silently shut the door behind them.

Inside, Bernice sat in an armchair under a painting of a fruit bowl. Her dress was a deep plum, with elegant ruffles suitable to her station. Her cane had even been spruced up for the occasion, polished to such a degree that the handle gleamed in the light. But even the shine on the cane could hardly match the gleam on the surface of the tinted dark glass of her spectacles.

"Would you like a drink?" Bernice said as a wine bottle poured liquid into the glass in her hand. "It'll raise your spirits."

"No need," Hetty said.

"More for me then." Bernice took a deep draw from her glass. "Take a seat. Don't stand on ceremony."

They sat. Hetty pulled her cape aside, her fingers running over the stitches.

"I suppose you're wondering why I invited you here," Bernice said.

"You want us to do something for you," Benjy said.

Bernice smirked. "I always did like you. Where most people dance around their words, you charge right through. Yes, I do have a task for you."

Benjy shifted forward. Nothing else changed. Not the placement of his hands, the set of his jaw, or even his gaze. Hetty realized then that there was no need for a change. He had known from the moment Bernice waved an invitation in front of them that whatever she wanted, whatever she asked, was not going to be worth the trouble they'd end up in. "I think you're misunderstanding things. We are not here to take an assignment from you. We are here for crucial information you withheld because you were moving pieces around on your chessboard, not realizing that there's a different game being played. What is it you want from us?"

Bernice slammed her empty glass onto the table. "The only thing you can do in this situation! I need your help with the Clarke Cipher. The ghost of Raimond Duval insists on it!"

A strangled noise escaped Benjy's throat, but he said nothing, leaving Hetty to speak up: "The Clarke Cipher is a well-crafted story."

"No, it has a good storyteller." Bernice poured herself another glass. She didn't drink it. She sat holding the glass, as she continued. "Most of what's in that star-forsaken pamphlet is true. I know Raimond and John Roberts are dead because of it. As is Valentine. And so many others. I didn't act quickly enough. Before he died, Valentine told me that he expected a threat on his life and that he needed my help. He wanted the names of the people who had helped Sarah Jacobs. He said he was trying to figure out who might have been in trouble, but I didn't quite believe him. I didn't want to believe him. But when I thought of Raimond's death, and the others I've taken for accidents, I thought he had a point, even before Valentine himself died. When Sarah's daughter arrived in town, I made sure to keep the girl safe. It was difficult. The girl did not trust me and gave my assistant the slip once or twice until we were able to convince her to stay with us."

"What convinced her?"

"The fire at Valentine Duval's home. The news about his death hadn't reached us yet, and Emily snuck out early that morning. Miss Murray went after the girl, and just in time. Fire was eating away at the house. A fire deliberately set by an intruder. Emily didn't see the man—she had hidden away in a room—locked herself in by accident. Luckily, Miss Murray found her and brought her back."

"That was a few days ago. Why stay quiet about all this?" Hetty said.

"I was hoping to handle this on my own. I also was trying to get information from the girl. Raimond and Valentine both were in communication with her. She knows something, but she won't tell me."

"Where is she now?" Benjy asked.

"You don't need to worry about her. She's under my protection."

"Then what do you want us to help you with?" Hetty asked.

"I need you to pretend that you've solved the cipher. Spread tales like you always do so that the murderer's attention falls on you while I make arrangements in the background. Once I have things in play, I'll let you know what you need to do next."

"Under what stars do you think we'll say yes to that?" Hetty exclaimed.

Bernice tightened her grip around her cane. "Don't you want your business to pick up at your funeral home? I can help with that. A few well-placed words do wonders. They bring business. They pull business away."

Whatever else Bernice had to say, Hetty didn't hear.

Magic crackled at her fingertips, as Hetty closed the space between her and the old crone.

"How *dare* you! I bet you are the cause of all our troubles! Raimond Duval dies, and you decide to ransom our business! All to get us to do your bidding. If it weren't for you I would have found my sister years ago and she'd probably be alive today! Now you're asking us to put ourselves in harm's way for you? How dare—"

Benjy put a hand on her shoulder. His touch, more than his magic, neutralized her roaring anger. Hetty's arm fell to her side. As she heaved, gasping for air, Benjy's words continued to be the only sound in the room.

"Miss Tanner would not waste her precious time meddling in our affairs," he said, turning each quiet word into a dagger. "She is far too busy. And far too aware of what it means to do such a thing to the people who did the impossible for her time and time again."

For the first time during the course of the interview, Bernice was silent, but Hetty had her answer anyway.

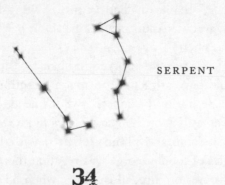

34

W<small>E NEED TO FIND EMILY JACOBS</small>," Hetty said the moment they were back in the ballroom. "Whatever Bernice has planned, I want nothing to do with it! All that matters is finding that girl."

"No arguments from me." Benjy's hand went to Hetty's arm, a gentle pressure once more holding her back. "But don't do anything you'll regret."

"I never regret anything!"

His expression said everything — his worries, his concerns, and the anger he held back, because one of them needed a clear mind.

"I won't do anything risky," Hetty said, responding to this unspoken sentiment. "But if Bernice ever asks anything of me again —"

"I know," he whispered, and let go. "But there is something else she said that bothered me. She said Valentine wanted to know everyone who helped Sarah Jacobs."

Hetty pulled out of her rage long enough to consider this. "You think we're in danger?"

"Not us," Benjy said.

"That's hard to say. I can't remember anyone who might have been part of all that who's still in the city, except for —" Hetty gulped, before she could say her friend's name.

"Darlene," Benjy finished grimly. "Didn't Penelope tell you Horace Duval was asking questions about her this morning?"

"And he's here!"

"Let's make sure he hasn't found her."

It would have attracted too much attention to use magic to find Darlene, but in the end, they didn't need to.

Standing at one of the small tables by the windows, Darlene, Penelope, George, and Thomas chatted, with drinks in hand and small plates of food. George was regaling them with some story, all of their eyes on him, all laughing when he said something in particular.

The sight brought a rush of calm over Hetty. All were attired in their finest. Serviceable suits for George and Thomas, although Thomas had tied a flashy orange scarf around his neck. Penelope was in a green dress, the fabric of which wasn't as poisonous as the deep color implied, not with the jeweled butterflies adorning her hair. Darlene wore an elegant gown of dark red, the cut and fall of the dress simple, but the embroidery was a fine netting of bronze. Her glasses were missing tonight, likely in the purse dangling from her wrist.

Hetty approved of all the sartorial choices, because in every stitch of clothing Hetty had left traces of her magic.

"I thought it might be you I saw earlier," George said in greeting when they approached. "I saw the trail of that dress and I thought: no one else would be so daring!"

"When you say you're going as guests, you do come in style!" Penelope added. "But here's the true test: What names did you give at the door? I owe Thomas five dollars if you used the Ross name."

Darlene frowned. "Why would you do that? Hardly anyone knows you're here."

"They like to keep their privacy," Thomas pointed out.

"So did you or did you not?" Penelope asked.

"If someone points us out," Benjy said when Hetty didn't move to answer, "tell them we are Iris and Sylvester Landry."

A little groan went through the group.

"Who gets the money?" Penelope asked.

"I do," Darlene said, "from both of you."

"You didn't take part in the bet," Thomas accused.

"Don't care—we got a baby to take care of," Darlene said.

Hetty cleared her throat, getting their attention. "Darlene, can we talk for a moment?"

Darlene nodded, and handed her drink to George.

As Hetty and Darlene left, Benjy turned to Thomas. "Where is Oliver?"

Hetty missed Thomas's answer as she led Darlene away from most of the crowd, stopping at a space where they could talk privately. "You and George need to head home."

Darlene looked on, rather surprised. "Is that all you were going to tell me? You could have told me that with the others."

"The others don't need to know because only you are in danger."

Darlene calmly took out her glasses and slid them back on. "Well, I'm not leaving this ball because of something like that. I have been in danger many times before. Maybe not as often as you, but still—I've been in my share of peril."

"This is different. You need to be somewhere safe just in case."

"In case what?" Darlene remarked. "You don't think I can handle things? I may not be as talented in magic, or have a bounty of potions to toss at things, but I'm more than capable of protecting myself. When the train compartment was attacked earlier, why do you think it was a sleep spell that got us all? Or even that no one came in to throw us off the train because of the magic being worked there? That was my spells at work! I'm not helpless."

"I know that, but—"

"Besides, I'm not that surprised that there is trouble brewing." Darlene looked around the ballroom. "Why do you think we are all here?"

"What are you talking about?"

"Hetty," Darlene said, with more than a fair share of exasperation. "You inform us that you're going to a ball, hosted by a woman you barely like, and kept those plans despite being in the middle of a case. Naturally, we came prepared. George brought one of his service pistols. Oliver has a knife with him. Penelope got potions, of course. And Thomas found this cane that has a sword inside it. We're here to help you, if you let us."

Hetty's heart warmed at these words, and it took her a moment before she could speak. "Do I have a choice?"

"No, you don't!"

"Then I suppose we should tell the others what's going on, if Benjy hasn't already."

"Yes, we should," Darlene agreed. She stopped as she looked up toward the mezzanine. "There's Oliver. I wondered where he went."

Hetty glanced up as well.

She saw Oliver's grumpy face peering out into the ballroom. But he was not alone up there.

Behind him stood Nathan Payne.

She should have come here as a servant.

This dress brought her too much notice. Even if Payne didn't expect to see her, even if he didn't recognize her, he would have remembered this dress.

"So did I," Hetty said to Darlene, hoping her voice betrayed nothing. "I'll go talk to him."

For a moment, it seemed Darlene was going to follow, but with a nod, she continued her way across the ballroom.

Oliver was still at the railing when she reached him, but Nathan Payne was gone. But not far. There was an open door behind Oliver that was swinging shut.

"There are far too many people here," Oliver said as he patted his pockets for his pipe. "They all talk too much. I can't believe Thomas convinced me—"

"You're not going anywhere, are you?"

Oliver's hands stopped moving. "What dangerous thing are you about to do?"

"Nothing. Just stay here. If you hear me screaming, come running."

Oliver blinked. "I never heard that before."

"You'll know it when you hear it."

There were several small tables set up in the room, with other people seated there. Despite the people around her, all Hetty could focus on was Payne and the memory of the promise she made many years ago. A promise with grim outcomes yet to be delivered.

Nathan Payne sat at a table a little farther away, with a checkerboard laid out in front of him.

He looked up. It was hard to tell if he knew her at all. Nothing in his manner said he recognized her from the train or from slicing up his face.

She was banking on the fact that her fancy dress and attire would give her some sort of protection, as he'd always seen her before in less pristine situations. It was a slim hope, but one she'd hold on to until the moment he tried to jam a knife into her stomach.

"Why is a lovely creature like yourself not out there dancing?"

"Bored," Hetty said, "and curious about what was in here." She looked around for decorations to point out, but there was nothing but the checkers spread out on the table.

"Would you like to play?"

Something that could be called a smile lifted the corner of

his mouth, but it was overshadowed by the intensity of his eyes. Hetty put her hand on the back of the chair to keep from pulling out one of her hairpins and jamming it into his eye.

"Just one round." Hetty took a seat at the table.

"What's your name? I feel as if we've met before."

"I doubt it," Hetty said, sliding one of her pieces forward. "My husband and I are fairly new in town. He's a teacher."

"Yet you're here."

"I suppose we know the right people."

Hetty moved one of her pieces in preparation to jump his in the next move. "What brings you here?"

"Work." Payne moved across the board, just where she wanted him to go.

"What sort?" Hetty jumped the piece, and then scooped up another.

Payne took one of her checkers in a move she didn't see at all. Hetty frowned. The move didn't allow him to snatch up any of her pieces in this turn, but it did limit her options.

"I'm in the business of acquiring goods on behalf of interested parties. Rare, expensive goods that I relocated from Canada and Boston to other places."

"Expensive goods," she echoed. "Such as ... musical instruments?"

"Nothing as fine as that. I'm quite practical."

"Nothing is more practical than something that brings a bit of good cheer into people's lives."

Hetty reached over to make another move, but this time, she hesitated.

There were more pieces on the board than there had been a moment or so ago.

More of his pieces.

Hetty studied them, wondering if she wanted to call out cheating. There were enough pieces on the board that adding a few didn't stick out like a red apple in a basket of green pears. These pieces were a red of a slightly different color, but a closer look showed how different they were. The marks on them—

Were like Raimond Duval's checkers.

Not like—they *were* the missing pieces from Raimond's set.

"Is something the matter?"

Hetty got another glimpse of his face, and realized she had been mistaken to think a fancy dress could fool him.

He knew exactly who she was.

His eyes said it, as did the smirk, like a spider who'd finally caught the prey it laid its web for.

Hetty jumped her pieces across the board and picked up one of the stolen pieces. She dropped it onto the pile.

If he was disappointed, he said nothing, moving the piece forward.

"We shall see." Hetty plotted her next move.

She wasn't going to lose to a murderer. Either in the actual game of checkers or this battle of wits he was silently waging.

She pushed a piece deliberately into danger, as she fell back to a strategy that usually worked. Instead of going after her opponent's pieces, she sacrificed hers as smokescreen for the efforts of a larger plan.

It was something she'd learned from watching Cora play chess a few times. Chess was a game about planning ahead and anticipating moves, and more importantly, baiting people to make certain moves.

Hetty could never quite master it with chess, but she'd gotten rather good at it with checkers.

She gave up pieces she could afford to lose to get her pieces in place. When that was won, she went on the offensive, clearing the board with only token resistance from Payne. Soon she had all of his pieces until only the last stolen piece was left. Then she swooped down, taking that as well.

"You win." Payne blinked. "How did you do that? I had you on the run."

"That was the idea." Hetty stood then, cupping the stolen checker piece in her palm. "Good game. But I must go find my husband. He'll be looking for me."

"Yes, I'm sure he will."

With his eyes boring into her back, Hetty left.

She might have won the game, but she felt like she had lost something on the way to victory.

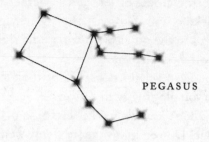

PEGASUS

35

Hetty hurried down the stairs to the ballroom's main floor, her mind focused only on getting as far away as possible.

The music in the ballroom was much more upbeat than before. Already, people were taking advantage of this shift, no more than Penelope and Thomas, who jumped and swung around, creating a wide berth around them that got them many glares and sour looks.

"There you are," Oliver said to Hetty. "That dress makes it easy to find you."

She looked back at Oliver, belatedly recalling telling him to wait for her. "I need to find Benjy. Have you seen him yet?"

"No, but I did see Thomas." Oliver pointed across the room. "His horrid scarf makes it easy."

"Horrid scarf that you gave him!"

Oliver shrugged. "I didn't think he'd ever wear it."

Hetty rolled her eyes. "Oliver, thank you for always being impossible to deal with."

"You're very welcome," he said rather grimly. "Now, what dangerous thing will you be doing next?"

"Dancing."

Before Oliver could protest, Hetty pulled him with her as she plunged into the crowd of dancers. Together they danced their way to Penelope and Thomas, the process getting easier the closer they got to the other pair. And at the right moment in the song, they switched partners.

"Ah!" Thomas exclaimed as Hetty took him by the hand. "What were you plotting with Oliver?"

"As if you don't know already," Hetty said. "You had him tail Nathan Payne! Do you know where Benjy went?"

"No idea. But he was asking questions about the medium. The one you girls saw."

"He's trying to find her?"

"Maybe he did already."

Before Hetty could say another word, they switched partners once again, Oliver grabbing Hetty's hand.

His scowl, rather impossibly, had deepened.

"Penelope says Benjy's gone looking for a medium. I thought he didn't believe in ghosts!"

Hetty shrugged. "He doesn't. I think he has questions about Horace Duval. Why were you tailing Nathan Payne for Thomas? I know you love him, but there are limits to supporting all his endeavors."

"It's nothing your husband wouldn't do for you," Oliver shot back.

Instead of answering, they made another switch. This time Hetty grabbed Penelope's hands instead, leaving both Oliver and Thomas stumbling awkwardly, taken aback by the switch in partners.

Penelope chortled a bit, as she stood there with Hetty while the dancing pairs moved around them.

"Where are Darlene and George?" Hetty asked.

"Not sure. They were talking with some teachers they knew. What's going on? Benjy said something, and Darlene said a bit more, but I'm not sure I got the complete picture."

"Darlene would neglect a few things," Hetty grumbled.

But Penelope surprisingly only laughed. "Well, what do you expect, you are friends, after all."

"Just keep an eye out for her. And Jay too. Just in case."

"I will."

Oliver pulled Penelope away and Thomas grabbed Hetty's hand, and they split back into mixed pairs once more.

"What do you need us to do?" Thomas asked.

"Find Darlene. She's in danger. And clearly she hasn't told you that bit yet."

"It seems to me that you're in trouble more than her. Nathan Payne is here."

"I played checkers against him. I won."

"And ran out, according to Oliver!"

"I'll be fine. It's Darlene you need to worry about."

They switched partners once more, but instead of Oliver taking her hand, she was grabbed from behind and spun neatly into another's awaiting arms.

"You vanished on me," Benjy said, pulling her close. "I don't like that."

Hetty could hear Oliver grumble, but such noise was already being overlooked as she gave Benjy her full attention.

Benjy led her away from the knot of dancers to the fringes. Here they danced just a tad slower than the music, so that they were in a world of their own. For a moment Hetty wished they could stay like that and pretend they were just invited guests here to enjoy themselves at the ball. But alas, this was not the night for such things. Rather ruefully, she said:

"There's a ghost in the ballroom. And his presence confirms our suspicion."

Benjy's expression did not alter beyond the slight narrowing of his eyes.

"Let's talk elsewhere."

Hand in hand, they moved to the fringes of the ballroom and quite smoothly walked up the stairs to the second level.

There were other places to talk without notice, but talking on the mezzanine was the best way they could watch the crowd as well.

Benjy leaned against the bannister as Hetty told him all about her checkers game. At the end of her tale, Hetty turned her hand over, revealing the checker piece. "Payne placed it on the board. On purpose."

"A cheat." Benjy shook his head.

"Look closer."

He looked at it again, and this time he saw it.

"The missing checker piece," Benjy murmured.

"Taken from Raimond Duval. If I had any doubts left, this proves that Nathan Payne killed him! And that he knows we're onto him! He wouldn't have put it down unless he knew of our investigation."

Of the reactions from her husband, puzzlement was the last one she expected to see. "How did he get the checker piece in the first place? And why bring it tonight?"

Ready to answer the first question, Hetty was tripped up by the second one.

This spoke of foresight and planning.

Hetty turned her gaze back toward the ballroom. The swirl of strangers soon faded away to the background as she spotted familiar faces. Penelope was drawing Cora aside to speak, a smile on the older woman's face becoming more frozen as Penelope spoke. Darlene and George were dancing in the crowded room, showing off their classical education with a series of smartly executed dance steps. And in the far corner of the room, Oliver and Thomas stood nearby, holding drinks but not sipping.

And in the middle of all that was Jay.

He stood in a cluster of men, likely generous benefactors to the school, laughing as he spoke with them.

If Hetty had her way, he'd stay there all night.

Because nearby was Nathan Payne, reaching into his jacket. Although the act could be seen as pulling out a pocket watch, the turn of his hand suggested a knife.

"Payne's going to attack!" Hetty cried.

"You can't aim a spell from here, Hetty, not without being seen first."

"Then I'll get closer."

Brushing her fingers against the lace at her neck, Hetty vanished from sight.

Benjy reached out to grab her, but Hetty had already climbed up onto the bannister.

Then she jumped.

Hetty fluttered down from the balcony, her spells like a gentle wind guiding her to the ballroom floor.

She landed with a soft thump, glad she had worn her boots instead of heels.

Grabbing the end of her dress, she moved into a run, dropping the invisibility spell so people would move a bit faster for her.

Jay had already moved from his friends. He was off walking by himself.

She needed to get to Jay. She needed to get there before—

Between the bodies that blocked her way, Payne drew out his knife.

No one seemed to have noticed.

Hetty watched in horror as Payne strode directly for Jay, closing the distance faster than Hetty could ever guess.

Payne raised his arm, ready to strike.

Something whooshed past, moving so fast that Hetty wasn't sure what it was.

But it had to be a spell.

Because the knife in Nathan Payne's hand shattered like glass.

The crowd lurched back as shards of metal flew in the air. A wisp of magic vanished in the air.

Hetty followed that wisp.

Benjy half leaned across the balcony, his hand outstretched. Their eyes met before he collapsed against the railing.

"Henrietta?" Jay stood before her, the shattered knife clearing the space between them. He stood shocked and aghast at the shards scattered on the ground around him. "What's going on?"

"Trouble," Hetty said as she caught sight of Payne pushing his way through the crowd. "Stay here. It's not safe!"

She had lost sight of Payne.

At first she thought he'd hidden himself in the crowd, biding his time like a leopard before striking. But then she spied a server apologizing to a guest with wine stains on their shirt and pointing to where Payne had fled.

Following similar gaps along the room, she left the ballroom behind and turned to the hallway and started opening each door.

The first two bore no fruit. The first was empty of occupants and the second held a pair whose mischief was amorous in nature.

Hetty shut the door without being noticed and moved to the next room.

Her hand was reaching for the third doorknob when something struck her on the shoulder.

"You will not find what you seek," Bernice Tanner said.

Hetty turned and saw her own glaring face reflected back at her in the dark shades.

"Because the North Wind is here to protect and safeguard all matters?"

The cane flipped up in Bernice's hand. "That was never a saying."

"You're in danger," Hetty said.

"That's hardly new. Why do you think I hired Miss Murray?" Bernice jerked her cane to the side.

On Hetty's right, Temperance Murray stood holding a pistol.

The gun was pointed to the ground and her face was a mask of professionalism as she looked around the hallway. At the sound of her name, Temperance nodded just once at Hetty before she pointed to one of the doors in the hall.

Grateful for this response, it was with full confidence that Hetty snapped back at Bernice, "Then why did you bring Emily Jacobs to this hotel?"

The cane swung out toward Hetty again but it didn't touch her this time. Instead it wavered in front of her as the old woman's lips trembled. "Because there is no safer place than at my side."

"Wrong. It's at mine!"

Bernice cackled. "You played checkers with a man who wanted you dead for many years now. If he hadn't been distracted by whatever charms you possessed, there might be a new story about you."

"If you're trying to keep me from opening this door, it's too late. Payne just tried to attack Jay in the middle of the ballroom."

"No, that's impossible!"

"It's only possible because your secrets and schemes made it easy for such a plot to unfold!" Hetty hissed.

Not interested in Bernice's reaction, Hetty turned back around. Her fingers skated in the air to form the Aries star sigil, and she shot it at the doorknob, blasting the door open.

As her eyes adjusted to the gloom, the moonlight that spilled into the room revealed a plush sofa and some chairs, some rumpled blankets, and a few books stacked on a small table next to an unlit lamp. She could smell wildflowers and sugared sweets.

"No one is here." Hetty touched the lamp. It was still warm.

"Impossible," Bernice cried. "I put spells on everything! Temperance, explain!"

As Temperance struggled to give an answer, Hetty continued her study of the room.

Wallpaper of neutral colors, newly laid. A window open to the night, and missing curtains. A chair moved out of place.

"I wouldn't worry. It looks like she made an escape. Which I don't blame her for. She came to you for help and you locked her up."

Bernice huffed. "It was the only way to keep her safe."

"You cannot keep everyone safe," Hetty said. "You may try, you may succeed. But you lose much in your efforts."

Bernice bowed her head, gripping her cane so tightly, Hetty thought it would snap in half.

"Why were you keeping Emily at your side?" Hetty asked.

"She holds the key to solving the ciphers," Temperance answered when her employer did not. "But she won't tell anyone but the Sparrow."

Hetty smiled. "Then I need to find her."

"There's a tunnel at the end of the hallway. It's hidden by a grandfather clock. You need to move the minute hand counter-clockwise to nine," Temperance said, even as Bernice started to protest. "It'll be the best way for you to exit without being seen."

"What are you doing?" Bernice grumbled.

"She has the best chance of finding Emily."

Leaving them behind, Hetty went deeper into the hallway.

She didn't have far to look. The hallway did not go for long, and the clock that Temperance had spoken of was easily spotted.

As was the other person lingering nearby.

A shadow moved around the grandfather clock, grunting as it tried and failed to move it. Hetty approached slowly, her fingers falling to find one of her hairpins.

Then the figure stepped out.

It was only Eudora Mason, looking lost and put out.

"Oh, dear stars." Eudora blinked. "Where did you come from?"

"Looking for some quiet," Hetty said. "It's very loud back there."

"It is," Eudora said. "But I suppose that's what happens at events like this."

They smiled at each other rather pleasantly. That's when Hetty took a closer look at Eudora. At the tense way she held herself as she watched Hetty.

Since Hetty had seen Eudora at the Duval home, she suspected the other woman was a thief, manipulating the gullible with fake séances, and gathering items of some value from homes when invited in. Hetty wouldn't be surprised now if she had caught Eudora doing the same here. But the grandfather clock was not something she could have absconded with. What was she really doing out here?

"How did you first meet Horace Duval?" Hetty asked.

"He came to one of my séances," Eudora said. "After his uncle died. He had regrets he wanted to share."

As Eudora spoke, the flower ring Hetty wore wiggled unmistakably. She wasn't sure the first time she'd felt it earlier, because she hadn't often encountered magic like this. But Hetty trusted her sister's skill and the accuracy of the note left in her book:

The chrysanthemum ring warns of liars who hold back the truth with their tongues.

". . . I just wanted to help all I could."

"That's a lie," Hetty said. "You wanted to get to know him for another purpose, for the access he gave you to the Duvals. Particularly about his cousin who was traveling, who you were very curious about meeting. Because he should have died instead of his father."

Eudora swallowed. "I don't know what you're talking about!"

"You do. Because you made that mistake several times until

you decided it'd be better to go after everyone who was there the night Alvin Jacobs was killed. The only question is *why*. Who was Alvin Jacobs to you?"

Eudora's eyes flashed. "Who was Alvin Jacobs?" she snapped. The whispery Southern accent she had been putting on this entire time melted away as she trembled. "He was my father! Joseph Reynolds, taken from me and my mother when I was a child! Valentine Duval was supposed to have freed him from slavery, but he didn't do that. He let my father die and then he printed the pamphlets! Raimond might have claimed that it wasn't the case when he went to see me. But I'm no fool! They killed him for the papers to the treasure, and when they couldn't find it on their own, they printed it out for the world to help with them! They deserved their deaths. They all did! They're all to blame!"

"You murdered innocent people. And you're working with a man who would have sold your father south!"

"You take help where help is offered, or in this case paid for." She sneered at Hetty. "I should almost be grateful to you. I was forced to peddle myself out as a medium to pay his fees, but now that Payne knows you are the one meddling with things, he was willing to do whatever I asked as long as I'd made sure he would be able to kill you without trouble."

Eudora flicked a spell at Hetty. The star sigil was crudely drawn, but it was strong enough that it rattled against Hetty's protection spells.

Through the floating star sigil, Eudora snarled: "Give me Emily Jacobs and the location of the treasure at Valentine Duval's funeral! Do that and I'll keep Payne from bothering you ever again."

"Never!" Hetty drew Ursa Major. The great star-speckled bear rose up next to her, filling the hallway with its magical bulk. "I never give up people who come to me for protection!"

Hetty directed the spell forward. The bear charged, but it was too late.

Eudora's spells weren't attacking—they were covering her escape! The false medium's magic destroyed the grandfather clock, revealing a hidden door. Ursa Major ran through the spells, eliminating the rogue magic, and in the confusion, Eudora slipped into the tunnel opening.

Hetty ran for the door. But Eudora had spelled it shut.

Hetty pounded on it, even when she knew magic would be a better help. Who knows where Eudora would emerge? She might have gotten a confession out of the medium, but there was no proof to tie Eudora yet to the murders except her willing accomplice.

Hetty readied to pry the door open with her magic, but then a gunshot pierced the air.

It came from the ballroom.

Hetty grabbed fistfuls of her skirts and started running. As she ran, she yanked off her cape, letting it fly behind her as she returned to the ballroom. All around, people were frozen in place, pointing toward at the balcony. Hetty followed their gazes.

She looked up just as Nathan Payne shoved Darlene off the second-floor balcony.

Time slowed as her friend fell backwards.

Hetty lifted her hand to perform a spell, but then something gold filled the air.

The winged horse, Pegasus, flew directly at Darlene, gleaming with starlight from its flanks to its outstretched wings.

It didn't scoop Darlene onto its back but flew around her, its large wings beating the air until a wind swirled up.

The wind caught Darlene, and only then was Hetty able to focus to see the figure in control.

With one hand aloft, Benjy slowed Darlene's fall, bringing her slowly to the ground.

"No!"

With an inhuman roar, Nathan Payne fired off more spells down into the ballroom.

Magic clashed with magic. Not just with Benjy's spells, but with others'.

Foolish others with good intentions but whose magic at the moment was as desired as fireworks over brittle bushes and parched soil.

"Stop this! You're not helping at all," Hetty called as she pushed her way through. "You mustn't—"

A large crash shook the room. Then screams rushed around her as the chandelier swayed and then plummeted to the ground.

URSA MINOR

36

ALL FIRES START SMALL.

Hetty learned that from her mother, watching a simple spark create a flame that would last for days as long as it was tended. Fire transformed the world, bringing light to where there had been none, and heat where only cold remained. But fires had to be contained, because once let loose, very little could stop them.

This fire in the ballroom was not a normal one.

Fueled by magic, it fed on the floorboards and quickly extended its reach. Then, of course, like the keen checkers player he was, Nathan Payne pressed his advantage and flung even more magic into the flames.

As people ran, Hetty pushed through to where she'd last seen Benjy. Darlene was sprawled on the ground, half held up by him. As Hetty reached them, George burst through the crowd, falling next to Darlene.

"Is she alive?" he rasped.

"She fainted." Benjy directed his words to them both. "She'll be fine. George, get her out of here."

"I can't!"

"You can, and you will," Benjy said.

He saw Hetty then, and he gently moved Darlene into George's arms.

"It's Eudora. She hired Payne," Hetty said in a rush. "Her father's name was not always Alvin Jacobs."

Benjy nodded. "I thought it might be. Should we attempt to find her?"

"I don't know. Can we trust that our friends will get out of here without trouble?"

Benjy looked up and muttered something under his breath. "No, we can't!"

Hetty looked up as well.

Through the flickering flames, she saw Thomas and Oliver on the stairs. They were near the top, stopped by the flames that were growing by the second.

As for Penelope, she was perilously near to Nathan Payne, shaking one of her potion bottles.

"I need to get up there," Hetty said. "But I'll be too late with this crowd in my way."

"Do what you did before," Benjy said. "Jump."

"Jump?"

"Yes." He knelt down with his hands clasped together, his meaning clear.

Hetty set a foot down atop his hands and in the next moment she was flung into the air.

For a brief moment she hovered, her magic lifting her up, and then she dropped down onto the landing just as Penelope threw the potion bottle.

Payne dodged it.

The glass shattered into a puff of pink.

He was still laughing when a glittering arrow struck the floor.

Hetty flung more arrows at him, pushing him back.

"Get out of here," Hetty said, without looking back at Penelope. "Go now!"

"No, I have this under control!"

"Do you want to die?" Hetty shouted. "Because that is how it happens!"

"Let her do what she wishes, Sparrow." Payne sneered at them. "I'll get to her sooner or later."

He had a knife pointed at them, but that was hardly a concern in the wake of so much magic flying around. Hetty flicked her hand, and a crow swooped in and pecked his face.

Payne howled in pain. The knife fell out of his hand. With him distracted, she pushed him with her magic into a nearby room and shut the door.

"That won't hold him for long," Hetty said, going to Penelope. "Time to go."

"Where? We're trapped."

The fire blocked their way back to the stairs. The flames weren't high enough to hide Oliver and Thomas, but there was no safe passage ahead.

"If I knew it would be like this," Penelope coughed, "I would have brought the ice pistol."

"Wouldn't have helped."

"This way!" Thomas called. "Jump, we'll catch you."

"No." Oliver drew Thomas back. "It's too dangerous. We have to get off the stairs before they collapse!"

"Go," Hetty called. "We'll be right behind you. I promise."

Thomas protested, but Oliver grabbed his arm, shoving him back. "Trust Hetty."

They vanished then, swallowed up in the smoke. Hetty went to the edge thinking they could jump down. The fire was too high, and most people, like Cora and Jay, were using spells to push the fire this way to help others escape.

Penelope had looked down as well, but the sight had frozen her in place.

"It's burning too quickly. How will we stop it?"

"Not our problem," Hetty said.

Spying the window at the end of the landing, she moved them toward it. The wood of the window was already unbearably hot. Hetty held on to it anyway and yanked it open. The cool night air struck her face, although she could see little outside.

"We'll get out this way. The drop isn't far."

When Penelope didn't move, Hetty grabbed her friend.

"If you don't jump, I won't!"

This got Penelope moving.

Hetty had just gotten Penelope near the window when the door behind them flew off its hinges.

"You need help," Penelope whispered. "I have to—"

"Worry about other things."

Hetty slapped a sigil on Penelope's back and the Crane flowed around Penelope as she fell, disappearing into the night.

Hetty thought she saw Jay head for Penelope. Hetty couldn't check. A blue light was the only warning she got. She jumped away from the window, missing the lobbed spell.

The magic, instead of destroying the window, created a barrier. Hetty snapped her fingers; the magic she tossed at it only fed the angry flames.

At the coarse laugh behind her, Hetty turned to see Nathan Payne.

"Here we are again, Sparrow," Payne called, his nose freely bleeding. "What did I do to deserve this fate?"

"There's a saying: you get what you deserve. You've gotten no less."

"And so have you," he said with deliberate slowness, "Henrietta Rhodes."

"Keep my name out of your mouth. I won't have it said by a man so low, the worms won't eat his tainted flesh!"

"We do what we need to survive."

"No one who sells out their own people to get ahead is surviving. I'd die first before I ever did such a thing!"

Payne sneered. "I'll give you some help with that."

He flicked more magic at her. Her wards repelled his hex, and he jumped back, barely missing being struck by the counterspell.

"Always in my way," he grunted. "Would have been an easy job if not for you."

"This won't be the first time you disappointed your employer. What happened when One-Eyed Jack found out we gave you the slip?"

Roaring, Payne charged at her again.

Her wards didn't shatter, but his heavier weight threw her backwards. Knocked on the floor, her ears ringing, she lost her focus, and this time the wards around her vanished. The moment they did, Payne didn't waste a second. He reached for her again. She yanked a hairpin out, and jammed it into his hand.

As he yelled, she slammed her elbow into his ribs and tumbled out of the way.

"I *will* kill you, Sparrow." Payne spat out blood. It sizzled in the flames. "Maybe not today. But one day. But before I do, I will slit the throat of every person you love. Your husband as he whistles on the bench in your yard, your friend and her daughter as they feed birds, your sisters as one digs in the garden while the other sketches the sky, your wizened parents waiting patiently on the doorstep, your brother and his anxious spouse as they argue about the time of day. I'll kill them all and leave them for you to find, just like I found my son!"

Hetty's hand fell to her side. Each of his words hammered against her heart, holding more power than any of his previous threats. "You were outside my house, watching us?"

A terrible grin filled his face.

"I was going to set your home on fire, but your magic stood

against even the potions I gave the alderman. But this is far better."

He threw a burst of raw magic at her.

Unable to react in time to counter it, Hetty jumped out of the way, only to scramble back when she remembered the flames.

Her foot caught on something. There was a crack, a shudder.

And then the floor collapsed under them.

Impossibly, it seemed to fall slowly. Maybe it was the pain that engulfed her. Maybe it was the flames crackling in her ears. But the impact she was expecting didn't come. She scarcely felt anything.

And neither did Payne.

He laughed as he approached her, spells flickering at his fingertips.

"This looks familiar," Payne taunted. His spell slithered around her, binding her in place. Focused as he was on tying her down, he didn't notice how the shadows grew taller and broader behind him. "But with some —"

Payne never got to finish.

A piece of wood swung out and crashed against his head. The board snapped on impact and splintered into chunks that fed the hungry flames.

Nathan Payne staggered, his magic vanishing at once.

And then Benjy emerged from the inferno.

The flames parted for him as he hurried to Hetty. His shirt and waistcoat were lit up in violet light — all the spells she'd sewn into clothes by habit, since her blacksmith husband always got too close to fire.

It was also one of the most beautiful sights she had ever seen.

"What have I told you about running into dangerous situations without me?" Benjy said.

The clever quip Hetty had on her lips was forgotten in a single moment as she saw Payne get back on his feet.

"Behind you!" Hetty called.

Benjy didn't even turn. He stepped aside and grasped Payne by the arm. And then *twisted*.

The piece of flaming floorboard in Payne's hand fell to the floor, but Benjy kept twisting until bone snapped. Payne cried out, although from the pain or rage, the chances were evenly split. With a grunt, Benjy shoved him to the ground.

It was only then as Hetty looked around that she realized the light around her wasn't just from the flames. Benjy's magic had melded with the wood, suspending the balcony in the air.

She couldn't tell how much he was holding up. But she knew one thing. He couldn't do this for long.

Not with Payne still able to work magic.

Hetty braced a hand to the floor and slowly began to push herself up.

She was nearly standing when she placed her weight on her right foot. A knife ramming through her ankle would have been less painful. But she swallowed back that scream. Grimly, Hetty drew a star sigil into the air, slowly taking the time to draw the most elaborate one that came to mind.

The telltale green glow of her spell drew Payne's attention.

And instead of tossing his magic at Benjy, he took aim at Hetty.

This was the last mistake he ever made.

With Hetty's spell in place to hold up the landing, Benjy was free to catch Payne's magic.

The snarling Wolf that Payne had flung in Hetty's direction collided directly with Benjy's wards and then rebounded back at Payne.

Payne flew backwards until a sharp wooden beam shortened his flight.

Hetty didn't look away.

Not at hearing the loud thwack when the beam burst through his chest. Not at seeing the blood blossom and stain the wood.

Not even when his face went slack and his hands fell to his side. Hetty didn't look away until the light faded from Payne's eyes, so she could be certain that his ghost would never return to haunt her.

"Hetty," Benjy had an arm around her. "We're going to have to jump."

"I can't."

"You're going to have to try."

"I can't." Hetty struggled to find something more useful to say. "I hurt my ankle."

"Is that all? I'll carry you out."

"How?" Hetty asked. "Wherever you came from, it's probably collapsed by now. Unless you know a way to fly out of here, it won't be in time for—" Hetty blinked, seeing through the flames.

She took a step forward, forgetting her ankle. Benjy caught her before she toppled to the ground.

"Time for what?" he asked.

"To find the clock," Hetty gasped, swallowing back another wave of pain. "The clock that blocks a tunnel entrance!"

"You're kidding!"

"It was in the hallway where we spoke to Bernice." Hetty pointed in one direction, but Benjy calmly pointed in another.

Not that it mattered. Beyond their little bubble of protection, the flames roared equally.

"If it's not blocked by the flames, parts of the building probably collapsed on top of it by now."

"Then we blow a hole through the floor," Hetty said.

"No," Benjy corrected. "You blow the hole. I'll make sure the rest of the building doesn't fall as you do."

"Always so logical." Hetty managed to laugh.

Benjy flashed a quick smile. "I love you too."

He bent down so he could carry her on his back. The magic stitched between their clothes blended together, and the unrelenting heat around them faded, despite the growing flames.

With the weight off her injured foot, the pain receded to a dull throb. The immediate danger held off by Benjy, Hetty turned her focus on one thing: moving forward.

The first sigil she chose was Andromeda. But she kept it in its raw state, channeling the magic behind it into the floor beneath them.

She had an idea of where the tunnel was. She just needed to clear a path.

And clear a path she did. Keeping tight control of her magic, Hetty knocked aside the worst parts of the still-burning building as Benjy carried her into the hallway.

What remained of the clock was long gone, but the door to the tunnel was untouched by the fires due to the glistening magic spun across it.

"Together," Benjy murmured.

Hetty held up her hand alongside his, and as one they launched spells at the door, their magic entwining in a way that made it hard to tell where her magic stopped and his began.

Benjy hurried inside and then shut the door after them. Hetty tapped it, adding a few charms in place to hold back the fire at their backs.

The passage was especially cool after the intense heat of the fire, and the more they traveled through it, the more all the aches and pains of Hetty's brawl with Nathan Payne settled in on her.

She was also finding it hard to keep her eyes open, now that most of the danger had passed. She was just starting to slip off into sleep when Benjy jostled her.

"A little light will be helpful."

"You do it," she muttered.

"No free hands," he said, although Hetty had a feeling he was lying.

With an effort Hetty ran her hand along his shoulder, and the stitches in his shirt turned a bright purple. She lifted her hand, pulling the magic like thread, shook it, and then tossed it out into the air before her. Light as bright as a lantern appeared as a pair of crows materialized next to them. As Benjy continued to carry her down the tunnel, the crows' wings silently flapped as they lit the way.

"Who told you about this tunnel?" Benjy asked.

"Does it matter?" Hetty frowned and the crows flickered but remained.

"I'm curious."

"You're curious about everything," she said, lying back down.

"I know," he said cheerfully. When Hetty didn't say anything, he jostled her once again. "Don't fall asleep on me. You have to keep your magic going."

"I can't focus," Hetty moaned. "I'm too tired."

"Tell me a story then, any story. Just stay awake."

Hetty swallowed, her throat dry. She couldn't deny anyone a story, let alone her husband. She began: "Once there was a tunnel, and in it"—she blinked and saw the glimmer of a star sigil that wasn't her magic—"there was someone who came here before us. Benjy, Eudora came through here. She might have left a trap for us!"

Hetty shifted about, nearly jumping down despite her broken foot.

The glimmer of magic came closer, threatening to swallow them up and their shadows. It stopped right in front of them, and in the center of the light stood a person.

"There you are!" Thomas said, grinning despite the ashes that streaked his face. "Temperance Murray said you'd might come out through here!"

HARE

INTERLUDE

June 1868

GERMANTOWN, PHILADELPHIA, PENNSYLVANIA

As HETTY STEPPED DOWN into the amphitheater tucked away in the tiny park, she could hear parts of the rehearsal for tomorrow night's play.

She was glad to hear it, because it was her first time coming to Germantown on her own. When she wasn't worried about losing her way, she wondered why this play her friends were part of wasn't just done back in the dance hall in the Fifth Ward. The Ira Aldridge Troupe had just performed there a few weeks ago, and it was a perfectly good place for a performance. But as Hetty thought about it, she remembered why the venue change might have been a good idea. The troupe had put on a minstrel show that had all the white folks acting like their milk had gone sour on them, because they'd expected blackface foolishness and got instead Black actors wearing greasepaint putting on exaggerated Irish accents.

But beyond that, Hetty did think using the amphitheater was a nice change. It was a very lovely space. With seats built into the gentle slope, it wasn't very large. Around two hundred people could sit here and enjoy the show. The stage was wooden and decorated to look like a sitting room, with a low table, a few chairs, the façade of a fireplace in the background, and a magnificent staircase that disappeared into the trees above. While there were a few people, such as Darlene, painting the set, Hetty and every person in the audience were transfixed on the actor standing center stage speaking about the changing of tides and life aboard a ship.

Hetty didn't recognize the speech, but there was something familiar in the voice and manner that didn't fall into place until she got close enough to see who it was.

"Benjy, what are you doing up there!" Her voice was louder than she expected, and it echoed in the air. Hetty's face grew warm as heads turned her way, and warmer still when Benjy slipped against the staircase, stammering through his next few lines.

This caused a scattering bit of laughter, mostly from Penelope, sitting on a stool on stage left.

The director was the only one who remained unamused. He fixed Hetty with a stern look and turned back to Benjy. "Let's continue on with a new scene."

Tempted to cast a spell to vanish from sight, Hetty sat down on the nearest bench, just hoping people would forget all about her.

"You look ready to crawl out of here." Thomas walked across the seats to settle next to Hetty. Oliver followed, slowly and pointedly, on the stairs.

"I was just surprised," Hetty whispered. "I knew he was helping build the set, not that he was acting in the show. He never told me about this."

"It was rather sudden," Thomas said. "There was an accident with the lead this morning, and Benjy knew all the lines. I always knew he had a good memory, but I didn't know he could act. He never takes part when we do the plays at home." Even though this was said with kindness, Hetty didn't miss the accusation in his words.

She looked down at her hands. "He has other interests that keep him busy."

"You can't keep looking for your sister every single moment of your life." Oliver sat down not in their row but one above, so he would be right behind Thomas. "And having a bit of fun won't change that you're still searching."

"*You* talking about fun? What nonsense is this?" Hetty retorted, hoping to shift the conversation away from her.

Oliver didn't take the bait. "Did you tell Benjy that doing plays is a waste of time? Because he's doing terribly now that you're here."

Hetty was doing her best not to pay attention to the stage before her, blocking out both sight and sound through sheer force of will. Perhaps what Oliver had said might have been true, but she was not going to give him the satisfaction of telling him he was right. "Why would it matter what I think?"

The couple gave her equally amused looks, as if they knew something she didn't. Hetty doubted that. Benjy was pretty honest with her. At times, a bit *too* honest, perhaps. If he wanted to act in these plays, well, she wasn't going to insist he stop or wish him to do poorly.

"If we have to explain it to you, I guess you aren't that great at solving mysteries," Thomas said.

"There's nothing to explain." With a huff, Hetty jumped up to leave, only to bump into George standing on the stairs.

He was fuming as much as she was, but for different reasons. "I can't believe this is going on," he muttered. "Why do this play when there are so many more important things happening? Did you hear the latest news about the proposed Wand Acts?"

"No," Hetty said. This was a mistake, since it meant George

now had a listener. He boxed her in, not letting her leave, plunging into pretty much the same rant about current events that had ruined dinner at the Richardsons' the other night.

"All this means we're lucky that wasn't the bargain made to get the South back into the Union. Let's not forget, with the Senate acquitting Johnson, we don't know if he's going to stop trying to obstruct efforts for Reconstruction. The House impeached him for a reason! He's playing too nice with the South, and it'll mean everything we fought for is at risk. Haven't you seen—"

"No, I haven't seen it!" Hetty cut in. "And if you have a problem with the play, tell your wife." Hetty gestured to the stage. "But if you ask me, she seems happy to get a chance to paint."

Lurching at this shift in topics, George grumbled, "Why am I even bothering talking to you? This city could be on fire and all you care about is your sister! You know after all this time it's likely that she's gone."

"How dare you—"

George gave her a look, the same one he gave his students when they spoke out of turn. "There's having hope, and there's clinging to false hope. You're moving toward the latter."

Hetty would have shoved him down the stairs if Benjy hadn't appeared just then, silently passing judgment on George.

That didn't deter George, as he snapped at Benjy, "Tell your wife she needs to expand her horizons!"

He stomped off down to the stage, clearly determined to fuss at Darlene too.

Not about to let her friend have her small joy torn to tatters, Hetty moved to follow, but Benjy shifted to block her path.

"There's trouble."

"I know, George is about to make a fuss about the play. We need to stop him before—"

"Not that sort of trouble, something more interesting."

Benjy turned and went back down the stairs, leaving Hetty no choice but to follow if she wanted her curiosity satisfied.

He led her to an area behind the stage, where crates of what looked to be props and costumes waited, including a trunk. But Benjy moved toward none of them. Instead, he went to a large rock. With care, he drew the Wolf star sigil. The mark flashed and the rock lifted up into the air.

"Is this about the morning accident? Thomas mentioned something happened." Hetty asked.

"I'm letting everyone think it was, because this is what I found."

With a handkerchief in hand, he picked up a dagger. Hetty could tell the blade wasn't really steel and merely a wooden prop, but he held it delicately for a reason. The threads in the handkerchief were a sallow yellow color, warning of danger. Benjy reached into a pocket for a vial of green dust. He uncapped it and sprinkled it over the knife. Hetty recognized the telltale glow of poison as the dust hit the blade.

"How did you know to check it?"

"Because it brushed against the arm of the person playing the lead and he fainted," Benjy replied.

"Is he still alive?"

"Yes, but he's very sick."

"What does it have to do with you taking his spot?"

Benjy looked away from her. "I may have been arguing with the actor at the time. He was getting his lines wrong."

Hetty took a moment to consider all of this. "It's a very good thing you showed me this yourself, because otherwise I'd be forced to consider you a suspect."

"That's entirely unfair." Benjy bristled.

She laughed at him. "Everyone's a suspect until proven otherwise."

"I would think the poor planning would make me above such

an accusation," Benjy grumbled, far from amused at having his own words flung back at him. "If I was going to poison someone, I'd do it during the performance, not rehearsal."

"Unless the point was to get the actor replaced to cause more trouble later on." Hetty followed this line of thought, and suddenly what had been an amusing distraction was no longer that. "Quit the play," she said. "You're not doing this. I refuse to become a widow because someone stabbed you with a poisoned prop knife."

"You're assuming we can't find the murderer by tomorrow night," Benjy said rather mildly. "This is hardly a difficult case."

"This could be an elaborate scheme to kill you!"

"I'm not worried," Benjy said, continuing to be insufferably calm as he put the dagger back into its hiding spot. "For starters, this knife was in a locked trunk donated by the person who's financing the play, Bernice Tanner."

Hetty blinked. "So I wasn't wrong about an elaborate scheme."

"I wouldn't say elaborate. A poisoned knife, an accident on stage, is very straightforward. She's sending a message, she wants to talk."

"But why? Why couldn't she tell us outright?"

Benjy lifted an eyebrow. "You're still wondering that after all these years? She likes to play games. And we just go along with it."

Hetty stiffened. "She has information about my sister."

"Does she?" Sarcasm dripped off his words. "How is this time different than the last dozen or so times?"

It wasn't. The way Bernice was getting their attention was different, but it would be the same in the end. "We can't ignore her; there's always a chance it might be true. Also, I don't think a poisoned prop will be the last thing she does if we refuse to talk."

"Only one way to prevent that," Benjy said, looking at her very seriously. "Take part in the play."

Hetty snorted. "You have said many ridiculous things, including trying to convince me a book that waxes poetry about sewer systems is good entertainment. But I'm not taking part in any play. I'll make costumes. I'll even paint a thing or two. But I'll not do anything more than sit in the audience and cheer you all on!"

"Why not?" Benjy challenged.

"This is silly. A waste of time." The words were out of her mouth before she could stop herself. She expected Benjy to argue with her right there about it, but as always he surprised her by laughing.

"Of course the plays are! That's why our friends all gather up at Oliver and Thomas's and throw things together! Frivolous and convoluted as these things are, it's about imagining a world a little different than ours. A little better, a little worse in some cases. Where the unexpected was expected in some fashion."

"And there was a swordfight or two somewhere?" Hetty added.

"Am I convincing you?" Benjy asked, with a small smile that broke the rest of Hetty's resistance to the idea.

"A bit," she admitted.

"Think of it as a special skill for solving mysteries. Sometimes to get the answers we want requires playing a part."

"I suppose that's something we've done for quite a while," Hetty said, thinking over their many adventures. "I suppose it's not much different than telling stories in front of a crowd."

"And you can do effects with your magic."

Hetty beamed at this. "Now you have convinced me!"

URSA MAJOR

37

After listening to Darlene recount what had happened in the ballroom, Hetty found herself both amused and a bit alarmed.

"You shot Nathan Payne?" Hetty asked.

"I did a poor job about it," Darlene complained as she looked up from the sketchbook in her lap. "The pistol was heavier than I expected, so I missed him."

"He didn't miss you." Penelope grimly sat back in her chair, with a bowl of puce-colored paste. "This should get the rest of the poison out so your cut will heal properly."

Ironically, despite Hetty hurting her ankle and inhaling a great deal of smoke, Darlene ended up hurt the worst. Although Benjy had caught Darlene before she plummeted from the balcony, Payne had scratched her with a knife coated with a particularly tricky poison.

Because it was on the list of poisons that had gotten stolen from an herbal shop, Penelope was well prepared for it. But she was not up to having multiple patients at once. Declaring that Hetty was not dying anytime soon, Penelope gave Hetty a healing tonic that would mend her ankle, ordered her to stay in bed half the day, and then retreated back to Darlene's home.

Upon arriving at the apartment that afternoon, Hetty made a few jokes about being poorly treated, but only when it was clear that Darlene was bored and restless at being confined to her bed.

"Luckily Payne got my left arm," Darlene said, as Penelope busied herself with checking on the bandages. "Or I wouldn't be able to help you now. I can draw copies of Eudora Mason if you like."

"Just the one will be fine. We're going to give it to Sy to carry around." Hetty leaned back in her chair, trying not to tap her foot. Her ankle was healed enough to walk all the way out here, but it was tender and she was conscious of the injury. "It's better for him to do it. He's got one of those faces people don't always remember."

Penelope snorted. "I'd keep that detail to myself."

"Why?" Hetty asked, rather puzzled. "It's a really good thing. It means you don't have to use elaborate disguises."

"Well, luckily for you, Eudora Mason does not." Darlene dropped her pencil and handed the sketchbook to Hetty. "Will this do?"

"Of course it will," Hetty said, glancing at the drawing. Darlene had only really seen Eudora back at the tent in Camden, but that glance was all she needed to render the woman now, and even strip away the trappings to reveal what the woman looked like when she wasn't putting on a performance.

"The case is mostly done. We just need to tie down one last loose end," Hetty said. "And if we don't do it soon enough, well, everything else is for naught."

"Think she'll skip town?" Darlene asked.

"I would have if I were her," Penelope said.

Hetty shook her head. "She wants something from us. Emily Jacobs."

"And this buried treasure." Darlene slumped against the pillows propping her up. "If I only knew back then—"

"It wouldn't have changed anything," Hetty said. "And I would have done everything I did back then all the same."

"I can think of a few things I would have changed," Benjy said as he poked his head in the bedroom. "Mainly not losing the air balloon."

"How did you lose the air balloon?" Penelope asked.

"In the worst way possible." Hetty sighed.

"Where's George?" Darlene asked, shifting forward a bit. "Didn't he go with you?"

"Don't worry." Benjy looked around for a place to sit, but then settled on leaning against the wall. "He just went to get the baby."

No sooner did he speak than George walked in with a cranky-looking Lorene. The baby was a few moments away from screaming her lungs out, but once she saw the adults gathered in the room, she was all smiles, even before she was placed in her mother's arms.

"I think she's getting spoiled by all this attention," Hetty remarked as George perched on the edge of his bed.

"She just knows something interesting is occurring whenever you're here." Darlene wrapped her arms around her daughter so the baby could face outward to the group.

"What did Adelaide say?" Hetty asked.

"Didn't see her at the house. Only her cousin was there," Benjy answered. "He doesn't know anything that's going on. And the address I managed to get from him for Eudora Mason leads to an abandoned lot."

"A fake to the very end," Hetty said.

"We asked around at boardinghouses, hotels, and the like. Couldn't get across the river, because it's Sunday," George added.

"No need to worry about that," Hetty said.

"I want to do this." George's eyes drifted over to Darlene. "This woman is free to do whatever she likes simply because she can't be found."

Hetty shook her head. "We know where she'll be next. She'll be at the funeral."

"You're still having it?" Penelope asked. "After all that's happened!"

Hetty shrugged. "Nothing changed, and Adelaide still wants to hold it. She wants to put all this behind her."

"What did she think would happen otherwise?" George asked. "Her brother's ghost shows up with a list of complaints?"

"It would be quite a spectacle," Benjy began.

"More entertaining than the last play we put on—and that included creating a shipwreck in your parlor!" George declared. "It'd be a rather haunting type of show, wouldn't it?"

He laughed at his poor joke. It was all Hetty could do to stop herself from rolling her eyes, which was why she was surprised when Benjy snapped his fingers, crying out, "You're absolutely right!"

George sat up, his eyes comically wide in shock. "You all heard him say that. I'm not imagining things?"

"Yes, and I think he must have inhaled too much smoke last night," Penelope said with a great deal of alarm.

"I'm fine," Benjy said. "It's just that George is right. A ghost would be perfect for the funeral."

"Penelope," Hetty said, growing greatly worried at these words. "Go get whatever potions you need. He can't be feeling well if he's saying that."

"No, no," Benjy laughed. "I'm talking about making the funeral a bit more theatrical."

"Oh," Darlene exclaimed. "You mean make it like one of the plays. Now, that's an interesting plan!"

"And easily done," Hetty said, seeing where Benjy was going with this. "It's one big trick, we just got to time it right."

"Whatever you end up doing, you'll need help," Penelope said.

"Well, putting on shows is what we do best." Darlene nodded.

"You need to tell Oliver and Thomas about this. They'll have some good ideas."

"Oliver will want to write the script," George snickered.

"They're back at Juniper Street," Hetty said, "and we'll need more than just their help. Penelope, what about your cousins? I know Sy will help, but what about Rosie, Maybelle, even Jobelle and the rest?"

"I can ask," Penelope said. She added shyly, "You should mention this to Temperance. Surely she'll help."

"Temperance? Who is Temperance?" George asked.

"I'll tell you later," Darlene said, patting his arm, "but it won't be as good as the story as Hetty tells!"

They talked a bit more about the plan, but not for much longer.

"Penelope is right, we should ask for Temperance Murray's help," Hetty remarked when they left Darlene and George's apartment behind. "She's been helpful this whole time."

"To talk to her, you know where we need to go," Benjy remarked. "Can you manage to walk there?"

Hetty knew she could, but that wasn't what Benjy was asking.

"We need to talk to Bernice," Hetty said, "and it's best to do so now, when she's primed to feel guilty about it."

Although Hetty had several stories ready for the occasion, she didn't need to use a single one.

Cora already had that handled.

Temperance Murray had answered the door when they knocked at Bernice Tanner's tidy little house on Society Hill. And before they could even tell her about the theatrics they had planned for the funeral, they heard Cora's voice in the parlor.

Cora and Jay sat across from their old friend, sitting in stiff-backed chairs. Although the summer evening was rather balmy, inside the room the air was quite frigid.

"Henrietta! Benjamin!" Jay said, being the first to notice them. "What are you doing here?"

"I want to ask the same of you," Hetty said.

"We've come to ask questions from my good friend," Cora said, not moving her gaze away from Bernice. "Like the important information she withheld. She might not be the murderer, but people are dead because of her!"

"You cannot expect me to take the blame for another's actions. Raimond didn't tell me everything. I don't even know about the pamphlet. I didn't think it was important."

"You moved the world to catch stars for Sarah Jacobs all those years ago. You knew it was important then!"

"Cora," Hetty said softly, "it's fine. The only one to blame is Eudora—Dora Reynolds. We have a plan to catch her, but we need your help. It's going to be done at the funeral. But we're going to do it like we'd do it in a play."

"A play?"

A new voice entered the room. Adelaide Duval had been sitting in the far corner, hidden by an overgrown potted plant.

Although she looked like she had not slept at all the previous night, her eyes were bright and alert.

"Darlene told me about the plays you put on. How will this work with my brother's funeral? Will it capture this woman who took my family from me?"

"If all goes well, we will," Benjy said.

"But if you don't want us to, we can come up with a different plan," Hetty said.

"Nonsense." Adelaide waved a hand. "I wanted a private ceremony for my brother anyway."

As Hetty looked on, puzzled, a thin smile appeared on Adelaide's face. "Do you really think I want my brother to actually be in the casket when all this occurs? There should be two ceremonies. The false performance, and the true one held afterward."

With this settled, they easily got a promise of help from Temperance, who offered it before it was asked of her.

On the way back home, Hetty and Benjy bumped into Sy Caldwell at their front door.

"Leaving or arriving?" Benjy asked the young man.

"Leaving," Sy said, "but I can stay. Thomas wasn't sure when you'd return, and I didn't want to linger here all night. Got news for you."

Oliver and Thomas were sitting in the parlor, and their conversation changed the moment the other three entered.

Sy sat down in a chair and settled in to tell them about his adventures for the day.

"I'll start with the biggest piece. The hotel is gone, all ashes," Sy said. "Nothing can be saved, and they say it's a miracle injuries were limited and there are no reported deaths."

"It shouldn't be gone," Benjy remarked. He sat at the window seat with his hand folded under his chin; his attention was far away as usual. "There should be something of the foundation left."

"I saw it with my own two eyes," Sy said. "Nothing's there."

"Then it was done on purpose," Hetty said. Thinking of Nathan Payne speared by the beam, and the threats to do the same or worse to her. "To hide what happened."

"Rumor is it's not enough. There is talk about a magical fire," Sy said.

"Well, it's not the only fire that occurred lately," Oliver pointed out.

"What about Emily Jacobs?" Hetty asked.

Sy shook his head. "Nothing. All this rain disrupted any magic I could use to follow her. I asked all over town, but no one I talked to heard anything about a young girl looking for sanctuary, or even asking around for you by name. The Duval name didn't turn up anything new, either."

"She's too smart for that," Benjy said. "She gave Bernice Tanner the slip several times already, and trust me, that takes some skill."

"From all you said, it might be best if she says hidden," Oliver said. "I would. I'd even go back home."

"But she came here for a reason." Hetty tapped her fingers against the couch. "Emily came here on her own. Something prompted her; no outside forces brought her here. It might be the Clarke Cipher or something else, but she's looking for us. So, I know she must still be in the city."

Sy looked to Benjy.

"It'll be dark soon, no need to keep searching," he said. "When she wants to be found, she'll turn up."

"I'm not sure," Thomas said. "I was here all day. No one's come around. Nor has your nosy neighbor complained of seeing anyone."

"Finding her is crucial, especially if we can do so by tomorrow," Hetty said.

"Isn't the funeral tomorrow?" Oliver cried. "Don't tell me you canceled it!"

"We haven't, we just tweaked a few things and need your help to do more."

Hetty quickly explained the plan. Because she had Adelaide's approval, Hetty added details she hadn't discussed yet with anyone else. She wasn't surprised that Oliver and Thomas asked the most questions. Coming together to put on plays had been their idea, and Thomas often served as the director, keeping everyone on task.

Which was why Hetty half expected less than enthusiastic reactions to this plan.

But she'd underestimated both her friends' willingness to help and the eagerness to embellish her plan further. Just as everyone else agreed with only a crumb of an idea, with more details, conversation moved swiftly about how much could be done before the night was over.

Sy left with a list of tasks, including recruitment of his family, if Penelope's overtures had not been enough. Soon Thomas and Oliver were preparing to leave, to go see Darlene and the others and inform them of the changes.

"Only you would come up with such a thing." Oliver shook his head as Hetty walked with him to the door. "But if it works—"

"It will," Hetty said.

"Not *all* your plans do," Oliver pointed out.

"This isn't just her plan. You also made several good suggestions," Benjy reminded him.

"So I did," Oliver laughed. "Thomas, are you going to meet me at home or George and Darlene's?"

"I'm coming." Thomas hurried, pausing only to tap Hetty on the shoulder. "I made you dinner. Eat it before you join the rest." He gave them very stern looks. "And it's good—you can ask your neighbor's daughter."

Hetty blinked at Thomas. "Our neighbor's daughter?"

"Might be granddaughter." Thomas shrugged. "Didn't ask. I had the window open to let out some steam. She peered around the fence and said it smelled good. So I gave her some. I flatter easily."

"Too easily," Oliver said. They exchanged a look, which meant Hetty had time to rearrange her features to something they wouldn't worry about.

"Go on," Hetty encouraged him with a strained smile. "We'll meet you later."

"We'll be there." Oliver pulled on his hat. "Happy stars over your heads."

Hetty shut the door behind them and locked it.

"Mrs. Holloway does not have any family in town," Hetty whispered. "I don't know who that could be."

"Only one way to find out."

Without needing to say a word more, they marched toward the kitchen.

The moment Hetty opened the door, crows flooded in. Not just the small family that nested on their roof, but it seemed like their entire extended family, with at least a dozen or more birds streaming through the kitchen.

Benjy pulled her back, and they were surrounded by feathers and flapping wings.

"I told you if you keep feeding them this would happen!"

"That can't be it!" Hetty called.

Instead of pecking at her, the crow pulled at her clothes urgently. A few others flipped around to point toward the open door.

"They're trying to tell us something!" Hetty said as she went into the yard.

The crows, realizing they got the message, reversed course. They rushed past her, and every single one landed on Benjy's new workshop.

The lead crow was the last to land. It perched atop the door and pointedly tapped its foot on the wood. The message was clear. This door shouldn't have been open, even by the tiniest of cracks.

Benjy padded softly toward the shed, his left hand engulfed with swirling raw magic.

Hetty fell back, although she stayed close enough to see.

He pulled the door open, and the magic that had been swirling around him faded.

Huddled in the middle of the shed was a tangle of limbs. A sight they saw only for moments before a hammer swung out wildly at them.

Benjy deftly caught it, as well as the slender fist that followed.

"I wouldn't do that," he said softly as the little intruder fought vainly against his grip. "You're the one that came looking for help. Why are you surprised that it found you?"

The struggling stopped. And the face that peered up at them had the same suspicious look as it had many years ago when they woke her one night from her bed in Tennessee, telling her they were taking her to her mother.

"So this is where you were hiding," Hetty observed as Emily Jacobs blinked up at them. "No wonder no one could find her. She was here the whole time!"

Emily had passed the day in their neighbor's cellar. That door was loose enough for her to get inside, unlike the door to their cellar. Emily had only had the names of Sparrow and Finch to guide her, but they were enough to get this far. When she'd arrived early in the morning, she'd seen lots of people through the window, but not any sign of Hetty or Benjy. It seemed she got the wrong place, but it started to rain hard. Mrs. Holloway's cellar door was propped a bit open, so she hid in there and fell asleep while waiting out the rain. She woke when she heard their neighbor heading into the cellar, so she snuck out, intending to return once danger had passed. But she smelled food, and she was too hungry to stop herself from asking Thomas for some. While his gift had staved off the worst of her hunger pangs, it left her locked out of the cellar, so she chose the next best thing: the shed.

"You went through all that trouble to find us, and you still attacked," Benjy pointed out to the girl.

Emily tapped her fingers against the kitchen table, her face betraying a trace of embarrassment. "You scared me."

"Why were you looking for us?" Hetty asked.

"Mama always spoke so highly of you," Emily replied, "and from her stories I knew I could trust you."

"Not Bernice Tanner?"

"Miss Bernice hears lots of things, but she doesn't listen," Emily said.

Hetty chuckled, appreciating the candor. "I can agree with that."

"Once she found me, she kept telling me to do this and that, and wouldn't listen when I told her I knew nothing about the key for the Clarke Cipher."

Benjy stiffened at these words, but it was Hetty who asked: "A key?"

"Not a real key," the girl insisted. "It's a book."

Benjy slapped his face. "A key text! I should have known!"

"What's a key text?" Hetty asked.

"A book is used to build the cipher," Benjy said in a rush. "Sometimes it's a single page, sometimes it's the whole book. Either way, the key text helps to decode a cipher, and it's nearly impossible to break it without it. What book was it?"

"*By the Archway's Light,*" Emily replied.

Benjy's face fell. "We don't have that book. I never even heard of it."

But Hetty was already on her feet, her heart racing in excitement. "I have. We have it. Sy and Rosie brought it over with all of Raimond Duval's books. It's in the study!"

ANDROMEDA

38

To say the key text revealed everything did not do justice to what occurred.

Once it was in his hand, Benjy did not take long to decipher the code. Using key passages in the book, he found matches in the printed cipher and uncovered a pattern that unraveled the entire thing. In fact, by the time Hetty visited her friends, informed them that Emily was found, and returned to Juniper Street, Benjy and Emily had written out the cipher's hidden message. It gave them everything they needed to know about the buried treasure along with the most important bit of all: its location.

With Emily balanced precariously on the back of Benjy's bicycle, they rode to the outskirts of town, the paved streets giving way to packed dirt, and eventually no road at all.

While the treasure was within a bicycle ride, it was far enough away that Benjy first said he would go alone, fearing Hetty would injure herself again.

But she would not consider that for a moment. She wasn't about to miss the big finale.

Moonlight gave them enough light to ride by, although they

didn't need it. Hetty had brought their lantern with them and had it propped up on her basket to light the road ahead.

As for knowing where to go, Benjy had taken their old compass and charmed it with a spell to point to the coordinates of their destination. A tricky but very convenient bit of spellwork that kept them from having to check a map as they traveled. Although by the time they had gotten deep into the countryside, there was little need for the compass. Hetty could guide the way using the stars.

The cipher mentioned a few markers that would identify the spot. However, as Hetty surveyed the moon-drenched ground, those markers were lost to time. They could be out here until dawn if they weren't careful.

"Is there anything else in the cipher?" Hetty asked as Benjy took the shovel from Emily. "Something else that could keep us from digging holes everywhere?"

"There isn't. But there are other ways to search for these things." Benjy swung the shovel up onto his shoulder. "Just set up some boundary spells, things that can be moved if needed."

"He doesn't know where it is, does he?" Emily whispered to Hetty.

"I think he has a glimmer of an idea." Hetty picked up the lantern from the basket on her bicycle. She tapped her fingers along it, drawing up familiar star sigils, to guard and protect from the ghouls that lived in this neck of the woods. Her spells flew up around them as they headed for the trees, glimmers of starlight as they passed.

"What sort of magic is this?" Emily asked.

"A warning spell. It lets us know if the boundary is breached."

"What about spells that come from inside?" Emily asked.

Hetty tilted her head in Emily's direction. The lantern revealed only part of the girl's expression, which looked like worry, and not because Benjy's method of searching was going to keep them out here until dawn.

"What do you mean?"

"Well"—Emily tapped her foot against the ground—"my mother told me stories about this. She said there might be magic left behind to stop people from digging the treasure up. A spell to keep you lost."

"Such a spell might have faded in time," Hetty said. "Magic fades with the caster's death, no matter what type. Everyone involved in that night is dead."

"But there was a charm involved," Emily protested.

Across from them, Benjy walked in a tight circle, stopping every few steps to tap the shovel against the ground. Instead of digging, he picked the shovel up, walked away, shook his head, and then walked back to the same spot. He repeated this several times.

"What sort of charm?" Hetty asked.

"A stone carved with a spell that was dropped in the treasure chest when Clarke wasn't looking. My grandfather never wanted Clarke to find the treasure. At least, that was in the story my mother told me."

"Such stories tend to be true," Hetty replied. "What else did she tell you?"

"That this was a gift from Grandfather." Emily pulled out a necklace with a smooth stone, which gleamed in the night. Perhaps it was the light of the lantern, but Hetty suspected something else at play. There was a simple line cut into the stone that looked like it could be Canis Minor.

Could this necklace be the reason why Sarah was pursued all those years ago? For a necklace that negated the magic that still protected the chest? Charmed to work only for the wielder? Did Eudora know about it?

"Let's take a walk, shall we?" Hetty suggested. "Keep an eye on that necklace."

With Emily at her side, Hetty walked right to the spot where Benjy had left and returned to several times already. They hadn't stood at the spot for more than a moment before the little glimmer of light on the necklace brightened to rival the lantern in Hetty's hand.

"I suppose you're right," Hetty called cheerfully to Benjy, who had swung back around by then. "There are other ways to search for these things. But they're hard to do when magic is making things tricky."

"What's this? A charm made by Alvin Jacobs?" Benjy grunted. He strode back next to them, but instead of looking at the necklace, tapped the shovel against the ground.

He hit the ground a few more times, then dragged the tip of the shovel across it.

"You need to start digging before it's too late," Hetty remarked.

Benjy tapped the ground again. "Do you want to help?"

Hetty had no plans to dig even the tiniest of shovelfuls, and was ready to say so in great detail when Emily spoke up:

"I'll help. You won't be able to find it without me."

"That seems to be the direction of things," Benjy said. "We'll trade off."

Hetty supposed Benjy could have taken the necklace from the girl and dug the whole thing up himself. But Emily clearly wanted to help—and they wouldn't have found it as easily without her. So they switched off, Benjy handing the shovel over to Emily every so often, although by Hetty's count, he did most of the work anyway.

As they worked, Hetty maintained the spells that cloaked them from the notice of any troublemaker who might be around at this time of night. When Emily was resting on the ground after finishing her turn of digging, Hetty asked for a fuller account of the girl's travels to Philadelphia and why Emily sought them out in the first place.

"I can't believe you remembered us," Hetty said. "You were a little girl. I didn't think you would."

"How could I *not* remember? You swooped in on an air balloon and brought me to my mother. I thought I would never see her again. I'll always remember that. She died last winter." Emily paused as if expecting Hetty to offer a token apology.

When Hetty said nothing, Emily continued. "She got sick, and there was nothing the healer could do about it. I wanted to go to school to study medicine, but that costs money. If I didn't have to take care of my sister I would have done it, but because I have to look after Lizzie, I got a job cleaning houses. The sapphires would have gotten us out of the boardinghouse. It's the only reason I responded to Mr. Duval's letter. Is that selfish?"

"No, it's yours, in a way," Hetty said. "Your inheritance."

"How?"

She was genuinely curious, and for once Hetty didn't have the words to explain.

"Your mother could have given up the information to the people who'd caused her so much trouble." Benjy stood in the hole, leaning against the shovel as he paused his digging. "Instead, she kept that secret and passed it on to you. It's yours. We only ever wanted to find it because it's a puzzle. If you hadn't shown up, we were going to donate the treasure."

Hetty coughed, choking back her less than charitable reply.

Benjy tapped the shovel against the ground and something hollow rang in the air. "I think this is it!"

It took a few more jabs of the shovel and a mighty tug, but Benjy wrenched a wooden chest out of the ground. He lifted it out of the hole and dropped it at Hetty's feet. Slightly rounded and the size of a traveling suitcase, it reminded her of a tale of a pirate who kept a heart hidden inside along with other precious things.

"Hold this." Hetty handed the lantern to Emily.

Hetty knelt down to the chest. It smelled strongly of the earth that remained packed along the grooves on the sides of the box.

She traced her fingers along them, expecting a stir of magic to rise up. But if there ever was magic, it was long gone.

"Bring the light closer," Hetty directed Emily. "Keep it overhead."

As the lantern swung closer, Hetty spotted the lock.

She twisted it, but it didn't budge.

"Can you break the lock on this?" Hetty called to her husband.

Benjy pulled himself out of the hole and knelt down to look at it. "That would only risk ruining the chest."

He lifted up the lock and then let it fall without touching it more. "Emily, your mother didn't happen to give you a key, did she?"

"No, and I don't think this necklace turns into one, either," Emily replied cheekily.

"Now don't be rude," Benjy remarked absently as he continued to study the chest. "I'm just checking to make sure no curses will jump out at us."

"It won't." Hetty tapped her choker, and the magic in her stitches spooled into her palm like spun gold. "I won't let it."

Benjy chuckled as he reached for her. Hetty smelled the earth as his hand caressed her cheek. "No, you wouldn't."

He plucked from her hair one of her pins, managing to find one she didn't care about. He bent it and used it to pick the lock, twisting it around until there was a click.

When Benjy opened the lid, nothing happened. No smoke, no light, not even dust drifted up.

Hetty lowered her hand, letting some of her protective spells fade as Benjy reached inside.

Still standing above them, Emily lowered the lantern even more without being asked.

Lantern light revealed the small bulging bag in his hand. The bag's contents clicked together when he tipped it over, and sapphires of many different sizes spilled out into his palm.

The treasure that had engrossed the city, that caused the deaths of several people and disrupted so many other lives, was real.

And it was in their hands.

"*Stars*," Emily whispered. "What are we going to do now?"

Hetty looked up at the girl and then back down at the piles of gemstones in Benjy's hand, Eudora Mason's threats loud in her ears.

"I think," Hetty said, "I have a few ideas . . ."

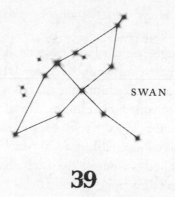

39

The easiest way to turn a funeral into a grand spectacle is by having a closed casket.

It allowed for some mystery, and cut down on the worry something might happen to the body. And it was something kept in mind for the future.

Hetty stood in the hallway, greeting people as they entered the Duval home and guiding them to the parlor, which had been rearranged for the event.

They had enough chairs for forty, split into two blocks with an aisle in the middle, and five rows. The chairs faced the casket, which was on a slightly raised platform. The parlor's usual decorations had been moved and changed around as needed. And the need was great, given what they had planned.

Though it would have been easier to do back on Juniper Street, they were doing the funeral at the Duval home because of the mirror tucked in the back of the room. The large oval mirror was covered with a white sheet and placed just behind the casket. Hetty had worried she might have to risk using magic to keep it hidden from sight, but luckily with so much to look at in the room, no one was giving it attention.

Of the many things they had to plan, this was the most crucial part, and the one Hetty fretted about the most, even as everyone assured her it would go well.

Still, even though Nathan Payne was dead, Emily Jacobs was safe, and the elusive treasure out of reach, Hetty didn't relax fully until Eudora Mason walked into the house.

She was accompanied by Horace Duval as always. While Hetty had her doubts about the man's innocence, they couldn't find anything that connected him to his uncle's death. He was a greedy snake, but he'd been used just as much as anyone else that came into Eudora's direction.

Eudora drifted past Hetty as if they had never met, her attention and conversation focused on Horace. The pair settled on the middle row on the left side, with Eudora taking the seat on the center aisle. As she settled, the fake medium glanced back at Hetty with a stern glare, as if questioning if Hetty would hold up her end of the bargain.

Hetty ignored that look, of course, as she entered the parlor.

"I thought she wouldn't come." Temperance Murray's voice was quiet as she stepped next to Hetty. "It would have been smart to leave town."

"People never do the most reasonable thing."

Hetty had gambled on that, as well as Eudora's desperation to find the treasure. Surely she knew by now that Payne was dead. And judging by those dark circles under the woman's eyes, she had been out looking for Emily herself.

This was the biggest gamble they were undertaking.

They didn't know what Eudora knew about them. Whether she believed the stories or made up her own based on what was said around town.

They did have one thing in their favor.

Help.

Her friends were placed in different spots in the audience. Darlene and George were in the front row on the right side, with

Penelope and Rosie seated directly behind them. All had vials and flasks at hand.

Oliver sat in the back on the left side with the alleged sword cane at his side. He leaned back, his slumped position hardly showing how nervous he was. Thomas sat on the opposite end of the room, the wind elemental pistol with him.

Sy milled around, settling people into their seats. While Rosie and Sy were the only ones of the Caldwell cousins to come, Maybelle had sent her son Gabe, which turned out to be a boon.

Adelaide, of course, was in a place of prominence, and thankfully had chosen calm stoicism to ride out the funeral instead of the boisterous tears she had first suggested. Cora was at her side, vigilant and prepared to whip out her pistol if needed. Jay was making idle conversation with some of the guests who had yet to take their seats. Of everyone, he was the person most at ease, since he had the easiest job.

Benjy was settled at the piano, off to the side but not out of reach. His soft playing filled the room, as the rest of the people in the audience were mostly made up of strangers — another request by Adelaide, either out of a desire to keep people she knew out of harm's way or to keep her disliked relatives out of the house.

Sy shut the door and nodded at Hetty. Everyone expected to be there had come.

"Looks like the show is about to start," Temperance said. "Let's hope this plan of yours works."

Hetty didn't bother answering.

Hetty went over to Jay and whispered: "Showtime."

The pastor made his way to the front, next to the closed casket. A silence fell over the room.

He opened the wake with the usual greetings he did for funerals. Then, quite easily, Jay moved into a personal story about Raimond Duval, with such skill that Hetty almost missed him saying "spirits abound."

Rosie didn't.

She twisted her handkerchief around and the magic Hetty had sewn into it came to life.

Nearby, the sheet slipped off the mirror and fell to the floor. It did this quietly, so that only those nearest even noted it.

But Jay kept going as he related his story. "My friend always said that his son—"

The mirror rattled against the wall, and at the proper moment, Valentine Duval himself appeared framed in the mirror.

The reactions came at once.

People got up, others pointed, and Thomas cried, "His spirit got caught in the mirror!"

But Hetty locked her eyes on only one person.

Eudora Mason had grown rigid, her head frozen and upturned toward the sight before her.

Just when the noise rose to a fever pitch, a voice cut through with chilling ease.

"My killer sits among you." The ghost of Valentine Duval leaned forward inside the confines of his mirror. "I know the truth, and I come to speak it."

Curtains billowed at the window, seemingly in reaction to his words.

The ghost lifted a hand, pointing into the crowd. "He's coming for you. Run all you like. You'll never be free of the truth."

Hetty stepped into the aisle, moving toward Eudora.

She was almost there when Gabe reminded her why he was never offered a role in their little plays.

Where there should have been silence, the young man added new lines that were not in the script Oliver had written.

"And I'm not alone. We only have to wait. The worst part is that you would have gotten your answers."

The ripple effect was clear at once. Penelope, ready to toss her first vial, fumbled at these words, missing her cue. This caused

George to drop his. It hit the ground with an audible thump, but didn't break as it should have.

But it broke the spell that had fallen across the room.

"I should have expected this." Eudora stood. She held up her hands, basking in the attention in the room. "Ghosts return to the place where they dwelled while living. Let me take care of this." She turned in a slow circle, her hands spinning around, clearly preparing for her next spell. She glanced over at Hetty, and her dark eyes gleamed with malice. "Don't want things ruined."

"I'm afraid they already are." Hetty pulled out a sapphire from the cache they'd found the previous night. She angled it so it glittered in the light.

Eudora froze.

Then she did the one thing Hetty hoped she would do.

She flung magic in Hetty's face.

But Benjy's magic sealed Eudora's orb in midair. The angry red magic bubbled, pressing against a ward that would not break.

Quietly, Benjy rose from the piano, one hand keeping the magic in place. For this plan to work, he could do no more than that.

Their goal was to rip the gloves off and reveal the blood staining Eudora's hands. They needed Eudora to act as vicious as she could be to make that clear.

Jay coughed, stepping off the dais and out of the way.

Hearing this, Darlene cracked the seal of the vial and dropped it to the floor.

Smoke spilled out, filling the room with fog.

Temperance ran for the side door at once, her footsteps covered by the outcry in the room. But the smoke didn't last long.

At the right moment, George dropped the diffusing vial.

All magic vanished from the room. The orb and Benjy's protective magic around it popped out of sight. The smoke evaporated, and the coy wind that moved the curtains stopped. The lights floating above their heads blinked out, leaving only sun-light streaming through the room.

And then the fake Valentine Duval stepped out of the mirror. He walked around the casket and stood on the dais.

Eudora shrieked, falling back.

"You're alive!" she cried as Horace Duval and half the room stood up, gaping at the sight. "You're supposed to be dead! I was told. I was promised!"

Gabe laughed, his voice echoed in the room as if coming from afar. Then he stopped, his face as blank and cold as the grave. "Don't you know that when you call, ghosts answer! And they are coming for you!"

Eudora's eyes fluttered, and she fainted, collapsing onto the floor.

Not part of the plan.

But it would work.

Hetty pushed her way through the crowd to Eudora's side. Luckily, people were moving as far away as they could from the fake medium.

Hetty was reaching for Eudora when a memory of a previous occasion made her take a hasty step back.

Just as she did, a burst of magic exploded in front of Hetty.

"I see I got your answer!" Eudora's hands were lit with flames as she stood. "Hand over the sapphire or I'll burn this place down!"

Hetty looked for Benjy.

Their eyes met across the room, and he nodded at her, answering her silent request.

A dome appeared around Hetty and Eudora, placing them apart from the rest of the room.

"Think that's going to stop me?" Eudora laughed.

"No," Hetty spat. "That's my job!"

She opened her hand, revealing the star sigil she hid. Sagittarius charged at the fake medium. With a swing of her bow, the centaur fired glittery arrows of stardust right at Eudora.

Eudora aimed her flames at the arrows. They overwhelmed the spell. But the arrows were only just a distraction.

A tap at the band of Hetty's neck brought to life the rest of the magic left in her stitches. The Aquarius star sigil appeared and dumped a bucketful of water on Eudora. The water bearer winked right at Eudora even as a scorpion's pincer shot through it, exploding the spell.

Scorpio lunged for Hetty, but while the spell was well crafted, it never had a chance. It ran headfirst into the wall of Hetty's personal protective wards, every thread stitched into her clothing coming to light. Contained in the bubble around them, the light was even brighter, masking the quick work Hetty put in as she created and fired off a series of spells.

And when the light faded, Eudora was surrounded by a glittering menagerie of star sigils.

"Give up yet?" Hetty asked.

"Never!" Eudora's hand slashed across Canis Major, disrupting the spell. "You will not take what's rightfully mine! My father died for that treasure! I'll pry it from your hands."

"I have only that one," Hetty said. "My husband has the rest. You'll have to get through me to get to him, but that's never going to happen."

Eudora screamed. It echoed loud enough that Hetty's concentration broke and the star sigils that surrounded Eudora faded —a bloodcurdling scream that showed the depths of the woman's soul, of the sorrow, of the loss, and of the righteous anger. A scream that might have plucked at Hetty's sympathy, if she forgot that not only had Eudora gotten someone to do her dirty work, but she'd hired someone that didn't care who he killed as long as he got what he wanted.

Hetty dodged the first burst of magic flung at her, but the second she let bounce off her personal protections.

Rage overtook Eudora's features then, and her magic became formless, erratic—and in the end, ineffective.

With ease, Hetty moved and ducked around Eudora's attacks, until she got under Eudora's guard.

A twist of Hetty's wrist sent Eudora hovering in the air, then pressed her up against the curve of the dome. "Do you give up?" Hetty asked.

Eudora's eyes burned with the hatred of a thousand flames. "You don't listen, do you? No wonder you lose people in the end."

"Don't try that trick on me again. You're not a real medium. No ghosts speak to you!"

"But I can see your past. There's no trick in that. You lost people, and risk losing people all the time."

"That's life. People are here for a moment, passing through your life. It's why it's better to enjoy what time you get and worry about everything else later."

"Such pithy phrases," Eudora said, her hands twitching.

"Are you trying to distract me as you work a spell?" Hetty declared. "I'm Henrietta Rhodes, and I'm the best practitioner of magic you'll ever meet!"

"I know. That's why I'm taking you with me!"

The telltale glow was just enough for Hetty to react. She shoved Eudora away and flung herself backwards, moving as far away from Eudora as she could.

Hetty pounded just once on the dome before she fell through. Penelope and Darlene caught and pulled her out of the way as the dome resealed itself.

"Below," Hetty gasped, but Benjy had already taken care of it.

Although a sheen of sweat shone on his forehead, Benjy cast another spell that turned the dome into a bubble, firmly encasing Eudora all around as it lifted her into the air.

Through the transparent shielding, Eudora's enraged face disappeared in a pop of bright light.

The bubble shook and something spattered inside. But the bubble held.

"Someone get the door!" Benjy called.

Sy jumped into action, the light from his spells flinging the chairs strewn about out of his way as he ran for the nearest door.

Knowing that nothing else was needed from her, Hetty sank to the floor, panting as she caught her breath.

"You're a fool, Henrietta Rhodes!" Darlene shook her. "Do you know that? You could have died!"

"I wouldn't have," Hetty gasped.

"Why are we friends with you," Darlene bemoaned. "Why do we put up with this?"

"Because if we don't, no one else will," Penelope added rather grimly.

Hetty shooed them away, but her friends hugged her, squeezing her from both sides.

Hetty patted them both on the back, touched and a bit overwhelmed.

"Were you wearing a brooch earlier?" Penelope asked. She had let go of Hetty and pointed to a small hole in the collar of Hetty's dress. Penelope frowned at it, clearly puzzled. As she should have been, since Hetty had slipped the brooch on when neither of her friends was looking.

"Was it the deadly butterfly?" Darlene whispered. "Did you use it on Eudora?"

Hetty looked at them both. "Do you really want that question answered?"

Darlene's face said yes, but her mouth said no, and it was left at that.

Hetty got up off the floor and took stock of the room.

The only major damage in the room was within the circle

where she and Eudora fought. It smoked with a bit of the magical aftereffects, but it could be fixed with ease, just like the wall that needed a splash of paint to cover the scraping from the chairs.

Most of the guests had fled, so it was only the people she knew that were still there. Some were explaining things to the curious, while some were tidying up. Horace Duval was nowhere in sight. Which was a good thing, because Hetty didn't want to deal with him. Gabe Lewis was rubbing at the makeup that had altered his features to resemble Valentine Duval, looking rather pleased with himself, even as Oliver fussed at him for going off-script.

Sy slipped back into the room, and a few moments later, Benjy was there.

Hetty supposed there would be words about nearly getting herself blown up, but for now, he smiled at her, just happy to see their plan had come together in the end.

Then his smile faded and he quickly hurried to her side.

Hetty turned around and she was hardly surprised to see Bernice Tanner.

"I have learned never to play the odds with you, Mrs. Rhodes. Your plan worked."

"I told you it would."

"And I should have known. You've done the impossible before. Temperance," Bernice said without looking back.

Temperance Murray, standing quietly in Bernice's shadow, took a half step forward.

"Take Henrietta's friends out of earshot. Distract them with conversation."

Temperance barely blinked. "Miss Tanner. They're right before you—"

"Temperance, I may be blind, but that doesn't mean I don't know what's going on. I know they're right there. I just have no mood for pretense and veiled meanings."

"Yes, ma'am."

Temperance inclined her head, and her gaze fell on Penelope. A smile made its way through Temperance's stern, if indifferent expression. "I don't believe we were introduced properly. Which one of you is a fan of baseball?"

"It's my favorite sport in the world!" Penelope declared. She was on her feet, and half ushering Temperance away, blathering on about baseball facts that Hetty knew were wrong. Darlene followed after, shaking her head.

Benjy made it over to her by then, and he helped Hetty up. His arm remained wrapped around her shoulders, though whether to give support or to hold her back from striking the old woman was yet to be determined.

"I like to think I know everything in this town, but you two reminded me, that's not always true," Bernice said. "One question. How did you get her to come? A woman like Eudora Mason must have known better."

"She probably did. But she didn't hear all the stories about us," Hetty said. "Somewhere along the line, she heard such tales that were less exciting, with several details changed. It's why she set her sights on Darlene at first, before she realized her error far too late. Can't imagine how that happened."

"Neither can I," Bernice said easily.

She tilted her head, and those dark lenses of hers seemed to dare them to ask.

The older woman had never apologized for the trials she put them through over the years. And Hetty might never forgive her for only giving empty promises. But this was a small step in the right direction.

"Greed brought Eudora here," Benjy said. "We found the treasure."

Bernice's mouth opened slightly, and then lifted into a rather amused smile. "Well then, you must tell me how you managed to solve the cipher."

"Emily Jacobs came to us." Hetty relished in the not unsignificant amount of shock that passed over the woman's face. It was a detail they worked hard to keep from Bernice and her rather efficient assistant. "The girl had knowledge of the key text that would unlock the cipher and a charm to help find the treasure. This is what people chased after Sarah Jacobs for, and Eudora must have guessed Emily had in her possession."

"And what of the sapphires? Do you have them?" Bernice asked. "You could set yourself up rather prettily with those in your possession. Never have to worry about money again."

"Now, why would we tell you what's happened to them?" Hetty asked.

Bernice went quiet for a long moment, and then she laughed. The sound was so unexpectedly full of sheer delight that it drew some alarm from Hetty.

Bernice turned away, swinging her cane around. "May we meet under kinder stars. And may your next adventure be just as thrilling!"

"I don't like the sound of that," Benjy whispered into Hetty's ear. "She's going to have another mystery for us to solve!"

Hetty watched Bernice move to speak with Cora and Jay. From the expressions of bemusement that passed between the trio, Hetty found herself viewing the prospects differently. "I wouldn't worry. We can handle anything she throws at us!"

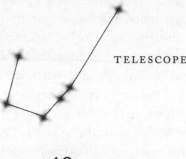

40

Hᴇᴛᴛʏ ʟᴇᴀɴᴇᴅ ʙᴀᴄᴋ on the stool in Benjy's workshop, polishing her telescope to the gentle rhythm of a hammer beating against metal. She had intended to work on a costume for next week's play, but dinner last night with their friends made it a moot point. Oliver announced that he and Thomas were going on holiday, which meant no elaborate plays would be put on for a while. To which George had remarked, with an annoying smirk, that they all had had their fill of putting on a show for a while anyway.

A week had passed since they put on Valentine Duval's funeral, both the spectacle and the private one held afterward, and things were as quiet as they usually got.

Hetty hosted the E. W. Harper meeting, and to her great surprise, it was rather pleasant. It had been a small group. Evie Wong, the glassmaker Violet Morrow, Hetty's old neighbor Willa, plus two others Hetty had not met before had come. Darlene had taken control of the meeting, guiding conversation to various topics with great skill. Penelope talked about potion making. Hetty even got a chance to read part of the astronomy paper she had submitted to the astronomy journal, and had a good laugh with everyone as she realized how convoluted some parts of her paper were.

An invitation to Adelaide Duval's gallery opening had arrived that morning, announcing not just the grand reveal of some of her statues, but the paintings Darlene had worked on. The opening would be near the end of the month, as Adelaide wanted to wait for the arrival of Emily Jacobs's sister, Lizzie, from Canada. Adelaide only had to hear Emily tell her story once before the sculptor insisted on taking the girls under her wing. The Jacobs sisters would stay with Adelaide, and of course take classes at Olmstead, a decision that was agreed to as easily as it had been made.

There were other smaller things at work too. Sy and Rosie finally opened up the bookshop, and currently planned to be open a few days out of the week. Penelope had yet to move into Hetty's guest room, although with all of Penelope's plants currently residing around the house, it was only a matter of time. Which was fine by Hetty, as there was one lingering problem they needed to deal with.

Nathan Payne had set some of the mysterious fires that plagued the city, to cover the murders he performed as directed by Eudora. But the rest of the fires had a different origin, and were still a major problem.

As Hetty and Benjy had told Jay previously, when it came to the fires, all roads led to Beatty Hose. Even with the resources Cora could provide through the Magnolia Muses, handling Beatty Hose was still a delicate matter. While directly confronting them was still an option, it risked bringing trouble on their heads as well as others. A less indirect route involving the courts and the rule of law was also out of the question, because there was no way laws could stop people who weren't following the rules in the first place.

Yet, despite these issues, Hetty was able to find an elegant solution to the problem.

"You should check the cauldron," Benjy called, pausing to wipe the sweat from his brow. "It's starting to bubble."

"You're closer," Hetty said, giving one last rub to her tele-scope.

"I'm busy. And it's your sister's spell that you insisted on doing and wouldn't accept my help."

Hetty rarely dabbled with brewed magic, and when she announced she wanted to try this spell, Benjy didn't even bother arguing with her. He carried the cauldron out to his workshop and kept one eye on it the entire time. She thought it a bit extreme since his experiments with magic had nearly set their house on fire before, but she had to admit, brewing the potion in here made things easier.

Hetty gently placed her telescope on the table and approached the bubbling cauldron sitting on the brazier.

The liquid inside had turned gold—it even had the sheen that Esther's note had mentioned it should have at this point.

Reaching for a ladle, Hetty ran her thumb over the Fox star sigil at the base, stirring the magic that would keep the utensil from melting in her hand. She scooped out the still bubbling potion and poured it over a small wooden box, making sure to get all parts of the surface.

That done, she replaced the ladle and drew the Phoenix star sigil next, igniting a small flame onto the box.

For the briefest of moments, the flames flickered on the surface before it vanished.

"It worked," Benjy remarked as he gently tapped the hammer around the object he was working on. "Are we selling the potion itself, or the knowledge?"

"We're giving the knowledge away," Hetty corrected.

He smiled, inordinately pleased. "What is the world coming to when you're not concerned about money?"

"A world in which I don't want to be tasked with making this potion all the time."

Benjy gave another whack to the object in his hand, snapping off a piece. "Isn't this a better solution than writing the alderman a stern letter?"

"It was never just a letter." Hetty set another fire spell on the box, watching the fire burn then vanish once again. "It was sending him a letter after we burned down all the warehouses he's been using, wrecked the entrances to the tunnels he'd slinked about in, and made sure he could never use that little clubhouse of his again. Then," she added with relish, "I'll set my birds on him, so he'll think he's being watched!"

"That's too dramatic," Benjy said. "No need to get the birds involved."

"We have to do something, or he'll just continue what Payne started."

Benjy picked up the metal rose he had been working on and held it out for Hetty to take. "I already collapsed the tunnels, and wrecked the foundation for both the warehouses and the old Beatty Hose station. With Sy's and Thomas's help, I stole the ledgers and disrupted the supply chain the alderman used for his business."

Hetty held on to the rose, unable to do anything more than grip it tighter, focusing on the fine details of the petals as she made sense of his words. "When did you do this?"

"During your E. W. Harper meeting."

"You should have picked a different time; that is something I wanted to be part of." Hetty pouted.

"Through Payne, the alderman messed with my friends," Benjy said. "You already had your revenge. I wanted mine."

"I suppose that's fair." Hetty absently spun the metal rose between her fingers. "Penelope's going to be very shocked to know I made the potion and that it worked."

"I'm surprised you didn't let her do it." Benjy turned the fire down under the cauldron.

"Esther tried to teach me brewed magic. I never had the patience for it. I still don't. But that doesn't mean I can't learn following the notes she left me."

Benjy picked up the tongs and pulled out of the pail on the floor the object he had been working on while they waited for the potion to finish brewing.

"Are you finally done with the sign?" Hetty asked, laying the rose down next to her telescope. "Does it meet your exacting standards?"

"Don't you mean does it meet yours? You were giving me suggestions even as I was pounding things out."

Hetty slid over to his side of the table, brushing up against him. "I had to make sure you got it right. Or you'd have to do it again."

Although she said this, from her first glance she knew the sign was perfect. Just like they had discussed, it was a large oval, with a sun cut into the metal on the left side and a crescent moon on the right. In between were two lines of text:

Mourning Dove Funeral Home
Inquiries Welcomed

A sign to speak to those who came here to bury bodies and to those who might come to learn where bodies were buried.

"Do you think this will work better?" Benjy asked.

"Much better," Hetty began, only to be interrupted by a series of sharp raps followed by their neighbor calling out to them: "Are you in there? Come outside! Both of you!"

Hetty groaned, and she pressed her head against Benjy's shoulder. "What does she want now?"

"We could ignore her?" Benjy whispered, but the rapping just continued.

"I know you're in there," Blythe called. "I saw you earlier! What are you doing in there anyway?"

Hetty stormed out of the workshop first. Her neighbor had a broomstick in her hand and was gleefully hitting the side of the shack.

"Mrs. Holloway, how can we help you?"

"Quite easily." Blythe dropped the broomstick as Benjy stepped into the yard. "I'm inviting you over for tea. There is something I wish to talk about." With a twist of her hand, the gate's latch lifted and swung invitingly open. "Don't look at me like that. I'm not going to poison you. Not on purpose."

Hetty had to admit, annoyed as she was, this sparked her curiosity.

It had sparked Benjy's as well, for he simply followed after Hetty through the gate and into their neighbor's backyard.

The only thing of note in Blythe's yard was a small table with a couple of chairs, all of which looked like it had been recently moved to sit in the shade of their shack. The lock on Blythe's cellar door was shiny. It and the hinges on the door had the honor of being the first items to come out from Benjy's workshop — and added without informing their neighbor of the houseguest she had unknowingly had.

There wasn't anything remarkable about Blythe's kitchen. It had the same layout as theirs except flipped. Hetty walked around with an odd feeling of walking in a mirror. Everything was in reverse, from the layout of the cabinets and stove to even the placement of the table.

Hetty bumped into the table by accident, not expecting it to jut out so far. Something rattled on it. But it was just a tray with a half-melted candle sitting in a dish. Everything else on the table wasn't breakable. Just letters scattered across the surface.

Letters all addressed to a Miss Carole. Just Miss Carole. No last name, and with an address that belonged to the *Eventide Observer.*

All at once, the dozens of letters Hetty read in the paper's advice column came flooding back to her, with something akin to horrified delight.

"You." Hetty turned to her neighbor. "You're Miss Carole!"

"I am." Blythe took a few mismatched teacups from the cabinet. "It's fun mostly. I used to do an etiquette and manners column back home, but I like giving out more general advice, as it gets me more interesting letters. But don't you know this, after you received some of my letters by accident?" Blythe frowned as she glanced over at Benjy. He was very quietly washing his hands at the sink. "Benjamin brought them over when they got in your box by accident. Ever since then, I go through your mail to check. The newspaper sends children with my mail, and your box is easier for the little ones to reach."

"I had no idea," Hetty said.

"Well," Blythe said, with a knowing grin, "surprises are good for everyone!"

With the tea tray in hand, she bumped the kitchen door open with her hip and headed out of the room.

"Did you know before you found the letters?" Hetty bristled.

"I didn't." Benjy turned around, drying his hands. "I didn't say anything because you liked the column so much and I didn't want to ruin your fun, since you don't like Mrs. Holloway."

"That's where you're wrong. She's rather vexing and nosy," Hetty said, "but I don't dislike her. I'd have to dislike myself, because I have similar qualities."

"I suppose that's why I get along with her," Benjy said, so sincerely that Hetty almost missed the amusement that lurked in his eyes.

"Well, you keep that in mind!" Hetty retorted. "She's about to spring a surprise on us. She took out four teacups."

Benjy tapped his chin. "She did say she wants our help. Any guesses why?"

Hetty leaned against the counter, her eyes drawn back to the letters on the table. "Someone came to her for advice, someone she's very close to and wants to provide the best help possible."

"A person who is resistant to accepting that help from her," Benjy added. "Why else bring us in?"

And it was with this confidence that they went into the next room, where Blythe was arguing with her houseguest as she poured tea.

". . . you just need to talk to them and it'll be fine."

"Auntie," Temperance Murray cried, "I don't care who your neighbors are. They can't do a thing about . . ."

Temperance blinked, looking younger and quite startled as she stared at Hetty and Benjy.

Hetty stared right back. Temperance was the last person she expected to see sitting in the upholstered chair. For a wild moment she feared that Bernice Tanner might have sent her. But there was a strain in Temperance's face and a deep worry creasing her brow that had never been there in any of their previous encounters.

"*You're* the neighbors!" Temperance exclaimed. "You live next door!"

"Oh, you've met before," Blythe said. "This shall make everything easier!"

Temperance reached for her aunt's arm, shaking it a bit. "No, it won't! I can't take their help!"

Blythe calmly lifted the younger woman's hand from hers. "You're going to have to take it. Because when you wrote to me saying you were seeking employment in Philadelphia because there was nothing keeping you in California, I thought you got your heart broken by that rich girl again. Not that three different people wanted your fingers for souvenirs for stealing a music box."

"What sort of music box?" Hetty asked, rather intrigued. "What can it do?"

"It's nothing special." Temperance glared at her aunt.

"If someone wants you dead, it certainly is special," Hetty said.

"Did you steal it?" Benjy asked.

Hetty turned to her husband. "Does it matter if she stole it? The item's lost. Doesn't it need to be found?"

"Or *should* it be found? Is it dangerous?"

"Or valuable? What can it do?"

Temperance held up her hands in an attempt to hold back their questions. "I don't need your help," she said quite firmly. "I'll manage."

"I don't know about that." Blythe was the only one actually drinking the tea. She sat there as if watching a rather amusing play. "You wanted my advice, didn't you? So here it is. I can't think of anyone else who is better equipped to help than Henrietta and Benjamin Rhodes. I know you haven't been in Philadelphia long, but haven't you heard the stories about them?"

Temperance's scowl only deepened. "I've heard plenty. Trust me: you don't want to be dragged into this mess. Don't you have other work to focus on?"

"There's always work to do." Hetty shrugged. "If you really didn't want our help, you would have walked out the room the moment we came in."

"If I did," Temperance countered, "would you still want to help?"

"Of course," Benjy said, so firmly that Hetty turned to face him—and saw the spell he cast with a gentle twist of his fingers. "Because you have a hex hanging about you. But don't worry. We know exactly what to do."

Acknowledgments

If a first book is the book of your heart, I think a second book is the one of determination and grit. Not because writing a second book is harder (it is in many ways, but also much easier in others), but because a second book is where you have to start growing as a writer, a person, and a teller of tales.

To help me grow, I'm lucky to have a great number of people supporting me along the way.

Thanks to my agent, Jennie Goloboy, who diligently listened to every random idea, question, and concern I volleyed her way.

Thanks to my editor, John Joseph Adams, for said two books and for letting me have room to figure out what that meant.

A big thanks to all movers and shakers behind the scenes, both at HMH and Penguin UK, who made things happen, and in particular: Jaime Levine, Kasim Mohammed, Fariza Hawke, Hannah Dirgins, Lisa McAuliffe, Heather Tamarkin, Alison Kerr Miller, Martha Kennedy, Liz Anderson, and Rachel Kennedy. With a special shout out to Hillary Wilson and Henry Petrides for their cover work.

Thanks as always to my parents, my sisters, and the rest of my family, who showed me all the various ways support and love can take form.